DEC, 2009
TO: Ms ARMEATHER GIBBS,

THE PERSON WHO GAVE YOU
THIS BOOK LOVES YOU AND
SO DO I.
MY BEST WISHES TO YOU

WWW.TAPMOSI.COM

Most Likely To...

T. Arnold Powell

authorHOUSE®

AuthorHouse™
1663 Liberty Drive, Suite 200
Bloomington, IN 47403
www.authorhouse.com
Phone: 1-800-839-8640

First published by AuthorHouse   7/18/2008

ISBN: 978-1-4343-6273-5 (sc)

Printed in the United States of America
Bloomington, Indiana

This book is printed on acid-free paper.

This book is dedicated to the memory of my parents John and Maggie Powell. Their love, devotion to family and life lessons are constant reminders to me every day.

In addition, I dedicate this book to others who are no longer here but played an important part in my life and development. They are, John Powell Jr., Theodore 'Sonny' Johnson, Ernest Sage, Mary Ponds, David Scott, Ralph Alford, Cassandra Jose, Ruby Kemp, Algernon Johnson and a very special young man, Kevin Shiflet.

I give thanks for the love and support of my family. I am fortunate to have the greatest brothers and sister in the world, Rick, Bob, Monroe and Andy. You have always been kings in my life. I have not met a woman more resourceful, enterprising, generous and just simply nice as my sister Mable Powell Sumter.

SPECIAL ACKNOWLEDGEMENTS

Otis McDaniel- If you are able to call this man your friend, you have all the riches this world can offer. You are a true friend. This book would not have been done without your help and support.

Annie Clowers- The world's greatest English teacher and my first editor.

Phyllis- It was you who encouraged me to get this done.

My Wall Street buddies - All of you are a best-kept secret. You are the real trailblazers who made your mark at a time when it was very difficult. I salute you George Patrick, Milton Brown, Ralph Wright, Don Washington, Roland Wyatt and Bill Franklin.

I give my sincere salutations to the following:

My life-long friends with whom I have shared great joy, good times and love for each other. Don Tyler, Joe Grayman, Richard Furel, Don Washington, Frank Shiflet and Bernard White.

To Great ladies, Meredith, Olive, Peggy, Curtese, Barbara, Betty, Karen, Dotty, Beatrice, Verdel, Sarah, Sharon, Arlena, Evelyn, Bernice and Priscilla.

To Rev. Dr. Michael N. Harris

To the finest doctors I have coughed for, Dr. James K. Bennett and Dr. William R. Osborne.

Roland and Lillie Wheatle; Rainmakers, who have touched the lives and hearts of many and will be my true friends forever.

A special note of gratitude goes to my friend Gary Riley. He is the most talented geek, computer guru and one of the nicest people I have met. Thanks Gary for keeping my computer running and the manuscript for this book safe from hard drive hell.

To my sons Kendal and Jeremy,

With God in your hearts and soul and always striving for excellence in your life endeavors, you too can be destined 'most likely to succeed'.

To Margaret

Thirty-seven years ago, you succeeded in making my life more rewarding, more meaningful, extremely full of joy and you gave me a purpose for living. For that, I will be eternally grateful.

AUTHORS NOTE

The investment instruments mentioned in this book reflect the manner in which they were similarly traded and regulated in the 1960s.

CHAPTER 1

Jay was pleased to get a taxi on just his first try for the ride up to Harlem- no easy task. The apartment building that he lived in on Columbus Avenue in Manhattan's upper west side did not have a doorman to hail a taxi for him. So, he walked over to Broadway where it is sometimes easier.

Perhaps it's because of the way he is dressed. He is wearing a navy blue Armani suit with a neatly folded white handkerchief in the breast pocket. His shirt is white; his tie is dark blue, and adorned with the symbols of the stock market; little bulls and bears in soft yellow and red. The dark oxblood wing tip shoes that he had on completed the typical Wall Street uniform. Jay learned the uniform dress of the typical Wall Street executive, broker, banker or clerk his very first day on the 'Street'. The taxi driver did not hesitate and stopped immediately. Surely this Black man, although young, was okay it seemed.

As Jay got in, he smelled incense emitting from the taxi driver's clothing. It appeared that he was trying to disguise the marijuana he obviously smoked. Oriental musk he thought; remembering the aroma from Sye's collection. "One hundred and Twenty-Seventh between Lenox and Fifth." Jay said to the driver. He sat back, rolled the window down and felt the warm breeze against his face as the taxi approached Central Park- the best route to Harlem

His mind wandered and he thought of Sarah, his mother's friend and the person he lived with when he first arrived in New York several years ago. She sounded anxious on the phone and he couldn't imagine what was so important that she had to see him tonight.

After all, he hadn't seen nor talked to her for a few weeks. He couldn't refuse her however; he thought she might really have a problem. Then again, she may just be lonely tonight; so instead of driving his Benz, he took a taxi. If she is horny or something, he planned to spend the night and his Benz wouldn't be parked in her block all night. He knew what could happen to a car like that on 127th Street in Harlem.

Sarah was exceptionally good in bed and Jay's mind gave rise to the very first time he was with her. It was right after he arrived in the Big Apple, fresh off the bus and just out of high school, from Charleston, S.C. Given the things that have transpired in his life the past few days, some time with Sarah is perhaps just what Jay needs.

Yes, Sarah was the person Jay's mother trusted to take care of him while he is away from home for the first time. She was to give him a place to live while he worked in New York for the summer. Sarah provided the opportunity for Jay to leave Charleston and earn some money until that scholarship came through. She took care of Jay just fine.

Jay had a job in Charleston, working at the biggest hotel downtown as a waiter in the banquet department. Mr. Earl, the headwaiter, who liked Jay's mother, got him the job.

Jay's mother, Diane Austin felt that it was a good idea that he should get away for the summer and New York was the place. He could make more money and get the feel of being away from home before college. That was the plan.

The taxi came out of Central Park and pulled on to Lenox Avenue and 110th Street. As always, people were everywhere; hanging out, trying to beat the nighttime heat on this typical Friday in Harlem.

It was early night but there was this rhythm that Jay loved about Harlem in the air. The taxi moved up Lenox Avenue approaching 116th Street; the sights and sounds were exciting and also frightful as Jay all too well remembered.

The music of Tito Puente was blearing from a bodega on 118th Street and Jay patted his feet to the beat. Yes, Latin music was one of the things that Jay learned to appreciate in New York. Sye introduced him to jazz. What a collection he had. Miles, Coltrane, Monk, Bird and of course, Ella. Sye had the music of all the great ones. And he spent many nights sharing a joint, his music, and his worldly experiences with the young blood from the south.

"Stop on 125th." Jay told the driver "I'll walk from here". He wanted to pass by Shirley's restaurant where he first worked when he came to New York. He could see if some of the regulars were out having their dinner. He would also pass by his first apartment where he sat on the stoop many nights and observed the street scenes.

Was Crip, the one legged wino in his usual place? He spotted Nick, one of many numbers runner making his rounds for the night action. The Liquor store on 126th Street was busy as usual. He noted that some things had not changed much, and he felt good as the warm air blew in his face and the sounds of Harlem filled his ears.

Jay decided to stop at the liquor store and buy a bottle of wine. He knew they wouldn't have Chardonnay there; his choice, but something that Sarah might appreciate; something that would help put her in the mood. He felt a little excited at the thought of being in bed with Sarah again. She was his real education.

Jay often wondered why Sarah never got married. She was good-looking, had a nice body with the biggest legs, and that butt of hers, always caught attention; especially from the White guys who often came to Shirley's for some soul food now and then.

Sarah just never got the country out of her; she always fell for the wrong guy. She made a lot of money at Shirley's waiting on tables and everyone knew that old man Mr. Frank, would give her all his money if she would just move in with him. Never mind that he was old enough to be her grandfather. She was just too nice to take advantage of this situation. Poor fool.

He didn't recognize any faces in the liquor store; after all he didn't go there often. He had been in there only a few times to buy Gordon's gin for Maxine. After some thought, he purchased a simple bottle of white wine and headed on to 127th Street.

The block between Lenox and Fifth Avenue was always full of life. He knew the regular faces would be in their respective places.

Mrs. Knowles, the unofficial block watcher would be sitting in her window where she often is day and night. She would be watching everything and everyone. Her husband left her some twenty years ago the story goes, and she has been waiting for him to come back ever since; so she watches the corner.

Neal, who had four kids; each with a different man, would be outside yelling at them, calling each the other's name. Staci would be waiting for her pimp to pick her up for her night's work downtown at one of the local expensive hotels, always with a skirt to short and heels to high.

There would be the dice game in front of 258; a group sounding like the Temptations singing on the stoop of 262; and Mitch, the numbers runner, taking action for the night track. You would be sure to hear the Greens, Richard and Thelma; drunk from drinking gin—each threatening to kill the other as they sit in the living room of their first floor apartment. And the ever-present Geraldine Geridau, the transvestite, sitting on the stoop of 275, watching the young men and trying to entice one into his room for the night. They would always be there; day after night, after day. Jay witnessed this scene daily for the year he lived with Sarah on 127th street.

His paced quicken now as he turned off Lenox and onto 127th. He looked up to his left and there was Mrs. Knowles in her second floor window. She was standing as she looked and Jay thought this was a little unusual for her but paid no further attention to this.

Jay passed a parked car with two men sitting in the front seat. Then he heard the car doors open behind him. Ahead and midway in the block, Jay saw two men get out of another car that was parked across the street. They started walking toward him. In the streetlights, he caught the gleam of a gun that one of the men held at his side as they slowly moved forward right at him.

A quick glance over his shoulder, Jay saw the two men that he just passed in the parked car were now out and walking behind him. Jay's heartbeat accelerated. This didn't look good. *Am I about to be mugged?* He thought, but then these guys didn't look like muggers. He had witnessed muggings in the streets of New York. They don't sit in cars and wait for victims. *Are they policemen? Why? Are they looking for me? Are they expecting me? Who are these guys?* Jay's heart was racing and his mind was trying to keep up. *Should he run? Could he make it to Sarah's apartment? Don't panic. Keep your cool. You are known for being cool under any circumstances.*

Jay's mind and body seemed to be moving in slow motion. And so did the people in the street and the men behind and in front of him. The man with the gun at his side raised his arm and pointed the gun at Jay from about thirty feet away. People started running run up the stoops and into apartment buildings. They knew something was about to go down. So did Jay.

Feeling an adrenaline rush, Jay dropped the wine he had purchased for Sarah and ran up the steps of the apartment building to his immediate left. He heard a voice cry out, "Get him, get him."

Almost instantly, a shot rang out and a bullet pierced the door of the building. "Shit, they're shooting at me. What's going on?" Jay said out loud but to no one in particular. He stumbled as he raced into the lobby and heard two more shots. Bullets shattered the glass behind him and he could hear the men running after him. His heart was about to bust out of his body.

Jay ran the first flight of stairs two at a time. As he reached the landing, he heard them bust into the lobby. Another shot hit the wall of the first floor landing. He was racing to the second floor. Stumbling as he ran, he reached the third floor. *Where am I going? Why are they after me? Can I get out of this building?* These questions raced through Jay's head as he raced up the stairs.

As he approached the fourth floor, he felt a sting to his leg, saw blood drip on the floor and realized he had been hit by one of the shots. He heard apartment doors open and close then locked. *Will someone let me in if I knock on one of these doors? Do I know anyone in this building?* Those thoughts came and went in an instant. Jay knew better. He also knew that he had never been in this building before. Jay lived on this block for over one year, had never been in this building and never met anyone who lived in it. *Where am I going?* was his dominating thought.

Not having an answer to his mind's questions, Jay kept running and falling up the steps. The men closely behind. His leg was starting to hurt now from the shot but he knew he would hurt more if he stopped and they got him.

He was now at the sixth floor and he would soon be on the roof. Again his mind raced. *Is this rooftop door locked? If it is, I'm a dead man. Is this how I am going to die? Shot to death and found in a pool of blood in a tenement stairway in Harlem.* This just didn't seem right to Jay. He felt that he deserved a more dignified death.

A quick glance back, Jay could see and hear the men on the fifth floor landing. He could also see his blood trailing behind him. *Why is this shit happening? What is this about?* "You're a dead motherfucker, you're a dead man tonight." One of the men shouted out.

Two feet away was the door that would determine whether he lived or dies tonight and he heard himself say, *'Please, God, please.'* He lunged at the door and it flew open. It's not locked, it's opened and he was now on the rooftop. *What now?* His leg was on fire and he was out of breathe, his heart pounding. *Can he hide there? No they would surely find him, could he jump to the rooftop of the adjoining building? Could he make the jump with the pain in his leg?*

He had no time to think of what to do. *Wait, the rooftop fire escape. No, they would just shoot downward and surely get him.* Jay ran and jumped to the rooftop of the next building. The pain in his leg nearly paralyzed him from the impact. No time to stop now. That door being opened was a sign that he just might survive whatever this is.

He heard the men reach the rooftop from his position on the rooftop of the adjacent building. He ran hard across the rooftop as his warm blood trickled down his leg. The men stopped running and cautiously searched the rooftop for Jay.

Jay also stopped running. He could hear his heart pounding. There was a pigeon coup on the rooftop and the pigeons started to flap their wings and take to flight as Jay startled them. "He's over there." One of the men shouted and they all ran in his direction.

As he limped away quickly as he could, he spotted a rope tied to the chimney that someone had left there. Without thinking, Jay grasped the rope and was over the side. Here he is, dangling on a rope six stories above ground- sliding down that rope that was burning the skin off his hands- three men apparently trying to kill him- his life in the balance, and Jay didn't have a clue why.

He could no longer feel the burning sensation in his hands; all he could think about was living. He didn't look down, but above him he saw the flash of light an instant before the pop of the gun; he felt the bullets whizzing past his ear. He had an angle on them so he was not an easy target.

I've got to get down this rope. If I can reach the streets, I might get away. This was the thought that now dominated Jay's mind. Near the first floor level, he let go of the rope and landed in the back yard of the building. The landing shot pain all through his body, but in a flash he was up and running. "You bastard" he heard from the rooftop follow by gunshots hitting the ground all around him. But he was not hit again. Jay ran, with throbbing pain in his leg back to 127th street. The block was now deserted, but people were in their windows, drawn there by the sound of the gunshots.

Jay painfully ran to Lenox Avenue. His lungs were just about out of breath when he saw a taxi going up Lenox. With all the energy left in his body, Jay ran right in front of the taxi. The driver slammed the brakes and the tires screamed. He fumbled to get the door open as he heard a voice behind him say, "There's the sonofabitch."

"Drive." he yells, "Someone is trying to kill me." Two quick shots smashed into the taxi door, the driver screech off heading up Lenox Avenue.

"What the fuck is this?" The driver says, "What is this shit?"

"Take me to Harlem hospital" Jay yells, "Those bastards shot me in the leg; they were trying to rob me."

While totally out of breath and his heart pounding, Jay realized that somehow he survived. His ears were ringing, sweat poured down his face, pain in his leg from the shot, his pants soaked with blood and he was in a taxi getting away. From what, he didn't know, but he got away from the bastards.

CHAPTER 2

CHARLESTON, S.C. JUNE 1961

Jay took the graduation cap and gown out of its box and put it on his bed. He looked at the royal   blue gown and held it up to look for wrinkles. Can't have that. Got to look good on this last day of high school. He inspected the cap and saw that the white tassel was just right. His mother, Diane, knocked on his bedroom door and asked, "Are you ready to go yet? "

"I'll be ready soon, I have to press this gown."

"Let me do It." she says, "I'll take care of my baby on his graduation day."

He opened the door and his mother was dressed and looking good.

She was thirty-four, looked twenty-four and is a single parent. Diane, with the help of her parents raised Jay after his father, a sailor, left town after Jay was born and never looked back.

Diane Austin was a very attractive woman. Like a lot of young girls in Charleston, she was impressed with the sailors stationed at the navel base in North Charleston. They made promises of marriage, security, travel, undying love and other lies. She wasn't bitter about the experience- and if anyone asked her about it, she always said, "I got a beautiful son out the deal, and I had a mother and father who never turned their backs on me."

Whenever Jay went out with Diane, he would see men look and stare at her. Her dark features were stunning yet soft. She had long jet-black hair and being a hairdresser, she tirelessly took care of it herself. She never weighed more than 125 pounds. She could get any man she wanted in Charleston, but Jay never saw any visit his house. She was contented to work and go to church. Her life revolved around her church, her mother and the life and dreams of her young son. Jay wanted to attend college and she was determined that he would. College life was one thing she did not experience.

Jay and Diane were hopeful that the scholarship he needs would come through in time for him to attend the fall semester of 1961. So the plan now is to go to New York, find work for the summer, save some money and pursue his dream to be an attorney. So, today is his high school graduation and his mother and grandmother, are very proud of him.

They really spoiled him; his mother and grandparents. They always made him feel special. Although Diane didn't make a lot of money they always had the basic necessities of life and lived in a house that was mortgage free. She owned and operated a beauty parlor. Her clientele were among the elite of Black Charleston. They didn't want for any thing and Jay always had decent clothes and always a few dollars in his pockets.

Other people spoiled him too; like Mr. Leland, his English teacher. He is arranging that scholarship for Jay. It will be at his alma mater Talladega College in Alabama. Word is Mr. Leland was gay. He never approached Jay in that way but he always treated Jay special. So Jay felt that if Mr. Leland gets that scholarship for him, he would have to find a way to thank him; other than the obvious.

See, Jay always had the ability to get whatever he wanted or needed with just his words, his sincerity, and little effort. That's why he believes that he will be a successful lawyer. He has the gift to gab. That gift, also worked with the girls in Charleston. Jay managed to have a relationship with a few; including his math teacher Ms. Mack. Jay really loved that lady. He is going to miss her. He did very well in her classroom and after some tutoring, he excelled in her bedroom. But he made sure that his grades were earned because of what he did in class and not in her bedroom.

They were very cool with the relationship and no one ever found out. She was not just some lonely, horny lady preying on a young man and using him for sex. Jay believed that she genuinely cared for him.

There were times he would sneak into her house and they would just talk, listen to her extensive music collection and laugh at silly jokes. Other times they would actually do some math. But then there was the sex. Like nothing Jay ever experienced in his young years, she taught him the difference between screwing and lovemaking. Jay found out later in life that some men never discover the difference.

Ms. Mack and Jay made plans for a meeting after graduation. He also has plans with Ruby, Janet and Harriet. Janet and Harriet were graduating also. Ruby was a junior in high school and a very sweet girl. Jay really liked her gentleness and shyness. She would believe anything he told her without question.

Janet, and Harriet on the other hand, thought that Jay was very much in love with them and in some young man way he was. He always respected them and never embarrassed them in any way. In other words, they never caught him with the other or caught him in a lie. They suspected that he was seeing the other but could never prove it.

The relationship with Ms. Mack started out quite innocently. Jay was leaving work at the hotel one Friday night about 10:00 p.m. He was waiting at the bus stop for the Belt Line for the shot ride home. It was a typical warm October night, not cold yet. A police car drove by slowly to check Jay out. They had seen Jay at this bus stop many times and knew he would soon be off their streets when the bus comes.

There were the usual White sailors from the naval base in North Charleston in the streets going in and out of the tattoo parlors on King Street. And cadets from the Citadel, the military college in their starched Grey uniforms going to have that last beer. The Citadel had just lost another football game earlier that night so they had nothing to celebrate.

As the police drove away, up pulls Ms. Mack. She rolled the window down on her Chevy Bellaire and said, "What are you doing out here Jayson Austin, why aren't you home doing my math homework?"

Jay leaned into the opened window and replied, "I did your homework early today and I'm on my way home from work. What are you doing out here Ms. Mack?"

"I'm driving down to the Battery for a while, pick up my usual ice cream then I'm going back home. Get in I'll take you home; you live near the Battery right?"

"Yes ma'am, on Pinckney Street off Anniston."

Jay got in and she headed up King Street towards the Battery. Charleston is located on a peninsula formed by the Ashley and Cooper rivers. The Battery is the point where the rivers join. In Charleston harbor, sits Fort Sumter where history says, the first shots of the civil war were fired.

"I usually get some hand packed ice cream at Dolly's. Would you like some?" Ms. Mack asked. Jay had money from the tips he made that night so he took this opportunity to show off a little. "I'll buy. I like vanilla. What flavor would you like?" Jay asked.

"I'm a vanilla person too, but I also like their cherry vanilla.

Ms. Mack stopped at the ice cream parlor on the corner of King and Society Streets and Jay got out to get the ice cream.

The clerk ignored Jay as he walked in. Two cadets from the military academy walked in behind him and the clerk immediately served them first. This treatment was some of the things Jay was used to in the South. After getting the ice cream, the two drove on to the Battery.

"What did you get for us?"

"I decided to get vanilla and cherry vanilla mixed."

"Excellent." She said and opened the glove compartment and unwrapped a metal spoon.

"I bring my own spoon because I don't like those wooden things. I only have one though."

"That's okay, I don't mind the wood." Jay said but feeling a bit awkward.

Ms. Mack parked her car at her favorite spot where she always had an uninhibited view of the river looking from East Bay Street.

The two sat in silence eating their ice cream and staring at the moon lit Cooper River. It was truly a beautiful spot and you can't help but feel a sense of history as you look at the surroundings.

There is a park square that had old cannons and cannon balls stacked in triangles that stood as a monument to the civil war; surely remnants from the historical fort.

This area of Charleston was a must see for the tourist who flocked to the famous city.

After a meal of fresh seafood like shrimp, crabs, oysters and fish, a visit to the battery was the next thing to do. You could walk or take a horse drawn carriage ride to absorb the sights.

On East Bay Street, were some of the finest homes that housed Charleston's rich and elite. They were all opulent townhouses; some dating back to the early seventeen hundreds.

The architectural motif, which Charleston became known for, is a house turned edgewise with a single room facing the street and a large porch overlooking a garden. It is a design, they say suited to the hot humid summers.

Jay and Ms. Mack sat eating their ice cream alone a row of such houses, about ten; each painted a different and brilliant color.

"You know Ms. Mack, where we are is called Rainbow Row. Just north of here is the area known as Catfish Row in Dubose Hayward's novel, Porgy. Have you seen the play Porgy and Bess?" Jay was trying right away to impress her with his knowledge; remembering a ninth grade book report.

"Why yes Jayson, I've seen the play and Gershwin's musical. I love it. When I come down here, I can always hear the music in my head. I can hear Sammy Davis Jr. singing 'It ain't necessarily so' or Dorothy Dandridge singing 'I loves you Porgy.'"

The historical waterfront was also very romantic, and many a couples can be seen holding hands as they walked on the elevated sidewalk that lined the harbor.

Some would stop and gaze into the dark stretches of the Cooper River that empties into the great Atlantic Ocean. Others would just simply act like lovers on a honeymoon.

Ms. Mack was about twenty-three years old and had been teaching at Burke for two years. She was from Greenville, S. C. and graduated from South Carolina State College. She was also very attractive. She wore her hair combed back with a ponytail and a bang in the front. When she first came to Burke, she was mistaken for a student and some of the senior guys hit on her. There were a number of embarrassed senior boys after they attended their first math class. She was no nonsense in her classroom and stresses the importance of math to her students. One of her favorite expressions was 'mathematics is the basis of all science.' Jay didn't appreciate that statement until much later in life.

She finally broke the silence in the car. "So, have you decided where you are going to college Jayson?"

Jay didn't quite have the answer to that yet, but he knew it would be somewhere. He replied, "I might go to South Carolina State, your alma mater, Ms. Mack. I understand all the women there are as fine as you."

Jay surprised himself with that response, and was immediately embarrassed. He was saying to himself. 'Stupid why did you say that?'

"Why Jayson Austin, I'm surprised by that statement. That is not a reason to pick a college. This could be the first defining time in your early life and choosing a college should have factors other than the quality of the opposite sex. I am however pleased that you describe me, as fine. I can't believe that I actually blushed when you said that."

Jay thought she let him off the hook. He put his foot squarely in his mouth and she let him off the hook.

"State was a very good school for me. I grew up in Greenville and didn't want to be far from home." She said. "State also had an excellent math department and that was going to be my major. I also wanted to be an educator and I was pleased with their teachers college. These were the major factors that governed my decision. My GPA was such that I had many choices but I settled on State to no regrets. Your decision should be based on what is important to you." She said.

Jay was feeling relaxed around her now and beginning to not feel intimidated by her beauty. "I know Ms Mack" Jay replied sheepishly. "I truly realize this will be an important step for me, but I guess my choice will be wherever I can get a scholarship. I don't know why I said that about women at State."

The teacher and student sat in an uneasy silence for a few minutes just eating the ice cream.

Jay was fighting the urge to do what he always did around girls, around women—that is, comment on their hair, or their dress, nails, their perfume. Tell women things they like to hear but not just a line. Sound sincere. In reality, this was a way to hide his shyness; It's flirting but not hard-core and obvious. He learned this from his mother.

In the case of Ms Mack, there was so much he could sincerely say to her and it was all true. She was drop dead beautiful. Her hair was dark black and silky. Her nails were impeccably polished a blush pink, and her perfume, intoxicating. He was drunk from it the moment he got into her car. He fought the urge to flirt because this was his teacher and this is not done.

Finally she spoke, "By the way Jayson Austin, you tell Harriet White she had better pay more attention in my class and not watch you so much. You are doing well and she isn't." Jay laughed and thought how did she know that.

"I didn't know she was watching me Ms Mack I didn't know anyone was."

"Now come on Jayson, I know what goes on in my classroom and some times outside too. But maybe you should not tell her that; she will want to know when did I tell you this, or where did I tell you this, or some other question might come to her mind. So don't say any thing to Harriet."

"Oh I wouldn't tell her any thing like that Ms Mack. I know you were just kidding." Jay replied.

"In fact perhaps it is best that you not even mentioned this meeting and the drive to the battery or our chat over ice cream. Charleston is a small town and there are small minds as such. As innocent as our meeting is, there are those who could or would misinterpret it. To be honest Jay, I wasn't sure if I should offer you a ride home. You understand what I mean of course."

Jay knew exactly what she meant and it was now important that he alleviate her fears. After all, this meeting was entirely innocent and just a nice gesture on her part. He knew how people could gossip in this town and a misplaced word by the wrong person could be the ruin of a nice lady who happens to be his teacher; besides, his mother would kill him if she thought...

"Ms Mack, I do understand; and while I'm only a high school senior, I'm not stupid. You needn't worry about that"

All of a sudden Jay felt somewhat confident, "I would however be the envy of probably every man in this state if..."

"Jayson." she cut him of, "It's time for me to take you home." She started the car, turned on the radio and the music of the Drifters filled the car.

"I didn't know you listened to this kind of music Ms Mack."

"And what kind of music did you think I listened to and just how old do you think I am Jayson?" she said.

"I just thought you were a Johnny Mathis person."

"I am, but I also like this music too. I'm only about six years older then you Jayson. I am not an old lady."

"I know that very well. In fact you could pass for a student. You look younger than a lot of girls in the senior class and none are as attractive as you."

"You have made me blush again Jayson and I don't know what to make of it."

Ms Mack was driving down Meeting Street and would be at Jay's house in a few minutes. Silence, but Jay's mind was racing. He had never been in the company of a woman so beautiful, dignified and intelligent. Don't hit on this lady. Don't make a fool of yourself.

"Do you work every night?" she asked.

"No, but whenever there is a banquet I do; and most are on Friday and Saturday nights. My mother don't want me to work on weeknights for obvious reasons, but I do- if I can be home by ten."

"Well maybe I'll see you again when I am out to get my ice cream and I'll pick you up if it is okay with your mother, and Harriet, and Ruby Brooks, and who else? I have seen Janet Smalls in your face too." She was laughing. "I told you I know what goes on in my classroom."

"I would like that very much Ms Mack but now you are making me blush."

She pulled onto Anniston Street. "Just up here on the right I'll get out here." Jay told her to stop. I was a block from his house. He wanted to demonstrate his discretion but wasn't sure why. "Thank you Ms Mack I really appreciate your kindness."

"Thanks for the ice cream Jayson, and I enjoyed you company."

Jay started the short walk to his house. He watched the car turn towards Meeting Street. The sweet smell of her perfume lingered in his nostrils. What just happened here, he thought. Why do I have the feeling that a man gets when he is sure of a new relationship beginning? This is the feeling Jay had with Harriet, Ruby, and Janet. This can't be the same or can it.

He walked up the three steps to the porch of his house and saw his grandmother sitting in the window. She always waited up for him to come home. He would always bring her some of the desert cookies from a banquet he served.

"Hi grandma, how you feeling"

"Just fine, how is my baby?" he gave her a hug and kiss as he always did.

"I brought your cookies, they are sugar cookies your favorite"

"Thank you sweetie."

His mother was asleep, tired from her long day at her beauty shop. He headed to his room tired himself but knowing he could not sleep.

The meeting with Ms Mack dominated Jay's thoughts for the rest of the night. His mind replayed every word uttered by her that evening. For the rest of his senior year, a relationship developed with her that influenced every fabric of his life then and forever. A high school kid became a man instantly. Ms Mack erased every notion Jay had that he knew what he was doing with the opposite sex. He was fortunate that early in his manhood he listened, paid attention and learned.

CHAPTER 3

Graduation was held at County Hall. This was the place where all big events involving Black folks in Charleston took place. With a graduating class of three hundred and seventy-four, this was the only place suitable. Jay, his mother and grandmother arrived early for the ceremony. Jay also had to perform with the band that day; his last as a high school student.

He got out of the car and joined the other seniors gathering outside the great hall for the procession. Mark, Bradley and Frank his cut buddies were also there early. The three of them were leaving for the army soon. Jay spotted Harriet. She was very pretty in her cap and gown. She had the nicest legs and he imagined them under that gown.

Outside the hall was now a sea of royal blue as the graduates gathered making small talk. Jay had plans to meet Ruby after the ceremony so he had to dodge Harriet. He would see her at the party later. He also had to avoid Janet until later because he really wanted this time with the sweet junior. The late night was reserved for Ms Mack.

His mother had made arrangements with her long time friend Sarah who lived in New York, to let him live with her for the summer and work. He was leaving tomorrow. So, after the ceremony, Ruby; walk her home, spend some time with her. Then Harriet later that evening; and then Ms Mack that night. Tomorrow morning he is on the Atlantic Coastline's train the East Coast champion to New York.

County Hall was packed for the ceremony. With a graduation class being the largest in recent history, it seemed that all of Charleston was there. It took forever for the graduates to march in. Jay did not have to endure the march. This was his last performance with the band and playing Pomp and Circumstances over and over was painful.

After the procession, Jay took his place with the class and his best friends, Frank, Mark, Charles, and JD. These were four of his buddies who made up the hip club in school. There were twelve members known as The Impalas; the best dress, best looking most popular, and the smartest guys in the senior class.

While the guest speaker was being introduced, the Impalas were finalizing plans for the last big party that night. Who was bringing the thunderbird wine; who was picking up the ice, punch and little sandwiches.

The Impalas were meeting at Mark's house; his parents were leaving Charleston right after the ceremony to attend the college graduation of Mark's older sister the next day. Jay was going to spend some time at the party with Harriet and then go to Ms Mack's house. His mother wouldn't mind if he was out late on this night. After all, it was graduation and he was leaving town the next day.

Being with close friends, some perhaps for the last time was important but Jay didn't really want the party. He would rather spend the whole time with Ms Mack. Harriet and the other girls in Jay's life didn't seem to matter any longer; that is, after the blossoming of the affair with Ms Mack.

He talked to them, mingle with them but it wasn't the same, and they knew it. Ruby still held a place in his heart because she simply adored him and would do anything for him. Somehow he felt he had to spend some time with Ruby, on his last night in Charleston for the summer.

The time came to acknowledge the achievement of noted graduates. There were thirty Honors grads. With his three point five grade point average, Jay was number twenty- five in the class. The brilliant, Bernard Wright was valedictorian and the lovely Dorothy Powers, was salutatorian. Jay had a big time crush on Dorothy. He took her to the sophomore class prom. He felt that she liked him too, but they were just good close friends.

The school administrators expected big things from Bernard and Dorothy, and a number of others in this class were destined to be successful in their life endeavors. Jay, however, by an overwhelming majority of the senior class, was voted MOST LIKELY TO SUCCEED. How about that? Of all the graduates, the distinction most likely to make it goes to Jayson Austin.

Maybe they recognized the drive of the young man, the leadership qualities, the affable personality, the charmer, the bon vivant, the decision-maker and the conflict resolver. These were the traits displayed by Jay Austin. In addition, Jay was perceived by a majority of the girls in the class as the most handsome. He won this distinction by a small margin over the class's heartthrob, John Bailey. He didn't have Jay's class and charm.

The ceremony lasted over three hours. After all the speeches, warnings, formulas for success, sermons and predictions; at long last, the class of nineteen sixty-one was now on its way to conquer the world.

Jay's immediate conquest was to get lost in the crowd as the throng exited County Hall. He must find Ruby; walk her home, then make it to the Impala's party. He told Harriet that he was going home with his mother to change his clothes and would meet her at the party at Mark's house. She said fine.

He found his Mother and grandmother in the crowd. She had tears in her eyes, tears of joy. Her baby had graduated and with distinction. This was the first step in the vision she held for her son.

"I'm very proud of you Jay, I'm also very happy, for you have been such a good son and I'm going to do all I can for you to be successful."

"Don't forget me," said grandma, "I'm going to help my baby too". The family engaged in a long group hug, Jay removed his cap and gown and gave it to his mother. "Mom, please take these home for me. I would like to meet some of my friends for a little get together to celebrate our graduation. I'll be home early."

"Okay dear, be careful and don't be out late, remember your train leaves at ten-fifteen in the morning".

"I won't." Jay replied.

He made his way through the thinning crowd slowing heading for the exit. Standing near the exit was Mr. Leland. He was smiling, arms extended ready to shake Jay's hand or embrace him. Jay didn't know which would come. He got the embrace, tight and a whisper in his ear.

"You are one of my all time favorites, I'll miss you." After the release, he said in a voice for all near to hear, "I'll let you know about that scholarship as soon as possible; here, give my number to your mother. She can call me while you are gone. Good luck to you."

"Goodbye Mr. Leland, I really enjoyed my time in your classes, you are the best."

Mr. Leland also led the dramatic guild and over the four years in high school, Jay had played leading and prominent roles in several productions put on by the guild. In fact, in a moment of idle daydreaming, he toyed with the thought of being an actor. His mother would have none of that. The experience however was extremely rewarding as Jay learned later in life.

Jay knew that Ruby would be waiting outside near King Street somewhat out of sight. There she was, with that big bright innocent smile that always captured him. It was now nearly dark outside and he was fairly safe that he could hug her close and not be seen. He did this, and she melted into his arms.

"Hi sweetheart I'm so glad you came."

"I'm sick Jay, what is to become of me if you are no longer here."

Jay took her small soft hands and started to walk. "Even if I'm not here. I'll always be thinking about you Ruby. When I get back from New York and before I leave for college I will see you. I know however as a senior next year you will have all the guys looking at you. You will soon forget about me."

She stopped abruptly and turned to look Jay straight into his eyes. She said, "I will never forget you Jay, I will never love anyone as much as I love you." He took her small round face in his hands, rubbed her curly jet black hair, looked at those big bright eyes, saw the sincerity in them and planted a light kiss; first on her forehead, then each cheek. He felt her swoon in his arms. Jay could feel the love of this dear genteel girl. He lived for moments like this; He could feel his control and he loved it.

They continued the walk to Ruby's house, his arms around her petite body. They moved in silence. Jay knew that the fact that he would be leaving the next day, Ruby would want him to stay with her as long as possible. In most times he wouldn't mind that because he always felt good around her and savored her devotion to him. Tonight, however, he had two other engagements so the thought in his head now is how to beg his excuse from her.

Ruby's parents liked Jay. They thought he had good manners, and was respectful; two traits that are a must to succeed in the South.

"I wish I could stay with you longer tonight but you know it's a week day and your parents work tomorrow so, I'll just stay a few minutes."

"Oh nooo Jay you're leaving tomorrow, I won't see you all summer please stay with me; and you know my mother loves you, she wouldn't care how long you stayed pleaseeee," Ruby cried.

"Sweetheart, I really don't want to leave you, but I also have to deliver some things for the senior party later which I really don't want to attend, but it may be the last time I see some of my friends; some I have known since first grade. I feel it's important that I at least spend some time with them. I will write you everyday over the summer."

She couldn't argue with that logic, so Jay knew he would be on his way after a few passionate kisses while sitting in the swing on Ruby's front porch.

Before leaving, Jay rang the doorbell to say goodbye to Mr. and Mrs. Brooks. Always a gentleman, he could not leave without acknowledging their kindness to him and to wish the best for Ruby.

"Would you please call a taxi for me? I don't want to walk to Mark's house."

"Yes I will, and I'll wait with you until it comes." Ruby said.

Jay reflected on his relationship with Ruby and thought he could really fall for her. She was just the kind of girl that attracted him. She had more than just great legs.

"You never told me what plans you have for the summer Ruby, what will you be doing?" She thought for a moment and replied. "I haven't told you what plans I have because I don't have any. What I would like to do is visit my aunt who lives in Brooklyn then maybe I will see you"

That thought intrigued Jay. For getting Ruby totally alone was one of his wishes. "That would be great, when will you know if it could happen?"

"If I could convince my father, I could be there sometime in July." she said.

The taxi came and Jay moved down the steps, Ruby grabbed him, wrapped her arms around him as tight as she could. He could feel the love. "Bye sweetheart, when I write to you, let me know if you do come to New York. I love you."

CHAPTER 4

As the taxi pulled away, Jay looked back to see Ruby blowing kisses to him. Sweet girl he thought. If she comes to New York this summer I'll make up for all the times I went home after leaving her with groin pain. He had never been able to get Ruby in bed. Although a virgin, She wanted to; it just wasn't convenient for them. Someone was always at her house and there was just no place they could go. He didn't force the issue of one of the local hotels. And there was the time when his mother was at her beauty shop and his grandmother was away visiting one of her friends. He took Ruby to his house only to discover it was the wrong time of the month. She was more upset than him because she couldn't please him.

Jay was cool however; he wasn't concerned. He used the opportunity for some very heavy petting and kissing; convincing Ruby that he was not just interested in sex but just to be alone with her and tell her how much she meant to him. She was overwhelmed.

The taxi arrived at Mark's house on Ashley Avenue. Jay saw some of his friends on the front porch drinking punch, which he knew, was spiked with thunderbird wine. As he entered the dark front room, he heard a song by the Flamingos on the stereo. *'Please wait for me.'* This was a nice slow song and perfect for the dance called the grind.

There were about eight couples on the floor dancing so close to each other that they could be counted as individuals not couples. Harriet was already there and rushed to meet Jay. She pulled him close to her and started to dance to the slow music.

"Where have you been? " She whispered in his ear. "I have been going crazy waiting for you." Before Jay could answer, she found his lips for a long hard kiss. She obviously had a drink of the spiked punch and was feeling it. He didn't say a word but just enjoyed the moment of Harriet held tight in his arms, their bodies one, and the sweet smell of her hair and perfume. In fact, the only sound in the room was the Flamingos with their slow melodic harmony and lyrics made for lovers.

When the song ended, Mark shouted out, "Play that again and don't play anything else." There was a loud 'Yea' in unison by all the guys and some of the girls. Harriet was quiet but in deep thought while in Jay's arms moving to the slow music.

Finally she said, "Jay do you realize that after today, it will be the first time since first grade that we will not be together in school?"

She was absolutely right. Harriet and Jay met in first grade at Henry P. Archer School. They were very close friends but it wasn't until they were freshman at Burke that they became lovers. She had a very light complexion, short curly black hair and hazel eyes, a little plump but a pretty girl. She had the look that people would say 'there is some white in that family.'

Like Jay, Harriet's father was a sailor who fled the port of Charleston when his tour was over but had no interest in the child he left behind. Her mother, who was also light-skinned, drank a bit but was a nice lady.

With the common thread of being the only child of a single parent and a wayward sailor for a father, Jay and Harriet bonded and were protective of each other. They were inseparable, did everything together from elementary to high school. Were it not for the difference in complexion, the two would have been considered brother and sister.

Harriet was a majorette; Jay played saxophone in the band. Returning from a football game in Columbia, S.C. one Friday night, they wound up sitting next to each other on the bus. She fell asleep on his shoulder and they were an item ever since. They walked home together that night, sat on her porch and talked for over and hour. When it was time for him to leave, he gave her a kiss on the cheek. It was perhaps at this point in their young life, sexual arousal and feelings became more than a curiosity. It was a natural trust they had in each other after all the interaction they shared from first grade. So their first sexual encounter as awkward as it was, were two people who knew each other and was experimenting with a trusted friend.

They met often at her house to study but always had time for the experiment that brought them even closer. Harriet professed her undying love for Jay. He, in turn was just taking notes on women and sexuality. Jay always suspected that Harriet laid sole claim to him because she knew him longer.

Harriet was fully aware of his growing popularity with other girls at Burke but she never exhibited any jealously over him. She instead displayed a quiet confidence in her relationship with Jay. In her mind they were destined to be together. Jay loved her, but only like a sister.

Yes, Jay realized he had known this girl since they were both six years old. Now they were eighteen, dancing cheek-to-cheek and contemplating life as young adults.

"I can't imagine being in school without you Harry, I mean we always had each other and now with you off to Hampton, and me, I'm not sure where yet, it just feels strange."

"Jay, we will always have each other; it only means we may not be in the same classroom or the same city for that matter. But you will always be in my life, Jay Austin, you know I love you."

The party was getting loud now and the degree of din was the inverse relationship to the spiked punch consumed. James Brown was wailing on the stereo, lies were being told and false promises made. The Impalas were having their last good time as the club of sophisticated dudes. All had their plans for life after high school, which included college for some and the military for others. All that is, except Jay. College was definitely in the plans but which one had not been decided. So he sat in a big arm-chair; Harriet snuggled close, and contemplated the scene. He was glad to be with his friends but was totally bored and wanted nothing less than to be with Carla. Carla Mack, that is. She told him please don't call her Ms Mack when they were alone. He had to make up an excuse to leave this party so that he could be with her before he left for New York.

Everyone knew he was leaving the next day, so if he said 'I haven't packed yet, I must go do that now since I'm leaving early tomorrow' would be okay. "Mark can I use your phone I've got to call my mom."

"Sure, Mr. Most Likely to Succeed, you can have anything in this house; just don't forget your good buddy when you make it."

Jay called his mom. He told her he was going to walk Harriet home and would be there shortly after that. She reminded him that the train leaves at 10:45a.m. and he shouldn't be out very late. He assured her he wouldn't, and then he dialed Carla.

"Hi Carla, this is the graduate."

"Hello Jay, how are you?"

"I'm just fine. I would be a great deal better if I was in your company." There was an uneasy silence.

"From the sound of that music and noise in the background, I would say you are having a great time." She said.

"No in fact I'm quite bored."

"Why? You're with your friends; some you may not see again for quite some time; and I'm sure Harriet is there celebrating with you. You should be happy Jay."

He didn't know what to make of that statement so he said nothing for a few seconds.

"I want to see you Carla, can I come over?" He heard a deep long sigh then she said,

"No Jay. I think not. You have graduated now and I'm proud of you and happy for you. I held back my joy when you got that award. But it's time for you to move on now. The last few months of my life and the experience with you will live with me forever. You are a mature and fine young man Jay, and you will do great things in life. I feel however, that what occurred with us should go no further. I will not say I regret it, far from that; the fact is, I enjoyed our moments very, very much. But, we must not forget our roles. You were my student, I your teacher. Use those moments, as I will, as an extraordinary period in your life when everything was wonderful and under control. I'm going back to school for my masters so I will be leaving Charleston. I don't know if I will ever see you again Jay, but I won't forget you."

Jay held the receiver to his ear and stood in stunned silence. He knew she was right and there was no disagreement with what she said. He also knew it would be useless to protest. She had made up her mind, and there would be no change.

"You are wrong about one thing Carla." Jay said. "I don't know when or where but I will see you again. I love you." Those words surprised him for they had avoided saying   things like that. At the same time, unspoken words described what was a truly remarkable relationship. "Goodbye Jay, you know how I feel"

Jay returned to the party. The room was very warm now and everyone was working up a sweat. The Platters was on the stereo, but Jay heard no music saw no one dancing and did not see Harriet as she approached him. "What's wrong Jay, are you all right?"

Jay stared straight-ahead not hearing a word. Harriet continued, "Jay, sweetheart what's the matter did you talk to your mother, is she okay?" She pulled on his arm and finally got his attention. "I'm okay Harry, everything is okay. I'm just a little warm and that punch is going to my head. I need to go outside, get some air, it is getting hot in here now."

Harriet said. "Yea let's do that."

"In fact I think we should leave now; are you ready Harry?"

Harriet looked at Jay curiously; sensing something was wrong. But what, was a mystery. "If you're ready Jay, I am."

They said their good-byes, hugs to everyone and were on their way. The two long time friends walked in silence holding hands as the warm June night air-cooled them down. "The party was nice. You Impalas will always be remembered at Burke; and I have the number one Impala in my heart" Jay smiled, looked at Harriet and squeezed her hand.

Words did not come so he said nothing. His mind was in another place, in another time with a different person.

"Hey, it's still early Jay, why don't I go home with you, I can help you pack. You can walk me home after that."

"Okay Harry" Jay said, not enthused by the idea because he really wanted to be alone. What the hell, Jay figured; he might as well let her come with him; maybe when he walk her home, her mother will have had a few drinks and would probably be asleep; then they would be alone in Harry's bedroom. They had done that many times before.

CHAPTER 5

The train was exactly on time. In a few minutes it would be leaving Charleston for points North and then New York. Jay had never been to New York before but he had heard the stories from friends who visited there in the summer.

Everyone in Charleston it seems had a relative who lived there. The great migration from the southern cities and cotton fields was still strong and ongoing. Jay saw many familiar faces of people making the migration trip with dreams of a well paying job, a better life, a sense of freedom, and most of all, getting away from disrespectful White folks.

Jay however, had no such dreams. His grandfather did not fear White people and instilled that same feeling in his family. Jay's trip was more of a vacation with work included- work to earn money for the fall semester in college. Jay had no plans to move to New York permanently like everyone else on that train. Like Jay, they all carried a brown bag that held their lunch for the trip. Jay's bag held his grandmother's fried chicken; eight pieces. No one could fry chicken better. She had been up before dawn cooking food for Jay's trip. The bag also included wrapped in wax paper, baked macaroni and cheese, corn bread and her unbelievable apple pie.

"Now baby all you have to do is buy you a drink on the train, I fix you enough food to get you there and for a couple more days." As his grandmother said this to Jay, she was putting a twenty- dollar bill in his hand.

The train started to leave the station and Jay watched his mother and Harriet waving goodbye to him. His mother had given him all the usual warnings about being away from home and being careful and responsible. "Listen to Sarah now, and be sure you call me when you get there."

What a night Jay had with Harriet. Her mother went home from the graduation, buried herself in a bottle of bourbon and was lying across her bed dead drunk. Jay had seen this scene before. She had no idea that Harriet and Jay was there. Harriet, no longer embarrassed by her mother's drinking, because she only drank at home, gently pulled the bed covers over her; turned the lights out and joined Jay in her bedroom.

He took this opportunity to show what he had learned from Ms Mack to his best friend and lover. Harriet said she fell in love with Jay all over again as he was leaving to go home.

Jay felt that his mother suspected that he and Harriet were intimate but she never mentioned it. She knew that they spent a great deal of time together but all she ever said to him was, "Jay, don't you bring no babies in this house."

The train was Jay's favorite mode of travel. His grandfather worked on the railroad as a conductor and during the summer months, he often took Jay along on his short trips to cities north and south of Charleston. He had been as far north as Fayetteville, North Carolina and as far south as Jacksonville, Florida. He was seven years old and he loved it. He had never been further, so he looked forward to seeing the countryside of Virginia, and Maryland traveling at more than eighty miles an hour.

The sightseeing didn't last very long for Jay fell asleep almost immediately since he didn't get much sleep the night before. The thoughts of Harriet, Ruby and of course, Carla played in his head. He didn't get to call Janet; too bad.

Sleep was deep and restful; the train's motion played the role of a sedative. Jay woke up feeling somewhat refreshed and hungry. He immediately reached for his grandmother's fried chicken and corn bread. The train was now approaching Virginia. Jay realized that he had slept through North Carolina.

In a few hours, Jay would be in New York and he had no idea what was in store for him. What he did know is that Sarah would be waiting for him.

He remembers meeting her when she came home to Charleston and visited his mom. Jay was about twelve years old at the time. He remembers very vividly that she had a gold tooth, short stout built, a rather jovial person and, she smelled good. He remembered that from the time she hugged him and said, "I chang your diapers when you wus a baby, and look at you now, you all grown up and handsome too—Girrllll, you is rais'ng a lady killer here"

Sarah had been one of Diane Austin's closest friends growing up in Charleston.   She was one of ten children. According to Diane, they didn't hit it off right away for Sarah lived in a part of town called the borough. This was where all the fighting, shooting, drinking and other crap that can engulf a neighborhood and brand the people as misfits- who happen to live there. Sarah was one of the people who were misjudged. Diane told Jay that Sarah was a sweet, kind, friendly person who worked hard and would do anything for you.

They met in cosmetology class in high school and did each other's hair. And when Diane got pregnant with Jay, Sarah was right there to help out. Sarah wasn't the brightest person but a good person, according to Diane.

Sarah decided to move to New York, partially to get away from her family, some of whom were true to form of the neighborhood. She had brothers in jail. The overriding reason was better jobs were available in New York, and she could make more money.

She sent a great deal of her money home to help support her parents; a disable father and a mother legally blind as the result of untreated diabetes. The friends remained in touch over the years. So, when the idea to go away for the summer arose, New York was first on the list.

Sarah told Diane that she could get a job for Jay at the restaurant where she worked, some place called Shirley's. This was natural for Jay; this was work that he knew. Having worked as a waiter at two of the finest restaurants in Charleston, Henry's and the Swamp-fox restaurant in the Francis Marion Hotel, Jay learned the art of service. Shirley told Diane that in New York, Jay could be an employee at the restaurant as well as a customer. That was not possible in 1961 Charleston. He could work at a restaurant. But the ones that he could be a patron of were limited to those owned by Negroes.

"New York Penn Station, next stop." The conductor announced as he moved through the train. All of the passengers in Jay's car began to stir and retrieve their suitcases from the overhead rack because this was their destination. This is where the dream would begin. He pulled down his large suitcase and put away his remaining chicken and apple pie for later eating.

The passengers were directed to a set of stairs leading to the waiting room of Penn Station. Immediately, Jay was in awe of this massive indoor station. There at the top of the stairs, in a too tight red skirt, stood Sarah. The gold tooth smile greeted Jay alone with opened arms.

"Well look at my big boy, ya have gron handsome jus like I knew yu would, how wus the trip how ya mom? Are ya hungry?"

She keep asking questions but not waiting for an answer. At first Jay paused, then said, "I'm fine Miss Sarah, the train ride was nice; no I'm not hungry, my grandmother gave me some chicken"

"Well come on, ya in New York now and I'm gonna take care of ya-but it don't look like ya needs no one to look after ya. We gonna tak the subway; you ever been on a subway? My lord you an't nev'r been here so you nev'r seen one. I'm so glad you here Jaysun you like to be call, Jay or Jaysun? When your mamma ask me if you could come the summer, I said sure, sure you my god son; did she tell you that? Well I made you my god son; I mean it ain't official but me and yo mamma, we real close and I'll do anything fo hur we like sistas even closer"

She stop talking just to take a breath but Jayson didn't hear a word she said; instead he just took in the sights and sounds of this huge place with all the people walking around. He saw a young couple speaking what he assumed to be Spanish but he had never heard it spoken like that before. He took Latin in school.

He saw other people that he knew were neither White nor Negro but what, he was not sure. This is some place he thought.

They made their way to the subway. "We'll tak the number three train; remember that Jaysun, to 125th Street. And I live on 127th, tween Lenox and 5th. I have tokens. Don't go lookin like you is visiting here people will tak advantage of you; act like you belong here; know what I mean?"

"Yes ma'am I know - my mother told me the same thing." In an instant, Jay heard this loud roar in the distant- a sound he had never heard before. That must be the subway he thought. The train raced into the station with a deafening noise that made your ears hurt. People spilled out the open doors and almost ran over Jay as he stood there with his big suitcase. The country boy was stunned for a moment until Sarah pulled his arm and said, "That's us this is yur first subway ride."

It is nine-thirty at night and the train was full of people. There was nowhere to sit down so Jay did as Sarah did and held on to an overhead handle. The ride was loud and jerky. Jay found himself almost falling as the train raced to the next stop. Above all, the car smelled awful. Sarah saw Jay's discomfort and said, "Welcome to New York, you get use to it."

Sarah proceeded to tell Jay about the job she arranged for him at the restaurant. She was talking above the noise of the fast moving train but Jay still didn't hear a word she said. He was too embarrassed to tell her he couldn't hear her so he just shook his head nodding yes.

The ride lasted about twenty minutes; then 125th Street. They exited the subway to a scene that although shocking, Jay did not show it.

He was on a sidewalk wider than most streets in Charleston. Then he saw people every where and cars blowing their horns and lights and taxies racing in and out of the moving traffic. He heard noises, sirens in the distance and music- loud talking; he saw trash everywhere.

Everyone was either in a hurry it seemed or just standing around waiting for something. This was Friday night in Harlem

Jay walked wide-eyed with a tight grip on his suitcase and stared at the people, the tall buildings, and the stores- the scene was captivating. "Now we on the famous 125th street and Lenox Avenue." Sarah said. "Down the street is the Apollo theatre, you heard of that right? And on Seventh Avenue is the Theresa Hotel; I'll take you to a show at the Apollo. You in Harlem now Jaysun, and you will probably see more Negroes here than anywhere else in the world. Hell you might see more in my block than in all a Cha'ston." She said with a laugh.

Jay was too overwhelmed at what he saw of this big city and its inhabitants to respond to Sarah's spontaneous guided tour. They turned into her block on 127th street and entered her building number 282. There were people sitting on the stoop and they greeted her.

"Hi Sarah, I see you done got you a sweet young thing, he moving in wit you?" Said one lady about Sarah's age. The other stoop dwellers all laughed. "You hush ya mouth, hussy; this my god-son, gonna stay wit me for the summer he just graduated yestaday and I want y'all to watch out for him."

"I'll watch out for him. I live in apt 3-E sweetie." said another lady.

"Oh no you don't tramp, he ain't coming near you. Com'on Jaysun, lem me get you off this stoop fore you get attacked on your first night here, your mother would kill me."

Sarah's apartment was on the fourth floor that had five other apartments. Her apartment was on the front and it overlooked 127th Street. There were two bedrooms, a small kitchen and bath. The floor was covered with black and white square linoleum; very neat. "Lem me show you around my place. It small but I like it and the rent is ffordable. Your bedroom is on the front and you can look out to 127th street."

Sarah obviously loved the color red. Besides the bathroom, which had bright red towels and red toilet accessories and curtains, the bedroom Jay was to sleep in had red bed covers and floor mats.

"Well Jaysun, this is your home for the summer. I don't have no rules. Your mama said you is a responsible young man, so that's good enough for me okay?"

"Yes ma'am, this is fine I like it. I really appreciate you taking me in like this, and I don't want you to treat me like company, I'm here to work and save some money for college so I hope not to be in your way." Jay said with all sincerity and a big smile.

Sarah laughed. "You won't be in my way. I glad you here. I don't go out much. I don't trust people here but maybe we'll go to the Apollo or do something when you is off. You want to start work tomorrow or wait until Monday? Shirley wants you to start with the breakfast, is that okay?"

"Oh I want to start right away so tomorrow is fine. What time should I be up?"

"We start breakfast at seven, so why don't you call your mom tell her you fine then you can get some sleep or watch television or whatever you want. I'm goin to bed, you sure you don't want something to eat? The refrigerator is full of food so help yuself. I don't cook much cause I get my meals at the restaurant, you will to and that's good."

"Good night Miss Sarah and thanks again" Jay realize he had to get used to Sarah's questions that don't need answers. He called his mother; assured her that he arrived safe and sound, listened again to her warnings and then went to bed. He soon fell asleep to the all night street sounds of Harlem, New York.

CHAPTER 6

Jay was up at 5 a.m. He was just finishing his shower and suddenly, the bathroom door opened and in walked Sarah into the steamy mist. He was completely nude. "Oh Jay, I forget you wus here. I'm so sorry; lord Jesus, I ain't use to nobody being here and I just furgot". Jay was frozen in his tracks not knowing what to do. Sarah made no attempt to leave but just stared at the graduate, talking but not looking into his face. After what seem like an eternity, Jay grabbed a towel and covered himself and said, "I'm finish Miss Sarah, I was just leaving."

Sarah was silent as she pulled her nightgown tight around her body. Jay brushed against her as he left the bathroom; towel pulled tight around his body. This scene would be etched in his mind for a long time.

They arrived at the restaurant at 6 a.m. After the short walk from 127th street to Lenox Avenue, Jay was even more amazed at the daytime scene of Harlem. It was Saturday morning and the remnants of the night before were visible. Trash was strewn throughout the streets as if there was an outdoor party. People; some coming home, some going out, and some still hanging out.

He had put on his starch white shirt and black trousers. He carried his black bow tie, not wanting to put that on yet. Mr. Earl, at the restaurant in Charleston always made sure his waiters were dressed in clean shirts and pressed black trousers when reporting to work. If you weren't prepared, that is not pass his inspection, he would say; 'You can't work in my dining room today, go home'

For the first time since Jay arrived the night before, Sarah didn't have much to say. They walked in silence to the restaurant. She appeared to be preoccupied. When they arrived she said, "This is the famous Shirley's. I been here gon' on six years now; it's like home to me. Most of the people here are very nice, Shirley don't tolerate no nonsense and I'm glad to be working fo her. There is usually a busy Saturday and Sunday morning breakfast crowd. You will start off being busy, you ready?"

The two walked into a large dining room that was bustling with activity. No customers were there yet but preparation was under way. "Good morning." She said to all within ear short. "This my god-son Jaysun, he got in last night and is ready to work."

The first person to greet Jay was Merle, Shirley's daughter. She is the cashier and in charge of the dining room. "Hello Mr. Jayson welcome aboard. We've heard so much about you. I need you to fill out some papers for me. You can take them home and bring them back tomorrow. Today, we just want you to be a bust-boy. So you'll work with Sarah to learn the menu and order taking procedures. I understand you have had some experience"

"Yes ma'am I know how to wait on tables" Jayson said with a shy look but at the same time confident.

"Good; then it won't take you long. Sarah, get him a jacket; you and Jay work section three. My mother is in her office in the back." Sarah took Jay to the kitchen and introduced him around.

The aroma of this kitchen was far different from Henry's and the Francis Marion hotel back in Charleston. Jay was greeted with the savory smell of collard greens, fried chicken, smothered pork chops, corn bread, peach cobbler and other soul food specialties.

First was CJ, the morning head chief. This is the man responsible for the famous salmon cakes that are popular at Shirley's. The menu was not unfamiliar to Jay, for he had grown up eating this food expertly prepared by his grandmother.

CJ, gruff and unshaven, appeared to be in his fifties. He was a cook in the navy. He looked Jay over and growled, "Young blood, just off the boat huh? So you from Charleston huh? You a rice eating geatchie like

Sarah?" Jay knew he was being tested so in his best Gullah dialect said to CJ, "Yus sur Mr. CJ. Ah is from Chatson, I loves my rice. I eats em evyday, yus sur, sho do."

The Kitchen help roared with laughter. CJ grab Jay's hand in a firm grip and said,

"Welcome to my kitchen, young blood. I control what goes on back here; just understand that and we'll get along fine."

Then Jay met the other cooks. There was Merion, who was preparing the scramble eggs, the hash browns, beef and pork and hot sausages. He then met Steve, who prepared the steaks, smothered chops with gravy and biscuits.

The Kitchen smelled heavenly and Jay was impressed with the set up. CJ was also the main man responsible for the lunch menu that would follow. This was not the kitchen of the Francis Marion Hotel restaurant but these brothers knew what they were doing.

Off into a corner office Jay spotted a woman whom he assumed to be Shirley Davenport. She was busy doing paperwork. She looked up, saw Jay and Sarah, and motioned them over to her office. She is a handsome woman, maybe in her fifties, Jay thought, and very elegant. She is the sole owner of the restaurant and had been in business for over twenty years.

"Come on in Sarah, is this the young man you've been talking about?"

"This him, my fine god-son; he ready to work today, is that okay?"

"Sure that's fine Sarah. He looks like he is ready and I like that. Jayson, is that right?" Shirley extended her hand. Jay gave her a hearty handshake and said, "I'm extremely happy to have this opportunity and I thank you very much. You will not regret it."

"And we're glad to have you. We don't usually hire summer help but Sarah said you are an exceptional young man. All I ask is that you treat my customers good, come to work everyday and every thing will be fine. Sarah also told me that you're experienced, is that right?"

"Yes ma'am" Jay said, ever mindful of his manners, "I have been a waiter and done some bar tendering also"

"Good. "We don't need a bartender just yet." Shirley laughed. "But we might one day. Well, I'm finished here. Got to get ready for a check of the kitchen; we open the doors in ten minutes. Good luck Jayson, let's all make some money today"

Jay spent the early part of the breakfast service following Sarah around. He caught on fast to Shirley's system. His job was to clear Sarah's tables after the meal was completed and place silver settings for new arrivals. He also had to see that water was served when the parties sat down. He brought biscuits, butter and other condiments to the parties. This was the work of a bus boy, a position Jay had graduated from years ago when he worked at Henry's. It was very busy that morning with families, couples and singles. There was a long waiting list of people out for Saturday morning breakfast at Shirley's. To Jay this was a piece of cake.

There is a term used by waiters to describe how busy he is, and has many customers waiting to be served. The term is, ' I'm up a tree.' Jay observed several servers 'up a tree.' He, however, performed his duties diligently and expertly. He also bused other server tables and received a nod of approval and thanks from them. He heard them say, 'Who is that kid? He is good.'

Back in the Charleston restaurants, Jay moved through the dining room with ease. He had a knack for this kind of work and was rewarded by his customers for his flair in serving a meal. He routinely made more tips than all the waiters at the hotel in Charleston. He did things like grip the water glass from the bottom with just his thumb and forefinger and placed the glass on the table with an outward flick of his wrist. He never placed a water glass on a table with a grip around the top of the glass like he had observed at Shirley's.

Mid-way through breakfast, he announced to Sarah, "I'm ready, I can serve lunch today. Tell Ms. Shirley." Sarah looked at him in disbelief but knew in her mind that he indeed was ready.

CHAPTER 7

The restaurant had a collection of regular customers. Some among them were real characters. Jay had learned them all and had waited on most of them at some time. He was at the restaurant now for more than a month and stood out from the other waiters, including Sarah. He was becoming very popular with the regulars who liked his style, manners, cool, wit, and sophistication. Among the regulars was Mason, the numbers banker who sat in one of the front booths for lunch everyday and worked on his receipts for the day's action.

All the restaurant employees played the numbers and Mason booked their play. Jay didn't play this strange thing because first of all he was saving his money. His tips were very good.

There were several Harlem businessmen from 125th street, White and Negro who came to the restaurant for lunch. Among these were Milton Brown and his assistants Gwen Myers and Sharon Mack. They were financial people. Milton ran a branch office for a Wall Street brokerage firm. The branch office was on 125th Street. He is a stockbroker, Gwen is his assistant and she too was preparing to be a stockbroker. Sharon was secretary to the two.

Jay never understood what they would talk to him about whenever he served them. He had never heard of a stock market or a stockbroker;

and the only Wall Street he was familiar with was a street with project housing in downtown Charleston.

What they would talk to him about was the same thing Mason the numbers banker was talking about and that meant taking chances with your money. Jay would have none of that.

Occasionally, Gwen came back to the restaurant to have dinner by herself. She would come to Jay's station to be served by him. Her conversation was not about money so much, but about Jay. He had an idea that she liked him but he played it cool.

She lived some place called the Bronx. Gwen was a night student at City College. She was from Atlanta; came to New York a year earlier and landed a job on Wall Street. When the firm opened a branch in Harlem, she took the opportunity to work there because it was not such a long commute from home. Plus, she liked the comfort of being around Negroes. After being exposed to the financial world, Gwen dreamed of a career as a stockbroker.

The firm that she worked for recognized that there might be an opportunity for business from the minority community, so they encouraged her efforts. Under the tutelage of Milton, she was on the way to obtaining her license as a Registered Representative.

One evening Gwen came in for dinner. She sat at Jay's station. After placing her order, she said, "Jay, you really need to come by our office one day and let me show you what smart people do with their money."

Jay replied, "I know what they do. They put it in a bank. I've got an account back home and my mother deposits money that I send to her"

"That's good Jay, but you don't grow real money there. The best place to grow money is the stock market. You're an intelligent guy, why don't you take some time and let me teach you something that you won't regret?"

Jay saw this as an opportunity for something else but not about money. He was clearing away her table and whispered to her, I'm off in about a half hour why don't you wait for me, you can start teaching me tonight."

Gwen was somewhat startled by this reply. She had considered Jay rather shy and this suggestion said something else. While she did have an eye on him and seriously wanted to talk to him about the stock market, she was not quite sure how to take his offer. She looked at him curiously and said, "If you like, I have the key to our office on 125th Street. We can go there and I can show you what I'm talking about. I'll go there and wait for you." Her heartbeat increased as she suggested this.

"I'll be there in forty -five minutes." Jay said. "I'll take care of your check. "

"No, that's nice of you Jay, but I've got it." As she got up to leave, she left her usual tip for Jay but felt ill at ease for leaving one. It was, she reasoned still the right thing to do.

Jay felt that Gwen was very pretty- Sharon too. They were not like girls back home. They talked differently acted differently and just seemed to be of a nature unknown to Jay. These were the girls his mom and Sarah had warned about. They both said, 'watch them New York girls' but he really didn't know what to look for. So he thought maybe tonight I'll find out.

Sarah didn't work the dinner shift that night so Jay was there alone.

It was not particularly busy so the other servers would not mind if he left early. After checking with Merle, he was on his way to 125th Street to meet with a New York girl- but in reality a southern girl, who had been in New York longer then he.

Gwen heard the elevator stop and the doors opened. The office was on the fifth floor and as far as she knew, no else was on this floor. It was after 10p.m.- Wednesday night. She told the security guard she was expecting a client and it was okay to let him up to the office. While she waited, she had gathered sales material that the office used to qualify potential investors. She put that away after second thought and would instead use a pamphlet designed to educate prospects on the merits of stocks as an investment.

"Okay, I 'm here." Jay said as he entered the office, "Teach me high finance."

"Welcome to my office Jay, this is the place where you can buy a piece of America." Gwen responded nervously.

"Do you know what stock ownership means"?

"No".

"Well." Gwen started, "You're familiar with companies like General Motors, right?"

"Yea, they make Chevies, Buick, Pontiac and Cadillac."

"That's right. In fact, GM is the world's biggest automaker and the world's biggest corporation. They sell a lot of cars and trucks. They make a great deal of money and as a result of that, there is an opportunity for investors, or people like you, to participate in their good fortune. One way to do that is to buy the stock issued by General Motors. The purchase of their stock actually makes you one of the owners of GM. You would profit if the stock that you purchased increases in value. With their cars and trucks sales and sound management of the company, there is good reason to believe that GM will remain profitable and thus the price of the stock will go up. You follow me so far?"

Jay was half listening. He looked directly into her eyes, but he also stole glances at her dark skinned bare legs. "Yea, I guess so. I do see a lot of their cars around. But why should I do this? Is this something safe for me to do?"

"There is some risk; but it is a risk that banks, insurance companies, pension plans and other institutions, as well as individuals take every day. They put their money in a situation where the best growth is possible and the risk minimal. I have some material here that I want you to read. It tells you about the Dow Jones Averages. It further tells you about the growth of the stock market and the historical return on investment that stock ownership provides. I'm sure you have dreams of becoming wealthy or at least not having to struggle to live and enjoy the finer things in life. The only thing that might prohibit you from having a good financial life is the lack of knowledge. Now I didn't plan to meet with you tonight and it's late, so I can't get into everything that I would normally discuss with you at this hour but, read this stuff and if you have any questions after that I will be more than happy to answer them for you. If I don't have the answers, Milton will. He has been in the business for some time. Okay?"

"Do you own stocks yourself?" Jay asked.

"Sure I do. I'm just getting started. Remember, I just graduated last year and I don't have a lot of money but I got my parents and some relatives involved and so far it's been good. Think about this. I'm going to take the test next week then I can be your broker, I'll make you rich"

Gwen said with a laugh. "Then you won't need a scholarship to go to college.

Actually Jay, this business might interest you. You might want to consider this as a career. It captured me. I was like you. I came here to work for the summer. - Got this Wall Street job and was fascinated with this world. It might do the same for you. You can make a lot of money"

"I'll think about it but I can tell you now, I'm going to college, I'm going to be a lawyer. I guess I should be going now. I'll read your stuff. Are you leaving now?"

"Yea Jay we can go now It's late and I've got to be back here at eight in the morning."

Jay and Gwen walked to the subway at 125th and Lenox for her ride to the Bronx. It was now after 11 p.m.. Jay pondered what this girl was really all about. She seemed all business but that could be a ploy he thought. At least, he thought, he didn't make the first move. He didn't embarrass himself. They reached the subway and Gwen said, "So Jay, what do you do when you're not working?"

"Nothing much," he replied, "I don't know the city yet and I'm not much into going out any way. My god- mother, you know Sarah, she took me to the Apollo a couple of times. I saw the Shirelles and the Coasters. I enjoyed that."

"Do you mean that you haven't been out of Harlem since you've been here?"

"Not really."

"Well, the next time you have some time off, call me, here is my business card. I'll take you on a tour. I'll show you New York."

"That will be fine." Jay said as he read the card   "Call your office number?"

"Wait let me put my home number on the card. You can call me there too.   Good night Jay, read those pamphlets now."

"I will and I'll call you soon. Will you be at the restaurant for lunch tomorrow?"

"Yes, I'll see you then."

Jay walked the two blocks to 127th Street. When he turned off Lenox, he saw Sarah coming toward him with a look of concern on her face. "Jay wher you been? I called the restaurant when you didn't come home and they said you left. I wus scared to death. You all right? Did you go som wher? I thought something-happened Lord Jesus. You know it bad out here sometimes."

"I'm okay Miss Sarah; I just went for a walk. I'm sorry I didn't mean to worry you. I wanted to see who was coming to the Apollo so I walked to 125th Street"

"Oh that's okay child; I worry all the time. Come on let's get home so I can call the restaurant and tell them you're okay. They all got concern too. You know Jay; everybody there loves you. Shirley, Merle, all the cooks and servers- they all think you a wonderful young man. Even the customers tell Shirley how nice you is. And the womens, well, we see um all go to your station. Them fresh heifers- all wants to be served by you. We don't make no money no more since you there." Sarah laughed out loud. "Course Jay, I think you wonderful too. Yo mamma is such a lucky women." Now don't you ever be a dog like some mens out here. You keep them down home manners, you hear?"

"Yes ma'am Miss Sarah" Jay said with a shy look.

They entered the apartment that had been the world of Jay and Sarah for six weeks now. It had been a period of the two bumping into each other in all forms of dress and undress. Jay also noticed that Sarah did not seem to have any male friends. When he did answer the phone and a male voice asked for Sarah, she put them off rather quickly. When he took messages for her from a man, she would say; "What dat fool want" or "Why that dog calling me, I told him don't call me no more."

From her grumbling, Jay learned that Sarah had some rocky relationships and was not going to be hurt again no time soon.

Tired after working the breakfast, lunch and dinner Jay showered and was off to bed. He was going to read the brochures that Gwen gave him but the feel of sleep was overwhelming and he was drifting off.

He felt as if he was in a deep dream as he sensed the bed covers move slowly off him. Then the warm kisses on his cheeks and the low slow breathing. The perfume unmistakably told him whom this was but not what was happening.

His body was now being caressed with tenderness and care. The light kisses now moving from cheeks to shoulders to chest and back to cheeks. His toes began to curl. Lying on his back, Jay opened his eyes to see Sarah as she kissed him long and hard; not the way a god mother would. Finally, she said in almost a whisper, "Do you want me to stop?" Jay responded in a choking voice "No"

"Do you think I bad?"

"No I don't."

"Promise me one thing Jaysun, and I want you to swear." Sarah was now off the bed and slowly removing the nightgown she was wearing. She revealed all that Jay had not seen of her before. "You must never ever tell your mother."

CHAPTER 8

Mrs. Linda Hall was one of the most distinguished regulars at Shirley's. Not because she was famous, but because she was a grand old lady. She was always impeccably dressed, exuded class and loved by all in the neighborhood. Mrs. Hall is a retired widow. The talk about her is that her husband left her quite well off financially. She lived alone in one of the great Brownstones that remained on 126th Street but was never converted into an apartment building. She was about 72 years old and walked with the help of a cane. Since she lived alone, she often came to the restaurant for most of her meals. She would say, "I'm taking Arthur for a walk." She was referring to her arthritic condition.

Mrs. Hall quickly took to the new waiter and informed Merle that he is to be her waiter when she came for her meals. She loved Jay's manners and class she told Merle and furthermore, he had good upbringing. Jay made sure that she was pleased with her meal and service and always made a fuss over her. He always complimented her on her dress, hair, and even said to her once "Mrs. Hall, the older you get the more pretty you are." She loved hearing this and Jay always got a big tip. The other waiters were resentful but still liked the young blood from the South; after all he is only here for the summer and would be gone in the fall.

There were times when Mrs. Hall would ask Merle to let Jay walk her home after her meal. Of course she obliged the grand old dame.

There was no fear that someone would dare do harm to the great lady of Harlem, but more fear that she might fall from her uneasy steps. Jay gladly did this. He would take Mrs. Hall by the arm and escort her to her home.

What no one knew because she never mentioned it is the fact that Mrs. Hall, the great lady, had developed heart disease in her advanced age. She was on medication, which she sometimes carried on her person but most times she left it in her medicine cabinet.

Another of the people Jay met in his first summer in New York was Sye- Sylvester Long. He lived in the apartment down the hall from Sarah. Sye had spent time in the army. He was retired and lived on disability. No one knew what the disability was because Sye still lived life to the fullest. Sarah introduced Jay to him one day as they met in the hallway. Sye also frequented Shirley's for meals with several different women.

One day as Jay was going home alone after working breakfast and lunch, he ran into Sye as he too was going home. "Hey young blood, how you doing?"

"I'm just tired, Mr. Long. I'm going in here and pass out"

"Call me Sye; come on to my apartment; you like jazz? I just bought a new Miles. I'm gonna put it now."

"Okay." Jay replied. He had heard some of the music coming out of Sye's apartment and wanted to know what some of it was. He liked what little he heard so this was an opportunity that he didn't want to pass up. He had heard of Miles Davis before and some of his music when he went to buy reeds for his sax at the music store in Charleston. He couldn't, like other customers go into the private room to listen to a record before purchase. This was available only for the white customers.

Sye's apartment was very tidy for a single man. He had shelves full of albums; most of them jazz. The apartment had a distinct odor of incense that Jay had never smelled before but it was nice and he liked it.

"Sit down man I'll be right back. Sye disappeared into his bedroom but could be heard as he said to Jay, "You related to Sarah?"

"No, she is my god-mother, she is a good friend of my mother." Sye came back with a little box, which he placed on the coffee table in front of Jay then went to his stereo to put on the Miles album.

"Your god-mother is a nice lady, she won't give me a chance though. I've been trying for that ass since I first saw it and she lives right next door to me. We get alone but she said I got too many women for her. I told her I would put em all down for her but she just laughs at me. But I'll get it one day."

Sye put the album on and handed the jacket to Jay to read. The album is entitled *'Miles Davis Kind of Blue'*. Sye sits down and opens the box as the album begins with a tune call, *'So What.'* Jay hears the melodic sound of an up right bass and piano in duet. "That's Paul Chambers and Bill Evans." Sye said.

The music moved into a sound and rhythm not heard by Jay before but he loved it. He moved his head and patted his feet to the beat and the hunting sound of Miles' muted trumpet.

Jay then saw for the first time someone roll a marijuana cigarette. Sye lit the joint, took a long drag and passed it to Jay.

"No sir, I don't smoke."

Sye laughed and said, "I don't either. This isn't tobacco this is herb. I always enjoy herb when I'm listening to my music."

Sye didn't need to tell Jay what it was. Although he had never smelled marijuana before or been around it, Jay knew exactly what it was as soon as he smelled it. He also now knew what the incense was for.

This scene repeated itself many times in the next weeks. Jay found himself going to Sye's apartment when he was off to take in the great music and listen to the world traveler expound his experiences with women, politics, music, religion, sports and just about every thing else that Sye had an opinion about. Sye never attempted to share his joint with Jay after that first meeting but Jay wished that he would.

And then there was Maxine. The alcoholic, who also lived directly across from Sarah's apartment. She was harmless, kept to herself, but just drank too much. Sarah told Jay that Maxine was once a singer with a famous band but she couldn't keep off the bottle and now lived a life waiting for the next disability check and the walk to the liquor store.

When Sarah introduced Jay to Maxine, he immediately thought of Harriet and her mother. One could tell that Maxine was once a person of class but the bottle made her a woman who could pass for sixty but was only about forty-five. There was little doubt among the tenants in Sarah's building that one day, Maxine would simply drink herself to death.

CHAPTER 9

The secret between Jay and Sarah that took place in the bedroom continued; there was more intensity and emotion involved now. They no longer slept in separate beds. Sarah was more protective at work and Jay felt that the other employees knew about them.

Jay had other thoughts on his mind also. His mom informed him that the scholarship would come through but the freshman class for Talladega College was full for the coming fall semester. This meant he would not be able to enter until the second semester in January.

Jay was not too disappointed and this surprised him. He was beginning to really like New York and had thoughts of another career path that he could pursue there.

He could enter City College as Gwen suggested. While he hadn't made up his mind, the problem would be how would his mother take this development.

Jay was working the lunch shift one day when Merle called him.

"Jay, would you mind delivering lunch to Dr. Weinstein? He is a dentist. His office is on 124th street. Sometimes he is busy and can't come in, he tips good too."

"Sure, I don't mind," said Jay.

"Good I'll take care of your station. Go see CJ; he has the order, Number 652 on the first floor."

Jay picked up the take- out package from CJ and headed to 124th street. The bright mid-day sun was high and almost blinding and Jay had to shade his eyes to the adjustment. As usual, the streets were full of people; it seems they always were.

He arrived at the dentist office and was greeted by a very attractive woman who appeared to be in her mid thirties. She looked like a virgin in her starched white uniform. Pinned to her uniform was a nametag with the name Barbara Cook on it. Her hair was pulled back in a ponytail that protruded from her nurse's cap.

Although she was sitting, Jay got a sense that she was rather tall. Her bright wide smile highlighted by the dimples in her cheeks painted a portrait of an elegant lady.

He immediately realized that he had seen her before. She occasionally had lunch at the restaurant and usually sat alone at the counter.

"Can I help you?"

"Yes ma'am, I'm from Shirley's, I'm delivering lunch here to a Dr. Weinstein."

"Oh yes, he did call in, wait here, I'll tell him." As she got up to go to his office, Jay saw that he was right about her height. He watched a perfectly proportioned body, about five- nine, on a gorgeous pair of legs walk away from the reception area. He watched in silence with his eye trained on her butt. He was always a leg man but appreciated a nice butt. She turned down a hallway that led to the doctor's office.

Jay looked around the drab reception room. There were several uncomfortable looking chairs and a small corner table full of very old magazines. It was immediately known that the doctor did not care very much for patient atmosphere.

She reappeared at the hallway and said, "This way please; he is on the phone but he said come right on in." Jay passed her in the narrow hallway and got a whiff of her perfume. Nice he thought.

The doctor's office was as drab as the reception area. There was a heavy order of some kind of disinfectant. The air conditioner was turned very high as Jay noticed the coldness of the room. There were papers scattered all over his desk and not much lighting.

The fiftytish White man with thinning gray hair was in deep conversation on the phone and mouthed to Jay to come in.

The doctor pointed to a table in the corner of the office for Jay to put his lunch.

He continued his conversation while reaching into his back pocket for his wallet. "Yea that one was good Neil, we did all right on that one. What's that name again? How do you spell that? M-E-G-A-N associates, what's it at now fifteen? Next week? Well, put me down for a thousand okay? Call me tomorrow; I'll be in around ten. I may have someone else for you."

The doctor took a notebook out of the desk draw and proceeded to write down information that must have been very important. He wanted to do this before the matter of his lunch was done. "There" he said. "Thank you young man, what do I owe you?"

"Five-fifty sir." The doctor removed ten dollars from his wallet.

"Thank you sir"

"You're very welcome young man and thank Shirley for me. I had to take a very important phone call and I was starved."

Jay pocketed the money and was back in the reception room. Barbara was on the phone herself with a patient. Jay waited until she was finished then said; "I didn't see you at lunch today."

"Oh I brought my lunch today. I might not get out much now. I'm by myself for a while. Ann is out; she is about to have a baby."

"Well if you find that you can't get out, I'll be happy to bring lunch to you, but it doesn't look very busy here."

"We have more appointments later today but Dr. Weinstein had this call he was waiting for all day and he was going to be tied up. So I had to be here to take other calls or just be in the office. When his broker calls, his patients have to wait"

"Broker? What kind of broker?"

"Lord knows I don't know. But it has something to do with Wall Street. That much I do know. Sometimes Mr. Weiss would call and Ann and me would hear Dr. Weinstein shout. You know like Whoooo."

As Barbara continued to talk, several thoughts ran through Jay's mind. First Barbara's beauty and this stock market thing again. He wasn't listening to her but looked straight into her hazel eyes. He thought- she is about the same age as my mother and just as good looking.

"Well I've got to get back to the restaurant, It was nice meeting you Mrs. Cook, I'll see you when you come to lunch again."

"It was nice meeting you too- Ah, what's' your name?"

"Everybody calls me Jay; see you."

Back outside, Jay realized just how cool the doctor's office was when the mid-day heat kissed him. His mind was racing, no; boiling was more like it. What did he just overhear? He knew that lunch service was over and the restaurant wouldn't be busy so he was in no hurry to return.

He looked towards 125th and saw Gwen exiting the subway station. She had been very happy the past couple of days because she had successfully completed stockbroker training. She also had passed the grueling, as she described it, series –seven, stockbroker exam.

She waited for Jay when she saw that he was heading for the restaurant. Jay thought, she looks so cool, even in this heat.

"Hi Jay, where you been?"

"Hi pretty lady, I'm also the take out guy. "You having a late lunch? Didn't see you earlier."

"Don't tell me you actually missed me"

"Well, yes I did. You know I look for you everyday."

"That's nice of you. I worked at our downtown office today. I had to finish some paper work now that I'm a registered broker. Hey, I want to celebrate, why don't you take me out Saturday I can show you downtown New York."

"I don't mind. I want to talk to you anyway."

"Oh good. I'm actually here on an appointment. I'm going to open an account for Shirley and Merle. When I'm through with them we can make plans okay?"

As Gwen headed to Shirley's office, Jay caught the look on Sarah's face as they walked in together.

"Jay," Merle called out, "Did the doctor take care of you?"

"Yes he did."

"Good, I've got some tips for you that your customers left. So, is Gwen going to be the one?"

Jay laughed. "She's a nice girl but you know I'll be going to school soon and—Merle cut him off- "Why don't you go to school here?"

"You know, she suggested the same thing, but I've got a scholarship to Talladega College and I'm sorta set on going there." As Jay spoke these words, in heart he knew that New York had gotten into his blood and it was going to be hard to leave.

"You know me and my mother have grown very fond of you so, one day, we, you and me, have to talk"

Sarah came over to Jay and said, "Honey I want you to go to church wit me Sunday, okay?"

"I would Sarah but I didn't bring a suit with me"

"That's okay. I got some money saved; I'll buy a suit for you. That'll be a graduation gift from me. I been wunderin what to git you."

"Oh no Sarah I can't let you do that."

"And why can't I buy my god-son a suit. We'll go on 125th Street after we finish here, pik you out a nice suit and you kin go wit me Sunday"

"Okay." Jay replied reluctantly

Shirley told Gwen that when she became a stockbroker she would open an account with her. Shirley had never invested before but had been solicited by a few White male stockbrokers in the past.

She had decided that if she did this, it would be with this young girl because she trusted her.

Shirley was concerned about the future of her granddaughters; Merle's two little girls. Merle's husband it seems is a drug addict and she hadn't seen him in years. They met in college and got married after graduation.

Merle was only going to work in the restaurant for just a little while to teach her mother the accounting and management principals that she learned in college. Merle's husband, also an accounting graduate, worked for an accounting firm until he lost the job. Soon after, hints of his lifestyle began to surface. He blamed the White man for his situation.

Shirley was not convinced that her son-in-law was victimized. She did believe that he, however, was the cause of his own failings. He used to work in the restaurant but Shirley fired him because he often missed work and was caught stealing from the till and pilfering the waiter's tips. He left home and simply did not return one day. He called once on his oldest daughter's birthday so they knew he was alive at least.

Merle went out with a man who owned a funeral home. He was quite well off financially but she couldn't get serious over him because she had a problem, she said, with him putting his hands on her.

Jay liked talking to Merle. He saw some of his mother's traits in her. He liked the fact that she didn't have a spoiled brat; my mother is the owner attitude. She worked as hard as anyone around the restaurant and was respected by all the employees.

She is twenty-nine years old, a tad overweight, but a pretty face. And except occasionally with the undertaker, didn't go out often. The male customers always hit on her at the restaurant but she gave them all that great smile of hers and ushered them to a table. She had all kind of job offers to leave the restaurant but turned them all down. Most people knew that it was her ideas and management skills that helped make Shirley's the successful operation it is today.

Merle has been at the restaurant over ten years now. She has graciously accepted the fact that this will be her life work. Her life is comfortable; she has two lovely children whose future will be somewhat assured by a check and her mother's signature on Gwen's new account form. And her own life is secured by the contents of her mother's will; which she has knowledge off. Jay looked forward to discussing his future with Merle. He trusted her judgment.

Gwen opened four accounts at the restaurant. Shirley opened a personal account for herself and custodial accounts for her two granddaughters. Merle also opened an account for herself. Gwen was delighted. She walked toward Jay with a huge grin on her face. "Jay, you can let me go back to the office with five new accounts if you opened one with me today."

"I might just do that Gwen. We can talk about that when we go out Saturday night."

CHAPTER 10

Sarah and Jay headed to 125th Street looking for a store that had a suit that Jay would like. From his passing and looking into the windows of some men stores, he was not impressed with any that he had seen. He was not looking for clothing so nothing captured his attention. He was a fairly decent dresser in Charleston and there was a certain style that he liked. He did not see that style on 125th street. He decided that he would not be difficult and perhaps hurt Sarah's feeling.

At 125th and Seventh Avenue, they spotted Sye. He was buying incense from a street vendor. As they approached him, he looked up and smiled and said, "Hi Sarah, hey young blood wher yall going, the Apollo?"

"No man I'm looking for a suit."

"Out here?"

"Yea."

"Now man, I could be wrong, but you don't strike me as the type. You wanna nice suite, your style? You need to go to Barney's downtown, Seventeen Street."

"Seventeen Street!" Sarah said, "We can find a nice suit here." Immediately, Jay cut Sarah off. "I would like to go downtown I have never seen any thing I liked on this street."

"I'll take him downtown Sarah I ain't doing nothing" Sye said.

Slowly Sarah felt in her heart that she was losing Jay to the influence of others. In just over two months she saw her control of Jay's movement change from dependent on her to following his own choices. She talked to his mother at least once every week. The conversation was always the same. 'Yes he's doing fine, yes he minds me, yes everyone loves him, yes he is a good young man.' It was all true.

Sarah managed to stop Mason, the numbers banker, when he offered Jay a job in his enterprise, as he called it. Mason, impressed by the young blood from the south, told Jay he could make three times what he made at the restaurant including tips, by working for him. Jay was not quite sure what his job would entail so he told Sarah about it. She was furious that Mason would do this and got into his face when she saw him at the restaurant.

Mason was not a handsome man. Were it not for his money, no women would look at him twice. He didn't have to be told this and as a result did not trust women. Except for Sarah. She never came on to him for his money, maybe because she knew it was from illegal activities. But Mason held a soft spot for Sarah.

"Now Mason, you know this my god-son and he going to college soon so leave him be with all this talk bout the money he could mak wit you. Did you tell him he could go to jail? Did you tell him, how many times you been locked up?"

Looking at the only woman who could intimidate him, Mason said sheepishly, "I only wanted the boy to make some real money. He got a good head on his shoulders and a good head for figures; I thought he could handle my books, I was gonna pay him three hundred a week"

"I don't care what you gon pay him he ain't workin for you, understand?"

"Sure Sarah, you know I ain't meant no harm, I like that kid. He reminds me of myself"

Sarah cut him off. "He ain't nuthing like you. I always thought you wus a nice man but you knows whut I don't like bout you Mason." And that was the end of that.

Now, Sarah sees the influence of this girl Gwen, and that Jay spends time in Sye's apartment listening to his music; that he talks to Merle at work quite a bit. She managed to control her jealousy over the long distance phone calls that he received almost every day. What is she to do; this is the son of her high school friend and she felt ashamed at her resentment. She reluctantly agreed to let Jay go with Sye. She handed Jay some folded money and headed back home.

Jay came home with a great looking blue suit. It was tailored on the spot. Sye told him to put cuffs in the pants but Jay was going to do that anyway. He saw that Milton, Gwen's boss, wore cuffs and Jay thought he was an especially good dresser. The suit cost two hundred and fifty dollars. Sarah had given him two hundred. He also purchased a shirt and tie to match the suit.

Sarah was pleased. It was decided that they would both take off from the restaurant on Sunday morning in two weeks and attend the church that Sarah went to most often.

Jay went over to Sye's apartment to listen to some music Saturday after lunch and wait until time for his date with Gwen. Sarah was going to get some sleep before going back to the restaurant for dinner service. Jay hoped that Sye would offer a joint during his visit but Sye never did since the first visit and if he were to partake, he would have to ask Sye. This might be the day to experiment.

Gwen took the subway from The Bronx. She sat in the middle of the ten-car train so that when it stopped at 125th Street, she would be at the turnstile entrance. Jay is to be there to meet her. He was there and they were able to get back on the same train together before it left the station.

She was in an exceedingly good mood and felt devilish. She had been on the phone all day telling her parents, other relatives and friends about receiving her broker license and that she was on her way to something special. Her parents were not happy about her decision to stay in New York.

They wanted her to attend Spelman College in Atlanta like her older sister did. Her sister was now teaching in the public school system in Atlanta.

Gwen reluctantly registered at Spelman but prayed that something else would happen. She did not want to be a teacher. In fact, she had no idea what she wanted to do. She knew what she did not want to do.

At the invitation of an aunt, one of her father's sisters, she went to New York to work for the summer. Her aunt Jennifer was the free spirit of her father's siblings and the favorite of her aunts. Her father warned her before leaving Atlanta "My sister Jenn is crazy, don't you be doing the stuff she does."

Gwen thought she was real cool. Like, she was the first woman Gwen ever meet who had an Afro. She came to Atlanta to visit them and was wearing a dashsheki, and talking about black power and black pride. This did not go over very well in some parts of Atlanta in 1960.

The subway was crowded as usual. After having traversed it for a few times, Jay could handle the swings, sways and noise of the fast moving train. He now looked like a typical unconcerned New Yorker. They rode to 50th and Broadway.

Gwen had decided on a restaurant called the Hawaii Kia.

Jay saw for the first time the New York he had seen in magazines. He was walking down Broadway; a street of lights and glamour. At first, he thought there were more people in these streets than he had seen in Harlem streets. They were going to the movie houses, the theaters and to the many restaurants that lined the streets. There was the traffic, and the street noise and the heartbeat of a very busy city. This scene was exciting, thrilling, and impressive all at once to Jay.

Jay was anxious to talk to Gwen. He had deep thoughts on his mind but was going to wait for the right time to broach his plan to her.

"Is anyone else going to be here?" he asked her.

"No, just you and me babe, does that bother you?"

"No I just wanted to know."

They entered a restaurant with the décor of a Hawaiian scene. As you entered, the Maitre'd greet you by placing a lei around your neck. Then they were led to a table lit by a candle sitting in a coconut like container. The waitresses were clad in grass skirts. They also had some kind of exotic flower in their hair. Very pretty Jay thought and he was immediately impressed.

Gwen had been here before so she told Jay to have the oysters on the half shell for an appetizer and tiger prawns for the main course. If she is trying to impress me, Jay thought to himself, she doesn't know. He has been in fine restaurants; although not as a customer. He has served and eaten oysters and prawns at Henry's, one of the finest restaurants in Charleston. He would say nothing however; he would let her have her fun.

Gwen also ordered drinks, something in a tall glass with a lot of fruit. The food was delicious and service excellent. Jay enjoyed himself and felt good in Gwen's company.

She had three drinks and was feeling no pain. Jay had two and was at his limit.

He really didn't care for alcohol and would never drink to the point that he would not be in control of himself.

After a very enjoyable dinner, Gwen suggested that they walk down Broadway to 42nd street and get the subway there for the trip back uptown. Jay agreed. He had to see more of this magnificent city.

Gwen took his arm and held him tight as she pointed out the scenes of midtown Manhattan. It was more than the southern boy could imagine. He thought about Harriet as they walked. She would love this city. She would relish the excitement, the lights, the people and the fervor of a bustling mega city. Then he thought of Ruby. She would be frightened just by the immense size of this place.

As they walked, Gwen continued to point out the places of interest. She pointed out some of the famous restaurants along Broadway like Jack Dempsey's, Mamma Leone and the Stage Deli. She pointed out the Empire State building in the distant but very visible. She was feeling good. She had been in New York for one year but had made it a point to learn the city, and visit the tourist attractions.

She announced their arrival into Times Square. Jay saw young men offering their services to whoever would pay for it. He saw a street with only movie theaters on both sides; about ten. He saw signs advertising live sex shows. He saw bizarre and outlandish things going on all around him. If all this moved him, he never showed it. He sensed that Gwen was waiting for some sort of reaction from him but he was cool. In his mind, he was saying, Damm!

It was now about nine-thirty. Jay and Gwen moved through the crowded train looking for two seats together.

"Well Jay" she started, "You have just had a very short tour of downtown New York City, whata you think?"

"Each day I'm amazed by what I see here. I love it"

"See, I told you, it gets in your blood, are you gonna stay?"

"I still don't know yet, I haven't discussed it with my mom."

They didn't talk much during the ride uptown. Jay didn't like talking, which seem like shouting, to be heard above the noise of the train. Gwen likewise was silent.

When the train roared into the 96th street station and came to a stop, Gwen said, "You feel like ridding to the Bronx, it's still early?"

"Yea why not, I've never been there; might as well continue this tour. Where we going?"   "I live on the Grand Concourse and 172nd street. There were once great apartments there. I use to live with my aunt, but now I have my own place. We can go there."

Again Jay was surprised by Gwen's invitation but did not show it. "Do you mean we will go to your place?"

"Yes, does that scare you? You think I gonna rape you or something Jay Austin?"

"No that's the farthest thing from my mind, I know you're not like that. I just didn't know what you meant. I don't like to make mistakes like that"

The train was now past 125th street and Jay knew he had better call Sarah when he gets to Gwen's house. She would be waiting up for him and it looked like he was going to be out a little late.

At 168th Street, the subway was no longer below ground but on elevated tracks above the traffic below. Jay could look into apartment windows from the fast moving train. He hid his astonishment and wondered, how did people living so close to these tracks deal with this noise all day. The thought quickly left his mind. He really didn't care. He was about to be alone with Gwen again and that was more important.

He wanted to talk to her but she had those three drinks at the Hawaii Kai and was still feeling good. This was not the time to talk about his business, although he was anxious to do so. This may work out fine later.

The train rumbled above them leaving the station and Gwen proceeded to point out scenes of interest in this part of the Bronx, but Jay wasn't listening. All he noticed is that it wasn't quite as busy and crowded as Harlem and as bright and exciting as downtown. It was still New York.

The buildings were definitely nicer than those Jay had seen in Harlem. Gwen's building had a nice lobby and elevator. They rode to the twelfth floor and entered Gwen's one bedroom apartment. This is different from Sarah's place was the first thought in Jay's mind. The parquet floors with the Persian rug stood out. One wall in the living room was decorated with four feet wide alternate chocolate brown and natural color burlap from floor to ceiling. The seams covered by black one-inch molding. "Did you cover the wall yourself?"

"Yes I did, I didn't want to paint and the burlap was cheap. You like it?"

"Yes it very different and stylish."

The hallway that led to the bathroom and bedroom was painted like a large mural with bright colors of green, blue and burnt orange in a pattern of waves. "I've always been atypical in my life Jay, my mother thinks I'm strange and I'm okay with that; I just don't do what everyone else does, you know what I mean. That's why when my dad said you wanna be a stockbroker? You must be going crazy in that crazy city. I was determined to do just that and now I am."

Gwen excused herself and headed to her bedroom. Jay went to the window to observe the view. In the distance, he saw the lights of Yankee stadium. He realized that he had never been this high in a building before. The Francis Marion Hotel where he worked in Charleston had fifteen floors but he had never been higher than the fourth floor banquet facilities. The view gave him a strange yet enthralling chill.

Gwen reappeared, put a Jackie Wilson album on her stereo and said "You like my view? See the Empire State building over there; and over there, is the Tri-Borough Bridge. I took this apartment as soon as I saw the view." She had changed into a loose fitting dress and wore no shoes. The drinks were beginning to wear off and she was somewhat relaxed but anxious.

Jay called Sarah. He told her he was going to a party with some friends of Gwen. He could hear concern in her voice as she told him to take a taxi home from wherever he was going. Jay was fairly safe in Sarah's block. Everyone knew he worked at Shirley's and furthermore, he was under the security of Mason the numbers banker. Mason employed a number of strong-arm types; men who had done time in prison and some who will do time eventually. He also employed women he had taken off the streets.

In spite of Sarah's warnings, Mason still had an eye on Jay. He told his people to make sure nothing happen to the young blood from the south. He still had visions of Jay working for him one day.

Jay stared out the window watching the traffic move up and down the Grand Concourse. Gwen slipped up behind him; gently rubbed his shoulders and gently kissed him on his neck. Jay did not respond outwardly but he felt the kiss in his toes. Another kiss and he turned to face her. Their eyes locked then their lips met and the deep kiss lasted for what seem like an eternity.

She whispered, "I have an aggressive nature, does that bother you?" Jay, ever the man of words softly said, "You called this being aggressive, I still have my clothes on."

She replied simply, "Why?"

They made love for hours. It was as if they had done this for years and no exploration was needed. They knew how to please each other. In a moment of silence while lying in Jay's arms, the lovers spent, Gwen said, "I don't do this Jay. I have been in this apartment for five months and you're the first man that has been here. In fact, you are the first man I've been with since I've been in New York."

The statement 'the first man in New York' stuck with Jay for a moment. "Is there someone back in Atlanta?"

"There was; he's at Morehouse now, gonna be a preacher."

"You loved him?"

"I was in high school, I thought it was love. How about you, who did you leave in Charleston?"

"One person in particular and I *was* in love with her." Jay knew he would say no more if she asked; she didn't.

"What's gonna happen from here for us Jay."

"Now Gwen you know as well as I do that neither of us have the answer to that. I really felt good being with you and that was *before* we went to bed. I like you Gwen. I think you know that, so why don't we just let what will happen, happen and don't worry about it for now."

"Sure Jay. I think you know that I like you too but even *more* now that we've gone to bed." As Gwen said this, she squeezed Jay's hand.

"So you just want me for my body, is that it?" Jay asked.

"Yes I do. Didn't you realize that?" They both laughed.

"Look, I have to go. I have to be to work at six; It's after three."

"I know. I'll go downstairs with you to get a taxi."

"There is something I want to talk to you about so I'll call you later."

"What is it Jay?"

"Later Gwen, I need to think about it some more, I'll call you after breakfast in the morning."

Jay arrived in his taxi to 127th street. Although it was after four in the morning, people were still in the streets. He hurried up the stairs to Sarah's apartment. He heard music coming from Sye's apartment as usual. He also suspected that Maxine was still up drinking, he heard her playing one of the albums she recorded when she was a young singer. She often did this when she drank.

CHAPTER 11

"Hi baby; you wus out late last night huh, can you work today?" Sarah decided, while lying in bed waiting to hear Jay's key in the door that she was not going to show her jealously any longer. She was going to be good-natured with him from now on. He was going to be there at least three more months. She decided that her feelings over Jay were simply, just dumb. And besides, she knew that she could crawl into his bed any time she wanted to.

"I'm fine Sarah, I'm always ready for work. My mom always told me, no matter what you do, always go to work. If necessary, leave early but never stay out because of the night before. "How you doing? I hope I didn't wake you when I came in."

"No child, I wus dead to the world didn't hear you. You had a good time?"

"It was okay. Have you ever been to this Hawaiian restaurant downtown?" Jay knew the answer but was merely making conversation with Sarah. He felt the uneasiness between them but he still realized, however, that she was still very important to him.

"No chil; ain't never been there, wus; it nice?"

"Yes it was; I'll take you there for dinner when we're both off."

"Oh that would nice Jay, we best get outta here you know Saturday morning breakfast. But don't forget, we're off next Sunday and we is going to my church. I can't wait to see you in that new suit."

It was a typical Saturday morning. There were the all-nighters, the families who made the trip to Harlem for breakfast, couples, tourists, and neighborhood regulars.

Jay really loved this scene.

He loved seeing the varied and multi-cultured people of New York. He found out by what people ordered, what part of the South they were from. He knew that people from South Carolina, always had rice with their meals. People from North Carolina had potatoes. People from Mississippi, Alabama and Georgia, always had collard greens, corn bread and always asked for hot sauce. Above all, he made a lot of money. He floated through the large dining room with grace and flare. It was hard not to notice this young waiter with a masters in customer service. He was a natural, and it seemed that he was the only server not 'up a tree.' Merle was constantly helping out some servers who had customers waiting for long periods of time. Not Jay.

Breakfast at Shirley's was served all day so it was not unusual to see people having a breakfast meal of grits, scramble eggs, hot sausage and pancakes at two p.m. and the table next to that having baked chicken with collard greens and black-eye peas.

Mrs. Hall came in not looking like the grand lady she was known to be but rather tired, drawn and ashen. Everyone was startled by her look. Her dress was still immaculate; she still displayed her polish and class; but she did not appear to be well. Merle knew to sit her in Jay's station.

"Well hello young lady, you just light up this place when you walked in." Jay didn't like her looks either but did not show it as he rushed to her side and help her into a booth.

"Now you stop messing with me Jay, you leave this old lady alone."

"I'll leave you alone when you go out with me; how about tonight?"

She laughed out loud and put her hand to her chest as she did.

"Okay Jay we can go out tonight. We can go to the Renaissance Ballroom and dance; I'll have to bring Arthur you know." Jay laughed.

"Okay it's a date. Pick you up at nine." He opened the dinner napkin with his usual flair; laid it across her lap as she liked, and said, "What do you wish my dear?"

"I feel like some fish, any more whiting in the kitchen?"

"Of course, you know we keep some here for you."

"Good I'll have fried whiting with a spoonful of grits and gravy; one biscuit and coffee."

"Now you know you can't have fried fish, I'll have JC bake it for you"

"No Jay, I don't like baked."

"I know fried is not good for you, baked."

"Jay, please make an old lady happy, give her what she wants."

"I'll tell you what, one piece broiled, one piece fried. How about that?" In the mock voice of a little girl, she said, "I'm going to tell Shirley you won't give me what I ordered. She will fire you. Make the biggest piece fried, please."

He was off to the kitchen with her order, laughing as he blinked at Merle. She shook her head and smiled.

Jay had been looking for an opportunity to call Gwen all morning, but because it was so busy; the right time had not come. He decided to take a break right after serving Mrs. Hall and call Gwen. He had made up his mind about what he was going to do when he went to bed after leaving her.

CJ hooked up a nice portion of fried whiting for Mrs. Hall. Along with the broiled piece, Jay added a salmon cake to the plate. She was pleased. He told Merle he had to make a quick call and would be in the back for a little while. His customers were taken care of.

"Hello Gwen, how are you?"

"I'm fine, been waiting for your call."

"You've been in here on Saturday morning. You know how it is."

"Yes I know. I started to come down for breakfast but you wore me out last night; couldn't get out of bed."

"I wore *you* out; you should see me today. I'm walking around like a zombie. You're dangerous lady." They both laughed. They really liked each other.

"Listen Gwen I don't have a lot of time; so quickly, I want you to open an account for me."

"Oh Jay, that's what it is? Why that's great; you had me thinking that you were in some serious shit or something, this is great."

"Gwen, watch your mouth"

"Yea I know Jay but shit, you could have told me this last night sweetie; then I wouldn't have been worried all night."

"I don't mix business with pleasure"

"Ohhhh I know you don't; you were all business last night, and I might add, you're good at your business honey."

"Gwen get serious please. What do you need from me?"

"Well I need your social security number, the address on 127th street?"

"249-57-3492; 282, apartment 3-E."

"How much do you make annually Jay?"

"I don't know I've been here three months, with salary and tips about two- fifty a week."

"That's not bad Jay"

"That's also about 12 to 14 hours a day; what else?"

"I'll fill in the rest, I know a little bit about you. What would you say is your objective and what do you hope to accomplish with this account?"

"You told me this is how you make money so that's what I'm trying to accomplish."

"Okay Jay, now our research department has identified several situations that I think would fit your...."

"Gwen!" he cut her off, "I know what I want, I want you to buy me two hundred shares of Megan Associates"

"Megan Associates? Where on earth did you get that from Jay?"

"I've been reading and that's what I want. Can you do it?"

"Why sure I can do it, but why?"

"It's about 15 a share now Gwen, so how much is 200 shares?"

"That's Three-thousand dollars plus commission, but Jay let me show you something that may be better for your initial investment. I don't want your first experience to be a bad one; I mean, last week you never even heard of the stock market and now you're reading and picking stocks; Jay, listen to me."

"Gwen I've got to get back to work; do this tomorrow morning, huh; now when do you need the money?"

"Settlement will be in five business days; so I'll open the account when I go in Monday morning. What does this company make Jay, what in the hell do they do?"

"Just buy it please; leave that to me."

"Okay. Monday morning, I'll make the purchase, you pay for it the following Monday." I'll have to mark your order ticket 'unsolicited,' which means I didn't recommend it. But if you change your mind, call me early Monday morning. Goodbye."

Jay hung up the phone and headed back into the dinning room wondering what had he done. At the same time he was thinking back to the times when he was getting a haircut in the barbershop in Charleston. He would listen to the older men talking about their missed opportunities when they were younger. They talked about the times they wished they had followed their minds and acted without fear. He remembered specifically Mr. Moore saying how he had a chance to make some real money but was afraid to take that chance. He heard Mr. Shepard saying 'don't be afraid but also don't be stupid.' Jay knew he was not stupid. So this was going to be his opportunity. He had a new feeling about himself when he returned to his customers; He knew that he had been changed that very moment, or did he always have this feeling of complete control and confidence.

Jay went immediately to Mrs. Hall's table; she had finished her lunch. "Well my dear, did you enjoy your food, is there something else you want, some peach cobbler maybe?"

"No I'm full Jay. That was very good; tell CJ the fish was great. I got to take this old body home now. I'm tired. Are you busy, can you walk me home?"

"Of course my dear, you know I take care of my favorite lady, you ready?"

"Yes"

"Okay, let me tell Merle."

The diners had thinned out and Merle agreed as she always did.

Jay took Mrs. Hall by the arm and led her down 126th street towards Fifth Avenue. The walk was very slow; she seemed to be laboring some.

"Are you feeling okay Mrs. Hall; you're not yourself today?"

"Oh I'm all right Jay, Just an old lady feeling a little poorly, I'll be fine."

Jay had never been in her house before, he would always walk her to the entrance and unlock the gate to the basement floor and left. Her home was one of the great brownstones on 126th street. Most of the brownstones had been converted into rooming houses, but not hers. She lived there alone since her husband died some eight years ago.

Jay took her keys to unlock the door and noticed mail in the box that hung on the gate.

"Linda you have mail in your box that you haven't picked up."

"Yes I saw it when I left. I was going to get it when I came back. Get it for me please."

"Come on inside Jay. You have never been in my house, have you?"

"No I haven't; I wanted to see what one of these buildings looked like inside."

"Well come on in. I'll show you around; maybe you'll buy it when you marry that cute girl Merle says you like; her boss calls me all the time wanting me to invest with him; Milton is his name, I think."

"You mean Gwen, I'm not thinking about marriage Linda; unless you'll have me." They both laughed.

He gave her the mail and paused in a narrow hallway that had stairs at the far end about twenty feet away. To their left was the doorway that opened into her bedroom. Not being able to climb the stairs any longer to the bedroom suits, she slept on the first floor.

"This house dates back to 1880. Harlem then had a lot of rich white folks living here. This floor was the dining room and the kitchen." Jay marveled at the beautiful parquet floor in the hallway.

Mrs. Hall sorted through the mail as she talked. "Oh, my granddaughter wrote me, bless her heart. "You should meet her Jay; She just went to college herself, out in Ohio; you would love her. When are you leaving for college by the way?"

"If I go, it will be in January"

"What do you mean if; I thought you got a scholarship?"

"I did, but I might want to do something else now; like what Gwen does, and go to school at night"

"Well you must get your education Jay, it's hard out here for a Negro without an education. I got to sit down; you go on through the house, straight back is the kitchen and up those steps is the parlor floor. The floor above that is the bedrooms and the top floor is another kitchen and bedroom; it use to be the nursery when rich folks lived here."

Jay took a quick look around the first floor; observing the great wood work in a sitting room between the dinning room, which now served as Mrs. Hall bedroom, and entrance to the kitchen. The room had a fireplace with an intricate decorative wood mantel. The highlight of this small room is an ornate chandelier. Stairs to the right led to the three rooms parlor floor above. This floor spoke volumes for the true beauty of this building and its elegance.

The wood floor, assembled in a design of triangles was stained alternately dark and light mahogany. The middle room between the front and rear parlor also had a magnificent fireplace, this one more resplendent than the one on the ground floor. The other two rooms also had an exquisite fireplace; each designed with tile and masterfully created cast iron grates. To the right was a majestic staircase that obviously led to the bedrooms. The two turns structure was surely breathtaking. Carved by a master craftsman, the banister was highly polished and glistens in the subtle light. Jay felt overwhelmed by the splendor of what he had seen so far.

"Wow I just love this." Jay shouted back downstairs for Mrs. Hall to hear.

"I knew you would." She said standing at the foot of the stairs.

Throughout this magnificent structure were examples of builders not lacking in detail and imagination. The rooms also had the original gas lamps that were in use before electricity. Of course she had furnishing to match the rooms. High back chairs, wing chairs, antique couches and other items of decoration from the 19th century complemented the distinctive parlor floor.

The rear of the parlor floor featured an intricate designed bay window. The middle window had been changed to a door and entrance to a deck built with treated wood. This was the only change the Halls made to this room. The deck overlooked a well-kept, skillfully manicured and fenced-in flower garden. Except for the beautiful garden, the view was limited to the rear of tenements whose front was 126th street.

The deck stairs took you down to the garden. The two outside bay windows were secured with iron casings that matched the splendid wrought iron door.

Jay had seen enough and was totally impressed. He went downstairs to join Mrs. Hall thinking I'm going to get me a house like this. The only house that he had ever been in that was even close to this was when he once worked with Mr. Earl at one of the mansion on the battery at a private party. He said to himself, those White folks had nothing on this.

Mrs. Hall was reading her mail. "Linda this is something else; I've never seen anything like it. I just love this, how long have you been here? I felt as if I was transported back in time."

"These old houses are nice Jay and one time they were all like this and better. All the brownstones and limestones in this block and all over Harlem were like this. Most have been converted into apartments; you know, they rent out the ground floor, add a kitchen and bath to the parlor floor and bedroom floor; the top floor already had a kitchen and bath and you got four apartments to rent."

She continued, "My husband and I didn't want that. We loved living in the whole house ourselves with our two children. Harlem was really grand then and we always gave parties and entertained a lot. We lived here over thirty years."

"Where are your children?" Jay asked.

"My daughter is in California. She did some acting and is still trying; chasing a dream they say. Her daughter is whom I just got this letter from. My son has been a big disappointment to me and to my husband. We gave that boy everything; too much I think. The more we did for him the more trouble he got into."

She went to the mantle where she had pictures of her family. Handing one to Jay she said, "This is my Edward. He was a handsome man. All the women loved him, but I got him. We both worked at the telephone company and in those days there weren't many of our kind working there.

We sort of gravitated toward each other and fell in love. We were married for over forty years until he died. Handing Jay two other pictures, she went on, "This is Grace and this is... I must have a picture of my granddaughter somewhere around here; oh, it's upstairs; her graduation picture. I'll show it to you another time. She is a very pretty girl."

"I know she is Linda, she is your blood." Jay said, never missing a beat.

"Sit down Jay, or are you in a hurry to get back?"

"No we're not busy now, won't be until about six, I've got some time." Sensing that she didn't want to be alone and she wanted to talk, Jay, ever the gentleman, obliged her.

He was about to sit in a chair near the front window and noticed two prescriptions that her doctor had just written maybe a day or two earlier in the chair. He picked them up and placed them on the table beside her bed.

"Mrs. Hall you need these filled. I can get them for you."

"Oh no, the girl who comes in to clean and dust for me will pick them up for me. She'll be in on Tuesday."

"Should you wait that long for your medicine?"

"I'm sure my doctor did not order the magic portion from the fountain of youth so I can wait a couple more days." She laughed at her little humor.

"I wondered how you kept this place so clean. This place is immaculate."

"Phyllis comes in twice a week. The lazy thing; she don't clean as much as she use to. She only gets the dust that she thinks I can see. I'll need her to ride down to the bank with me on Tuesday; my grand-daughter needs some money for school. You know, I pay her tuition. She is a sweet child; I'll probably leave this house to her. It's paid for. My daughter is so irresponsible; she drinks a bit. And that rogue son of mind, well I just don't know. Tell me Jay, you love your mother?"

"Yes ma'am, my mother is my best friend; my grandmother is very special to me also. I love them both dearly."

"Well don't ever break their hearts you hear. You don't appear to be that kind of person. I knew my son was going to be trouble when he was in first grade. Isn't that terrible?" Jay noticed that Linda never said where her son was and he didn't asked.

"My husband was a very smart man. He worked in the technical department at the phone company. I was one of the first Negro operators that they hired. We had a lot of White friends and we entertained them here and we were invited to their homes too. One of our dear friends Stan Marcus told Ed he should buy the company stock. We did and we made a nice sum. He also told Ed to buy some bonds. The bonds have been the cash I use to live on besides my pension and social security. Those bonds pay Joyce's- that's my granddaughter, tuition. She gets everything when I'm gone; the stocks, the bonds, and the house. I hope she don't find some no good man and he take it all from her. She's got a good head on her shoulders, I hope she finds somebody like you Jay; a nice young man."

"Jay, would you do me one more favor before you leave? I keep the bonds upstairs in Ed's strongbox. Would you go get it for me? I got to take a coupon down to the bank to cash in the interest. I don't trust that Phyllis; some of my jewelry is missing but I won't accuse her, you know getting old, you can misplace things."

Mrs. Hall told Jay where he would find the strong box in her upstairs bedroom. He hurried up the steps to the third floor and found it where she said it would be. He looked quickly into the unlocked box and saw several certificates reading 100 shares American Telephone and Telegraph Company. There were about twenty. In another envelope tied with a blue ribbon were certificates, reading U.S. treasury bonds. He saw a caption on the bonds that read 'bearer bonds.' He had no idea what all of this meant but he was sure it represented some wealth. He remembered the gossip that Mrs. Hall's husband left her well off.

He gave the strong box to her and announced that he must get back to work. "Wait one more minute Jay, I just want to get a coupon off this bond then you can take the box back upstairs for me. Can you do that?"

"Sure Mrs. Hall, I can so that."

He watched as Mrs. Hall untied the blue ribbon around the envelope that he knew contained the bonds that he had just seen. He watched as she detached a coupon from one of the bonds. She retied the package, put it back into the box and handed the box to Jay. "Now you can put it back. Thanks Jay thanks for helping an old lady out. It's a good thing you were here. I don't know how I would have made it up those stairs."

"You're very welcome. Is there any thing else you need?"

"No dear you have been a sweetheart. Tell Merle and Shirley thanks for letting me have your service."

Jay ran up the stairs to return the strong box. He was then saying goodbye to her. "Just pull the gate shut; it will lock. I'm going to take a nap now."

"Bye Mrs. Hall, if you need anything just call Merle"

Slowly walking back to the restaurant, Jay was trying hard to remove thoughts that were creeping into his mind. Hard as he tried, a picture kept reappearing.

Merle greeted Jay as he came in. "Is she okay Jay? She didn't look good."

"Yea she seems okay now; said she is going to take a nap."

"You know, she really likes you. She has been eating here for many years. She and her husband, when he was alive, have been coming here since mom first opened and that's been over twenty years. I have never seen her take to anyone like she has to you. Maybe she'll put you in her will." Merle laughed.

"Yea, sure, I've know her all of four months and I'm in her will?"

"It happens Jay, don't laugh it off.   Did you like her house? Isn't it nice?"

"Yea, her house is really spectacular. I like it."

Although conversing with Merle, Jay was still fighting off this picture that entered his mind. Then he thought, yea I guess she does likes me. She just shared a little secret with me. I wonder who else knows.

CHAPTER 12

Gwen was in the office at eight a.m. as usual. Sharon would arrive a few minutes later. Milton, the office manager, was already there as usual. He was always in at seven.

Gwen had gotten off to a good start as a new stockbroker; she opened six accounts the first week. The seventh account was going to be Jay's. Her day would be spent making prospecting calls; smile and dial it was called. She was trained to ask people that she had opened an account for if they knew anyone who might benefit from her services. If they gave her names and phones numbers, she would ask for permission to use their names when talking to those individuals. Stockbrokers grow their business from referrals. Shirley had given her several names and so did Merle. Milton always had prospects for her also. These were prospective clients from a list provided by their firm.

The first thing she had to do today is to check the stock guide for information on this Megan Associates that Jay wanted to buy. She didn't know a thing about the stock. This wasn't unusual for a new broker. With over two thousand corporate stocks listed for trading on the New York Stock Exchange, several hundred on the American Stock Exchange and several hundred more traded in the unlisted or over-counter- market; brokers did not know all of them.

Her first recommendations were limited to stocks that her firm had done research on and recommended for their clients.

"Ready to have a great week Gwen?" Milton greeted her.

"Yea, I'm pumped." She replied.

"In fact, I'm starting the day with a new account. Over the weekend, I opened this young man who works at Shirley's."

"Who?"

"You know, that waiter name Jay."

"Oh yes, I remember him; I've had my eye, I mean, I was going to prospect him; he's very intelligent. He has money?"

In her mind, Gwen knew that Milton indeed had his eyes on Jay. It was known that Milton is gay. She knew that the first time his roommate came by the office to meet him after work one day.

Milton was a good-looking man and so was Tony, his roommate. Milton was a native New Yorker; about 36, had graduated from NYU and immediately landed a job on Wall Street. There were not many Negroes in this business. Milton's family had a lot of money and so did his family friends. He was successful just doing business with referrals from his father. He is a doctor who had a large and successful practice.

If he didn't prefer men, Gwen knew that Milton could be a lady-killer.

"So what are you going to start him with?" Milton asked.

"Well he got this idea from somewhere; I'm trying to find information on it now. He wants to buy two hundred Megan Associates."

"He does? It's an electronic data processing company; MEA, trades on the New York. Punch it up. I don't know what it's selling at now; last time I saw it, it was about 12." Milton liked showing off his knowledge of the market.

Gwen turned to the small TV like terminal with a keyboard on her desk and put in the symbol MEA. "It closed at 13 and one-quarter Friday, The high is 14 and three- eighths. He thought it was about 15, so I guess I'll just put in a market order."

"Yea you should get it at much less than 15." Milton said to her. "Make sure you mark that order ticket unsolicited; if this thing should go bad it was not your recommendation."

Gwen completed the information form for Jay's account. An account number was assigned. Then, Milton signed and approved the purchased transaction.

She then typed into a teletype machine; Buy 200 MEA MKT; followed by Jay's account number. Her transaction was transmitted to their firm's order room downtown and then forwarded to the trading floor of the New York Stock Exchange. There, a floor broker for Gwen's firm would receive the transmission for Jay's order, and in an auction like procedure, buy 200 shares of Milton Associates at the best price available at that time from a seller.

The market opened for trading at 9:30 each day. Jay's order would be executed immediately after trading begins and a report would be transmitted back to Gwen's office. There is always a buyer and seller in this auction market. This system has in place another floor broker; a middle- man; called a Specialist. This individual's primary responsibility is to ensure that there is a fair and orderly market at all times. His duties include executing orders left in his care by sellers and buyers. Some of the orders were good only for that trading day and some were good until a certain price was met. In addition, the Specialist stands ready to buy from sellers, or sell to buyers at the prevailing price at his own risk of capital. So if there were no sellers of Milton Associates at the auction at the time Jay's order reached the trading floor, the Specialist would sell the stock to Gwen's firm for the account of Jayson Austin. The entire process would be done in minutes.

"By the way Milton, I talked to Jay about working here; thought he would be good for our training program."

"Why yes Gwen that's a good idea. I'm behind on recruiting and I've got to add three more brokers here in the next few months. I just couldn't find decent candidates. Have him come by for an interview. Does he seem interested?"

"We've talked about it; I would think that opening this account says he is somewhat interested. He is thinking about going to school in the winter semester. I'll have him call you."

CHAPTER 13

Jay did not work Monday. It was his day off. He had received letters from Harriet and Ruby some days past and had not answered them. Harriet spoke of her arrival at Hampton Institute in Virginia to begin her freshman year. She said how excited she was and how much she misses him. Ruby's letter spoke of her undying love and the boredom of her senior year without him there.

Jay would take this day to write to all his friends. He thought that writing would take away the thoughts that repeatedly entered his mind. Tried as he did, it was difficult.

After scribbling short notes to Harriet and Ruby, he wished he had a way to get in touch with Carla. But she disappeared from his life on his graduation day. She did not however, disappear from his heart.

He decided to visit Sye to past away the time. Listening to his music was always good. He stepped out into the hallway and was about to knock on Sye's apartment door when Maxine suddenly appeared. It was obvious that she was waiting for someone to emerge into the hall; perhaps she thought it might be Sarah. She looked a mess. Her eyes were swollen from lack of sleep. Her hair was matted and unkempt; her hands shaked. Jay could see in this pathetic figure a woman who was once beautiful. But now she was just a shameless drunk. He thought of Harriet's mother and felt pity for her.

"Hello young man is your aunt home? I was just coming over there." Her speech slurred.

"No, she's at work Miss Maxine, she'll be home about two p.m. He could see disappointment in her face. He knew what she would say next so he was not surprised when she did say, "I was gonna borrow a few dollars from your aunt until my check comes. Do you have any money you could lend me?" Jay knew that Sarah did give money to Maxine; he didn't know if she ever paid Sarah back.

"Yes I have a few dollars, what do you need?"

"Just five dollars, I'll pay you back."

He reached into his pocket and gave her ten. "Here take this."

"Oh thank you sweetheart, thank you very much, I'll pay you back as soon as my check comes."

Jay watched as she went back into her apartment, and then he knocked on Sye's door.

"Hey blood, I thought I heard you out there; you talking to Max? How much did she hit you for?"

"Oh just a couple dollars, no big deal."

"Come on in, I've got MJQ on."

"Who's that?"

"The Modern Jazz Quartet; John Lewis, Milt Jackson, Percy Heath, Connie Kay.   Sit down, listen to the masters."

The names were not familiar to Jay and he felt embarrassed that he had not heard of them. He loved the music that Sye introduced him too and felt as if he was getting an education. This guy knew so much about music; and not only jazz, he heard Latin music, R&B and some classical now and then. Sye just loved music. The joint was also a part of his compulsion.

Handing Jay the jacket cover to an album entitled Pyramid, Sye proceeded to roll his joint. Jay heard a tune called *It don't mean a thing;* a song he recognized by Duke Ellington. MJQ's arrangement was engaging.

"You know, Maxine was a beautiful broad before she found the bottle. I've got an album by her some where in here. When I find it, I'll let you see how fine she was. You wouldn't believe that she is the same person."

"How long have you known her?" Jay asked,

"Well I've been in this building over ten years. She was here when I came. We hung out a little but she became a pain- in the ass, you know what I mean? She wasn't fun to be around."

Sye was never lost for words, especially after a joint or two so Jay was prepared to listen to the sage expound. "Are you a basketball fan?" He asked Jay.

"Yes I love basketball."

"We'll, we got to go to the Garden and see a Knicks game."

"Oh man, that would be great. I would love to see a pro game."

"Did you play in school?"

"No I didn't play sports. I could have, but I just didn't. I was in the band. I played intramural ball but never went out for the school's team."

Sye took a long drag on his joint and said in a hoarse, choking and heavy nasal voice, "I played a lot of ball in school. In fact I got a scholarship to North Carolina A&T down in Charlotte."

"You did?"

"Yea I was pretty good. I was sure I would play for the Knicks one day."

"So what happen?"

"Stupid." Sye said, "I was this hot shoot kid from New York, been in all the newspapers here since my freshman year in high school, and I just had a big head. I also couldn't get use to the South. Some of the shit I went through fucked up my head. At least that's the excuse I give myself. The truth is, I fucked up. I wouldn't listen to the coach and we just didn't get along very well. To this day I regret my attitude."

Jay didn't know what to say so he said nothing. He could see the deep remorse in Sye' eyes. Sye went on, "The school and coach had taken enough of my shit and even though I was their best player, they sent me packing. Took away my scholarship after my sophomore year. Shock the shit outta me."

"What did you do?"

"I was scared shitless; didn't know what to do. I knew I couldn't go back to New York, my father woulda killed me. So like a dumb ass, I joined the army. This turned out not to be so bad. I spent ten years in the army; woulda made it a career but I got hurt."

Jay would not ask about that. He figured that if Sye wanted him to know about his injury, he would soon tell him.

"The army taught me discipline; made me a man. I had it made. I was smarter than a lot of guys in my company so I became the clerk. The Sergeant took care of me and I took care of him. Shit was good until I went to Korea; saw some serious combat. Korea is the world's best-kept secret. While you could get sent home in a body bag; if you played your cards right you learned how to survive the motherfucker." Jay felt, as he always does, around Sye that he was getting a contact high. Why doesn't he offer me again he said to himself.

Sye was at his best now. Jay had witnessed this before. He would have that mellow out joint, his mellow out music, and he would talk non-stop.

"I had this Korean woman that loved the shit outta me. Nineteen years old and fine as wine. Did anything for me. For a brief time I thought about bringing her here but there was so much fucking red tape, I just gave up. I was hurting too at the time and just didn't have the energy to fight the shit. I know she was disappointed but I just couldn't help it. I think about her to this day. I'm sure she was pregnant when I left there but she never said a word."

Jay saw a sensitive side to Sye that was not evident previously. He never spoke of a family before, and to think that he may have left one behind in his military days made him a little moisture eyed. Except for the many women in his life, he never spoke of his relatives. Sye changed the music to some Latin music. "I know you never heard of Eddie Palmeri; you'll love this shit."

The stereo came alive with an Afro Caribbean rhythm that immediately made Jay bob his head to the beat. He indeed loved the sound. Jay thought to himself, I've got so much to introduce to my friends back in Charleston. He was surprised that he thought of Charleston—he hadn't done so in a long time.

Jay soon grew tired of Sye's continuous monologue of information and declarations and just plain bullshit, intermingled with the great music. If he would just play the music, the visit would be more enjoyable.

CHAPTER 14

Jay took leave from Sye's apartment and was going home to call his mother at her shop. Surprisingly, she wasn't too upset that he would not be in college until the second semester. She did express her indifference to his idea about staying in New York and attending City College, and, she did not like this Wall Street job idea at all. Jay knew that somehow he would soon convince her before January came around.

He missed his mother and grandmother but felt that he was capable of making his own life decisions. He would use her training of him as the reason he will do the right thing. He would tell her that he is still the responsible man that she made him and to trust his judgment. He could sense from this most recent conversation that she was softening some. One more conversation should do it.

Jay was about to take a nap and sort out in his mind the ever-present thoughts that the visit with Sye did not erase. The phone rang and it was Gwen.

"Well my dear, I bought your stock today. I got it on the opening at fourteen and three- eighths."

"What does that mean?" he said.

In spite of her doubts and concern about his transaction, she was in a good mood.

"It means sweetie, that I placed an order to buy your stock at the first price of the day, the opening. You thought it was about fifteen. When I saw that it closed at less than that on Friday, and the quote was fourteen and one- quarter bid and fourteen and three- eighths ask, I put in a market order."

"I don't know what —in-the —hell you're talking about, but you did say you bought it, right?"

"Yes."

"What kind of price is fourteen and three- eighths?" he said.

"That's fourteen dollars and thirty-seven and one- half cents per share." She replied.

"Lem me explain. The bid price is the most someone is willing to pay for the stock. The ask, is how much someone is willing to sell it for. You therefore sell, at the bid and buy at the ask. It's called a quote. The quote will change by the force of supply and demand for the stock. You'll learn all this shit when you join us. By the way, Milton wants to talk to you."

"I still don't fully understand yet, but I'll get it" Jay said. He continued, "When do I pay for it?"

"Settlement is five business days from today so you must pay for it by Monday. You'll get a confirmation in the mail. It will show your purchase price, my commission, your account number, and the date payment is due. Two hundred shares plus commission is two thousand – nine hundred-eighty one dollars. If there is anything you don't understand just call me, okay?"

"Yea, I'll do that.

Gwen went on, "And call Milton, he's got the hots, I mean he wants to talk to you.

When Jay hung up, he thought, 'what the fuck have I done?' Three thousand dollars! He had the money. He had been sending most of his earnings home to his mother to bank for him. He had about four or five hundred with him that he hadn't sent yet but this money was for school. How am I going to get three thousand dollars from her, he questioned himself. Shit.

And then, he didn't worry about it any more; never gave it another thought. Somehow this will work itself out; he reasoned. After all, he had a few days to plan. One thing Jay knew for sure as he laid across his bed for that nap; he was going to lie to his mother for the very first time.

The next two days at the restaurant were uneventful. It was Wednesday morning and Jay was working the breakfast shift. About mid –day, Merle told Jay that there was a telephone call for him and to take it in the office. Jay hurried through the kitchen, which was loud and lively as always. JC was telling lies and barking orders to his cooks and the waiters shouting even louder. Jay loved it back here.

Shirley was not in the office as Jay took the phone. It was Gwen. She screamed, "Jay, you sonofabitch, you, you…"

"What's wrong Gwen?"

"I can't believe this, I can't fucking believe this." She was breathing heavy into the phone. Jay had a puzzled look on his face as he held the receiver closer to his ear.

"Gwen, calm down. What are you so excited about?" He heard Milton in the background saying, "Twenty eight and one-half." He heard Sharon the assistant scream. Gwen yelled to Milton. "What is it?" He heard Milton repeat, twenty-eight and one- half. Gwen shouted in the phone to Jay, "Did you hear that, twenty eight and one half."

Jay was looking out into the kitchen; his heart racing, not quite sure what was happening but he felt it was good. He knew from this phone call that his days in this kitchen, this restaurant was limited. He watched JC, a master at his craft going about his business of preparing his famous dishes. He watched the waiters and other kitchen help doing their life work and suddenly felt superior to them. He had a calm feeling in his body that said you are going to be okay. The shouting and screams of joy continued from the three people at the other end of the phone call. This is something big; this is your first crowning moment and there will be more to come from Mr. Most Likely To Succeed.

He decided to wait until Gwen told him what was happening, he would not ask again. He heard, "Twenty-nine."

Finally, Gwen said, still out of breath, "Jay, you hit it man; Megan is up to twenty nine, you hear me, the stock opened up five points today on rumors of a take-over. Then it was announced that General Motors is buying Megan at thirty dollars a share. The stock took off. Where did you hear this shit? How did you know?" He heard himself say in his mind, 'none of your dam business'.

"Jay, Jay, tell me how did you pick this stock?" Jay was still absorbed in his euphoria, and he saw himself in Dr. Weinstein's office. He wondered had the good doctor gotten his call yet.

"I told you I read about it." Jay said, with a touch of sarcasm in his voice. He was arrogant from his success and could only think at the moment, how will he do this again.

"So tell me Gwen, what happens now?"

"Well, you sell. The stock is not going higher than the take-over price of thirty. Unless another buyer comes along and offers to pay more for the company, thirty is the top price; it's just about there now. You've more than double your investment in less than two days. Holy shit. I tried to talk you out of this dam thing and it doubled in two days; are you lucky or what."

Arrogance aglow, Jay said, "Luck had nothing to do with it. I approached this thing very carefully, like I always do with something new. I liked what I saw and made a decision."

Gwen whispered, "You are full of shit Jay Austin, and I love you; we'll be over for lunch and it's on you," she laughed.

"Are you going to sell it now?" Jay said,

"Yes, I'll enter a order now. When I see you, I want you to tell me how you did this."

Jay hung the phone up and headed back to the dining room. His walk now took on the appearance of a monarch on the way to his coronation. His thoughts were, so, this is how the white man makes his money. Somehow he felt this was just a first step in a master plan that has not unfolded in its entirety yet. In fact, he had no idea what that plan was, but he did have a vision.

Merle came over to him and inquired about the nature of the phone call- that it wasn't bad news. She was concerned because of the look on his face. "No, I'm fine. The call was actually good news. I do have a toothache that's been bothering me since last night."

"Oh, why don't you go see Dr.Weinstein, maybe he'll do something for you." Merle advised. "I'll call him for you."

That's exactly what Jay wanted to hear; he had to get back into that doctor's office. What he was going to do he was not sure, but the compulsion was overwhelming.

CHAPTER 15

When Merle picked up the phone, Jay headed to the kitchen; an important item must be taken care of first. Remembering that Barbara was a vegetarian, and the fact that she was in the office by herself and unable to get out to lunch; he hadn't seen her at the restaurant. Jay went to the kitchen and ordered a veggie plate to go. He prepared the plate himself. He put generous portions of the day's veggies into a takeout container. Carrots, green beans, squash, broccoli and a spoonful of collard greens. He was careful not to take any of the meat used to season the greens. Shirley's vegetables, prepared with lot of herbs and spices were just dam good. He added a slice of corn bread and a large unsweetened ice tea. She would have enough for her dinner as well.

Jay made out a check, paid Merle, who gave him an inquisitive look, but said nothing. Sarah saw his haste out the restaurant door and wondered what was he up to now; they hadn't talk much lately. Just the usual pleasantries.

When she had been alone in the apartment, Sarah sat in the window over-looking 127th Street. She sat there so she could see Jay if he was coming home. With this apparently safe location, she could read Jay's mail. She had read his letters from Harriet, and Ruby. There was the letter from Talladega College notifying him of his acceptance there in the spring semester. And now, there was this letter, a bill about something with the name Megan Associates. The bill was for Two thousand nine hundred and eighty- one dollars. What is this boy doing, she thought, what is he doing.

On the way to 124th Street, Jay saw a crowd of people listening to a man standing on a ladder at 125th and Lenox Avenue. He was talking through a bullhorn. The tall, light-skinned man with reddish hair and goatee was a very eloquent speaker. He was talking about the plight of the Black man in America. Jay had heard and seen this man before but had never stopped to listen to him. He learned that the man called himself Malcolm X. Jay was intrigued by the little that he heard and decided that he would one day listen to his speech. Not today, however, he had other business.

Barbara was seated at her desk when Jay walked in. She greeted him with a warm smile. Merle had called and said Jay was coming to see the doctor and she couldn't quite understand the shameless excitable pang that hit her body. She recalled the last time he came to bring Dr. Weinstein's lunch and how charming he was.

"Hello Ms. Barbara, I hope you didn't bring lunch today, I brought some for you compliments of Shirley's."

She started to blush and tried hard not to show her total rejoice with his gesture.

"Oh my goodness, what have you done, I didn't bring lunch," she lied, "I didn't know what I was going to do. Thank you so very much; what did you bring me?" she said, gushing like a school girl.

Jay turned on the charm. "I know you only eat vegetables so, I made up a plate of Shirley's finest. I hope these are ones that you like." Jay knew that. He had seen what she ordered when in the restaurant.

Barbara nervously opened the container and said, "Ohhhh, this is just what I love; and you brought so much, I can't eat all of this, thank you so much. And you brought ice tea, and corn bread. Ohhhh this is just great. We open until seven tonight so this is more than enough for later. How did you know what I like?"

Jay said triumphantly, "I watched you when you were eating in the restaurant." Barbara felt her light-skinned complexion turn beet red and sweat form under her arms. "You do? Well you sure paid attention." She was embarrassed and thought she had better change the subject. "Ahh, Doctor Weinstein has one patient with him now and two more waiting, do you have time?"

"Yes, I don't have to be back to work right now so I can wait a while."

"Okay have a seat he won't be long."

Jay found a seat not entirely visible to Barbara but to the right of the reception desk. As She took her lunch in the back, his eyes were trained on her great legs and the way her skirt hugged her hips, nicely.

Two other people were waiting in the office trying not to show interest in the scene they just witnessed. Jay found a five months old Sports Illustrated magazine and began to turn the pages, not really reading anything.

After a few minutes she came back to her desk. She peeked over her shoulder at Jay and tried to get back to her work updating the records of patients. It was obvious that she freshened up her make-up while in the back her face was aglow. She was flustered.

The last of the two patients ahead of Jay went in to the back and Jay was next. Barbara came over to Jay and said cheerfully, "Come with me, Dr. Weinstein should be finished with this patient in a little while, and I can get you ready for him." Jay followed her to the treatment room and sat down. This is where he wanted to be but this was not the room. Barbara was saying something but Jay was not listening. His mind was churning. He noticed that he was directly across from Dr. Weinstein's office. He looked at the desk where he knew the doctor kept his information; information that he had to see.

Barbara left Jay in the room after making out a file for him that she placed on a table.

"He'll be in here shortly, make yourself comfortable. I'm gonna eat my terrific lunch while I have time."

Jay didn't know why, but he asked her, "How is Dr. Weinstein?"

She answered, "Oh, he's feeling good, he's been in a good mood all day, something has him happy."

Jay knew why. He watched her leave and left the door to the treatment room opened. Jay waited for a moment and when he heard the low buzzing of a drill at work, he made his move without thinking. He rushed into the doctor's office and picked up a magazine. He would say if discovered, that it was one that he took interest in when delivering the doctor's lunch last week and wanted to read it.

He quickly opened the desk draw. The drill was still buzzing. He removed the journal and read the last page. He saw the last entry;

two thousand MEA. Then he saw other entries, with dates; five thousand OXY, two thousand RCA, three thousand MAT, five thousand FNC and so on. The journal had pages of information like this. Jay hurriedly took out his order pad and wrote down the symbols that he saw. He wrote down the dates and quantities not knowing what it all meant.

Just then, the drilling stopped in the treatment room; he heard the muffled voice of Dr. Weinstein say something like, 'okay that'll be it for today.' Jay calmly left the office and returned to his treatment room pocketing his hastily scribbled notes.

Dr. Weinstein soon came to the treatment room and was indeed in a good mood. After accomplishing what he set out to do, Jay wanted to just leave with his new information.

His next task would be what should he do with it. He decided to sit through his mock tooth trouble. It was, he decided, time for a check up and cleaning. So he sat through forty minutes of x-rays and probing and light teeth maintenance. All the while the good doctor was happy as a Lark.

Finally, he was finished and the x-rays provided no new potential problems. Surprise.

Jay said goodbye to Barbara who continued to voice her appreciation for the lunch. He headed back to the restaurant.

What to do? That was the thought on Jay's mind as he walked up Lenox Avenue. The early afternoon was not without the usual activity that Harlem was noted for. Yet, Jay neither heard nor saw anyone in the streets. Then an idea rose in his head. He decided to walk to the library on 135th street. He recalled a project that he had to prepare while in high school and the source of information came from old newspaper articles. Articles stored on microfilm.

The young lady at the desk looked surprise when he asked for back copies of the Wall Street Journal. "We don't get much request for that here, you must be a student at Columbia University."

"No, I'm just doing some reading about the stock market." He replied. She was pretty, and any other time Jay would do his flirtatious thing but he had stuff to do and ignored the overtures she made with her big brown eyes. She led him to the microfilm room and instructed him how to look for old copies of the newspaper.

Jay had only seen copies of the Journal after hotel guest in Charleston discarded it. He had never seen more than the front page so he had no idea what he was looking for. Realizing that this may take some time, he went back to the desk and the young lady who now greeted him with a bright smile to go with the eyes, and asked if he may use the phone. She told him it was not usually done but for him she would make an exception. He was in reply the usual charmer and affable Jay Austin. He thought it best that he call Merle and tell her he would take the rest of the afternoon off and come back for dinner service. She agreed after inquiring about his visit at the dentist.

The first thing Jay did was read the table that explained how to read stock prices. He then was able to discern what close meant and open, high, low and last. The other shit didn't matter today.

Armed with this knowledge, and stock symbols, Jay set about looking for prices that corresponded with the dates found in Dr. Weinstein's Journal. One more trip to the now drooling young lady to get a legal pad. After two hours of recording dates and prices for the stock symbols, Jay began to see a pattern developing that he found astounding.

For each of the stock symbols and the date recorded, there was a dramatic increase in price from five to ten days later. A dramatic increase. He didn't need to be a Wall Street veteran to conclude what was going here. A grand analogy would be to know what numbers to play before it came out. Another would be to bet on a horse and know the winner before the race was over. Horse races have been known to be fixed. Can someone fix a stock rise? This was the kind of crap that numbers players who frequented the restaurant dreamed about. 'What's the number gonna be today?' They would ask each other. It appears that White people could answer that in their world. Damm. Jay heard the voices of the men in the barbershop in his head again. Don't be afraid to take risk, take chances.

He sat at the microfilm machine in silence. Boxes and boxes of film surrounded him. What was certain from this non-expert research is, the doctor had someone who was giving him, no; telling him when to buy certain stocks before they increased in value. That's fine. That was the sole purpose in buying stocks. The price is supposed to go up and then you sell and that's how you made money. What was wrong with this?   Well, Jay surmised, if everyone had this information, then everyone would make money. That apparently was not the case. So the doctor and his friends had an advantage not available to others. There must be some rule or law against this Jay thought but shit, the bastard is getting away with it. This was evident by the pages and pages in the notebook kept by Dr. Weinstein.

It was nearly six p.m. when Jay left the library. He headed back to the restaurant for the seven o'clock dinner service.   He walked slowly. He now had two thoughts dominating his thinking.   One he didn't like, and the other daring.   He knew he would never be in position to get information from Dr. Weinstein again, that was just luck.   He would not have access to the notebook again and he would also not know when the doctor would get another call.   But he thought, Barbara would.   She could be the key for him. The other nagging thing would have to happen in its own time. Jay was supposed to take advantage of this situation. It was destined. After all, he was just deemed most likely to succeed just a few months ago.

Lenox Avenue was preparing for the nightlife of Harlem. Steady streams of people emerged from the 135th Street subway station on their way home from work.   Merchants were pulling down the protective metal gates and doors that guarded the windows of their business over night.

The fish and chips were being prepared; the wine chilled in the liquors stores, the number runners were taking action and mothers were picking up their little ones from babysitters and day care centers.

He noticed a florist shop that hadn't closed its doors yet and an idea hit him. Surely they would take one more sale.   What did she say, she was working until seven tonight. Time for over kill. Armed with a dozen red roses that the owner sold at a discount, displayed in a green vase with white ferns and some other cute stuff, Jay raced back to the office of Dr. Weinstein.   There were three people waiting in reception and Barbara was not at her desk. Perfect. He didn't want to draw attention to himself if that could be avoided. He quickly placed the roses on her desk, wrote a note that said 'thanks for making the appointment for me today', J. In a few minutes, he was back on Lenox Avenue, smiling to himself.

Sarah was busy getting her station ready for dinner service when Jay walked in. She went over to him as soon as she saw him. "You okay honey? How's your tooth? You been gone all day, you gonna work tonight?" She still asked questions but didn't wait for answers. "Yea, I'm okay Sarah; I just had a little infection in one tooth; it will be okay."

Merle was next to inquire about Jay's dental problem and he assured her that all was fine. "By the way, Gwen called you a few times; you should call her back. Milton called too."

"I doubt if they are still in their office now so I'll call them in the morning." Jay said.

"I've got to get my station up now."

Jay tried to act as if there wasn't and will not be a change in his life. But he knew a metamorphosis had taken place, but it must not be noticed. So he put forth that energetic, lively, spirited personality that everyone in the restaurant had come to know and love.

Early the next morning, Jay called Gwen. She was in a very good mood. " I've sold your stock sweetie, at thirty, the take-over price. There is a problem however; I sold your purchase before you paid for it. Settlement isn't until Monday, but you still have to pay for the two hundred shares."

"Why? " Jay asked.

"Because sweetie, that's the rules."

"Can't you take the money out from the proceeds of the sale, the profit? You said I doubled my money."

"You did Jay, but, if you profit from a trade without paying for it, it's a thing called free- riding and withholding, you can't do that."

"I don't understand Gwen, why should I have to bring in three thousand for you to give me six thousand?"

Gwen started to show some frustration with Jay. "Because that's the way it works. We have a right to take your profit because you haven't paid; now don't mess up; you do have the money don't you?"

"Of course I do, it just doesn't make sense to me"

"If you don't pay, your account will be restricted, which means any future purchases, the money must be in the account first."

"Well go ahead and restrict it. There is money there, and I don't plan to take any out. Do you pay interest like a bank?"

"No this is a cash account no interest is paid. If you had a margin account..., shit, Jay I don't feel like going into this now. Milton will probably call you to talk about this. He will decide what we should do. I'll get back to you okay? This is going to cause me some grief."

"I don't want to do that Gwen, but the way I see it, you take your three thousand out of my six thousand and we're even."

"Oh Jay, I love you, but you're being a pain in the ass now. By the way, do you have any more ideas?"

Jay laughed. "So now you want advice from me huh, you think I know my shit. Oh you got me talking like you now."

"I'm not proclaiming you an expert just yet, but that was simply amazing."

Sounding boastful, Jay said, "Well you listen sweetie, I'm just getting started."

As Jay hung up the phone, he immediately thought of Barbara and how the flowers impacted her. He thought what should he do next, and what after that for she is going to be the key to additional information. He said to himself, 'I'll think of something. I always do.'

Barbara was indeed impressed. She was totally beside herself when she saw the flowers on her desk. One of the patients, a woman in her sixties volunteered, "A delivery boy left em, left you a note too, you see it?"

A delivery boy Barbara thought, *what is he trying to do? I'm old enough to be his mother I think. He can't be more than nineteen; my daughter Cheryl will be nineteen in two months. The boy is almost half my age and I'm blushing.*

It had been a while since any man had express interest in Barbara; at least any man that she would want too. She had to admit the attention, although from someone so young, felt good.

And that's about all it will do is make me feel good, I would never expect anything from this, but he is fine. I don't know if I can go to the restaurant now, I don't want to encourage him and there is something in me that say go for it. Don't be silly. What does he means he watches me, what is he doing watching me, Oh I can't stand this. I don't know when the last time someone gave me flowers.'

Not even Mat her former husband of six years and Cheryl's father ever gave her flowers.

Barbara's day dreaming was interrupted by Dr. Weinstein saying good night to her and Cheryl, her daughter, coming into the office. They had made plans to go downtown to Macys for some early Christmas shopping.

"Hi Dr. Weinstein, hello mom, ready to go?" Weinstein still in his good mood said to Cheryl, "Young lady you are really growing up. How is School? Cheryl is tall like her mother. She has her father's complexion, which is dark skin. She has long hair and hazel eyes like her mother that sparked when she smiled. The dimples in her face were pronounced and really gave her a stunning look like a model. Barbara was always attractive to dark skin man and the best thing she got out of her marriage she says was a dark skin beauty, Cheryl.

Cheryl did not think she could make it as a Black model and instead opted to be a fashion designer. She was enrolled at Westchester Community College in the school of arts and fashion design. She had no boy friends and not looking for one. She had time she said.

She and her mother had a good relationship and were good friends as well. She was not going to make the same mistake her mother made; that is marrying young to a no-good man. She loved her father but he was no good. One woman was not enough for him. She is in touch with him and he helps with her tuition but that's as far as the relationship goes. She will not forgive him for the many nights she heard her mother crying when Mat didn't come home." Barbara had made it a point to never bad-mouth Mat to Cheryl. She would not influence Cheryl's relationship with her father. Everyone knows he was handsome but a pure-breed dog.

After Weinstein left, Cheryl noticed the flowers. "One of your patients gave you flowers? They are beautiful."

Barbara had never lied to Cheryl and she wouldn't be now. Jay is a patient. "Yes. A patient did give them to me. He was thankful that I arranged an appointment for him."

"Is he cute? Is he old and bald?" Cheryl laughed.

"What makes you think I only attract old bald men?" Barbara said.

"Mr. ahh what's him name, yea, Mr. Thompson, he was old and bald."

"And he was a very nice man Cheryl. Looks isn't every thing and you should know that."

"I'm only kidding mom, don't take it so seriously; gee who is this guy?"

"Someone you will probably never meet. Now are we going shopping or what?"

Clearly, Barbara was embarrassed to feel the way she did. And she knew that Cheryl must never even think that a young man had aroused dormant feelings in her, and that this young man is her age. She would think that I've completely lost my mind.

CHAPTER 16

Early the next morning, Milton called Jay at the restaurant. He was rather jovial. "Hi Jay. Congratulations. Look, I'm going to let your transaction go. Gwen and I talked it over. This was your first investment, and I'm going to assume that you didn't know. We do have rules that state a purchase must be paid for even after a sale. This was a most unusual situation, but this must not happen again okay?"

Jay, never at a moment to not be congenial replied, "Thank you Mr. Milton, I hope I didn't get Gwen in trouble. I have the money; I just didn't understand why; you know what I mean?"

"It's okay and call me Milton. I'll be brief Jay. I wouldn't do this ordinarily, at least, without a formal interview; but I want to offer you a position with us. You have proven to me that you are capable and Gwen speaks very highly of you. We can pay you a small salary while you're in training. And when you take the test, and become a broker, you have the ability to make a lot of money. I know you have the personality, so I believe you can become quit successful. What do you think?"

"I don't know Mr. Milton, I have to think about school and I really don't know a lot of people here. I wouldn't know who to call for business."

"I'm sure that won't be a problem for you Jay. I think you have the gift. You know how to talk to people; and I can make you a salesman. Think it over and get back to me. Okay?"

"I sure will Mr. Milton and thanks again."

Jay knew right away what he was going to do. You have a gift he said, you know how to talk to people, you can make a lot of money. This was predestination. *I'm gonna take that job.* The problem is, what to tell his mother, Sarah and Shirley. And will he continue to live with Sarah. He loved his mother and was fond of everyone in his life in New York, but it was time to move on. *Yea, my mother knows I'm not stupid, she knows I think things through; yea I'll get my own apartment. Gwen did it. I can do this. I'll go to night school just like she does. Yea I can do this. I'll give my notice to Shirley tomorrow. Gotta tell Sarah first. Tell her tonight.*

The breakfast crowd was brisk for a Thursday morning. Jay was having a good day. He worked hard as usual and was getting good tips as he always did. As Noon approached, Merle came to him and said. "Hey Jay, your girlfriend wants you to bring her some lunch."

"Who?" Jay asked.

"Mrs. Hall, she don't feel like walking here so she asked me to let you bring it. She wants Fried chicken, black eye peas, rice and gravy, corn on the cob and ice tea. You got it."

"Sure I got it, but she shouldn't have fried foods, I'll take the baked chicken."

"She said you would say something about that," Merle laughed, "Take her what she wants, it can't hurt her now. Tell her it's on me. She must be hungry. I haven't seen her in a couple days."

Jay replied, "I've got two check-outs. When they leave, I'll take it to her."

After his last customers left, Jay went into the kitchen to get Mrs. Hall's order. Sarah was sitting down and massaging her feet. "My feet is killin me, I jus can't... I musta walk five miles in there today. Jay went over to her and whispered in her ear, "I'll message them for you tonight." She responded with her big gold tooth smile and said, "That be nice sweetie, you sure you got time?"

"We'll see tonight."

I've got a lot to do tonight.

He didn't use the take out containers for Mrs. Hall's food. He took regular plates, one for the chicken, one for the black eye peas, rice and corn and a dessert saucer for the peach cobbler. He neatly wrapped them in aluminum foil.

He arrived at Mrs. Hall and rang the bell on the gate. She looked out her bedroom window, saw it was Jay and started to make her way to the basement gate. He heard her say, "I'm coming Jay, the old lady can't walk too fast."

He started on her right away as she slowly opened the gate.

"Why didn't you have Phyllis come and get food for you?"

"Oh that lazy child, I haven't seen her since Tuesday. She called and said she was sick." "Well how are you doing? You okay?"

"I'm fine Jay; I just didn't have the strength to walk to the restaurant. He took her by the arm and ushered her back into her bedroom.

"What have you been eating? Did you get your prescription filled yet? Why didn't you call earlier? You know I would have brought you food." He was taking on a trait of Sarah's; asking questions but not waiting for an answer.

"I can still take care of myself son, don't be fussing at me. I just didn't feel like cooking today. Now what did you bring me?"

"Just what you ordered, I also added some peach cobbler. You know I wasn't going to bring fried chicken but Merle insisted."

"Bless her heart, she knows how to treat an old woman." She was smiling. She still radiated the air of a grand lady but Jay could tell that she was not well.

Jay unfolded a small metal table and brought the food to where she sat down. He snapped open a linen dinner napkin and gently laid it across her lap. She was always impressed with that.

"Thank you sweetheart, you are so good to me."

"Eat. I'm upset with you; you know I worry about you. I'm going to bring your food everyday from now on. Did Phyllis say when she would be back to work?"

After taking a bite of chicken and laboring to swallow, she said, "I don't know. Saturday is payday so I think she'll be better by then."

"Well I'll bring you something tonight, about seven o'clock."

"On no Jay this'll be enough for me today, I don't eat that much, but you can come back for the plates. I'll be in bed by eight."

"Okay I'll be back at seven. If you want any thing, just call."

"Thank you dear; you wanna take the key so you don't have to ring. It's hard for me to come to the door. I get tired." Jay spotted the unfilled prescription still in the same place on the mantel.

"Okay I'll take the key, but I'll ring so you'll know its me coming in."

"Okay dear, thanks again."

Jay headed back to the restaurant. The nagging scene once again firmly in his head.

I have a key... she is asleep by eight. I could... no I couldn't... I'm not a thief; she obviously trusts me, I'm not like that.

He felt himself shaking, and his walk unsteady.

Forget this shit Jay. What are you thinking?

"How is she?" Merle asked

"She is okay but she doesn't look good. She was supposed to get some medicine but her girl hasn't been in so she didn't get it. I told her to call if she needs anything."

Sarah had left the restaurant and went home to rest. Gwen came in and Merle knew to seat her in Jay's station. She ordered a hamburger with the works, fries and a vanilla milkshake. Jay came back with her order and she said, "Milton told me that he spoke to you; so what do you think?"

"I've made up my mind Gwen. I did as soon as I hung up the phone. I'm gonna do it. I'll tell Shirley tomorrow morning."

"Oh that's great Jay; we're gonna be great. We'll make a lot of money. I have trouble getting some accounts because people think that a woman can't do this job. They think that a woman can't manage money. Thank God for people like Milton and Shirley. But with you Jay, I can go back to some of the men who turned me down because I'm a woman but at the same time they wanted to take me out. We are gonna kick ass Jay Austin; I can't wait"

"Eat your lunch before it gets cold, I ain't taking nothing back to warm up for you. Milton said you spoke highly of me; I appreciate that. I also need your help getting into City College. My mother will kill me if I don't."

"I'll give you all the help you need Jay; what are you doing after work, why don't you come over, you remember how to get there don't you?"

"No I can't tonight I have something to do. I also have to find an apartment; are there any that you know of?"

"Jay you can"....

He cut her off, "No Gwen that's not a good idea."

"What's not a good idea, I was about to tell you that you can get an apartment in my building. There is a kitchenette available for thirty-five dollars per week."

"Okay, I might look at it. Thanks."

Gwen left after her lunch. There were few people in the restaurant. Jay went in the kitchen to chat with the cooks. He loved it back here. JC was one of his favorite people and enjoyed talking to him. He was going to miss everyone there, but he knew that his immediate future was promising. So there would be no regrets about leaving.

As he talked to the kitchen staff, he kept playing with the key in his pocket that would open the door to Mrs. Hall's home. There were times during the afternoon when he completely forgot that he had the key. He would reach into his pocket only to discover what it was and the haunting thought returned.

Merle came into the kitchen looking for Jay. She said to him, "I called your girlfriend to see how she was doing. She sounds different. She said bring her some more cobbler when you come back for the plates. She said she will be listening for your ring, okay."

"Maybe I should take it now." Jay said.

"Well, no." Merle said. "She said she was going to take a nap, so I wouldn't go now."

"Okay. I guess if she wants more food, she must be feeling better."

As the evening time in Harlem made its' auspicious entrance, days becoming shorter, nights and nightlife longer, Jay now stood in Shirley's front window staring at nothing in particular. For some strange reason, Carla, his high school math teacher and love of his young life, dominated his daydreams. He wondered where she might be. He asked Ruby during one conversation, if Ms. Mack is her Geometry teacher only to be told that it is somebody else, he didn't really hear the name, what he did hear Ruby say is, Ms. Mack did not come back to Burke this year. Jay wanted to write to her, let her know that he was okay and that he would never ever forget her.

His next thoughts were of Barbara. He wanted to call her but he cautioned against that.

No, I can't appear to be too aggressive. I should stay on a subtle, low key, non-obtrusive, approach. In fact, unless she comes in the restaurant,

I should not come in any contact with her unless it's accidental. Then I'll find a way to make a date with her.

He was fingering the key in his pocket. Maybe it's time for the peach cobbler.

Jay prepared a bowl of cobbler to take to Mrs. Hall. JC, observing him said, "Youngblood, you are gonna work your way into the lady's will."

Jay replied, "No JC, that lady will outlive all of us." There was a chorus of laughs from the kitchen staff.

It was nearly dark outside and a chill in the air. Jay was about to experience a New York winter for the first time in a few weeks. He thought that he should have worn something other than his waiter jacket out in the chill. He hurried his steps, wanting to get there and back to work. He sensed that someone would be watching him; there were always people in their windows watching the streets and someone would surely see him enter Mrs. Hall's house.

He rang the bell on the gate and waited a few seconds to see if she would answer. He saw the curtain move back from the window and Mrs. Hall motioned him to come on in. He took the key from his pocket and entered the hallway and then into her bedroom. She was watching television, the Ted Mack Amateur Hour.

"Hello My dear, you must be feeling good, wanting more dessert. Did you eat all your food?"

"Yes I did Jay, I don't know why I told Merle to send me cobbler, I'm full, and I've had this pain in my shoulder all day. Be a dear and put it in the refrigerator for me. Maybe I'll eat it later. The plates are back there in the sink. Thank you so much Jay."

"Oh you're welcome Mrs. Hall."

Jay put the cobbler in the empty refrigerator and retrieved the three plates from the sink. She had washed them. Returning to her bedroom, he saw her standing and looking into her handbag. She handed him a twenty-dollar bill.

"Thank you sweetheart, you are so kind to me."

"Oh thank you Linda, you know I didn't do this just to get a tip from you, you're special to me."

"I know Jay."

Just as she uttered his name, she clutched her chest and gasped for breath. She reached out for something to hold on to as she was falling and still gasping. She tried to call out his name but could only managed a deep guttural sound of someone suffocating. Jay was momentarily frozen in horror. Catching her, as she was about to collapse on the floor, Jay nearly fell himself from her weight. Unable to speak clearly, she mimicked putting something into her mouth. She said in a whisper in between gulps for air; "My medicine… kitchen, table." Jay gently laid her down on her bed and ran to the kitchen. He could hear the desperate and deep fight for breath from her.

He found a little bottle on the kitchen table. He read the label; it simply said nitroglycerin. He could still hear her fight for life but he could also hear that she was losing. And then he just stood there. He stood motionless as he heard life slowly oozing away from her.

After about two minutes the only sound he heard coming from the bedroom was the TV.

His knees started to shake, but there was no panic in him. No urgency to help this woman who had taken dearly to him. What was he doing? Is he just going to let her die there?

It seemed like an eternity before Jay slowly and deliberately walked back into the bedroom. He looked at the face of death. Mrs. Hall had a peaceful calm in her face, and he knew that she was gone. Still clutching the bottle until his fingers started to ache, Jay wondered what should he do. He knew the answer. He put the medicine back where he found it.

He raced upstairs where he knew the strong box to be. In complete control, Jay took the stock certificates from the box. He then took the bond certificate and her passport. He carefully stuffed them into his shirt at the back and down into his waistband out of sight. He made sure there was no bulge and his waiter jacket did not reveal anything. He glanced at his watch and realized the he had been there about ten minutes. For some reason, he didn't know why, he took out his handkerchief and wiped the strong box of any possible fingerprints. It just seemed the thing to do. After all, in his mind, he had just committed a crime. He went back to the kitchen and wiped the medicine bottle also.

He returned to the bedroom. Jay picked up the plates where he had let them fall when he tried to assist Mrs. Hall. He looked around the grand bedroom and again admired the splendor of this house. And then he looked at Mrs. Hall. The look on her face now was total serene. She was going to die soon anyway and there was nothing he could do that would have prevented that.

He put the key back on her mantel and was out the door making sure it was locked. He stopped out front and waved into the window, saying goodnight loudly as he walked away. He was sure someone saw and heard him. They will say that she must have been alive when he left.

He slowly walked back to the restaurant. He did not avoid the gaze of people that he passed. There were always familiar faces in the street; faces of people that he had never met but had seen before. He felt that they recognized him too. So there was no need to hide his presence in the street. He had just visited Mrs. Hall and left her in good spirits. There was nothing to fear. They will discover her and determine that she died from a heart attack

The street was quiet on this evening. Quiet to a point that it seemed mysterious. The temperature had dropped a few degrees in the few minutes that Jay was in Mrs. Hall's house and the cool air made his eyes water.

He walked with one hand stuffed deep into his pockets. His other hand was getting cold holding the plates that held Linda's last supper. He checked his back to feel that his package was secure at his waistband and in no danger of falling down to his hips.

Jay thought he had done nothing wrong. He had not killed Mrs. Hall; he just did not help her live. No one would know about the securities, he reasoned. She had told him that her children were not told that she and her husband had been buying stocks and bonds since early in their marriage. The picture that he could not erase from his mind was having the securities in his possession. Now they were... as if by fate.

Jay was amazed at the complete control of his emotions. He was so cold and uncaring. Lying dead in her bed was a woman who genuinely cared for him. And he cared for her on a real basis. Yet, when the occasion arose for him to help her, he was overcome by the thought that had dominated his mind for the last few days. He knew that he wanted to take possession of her money, and that feeling was stronger than the will to do what he could to save her life. He would have her money now and that was that. It was predestined. But what had he become. He never before displayed greed for anything; much less money. Only he knew and only he would ever know. His demeanor, behavior and deportment were not readable.

CHAPTER 17

At the restaurant, Jay was Jay. The only thing he talked about was to tell Merle that Mrs. Hall had given him a twenty-dollar tip. Merle was impressed but not surprised at Mrs. Hall's generosity. "That's the kind of lady she is Jay. She has done a lot of good things for people around here. Most people don't know that but, but mom and I know."

That night at the apartment, Jay kept his word. He was going to tell Sarah that he is leaving the restaurant and maybe get his own apartment. He went to his room to find a place to hide his bounty. He knew that Sarah was reading his mail so he would not have a safe place in the apartment. For the time being, he merely put them into the jackets of some jazz albums he had purchased. This would be a safe place because Sarah didn't care for the music and would never think to look in the jackets for any reason. Then he directed his attention to her.

He went to her bedroom, which he hadn't done for a short while. He started with a soft and gentle message of her feet. She swooned with pleasure. He then moved to other parts of her body and placed warm and wet kisses on her moist skin. Sarah was a woman who responded to sexual advances in record time. She could go from cold to hot in seconds. It seemed that she was like a man in that respect; that is, always ready. With Sarah, there was no need for foreplay. Jay knew this. But tonight, he was going to be slow and deliberate. He would arouse her to new heights; he would give her a night that she would not forget, if this was going to be their last.   So, he imagined that he was in bed with Carla.

She screamed and cried out in absolute pleasure; a pleasure place that no man had ever taken her to before. Sarah was in shock over the sexual experience from someone so young. She was in love.

"Jay," she whispered, "What is you doin to me boy, you is killin me, what is you doin to this old lady."

"What old lady?" Jay said. "You're the same age as my mother and she ain't old."

After she caught her breath and could talk, she said, "I wish you hadn't mentioned your mother Jay. I feel so ashamed when I think about her. You know, she calls me all the time, concern bout you, she called yestaday, wants to know what I thinks bout you wanting to stay here."

Jay looked at Sarah curiously and said, "So what did you tell her?"

"I says it could be good for you. You knows how to tak care of youself and you is smart and everybody loves you; I know I sure do. But I couldn't tell her that."

After a moment of silence Jay said, "You know Sarah, I'm thinking about leaving the restaurant. That man Milton, offered me a job working for his company, I could be a stockbroker, learn about investments. I could make a lot of money."

Sarah was surprised but knew in her heart that Jay would be leaving one day. She figured that he would be leaving for college soon but this news she wasn't prepared for. She was at once filled with joy but couldn't show it. She also knew that Jay staying in New York and working with Milton, meant that girl Gwen would be in his everyday life. He would soon forget her.

"Why that's nice honey, you could do that. You can do anything Jay, and I think that's a good move for you. You is too good for that restaurant. Shirley will be disappointed but you hafta think bout your future. You was going soon anyways."

"I really enjoyed the restaurant Sarah, I mean, I liked it there. I've met some really good people and everyone has been so nice to me, thanks to you. Although I've been there such a short time, it will still be hard to leave."

"They liked you for you Jay and I had nuting to do wit it. So you tell Shirley you is moving on, she'll understand."

The first step went smoothly Jay thought; time for number two.

"I've been thinking too Sarah, that maybe I should get my own place. I've been in your way for too long and I'm sure you want to get back to your own way, you know what I mean?"

Sarah had a look of surprise in her face. "Oh no Jay, honey, I don't want you to leave; you can always stay here. You can save the money you would need for a apartment by stayin here. Sides, your mother would feel better knowin you is wit somebody you knows. So please stay."

"I guess it would make sense to save some money; I don't know how I'm going to do in this business. I need to meet people and get them to invest with me I think, I'm not sure yet."

"That's, why maybe you shud stay at the restaurant a little longer Jay. Shirley knows lots of rich peoples she could intraduce you to em she'll do that for you."

"I plan to talk to her in the morning, tell her about what I want to do maybe she'll help me I'll see." Jay added.

Sarah pulled him close to her and nestled into his arms. She discovered all over what lovemaking was all about. Now for the first time since being in New York, she knew that she could never live alone again. She was going to find a man; she was going to get married. Losing Jay was going to leave too large a void in her life.

Jay closed his eyes hoping to go to sleep. He knew it would be difficult as the image of Mrs. Hall crept into mind. He was planning his response to the discovery of her death.

CHAPTER 18

The next morning, Jay went directly to Shirley's office after he and Sarah arrived at the restaurant for breakfast service. As always, Shirley was in a good mood. Jay developed a great deal of respect for Shirley in the five months he had been working for her. She was a good businesswoman and totally devoted to her restaurant and her employees. She was always open to a cash advance for the kitchen staff when those needs developed. With an exceptionally big heart, she had only fired two people in the twenty years that her restaurant was opened. She was quick to forgive and the results were loyal employees who worked hard for her. Jay sensed that she would be disappointed with his decision but not upset by it.

After Jay told Shirley about the offer from Milton and his immediate plans, she said, "Jay, you know I love you; you have proven to be one of the most important persons I have hired here in the last five, ten years. Besides Merle, C J and Sarah, no one has been more productive here, and in such a short period of time. I think you will be successful in any thing you attempt to do. You have that drive. I am disappointed that you will leave. After all, I thought you would be here for the summer only, and you would be going to college. I had visions of you working here every summer until you graduated. Merle and I discussed that possibility. We were both impressed with your attitude and your work.

All my customers just loved you. I want you to promise me that you will go to night school like you said. You will need that degree. To be a successful Black man, you must have that."

Jay replied to her "Oh yes ma'am Ms. Shirley. My mom would kill me if I didn't. The only reason she is letting me do this is, I have to be in school, so I'm enrolling at CCNY the next semester."

"That's good. I have a proposal for you Jay; maybe it will do both of us some good. How about you work here on the weekends. You can pick the time you want to work; whatever is convenient for you. I 'm sure you can use the money for school."

"Why that's great Ms. Shirley. Sure I'll do that. I'll be in training for eight weeks and I won't make a lot of money so that'll be great, thank you."

"There is something else I can also do Jay. I know a lot of people; some have a lot of money. Some have a little money but none of them know any thing about investing. I didn't either until Gwen made that proposal to me. I wished I had been exposed to this years ago. I was going to introduce her to them after I did my thing, you know, see how it was going. Now you learn that business Jay; and you learn it like you learned the restaurant business. You keep that same personality and that killer smile; I'll introduce them to you. Okay?"

Jay rose from his seat; his eyes began to glisten as he reached out to shake Shirley's hand. He grasped her hand with both of his and gave her what can be described as a firm and warm handshake. She pulled him into a hug and said, "If you left, all my female customers would stop coming here." She laughed out loud as Jay felt her gentleness.

"And Linda Hall, she would stop talking to me. So you must stay, just for her."

"I'll do anything you want Ms. Shirley; and you know Mrs. Hall is my favorite customer. In fact I've got to take her some lunch today. Thank you again Miss. Shirley."

Jay left Shirley's office feeling good. He felt the comment about Mrs. Hall was very good. He marveled at his quick response and coolness. What did Shirley say, 'you will be successful at anything you attempt.' Time will tell if she is right. Jay was confident that he indeed is most likely to succeed. Today he must go see Barbara.

Mason was at his usual table with two of his runners going over the night receipts. Sarah had just served them their breakfast of grits, bacon, scrambled eggs, biscuits and coffee. Another of Mason's runners came in and casually said there was an ambulance on 127th Street and the police were in the block also. This was no news in Harlem, but for some reason, Mason told his runner to see what was going on. "Can I eat first?" The young man said, and Mason replied, "The food will be here when you get back, see what the cops are doing in the block."

Phyllis entered Mrs. Hall house with her own key. She came to pick up her pay and do a little cleaning up. She didn't plan to stay long. Her man was waiting for her to come back with some money. The two of them had early plans for the little change. She also planned to look into Mrs. Hall's purse for a few dollars more, which she often did. She knew that Mrs. Hall was not as alert as she was when she first started working for her. She had been able to pocket up to fifty dollars at some times and had not been caught.

She heard voices coming from the bedroom and wondered who could be visiting her this time of the day. "Shit, I may not be able to get to her purse." Phyllis said to herself. She listened intently trying to recognize the voice when she suddenly realized it was the television. She was relieved.

"Good morning Mrs. Hall, how you doin today?" Phyllis said through the closed door to the bedroom. She waited for a reply but got only silence and the television voices. She stood at the door for a few seconds. "Are you awake, I'm going to dust upstairs and clean the kitchen and bathroom. Anything else you want done today? I got a doctor's appointment today so I'm gonna leave early all right?" There was no response.

Phyllis became agitated because it meant she would have to wake up Mrs. Hall to get her pay. Well, she thought, I'll do what I said, then she might be up by the time I'm finished. She went about the work half heartily.

She finished in about twenty minutes and hurried back to the closed bedroom door. She still heard nothing but the television. "Damm, she still sleepin." Phyllis began to knock on the door. "Mrs. Hall, I'm finished, I got to go now." She still heard only the TV. Annoyed, Phyllis opened the door and entered. "Mrs. Hall, you all right, I did the work and..." Phyllis looked at the still body lying on the bed motionless and not breathing.

She moved closer to confirm what she feared had happen to Mrs. Hall- the reason for the silence. Then, the realization came that her silenced is now eternal. Phyllis, amazingly, had the presence of mind to rifle Mrs. Hall's purse. "She did owe me my pay anyhow, I'll just see if it here."

The news of the neighborhood drifted into the restaurant. Merle was upset to a point of near fainting. She cried uncontrollably in Shirley's arms. All the restaurant staff was in disbelief and instant grief. Jay sat down in one of the chairs in the kitchen with his head bent into his hands. Tears rolled down his cheeks. Sarah came over to him and rubbed his shoulders in an attempt of consolation.

Shirley felt obligated to go to Mrs. Hall's home. She had been friend to her and her husband for many years. After Mrs. Hall's husband died, she gave Shirley her daughter's phone number in California in case of an emergency. Shirley knew that she would have to make that call.

The ambulance attendant told Shirley that from his observation, Mrs. Hall died in her sleep from an apparent heart attack. He found her medicine on the kitchen table and surmised that she could not get to it. He saw no need for further investigation and would write in his report, her death, the result of natural causes.

Phyllis was still there but anxious to leave. She recounted to Shirley her discovery of Mrs. Hall when she arrived. She also told Shirley that she was to get paid that day but now she would be out of her money, eighty-five dollars in total. Shirley assured her that it would be taken care of and to just wait a few days. She was sure that Grace, Mrs. Hall's daughter would meet with her.

Jay was quiet throughout the breakfast. He was showing his grief. His thoughts, however, were of Barbara. He had not talked to her since leaving the roses for her. Now two days later, it was time to call her. The next stage of his plan was ready for unveiling.

"Hello Miss Barbara, this is Jay Austin from Shirley's restaurant. I was..."

She cut him off. "I know who you are; how are you? Those roses are beautiful. I'm staring at them now; thank you so much. Why did you do that?"

"I just wanted to show my appreciation for your kindness and to let you know that I think you are a special lady."

"And you're a special young man, I don't know what to make of you."

"I called to tell you that I'm leaving the restaurant; I've got another job. I was hoping that I could take you out to dinner, not at Shirley's but some place downtown. I wanted to discuss my new job with you. Are you free Thursday night? I'm off that day."

Barbara was surprised again at her blushing and bubbly feeling that this young man managed to rise in her. "My intuition tells me to politely decline your invitation Jay, but I do find you to be a very charming and mature young man so I'll say yes with caution. I would rather not go downtown; there is a chicken and waffle restaurant that I've secretly wanted to try. I can cheat a little, so do you mind?"

"Chicken and waffles. That sounds good. Where is it?"

"134th and Seventh Avenue."

"So where should I meet you?"

"I'm off at seven Thursday so I'll meet you there at seven-thirty. Tell me one thing Jay; first you brought me lunch, then flowers, and now an invitation to dinner. Are you flirting with me?"

"Yes I am Miss Barbara and I won't apologize for it. I do find you extremely attractive and any man in his right mind would feel the same as I do. I realize of course, that you think I have what you might call a schoolboy crush on you, but it is a great deal more than that. I'm mature enough to know that because of our age difference, you would feel uncomfortable with a relationship. So to put you at ease, I'm not pursuing a relationship or an affair with you. I would like to be your friend and maybe you can help me in my new business, and I can help you in some way. Is that okay?"

Barbara was slow to respond; absorbing all that Jay had said, and then with a deep sigh said, "I'll admit the attention is flattering; everyone likes to get attention and I'm no different. I don't mind being your friend and if I can help you as you think, I'll be glad too. I should tell you also, that I have a daughter about a year or two younger than you so you know how I feel about your.... Oh, we'll talk more later."

It was seven-thirty a.m. when the phone in Grace's Los Angeles apartment rang. She was immediately annoyed at the intrusion. She had just gotten home after working the graveyard shift at the Los Angeles Hilton where she was the night auditor. She had just begun her morning exercise routine.

The few friends she had in LA knew not to call her at this hour. It can't be her agent or a casting director she thought, they haven't called in months. In fact, it has been a very long time since her last small part in a B movie that lasted about one week. LA has not been kind to Grace, and she was beginning to think seriously about going back to New York and perhaps the stage again.

It has been several weeks since she last had a drink- cold turkey. In spite of her addiction to alcohol, drinking had not damaged her good looks yet. The morning workout did two things; help her get through the day and tone her still attractive body.

She thought she had one more role in her and she wanted that last opportunity. Another reason New York was on her mind is, it's about time that she repairs the relation with her family, especially her daughter, Joyce   She is in her first year of college and she needs me now Grace reasoned. It's also about time she spent some time with her mother.

After graduating from the high school for the performing arts in New York, Grace's good looks and talent had landed her parts in several off- Broadway productions. The productions provided steady work and income for over three years and prospects were good for a successful career. She was selected for a touring company with the production of "Hello Dolly", an all black cast, of course. The role took her to fifteen states, forty cities, in the USA and a month in London.

It was during this tour that she met and fell in love with a musician name Harry Stephens. Against her parents' wishes, Grace married Harry after it was discovered that she was pregnant. Her career was put on hold for two years. Two years out of the business was not good for Grace. In show business, you must be seen, and she was busy being a new wife and mother.

Doors were not wide opened to her and other Black performers in the early fifties and the lack of work forced her to take odd jobs to make ends meet. Harry however, did not have the same attitude. If he could not make money in his trade, his ability to play several instruments, he would not work at all.

Naturally, this put a strain on their marriage and after a short time, one day Harry just never came home. He called weeks later to say he was alive and trying to get work in Paris. Imagine that. Grace said, the bastard is in Paris trying to get work. It's been sixteen years.

Grace read an article in Variety, the trade newspaper weeks back that detailed plans for a new Broadway play featuring an all Black cast. Surely, she thought, there will be a part for a mature and still good-looking lady in this production. Auditions will start in two months the article stated.

Grace's morning workout had intensified after reading the article and now this phone call would interrupt her.

"Hello Grace?"

Wanting the irritation to show in her voice she replied dryly, "Yessss"

"Grace this is Shirley Davenport from New York, I have some bad news for you."

Grace knew immediately what the bad news would be. Shirley would only call her for one reason. Grace was making plans to go home and make peace with her mother- take care of her. Tell her how much she really loved her, but now she was going home to bury her.

Jay left the restaurant early Thursday evening. The wake for Mrs. Hall was going to start at seven p.m. so he called Barbara and changed the time of their meeting to 6:30. He would have time to discuss his plans and then go to the wake after.

He dressed in the suit he got at Barney's. This would be the first time that he wears it. After deciding on a white shirt and burgundy and blue strip tie, he was on his way. He was about to open the apartment door to leave when he decided to add a white handkerchief to his breast pocket. He noticed that Milton did that; he always had one in his pocket; very white and very skillfully folded. One more look in the mirror for approval and Jay was pleased. He looked distinguished if not handsome, he thought.

No topcoat, he decided to brave the night chill for the short walk to the Chicken and Waffles restaurant.

Jay arrived at the restaurant just as Barbara was getting out of a taxi. Great timing. She was stunning as usual. He rushed to the opened taxi door and reached for her hand to help her exit. She smiled, placed her soft hand into his and gently stepped onto the sidewalk. Her perfume was already working as soon as it kissed Jay's nostrils.

"Well I see you're on time." Barbara said.

"Yes, I would not keep you waiting, in fact I have been anxious to get here all day. You know the wake for Mrs. Hall is tonight, did you know her?"

"No I didn't " Barbara answered. "I think I have seen her in the restaurant. I heard just yesterday that she died. I guess you are going."

"Yes" Jay replied. But first let's eat."

The Chicken and Waffles restaurant had the appearance of a railroad car when you entered. There was a bar the length of the room on the right. Across from the bar was a row of tables for four against a wall. The tables were covered with fresh clean white tablecloths and each had a dark purple vase with a candle burning in it.

A waitress greeted Jay and Barbara. They had to walk single file down the narrow way to a dining room at the rear and to the left. There was a stage in the back of this room where jazz bands performed on the weekends.

This room had more tables with the same candle burning vases and the starched white tablecloths. Around the walls of the room were booths. There were not many people in the restaurant; only two of the many tables were occupied.

It was rather early for dinner so they had their choices of seats.

Jay pointed to a booth in the rear of the dinning room and the waitress led them there.

"Is this okay?" Jay said to Barbara and she shook her head okay. Always the gentleman, Jay waited until Barbara was seated then took his seat across from her in the dimly lighted room.

"Welcome to Chicken and Waffles, is this your first time here?" The waitress asked but didn't wait for an answer, "My name is Ida."

Jay answered, "Yes, this is our first time here and guess what we are going to have?"

"So you don't wanna see the menu?"

"No, we'll both have the chicken and waffles, and she'll have white meat and I'll have dark. Okay?"

"Got it. Would you like something from the bar?"

"I don't know, would you?" Jay asked Barbara. She thought for a moment and was trying to read the face of the waitress to see if she was aware of their age difference and was she making someone out of it.

Barbara would love to have rum and coke; a drink that she enjoyed in the past but would not dare order something like that now for fear that it would not look right. She was self-conscious. "No" she was finally able to say, I' ll just have water."

The waitress left for the kitchen. "How did you know I wanted white meat Jay?"

"I didn't. But I figured for a person who hardly ever eats meat, but might try chicken, then white is usually the choice. I've worked in restaurants for a few years you know."

"And just what else do you know?"

"I know that you are nervous and wondering what on earth this young man wants with me."

"Right again."

"Don't be, I told you I'm not looking for an affair, but I do need your help with something."

"What can *I* do for you Jay?"

The waitress returned with a basket of warm cornbread, diner rolls, butter and water. "Your order will be ready shortly, would you like warm syrup?"

"Please, that would be **nice**." Jay said.

He took a warm slice of **cornbread** from the basket, broke off a piece and slowly spread a piece of **butter** on it just the way he had seen well-to-do White folks do in Henry's back in Charleston.

"This is good; not like Shirley's but good. Have a piece." Jay said. Barbara complied and did the same thing just like Jay.

"Well, I'm waiting." Barbara said

"I told you that I'm leaving the restaurant. I'm starting a new job next week at a stock brokerage firm on 125th Street, you know Wall Street; I'm going to be a broker."

"That's great Jay. I figured the restaurant was not for you, I knew you were too smart for that. Is this why you're dressed so professionally? You look great in that suit. But I thought you were going to college."

"I am, but I will be going at night."

"I don't know a thing about stocks. You know, Dr. Weinstein is involved in that; remember I told you."

"Yes, I remember, but I'm a little worried about it; I mean I don't want to make a fool of myself."

"Why would you do that? You're a smart guy- you'll do well once you learn it."

"Well that's how you can help me."

"I don't understand, I told you I don't know a thing."

Just at that moment, Ida returned with two platters of the most exquisite fried chicken Jay had ever seen. A golden waffle with a pat of butter in the center made it a most appealing and picturesque meal.

"This does look good." Jay said as he handed the warm syrup to Barbara. "How do you make the chicken so golden brown?" Jay asked Ida.

"Well, we marinate the chicken in milk before frying and that gives it the deep golden color."

"So that's the secret huh?" Barbara said.

"Yea, Mr. Pete our chef said his mamma taught him that."

Barbara cut into her chicken breast, ate the small piece and while still chewing said,

"Ooooh this is gooood."

"Well let me see," Jay said, "I love waffles"

The two quietly ate their meal. The only sounds made by Jay and Barbara for a few minutes was the approval lament from savory food.

Ida returned to remove the two empty platters. "Was everything all right?"

"Yes, very enjoyable." Jay said.

"Very good." Barbara chimed in.

"We also have the best peach cobbler in New York, not just Harlem, shall I bring you both some?"

"Oh not me." said Barbara

"But you must, I want some. Can I have a scoop of vanilla ice cream with that?"

"Sure you can"

"I'm full Jay, I can't eat another mouth full."

"Tell you what Ida, bring two plates in case she changes her mind, she can have some of

mine." Ida was off to the kitchen again.

"I know you must be wondering what is it that I need from you to be successful in my new business. I'm also thinking of you. You see, we both can do well."

"Jay, I have no idea what you are talking about. Why don't you just tell me?"

"Okay. You told me that Dr. Weinstein is into this business, well he told me also. But I found out when I was in his office, that this guy Neil, I think? Neil tells Dr. Weinstein what stocks to buy and he writes it all down in this little book that he keeps in his desk drawer. All I want you to do is when he gets a call from Neil, just look into his drawer when you can and tell me what stock is written there. Now if you don't feel comfortable doing this, then don't. But your doctor makes a lot of money. And we can too. I will buy the stocks he buys, and I will open an account for you and do the same thing."

"Is that it? You want me to snoop on my boss."

"Well yes, if you want to call it that. But only if you feel you can. I don't want you to get in trouble."

"Oh I can do it when he leaves, I lock up you know."

"Yes I do know, I just didn't know how you would feel doing this."

"I don't have a problem with it if that's what you want but I don't see how I can make money; I can't open an account I don't have that kind of money; I only have a small saving account."

"I'll take care of that for you. I'll open an account for you and your daughter; what's her name?"

"Her name is Cheryl."

"Is Cheryl as beautiful as you?"

"Jay, don't…"

"I won't Barbara, I told you, this is business and I promise to keep it that way."

Ida returned with a bowl of warm peach cobbler and a bowl of vanilla ice cream.

"You are going to love this. I bought a extra plate for you Miss, just in case."

Jay didn't wait for an indication that Barbara might want some of the dessert. He just made a plate for her, cobbler and ice cream and slowly pushed it across the table to her. She just looked at him and smiled. "You seemed to take charge quite a bit, don't you?"

"I didn't look at it that way; does it bother you?"

"No in fact I like it. It is rare to see a Black man, especially one so young, who seems to know just what he wants and will go for it."

"Then you won't mind if one day, I decide to go for you."

"That's not what I meant, and you know it."

Jay laughed and said, "The dessert is good, are you sorry you tried it?"

"No; so does that mean you know what's good for me?"

Jay looked into Barbara's face; lit by the candle in the vase and thought, again there is an older woman in my life that I like. He didn't know why but it felt good. He liked Barbara and they were going to make a lot of money is this new adventure. He did not answer her question.

"Hey Barbara, I've got to go. Can I put you in a taxi? I'm going on to the wake."

They exchanged phone numbers and Barbara promised to call him if and whenever the good doctor got a call from his cohort, Neil.

CHAPTER 19

Jay left the restaurant feeling pretty good. He was surprised that Barbara offered no resistance to his plan. And yes, he will open an account for her and fund it. While he didn't know what he would do with the securities he took from Mrs. Hall's strongbox at the moment, he felt confident that it would come to him. It always did for the man most likely to succeed.

It was nearly eight p.m. when he arrived at the funeral home just two blocks from Shirley's. He had passed the building many times but had paid little attention to it.

There were a few people standing outside smoking cigarettes. He quickly passed them and heard somber organ music playing as he entered the lobby.

The lobby floor was covered with a lush dark burgundy carpet and the walls were of a light brown imitation wood grain panel.

Just in front, he faced three rooms. Each room had a metal stand that announced on a black felt background in white lettering, the viewing of the deceased. The room to his far right, the largest of the three, announced Mrs. Linda Hall.

Jay entered the room and was surprised at the size, about twenty rows on both sides of a center aisle. He did not see an empty seat.

There were familiar faces from the restaurant and neighborhood present. He saw JC the cook, other kitchen workers, and most of the servers.

Sarah was not there but had told Jay that she would go to the funeral. She said Mrs. Hall had treated her nice when she first started at Shirley's.

He immediately saw a mound of flowers arranged around a coffin that held the great lady. He stood motionless for a few seconds just staring ahead. He could barely see her face from where he stood, but there was no doubt about that profile.

He was surprised to feel the shaking in his knees, and the dryness that suddenly took over his mouth. Just inside the room was a stand that held a book that visitors signed, he quickly surmised, to record their presence. He picked up the pen and felt it slipped from his grip due to the perspiration on his hands.

He struggled though his signature and as he looked up, he saw Shirley from her front row seat motioning to him to come forward; there was apparently a seat up there.

With a great deal of effort, he was able to put one foot in front of the other for the long walk he was about to take. Slowly, he saw the figure in the coffin take on the look of Mrs. Hall. She looked so peaceful and tranquil as he got closer.

He paused a few seconds to look down on her serene face and the image of her last living moments came vividly into his mind.

I should have done something to help her. Maybe I should have gotten her medicine from the kitchen. maybe.

Slowly, Jay turned away from the coffin and looked to his right for Shirley. The first two seats on the front row reserved for family were occupied. The third seat was empty and Shirley sat in the fourth. Shirley pointed to the unoccupied seat between her and the two women.

Jay immediately recognized from the photographs that he had seen, Grace, Mrs. Hall's daughter and the younger woman he assumed to be Mrs. Hall's granddaughter, Joyce. There was no doubt about family because they both displayed the elegance that described Linda Hall as well as the facial features.

Shirley patted the empty seat and Jay sat down. She smiled at him and took his hand and squeezed it. She then leaned forward in front of Jay and whispered to Grace; "I think Jay here was the last person to see your mother alive. He works at the restaurant and took your mother dinner the night before. Linda loved him. She would not have anybody else wait on her after Jay started with me."

Then Shirley introduced the two to Jay. Grace spoke first. "Merle said the same thing about you. She told me how much my mother cared about you. Thank you for your kindness to her."

Jay replied, "She reminded me very much of my grandmother and I loved her. She was such a nice person"

Jay felt at once awkward. These words were not appropriate for the great lady but it was all he could think of to say. And, there was something about Grace that unnerved him. He stole quick glances at Joyce and saw her young beauty. Definitely in the family.

Shirley whispered to Jay, "You look handsome in that suit Jay. This is the first time I've seen you outside the restaurant. You *are* going to the funeral tomorrow, aren't you? It's at Abyssinian on 135th street. I'm going to close the restaurant after breakfast till four o'clock."

"Yes ma'm I'm going. I'll be there."

Grace then got up and moved among the seated people and thanked them for coming. Joyce just stared at her beloved grandmother in the coffin and occasionally wiped tears from her eyes.

The people in charge of the funeral home soon came to the room and announced the wake was over and where the funeral would be as well as burial. People slowly made their way to the exit.

Shirley asked Grace and Joyce if they were hungry and would they join her at the restaurant. She also asked Jay to join them.

Mother and daughter hand in hand, walked to the restaurant. Shirley and Jay a few paces behind, walked in silence. The neighborhood people and restaurant employees were all not far behind as if in a procession; headed to the place where Linda spent most of her time when not at home.

The restaurant was not busy. It was after nine and Sarah the lone server was starting to clean up. Merle ushered Grace and Joyce to a booth. Jay removed his jacket and told Shirley that he would serve them.

"Is there anything special that you would like?" he asked.

"You know what" said Joyce, I'll eat whatever you bring out here."

"Yea" said her mother. "I *am* hungry. I don't think I have eaten since I got here, just bring whatever is good."

"Everything is good at Shirley's," said Jay, not missing an opportunity to score with his soon to be former boss. "Leave it to me."

Jay and Shirley both headed to the kitchen. She told him to give then whatever they wanted and don't make up a check.

Jay made up plates of fried chicken, smothered pork chops, potato salad, collard greens and other restaurant specials. They were delighted with the food.

Jay paid no special attention to the two beautiful women. In particular, he did not even look Joyce in the eyes. He went about this chore in rather businesslike fashion. He treated them like they were just regular customers. He was not going to give the impression of being a masher. He left the women to eat in solitude and grief.

He knew this would not be the last he saw of them. Grace was especially attractive and the older women thought came to mind. He decided to help Sarah clean up. He would stay with her to close up. As he wiped down tables, he felt that Grace and Joyce both would play a part in his life one day but now was not the time to set the stage for that.

The funeral ceremony for Linda was very stirring. The church was packed; reflecting the love and respect people had for the great lady. Not only did people from Harlem attend, there were also people from out of town, some local politicians and White folks present. Jay guessed that some might have been people that Mrs. Hall and her husband worked with.

Sitting with Sarah, Jay was moved to tears by a women singing the song ' *Swing low Sweet Chariot* '. Sarah clutched his hand tightly. He looked around the audience. He saw Shirley and Merle sitting directly behind Grace and Joyce. He also saw a man who appeared to be about thirty sitting next to Joyce. He is too young to be her father Jay thought, but whom?

The ceremony ended in about an hour. The coffin led a procession out of the great church followed by Grace, Joyce, the stranger and the attendees. The mysterious man walked holding hands with Joyce. As he approached the door, two other men, one White one Black took him by the arms and escorted him to a car parked not far from the church. As the coffin was being hoisted into the hearse, Jay suddenly noticed the two men were now placing handcuffs on the mysterious mourner and Jay did not quite know what to make of that.

Jay was not going to the burial. Shirley asked that he and Sarah go back to the restaurant and prepare for the reopening. The picture of the man being placed in handcuffs did not leave his mind. Finally he asked Sarah.

"That wus her son. Dey musta let him cum to her go'ng home. Dat boy give her the dickens. He doing big time; 12 years I think."

"What did he do?"

"I don't rightly know you haf to ax miss Shirley, she kno. but talk is, he done kilt some man over drugs."

Jay had his answer. He immediately recalled Mrs. Hall telling him that her son had been troubled.

Shirley and Merle agreed to provided food for mourners who came to Mrs. Hall's home after the interment. Church members, who belonged to church organizations that Mrs. Hall was a member of, also brought various homemade dishes. Jay and Sarah prepared large trays of food that would be taken to Mrs. Hall's home. Jay was looking forward to meeting with Grace and Joyce again. But, this would have to wait.

Ed Jr. sat in the back of the car next to corrections officer, Charles Bradley. The handcuffs around his wrists were cutting into his skin and he was hurting. Officer Mack was driving. "Hey you guys, can you takes these cuffs off for a little while, this shit is killing me."

"You know the drill Hall, the cuffs stays on." said Bradley.

"But you have them on too tight; the dam things are cutting my skin, see, I'm bleeding. I could bleed to death by the time we get back." Bradley took a look at Ed's wrists and proceeds to loosen the cuffs.

Bradley sits back and scowls, "It looks like you came from a nice family, Hall, why did you fuck up?" He went on, "Your mother had a big funeral, a lot of people; which meant she was well respected. You didn't come from a poor family or had the usual shit, like, no father, or a family to feed; it was just your dumb ass. You weren't abused, you are educated; why did you think you could get away with your shit, asshole?"

"Yea, I know I fucked up, but it's none of your business, so don't ask."

Officer Mack turned around slightly to look at Ed and says, "And that sister of yours is fine. Is she married? I didn't see any man with her; the young girl; was that her daughter?"

Ed didn't answer any of the questions the two CO's asked him. Instead, he was deep in thought thinking about the life path he choose and where it had led him.

He had been a spoiled brat kid growing up to two loving parents who gave him everything that he wanted. Maybe that was the problem. After private elementary schools, he went to Rice high school, the private Catholic school in Harlem that graduated some of the city's finest young men. He went to NYU for two years before dropping out. Then he began experimenting with heroin after a White girl he met in Greenwich Village introduced him to the drug.

The village was an area in lower Manhattan not far from the NYU campus, where New York's vanguards of the beatnik generation lived.

The area was home to artistes, the pseudo hip, jazz clubs, jazz musicians and coffee shops where wanna-be poets spouted their verses.

Ed loved the village and soon moved out of his parents' house to live there. He told his parents that he would take a year off from school, get a job, learn about self- support and then decide what he wanted to do for the rest of his life. His big sister had found herself in her talent and had performed on stage in New York and other cities. This was going to be his self-discovery.

Mr. and Mrs. Hall agreed. They paid the rent for the one bedroom apartment he found just off the campus. All Ed Jr. had to do was find a job and find himself.

What he found instead was the white lady, the street name for heroin. The lady took a firm hold of Ed. Jr. and made him almost unrecognizable to all who knew him. What little jobs he found, he couldn't keep. He was either late or failed to show up at all and was soon fired.

While his rent was paid, his habit suffered. To fund his addiction, he became a dealer. This arrangement worked out fine. He was a smart guy and a decent businessman. He became very successful and well known on the streets of the village. Too well known. He became a target of the police and the low- lifes that the culture brings.

He needed protection from the low-lifes, so he began carrying a gun. It was on one of these occasions that having the gun was not a good idea. He shot and killed a would be robber. Ed told the authorities that it was self-defense. The police did not find a weapon on the victim and there were no witness to the shooting. Subsequently, Ed was sentenced to serve twelve years at the Peekskill Correctional Facility in upstate New York. He had just completed eight years.

He was not allowed to attend his father's funeral and had just seen his mother in her coffin. This was not the life his parents envisioned for Ed, but he was going to put everything right- especially with the money his parents had left him and his sister. It should be a sizable sum he thought. His father had told him about the t-bond and the stock certificates. Mrs. Hall didn't know that her husband told Ed Jr. about their investments and the subsequent inheritance. But, Ed Sr. did not tell their daughter Grace.

Ed Jr. didn't get a chance to talk to Grace about their inheritance. The funeral was not the right time. He would speak to her when she comes to see him as she promised.

For now, he was going to be a model inmate and hope for early release.

CHAPTER 20

Jay arrived at the Harlem office of Hamill, Rhodes and Peck at 7:45a. m. He expected to wait outside the office because no one would be there. He wanted to be early, like his mother told him. Make the first good impression.

He was surprised to find the office open and someone there. Milton always arrived at 7:00 a.m.

"Well good morning and welcome aboard," said Milton; taking Jay's hand and shaking with both of his. This reminded Jay of the way Mr. Leland shook his hand.

"Good morning Mr. Milton, I didn't know if anyone would be here this early. I'm used to being at the restaurant at six or seven; I couldn't stay in bed any longer so I came in early. Gwen told me she is usually here at eight."

"Yes, she and Sharon get here about eight. I'm usually here at least by seven. I try to read a few things in the papers and prepare for the day's events."

Jay noticed copies of the New York Times and The wall Street Journal on Milton's desk and remembered his first review with it just a couple weeks earlier.

"Would you like some coffee?"

"No sir. I don't drink it"

"Jay please, call me Milton; we are very informal around here. Only when we have a client or visitors in the office do we tend to clean up our acts. I appreciate respect and it goes both ways."

"Understood." said Jay.

"We're excited about you joining us Jay, I think you are going to do well. Gwen and I noticed your outgoing personality when we came to the restaurant. Part of this business is personality. A great deal of it is knowledge and we will help you with that. Then your personality will take over to open doors for you. The key is to open doors to opportunity. An opportunity is to have a prospect give you time to talk to them about what you can do for them. I don't want to get ahead of myself, so what you will be doing for the next few weeks is work with Gwen. She will give you some study material for the stockbroker exam. I wouldn't start reading it right away. Give yourself a couple of weeks first; you'll pick up some terms and words that won't be familiar to you if you start reading it now. We're going to pay you $320.00 per month while you are in training. It's called a draw. The draw will extend up to a year, if I see the effort put forth by you to bring in sales. I'm sure Gwen told you that our income is commission income. The draw is against your future income. Understand?"

"Yes sir"

"By the way, I think your learning curve will be substantially less than usual judging by the success with your first trade. I'm impressed."

"Well there was some luck involved."

Gwen and Sharon came into the office at the same time. Gwen spoke up,"Hi Jay, hello Milton, Ohooo Jay, nice suit."

Sharon was quiet as she always is. She went to Jay and said, "I need you to fill out these papers for me so I can get you on the payroll. Get em back to me when you can."

Taking the papers, Jay looked Sharon directly in the eyes but she avoided his gaze.

Milton spoke up, "He will work with you Gwen. Take him on any appointments you may have and show him how we prospect. Turning to Jay, Milton said, "If you have any questions, just come to me. Take your time to learn. You won't get it all in one day or one month for that matter."

"Yea Gwen replied, this stuff will fill your head, you won't have room for anything else." she laughed.

For the next several weeks, Jay and Gwen were always together; at work and after work. She has targeted small business owners in Harlem and the Bronx for prospective clients. Hairdressers were on her list. She had not been successful at getting time to talk to owners and operators at most of the hairdressers- all women. But when she took Jay alone, she found doors were opening to her. She did all the talking but Jay, with just his presence, made it all possible. She was starting to get more business opportunities.

Recognizing this, she decided to take advantage of this newfound tool. She had Jay call to make appointments. He read from a script that Gwen got from Milton; Jay would call prospects and tell them that his firm was dedicated to helping Black business owners manage their money and increase their income through the stock market. He went on to say; successful and savvy people as well as banks and insurance companies use the market. Jay was going through the phase of a cold-caller. He spent most of his day smiling and dialing and telling people about Milton and Gwen. He also qualified prospects by asking probing questions about funds that they might have available to invest if a plan was presented to them. Getting qualified prospects, helped prevent stockbrokers from wasting time with individuals who did not have funds. Jay was good at it. The line that got him in was 'if I can show you how you can make money for your retirement, or save for your children's college education, or even money to take a long trip, would you be interested?' Invariably if the answer was yes, he would then asked 'how much funds can you commit to such a plan?' Money talks.

At the appointment, Gwen did all the talking; Jay observed and listened. He was not allowed to open accounts yet so all the business went to either Gwen or Milton. It was a good arrangement and Milton and Gwen were indeed happy with this new addition Jay. He was all that they thought he might be. In the meantime he spent his nights studying. He was anxious to take the test.

Then the opportunity came that he planed for. Barbara called and told him that Dr. Weinstein had gotten a call from Neil that morning. She went on to say that after Dr.Weinstein left the office, she discovered that he kept two books; one book had his wife's name written on it and the other had no name. In the book with his wife's name he wrote today's date and 200 SO. In the other book he wrote 1000 SO.

"Do you know what this means?" she asked Jay.

Not wanting to show his excitement, he coolly replied, "I think so, but I will let you know. How have you been Barbara? I've been thinking about you; did you have any trouble getting this?"

"No it was quite easy as I told you. The desk wasn't even locked. How is the new job?"

"It's coming along, I'm studying now. I still have so much to learn"

"You'll get it."

"How is your daughter?"

"Just fine. You still at the restaurant too?"

"Yes, only on the weekends. I'm too tired most days to work but that's the arrangement I have with Miss Shirley. Look Barbara, I really appreciate you doing this. I'm not sure how I will use it, but as I told you, you'll benefit from this also. I'll call you soon maybe, we can go back to the restaurant again for chicken and waffles again."

"Okay Jay, goodbye"

Jay was extremely excited. From his minimal experience, he knew that SO was the stock trading symbol for a major oil company. He also knew that, Dr. Weinstein was going to buy that stock. He also remembered from his trip to the library and the pattern he uncovered, that stock was going to have a dramatic increase in it's price within the next three to five days.

He quickly looked up the price in that day's Wall Street Journal. That would have been the prices from the previous day. He noted the stock closed at 37 5/8 the previous day. He would not know its current price until he went into work in the morning. He couldn't wait and sleep did not come easy.

Jay arrived at 7:00 a.m. Milton was unlocking the door. He went straight to the quote machine and punched in the symbol. It read 37 5/8; thirty-seven dollars, sixty- two and one half cents. He could buy 100 shares from the money in his account. He had to set Milton and Gwen up.

"How can I get some research on Solid Oil?"

"You mean SO."

"Yes, I'm thinking about buying some for my account."

"You like that. Why?"

"I was at the library studying last night and I read something in an old Wall Street Journal about the founder Frank D. Maynard. He is quite a smart man and I think an investment in his company is a good idea."

"I can get some research from downtown but it'll take a couple days."

"Well, I think I'll buy 100 shares today; I see it closed at 37 5/8."

"You know how to do that now but you know, it has to be under Gwen's broker number."

"Oh I know, that's not important to me now."

Milton went about his normal early morning routine. He retreated into his office and started pouring over a list of prospects, reviewing the previous day office transactions and reading current news. Out of the corner of his eye he watched Jay. He was determined to keep their relationship on a professional basis, but it was getting harder every day.

Gwen and Sharon arrived shortly after. Milton greeted them. "Jay has an idea about SO, He put in an order to buy 100 shares, your number."

"Shit, I'm making money before I even sit down, where did he get that?"

"He read something. That's good."

Gwen approach Jay, "Good morning Mr. Stock Picker, why SO?'

"Just a hunch, I learned from you that some stocks are good capital builders, so I'm looking for some price appreciation and income from the dividend the stock pays."

"So you have been studying- you ready for the test?"

"I'm not sure- there is so much stuff."

"I'll give you the practice tests that I have, see how you do. Well, let's break this day open; we have several appointments today."

"What ever you say Teach." Jay said.

Three days after the funeral, Grace and Joyce made plans for their new future. They spent two days just looking through papers found in various places on the three floors of the brownstone. Eventually they found the strong box that Mrs. Hall kept upstairs. In it, they found a will, an insurance policy, a savings account book with a balance of $18,000.00, jewelry that belonged to Mr. and Mrs. Hall, some letters and photographs.

The ladies did not know if anything was missing and neither had knowledge of the Treasury bond and stock certificates.

Mrs. Hall had an adequate life insurance policy which paid Grace and her brother $62,000.00. Grace put Ed's portion in a bank account that would be available when he got out of prison. Like she told Jay, Mrs. Hall willed her home to Joyce. Her college education was also assured by the cash proceeds Grace would receive from the insurance.

Joyce told her mother that she was going to keep the house but in the meantime her education was foremost in her plans. In a few days she was going back to school. Grace felt them growing closer even though it took the death of her mother to bring that about.

They both thought Ed Jr. looked good in spite of his predicament. Grace called on some influential family friends who made some phone calls to arrange for Ed Jr. to attend their mother's funeral. They were unable to converse with Ed at length and he was not allowed to attend the burial. Immediately after the funeral, they each promised him that they would come see him soon.

Grace had not decided if she should stay in the house or get her own apartment. She didn't know if she had to the strength to live in the big house by herself. She was leaning to an apartment and the house would be closed up for now. She still had visions of another stab at the Broadway stage and plans for casting the production she read about was only weeks away. Joyce encouraged and urged her to give it another try. They would talk about it more over dinner at Shirley's the night before Joyce leaves for school.

CHAPTER 21

Jay decided to stop by Shirley's on his way home. He found himself buying lunch on a regular basis and this was something he was not used to since arriving in the Big Apple six months ago. He was hungry for some of Shirley's food, and, he hadn't been there since the funeral.

There was a rather busy dinner crowd. Merle greeted him at the entrance, "Well hello Mr. Stockbroker, so nice of you to come to our humble restaurant. We know you are used to Del Montico, so what brings you here?"

"That is not nice Merle, I'm not a broker yet; you know this will always be home to me and I never heard of Del, what you call it?"

"Del Montico, a famous restaurant on Wall street"

They hugged, and Merle whispered in his ear "You've just left and I miss you already; women don't come here for lunch anymore, see what you did?"

"Don't say that Merle, especially since I know it's not true; you trying to make me feel good?"

"Come by here for lunch if you don't believe me." The two friends laughed out loud.

"You want dinner sweetie?'

"Yes. I'm hungry; Sarah working?"

"She just left. Go on in the kitchen, get what you want."

"No I want to be a paying customer, I can't keep taking advantage of your goodness; I'll sit out here. I've never done that. I'll sit at the counter and give Mitch a hard time."

At this usual table, Mason was doing his night track numbers receipts. Remembering the warning he received from Sarah, Mason only waived at Jay and smiled. Jay returned the greeting and thought to himself, that he should prospect Mason when he gets his license. Mason has plenty of money Jay reasons and he will make more for him.

He'll introduce me to his cohorts. Gwen and Milton thought not to approach him, but I will not rule out people like they do just because of what that person may do. Jay did not see a victim to Mason's crime.

As he turned to sit at the counter, Jay saw Grace and Joyce having dinner in a booth. Grace looked up, saw him and called him over to join them. He hesitated at first but he could not be rude. He would go over, say hello, excuse himself and eat at the counter.

"Good evening ladies, how are you doing?"

"Fine, you having dinner?" Grace said.

"Yes, ma'am just got off work."

"Sit down eat with us," said Grace.

"Oh no, I don't want to disturb you; you probably have a lot to talk about.

"Sit down, please." Joyce said, trying to mask the excitement that entered her body.

"How do you like your new job?" Grace asked.

"Oh, I love it- still have a lot to learn."

"What do you do?" Joyce asked.

"I'm training to be a stockbroker."

"Then you must eat with us and tell us about it. Order what you want." Joyce replied. Surprised again by her anxiousness.

Reluctantly, Jay sat down. This was not in his plans at this moment, but what the hell; won't do any harm he reasoned.

Merle observed the scene and overheard the conversation. She hurried to the kitchen and prepared a plated of fried chicken, mashed potatoes, candied yams and lemonade for Jay. She also brought more corn bread for the table.

"You are so nice Merle." Jay said. Turning to the ladies at the table, he said, "See how they spoil me."

They continued to eat in silence for a few minutes then Grace said, "This food is so good, I think I have gained ten pounds since I've been home. I've got to get back to my workout."

Joyce said, "yea, I have been loving this food, I don't know how I'm going to go back to that dining hall food at school."

"So Jay, mom left a little insurance money, I was going to talk to her banker but what would you do if I wanted to invest it?" Jay wasn't quite ready for this development. He knew there would be some insurance money, but he would not dare approach them about that now. It was too early. And after all, he was responsible for them getting the money.

"Well Miss Grace, like I said, I'm still in training, but between Mr. Milton, my boss and Gwen who I work with, we could come up with a plan. It would depend on what you want to do, you know, your objective and your risk tolerance." He thought he would show some of his training to impress her and not show eagerness for her business.

"Well I don't want to gamble it if that's what you mean by risk tolerance. I want something safe and something that is going to make me money. My dad did some of that stuff, but I never learned."

Joyce said, "We've touched on it a little in my economics class, but I don't know a thing either."

"Then, why don't you come by the office if you have time. Mr. Milton is good and so is Gwen, they will help you. I know that for sure."

"Will you get credit, I mean will this benefit you? Shirley and Merle both have said how much my mom loved you and how you cared for her. Maybe she saw in you the son she wished she had. I want some way to show my appreciation. In fact, I was going to open a bank account for my brother. Can you do something like that so the money is there for him when he wants it?" Grace looked at Joyce, who had a big grin on her face.

Joyce says, "Why don't you do it, mom."

"Thank you for the opportunity Miss Grace. You know, I only knew your mother for a few months, and she was the type of lady that was hard not to love. I mean, look at the people who came...."

"Yes they did come out."

"And yes, I'll get credit. Thank you very much."

"Okay, I'll come by your office; 125th street?"

"Yes ma'am"

"Maybe, I'll do something too. Do you have a card? I can call from school." Joyce says.

Jay reached into his pocket and gave her one of Gwen's card.

"I can be reached at that number. Maybe when you do call, I might have my license then I can open an account for you myself."

The three diners finished their meals and left the restaurant. Jay went home to Sarah; Grace and Joyce went to Mrs. Hall's house, which now belonged to Joyce.

Entering Sarah's building, Jay thought of Sye. He didn't know why. He hadn't seen him in a few days. He wanted to stop by Sye's apartment just to say hello, but anytime he did that, the visit turned into a marathon. He didn't have time for that tonight. He needed to study for the broker's test.

Then Maxine came to his mind as he passed her apartment on the way to Sarah's. As usual, jazz was blearing from Sye's apartment. He recognized the sounds of the genius, Charles Mingus. This was a recording that Sye had played for him on one of his visits.

Jay stopped to listened at the door to Maxine's apartment. Only sounds audible came from a radio tuned to a local Black station. For all Jay knew, Maxine could be peering at him through the peephole in the apartment door. Jay was no longer surprised when she opened the door to her apartment just as he was about to walk past it. It was no longer considered a coincident after the chance encounter happened so often.

The meeting in front of Maxine's apartment would always lead to a plea for money until her check came. No such meeting happened this time and Jay was curious. Maxine probably had money and was already obliterated or she was on her way back from the liquor store. As he stood with his ear against the door, listening for sounds, the plan that he needed came to him crystal clear. Maxine the drunk might be the answer.

Sarah was watching television when Jay arrived. He greeted her but headed to his room. He was tired and just wanted to relax for a few minutes and then study the stockbroker exam. He had two practice exams that Gwen gave him and was anxious to see just where he stood with knowledge of the material.

He was feeling good about his decision to work with Gwen and Milton. The future seemed positive, with Barbara giving him Dr. Weinstein's information and with the bounty from Mrs. Hall's strongbox. The final means of taking advantage of her money, however, had not entered his thoughts yet, but he was in no hurry.

Jay had good vibes from Grace and Joyce and the possibility of being with either or both of them brought a smile to his face.

He closed his eyes to bring forth a picture of himself with Joyce and the phone rang. After a few minutes, Sarah called out, "Jay, pick up, it's your mom."

"Hi mom, I was just thinking about you."

"Then why haven't you called me?"

"This new job; I was just about to study before I fall asleep; I'm so tired. How are you and Grandma?"

"I'm fine; tired like you. But mother hasn't been feeling well lately. I'm probably going to take her to the doctor in a couple of days. The shop has been very busy. She said she is okay, but I can tell something is bothering her."

"What do you think it is?"

"She is seventy-eight, Jay. Could be anything, but she just hasn't been herself lately; maybe she misses her baby."

"Let me talk to her."

"She is asleep now, but I'll tell her that I talked to you."

"Maybe I should come and see her"

"Can you get away from your new job?'

"Oh sure. Hey, maybe I'll fly home."

"You? On a plane?"

"Sure Mom, I think I will; I miss both of you; so I'll talk to my boss in the morning and see when I can get off. Okay? I'll let you know"

"How are things there Jay? Are you getting set for school next term?"

"The job is great mom, I'll be a broker soon; make lots of money. I'm meeting so many important people."

"That's not all I asked you Jay."

"I'm set for school mom. I'm registered at CCNY for the night school. Just like I told you. Mr. Milton, my boss and Gwen helped me. They both made sure I got in."

"Who is Gwen?"

"I work with her, she is very nice and she is helping me."

"Helping you do what?"

"Oh mom, you know, learn the stuff I need to know, meeting people; she is a southern girl, from Atlanta."

"Some girl name Ruby came by the shop. I did her hair; She said she was a friend of yours- you know her?"

"Yes ma'am, she is a year behind me. Nice girl."

"Jay, how did you ever graduate?'

"Mom you know I did my work"

"Have you heard from Harriet?"

"Yes ma'am. We talk. She is doing well at Hampton." ·

"She was home last week. Came to take care of something about her mom. She has gotten worse since Harriet ain't here to get on her."

"Have you seen her mother?"

"Yes and she didn't look good. Harriet came by to say hello. She looks great Jay. I think she is just happy to be away. But I can tell, she also loves her mother very much."

"And I love my mother very much, but I've got to study mom. I'll call you and tell you when I'm coming."

"Well ... Bye honey."

CHAPTER 22

Four days had gone by since Jay entered his order to buy the SO stock; two hundred shares.

On the fifth day, Jay was making cold calls from a list Milton gave him; Gwen was calling prospects that Jay had qualified.

The news came from Sharon. The office had an antique ticker tape machine that still worked. The machine was a gift from the regional manager of the company. He thought the machine would be a novelty in the office. Still plugged into the Stock Exchange Price Reporting Authority, which is responsibly for disseminating last sale prices promptly after each transaction, the tape also carried news- news that would affect the market as a whole or individual stocks.

Sharon was putting used tape into the wastebasket that gathers it when she read just a portion. "Look!" she screamed, "Look at the news on the tape." Milton, Gwen and Jay rushed to the machine. Gathering the tape into his hands, Milton yells out "Holy shit, Jay look at this"

The story announced the discovery by the oil giant, SO in a tract of land located in the Pacific Northwest, a field that early tests promise to be a major supply of crude oil.

The story was followed by prices of the stock going from 38 and rising. The stock was hot. Transactions of SO painted the tape. 40, 40

½, 40 ¾, 40 7/8. All transactions were for substantial amount of shares; thousands, and blocks of ten thousand.

"Dam! Jay, you hit it again; what do you know man? I don't believe this, look at the sales," Gwen screamed. In his mind, Jay could see Dr. Weinstein in his office equally overjoyed with this latest news about a company stock that he knew was going to release good news. Jay is now sure that the good doctor and his friends were buying stocks with what he has learned in his studies for the stockbroker's exam as, inside information.

"You've got the gift Jay." Milton said. "You keep this up, you'll have my job." Jay heard nothing. His head was full of thoughts.

I've got to prepare for the next one. Dr. Weinstein surely will get another call from this guy Weiss, and what about Barbara, will she continue to get the information; I've got to take care of her. How much should I give her? When can I open an account for her? I'll give her $2000. Then she can open an account with say, $1500. She'll be pleased.

Jay retreated to his desk to think. The stock continued to fly with the news. It was now at 42 ½. Gwen, Sharon and Milton stood at the ticker tape shouting at each price increase and block of shares. Jay maintained his cool throughout the celebration. He had close to $900 profit so far but he could only imagine what Dr. Weinstein was making. The doctor probably purchased his usual 1000 shares. Jay knew he had to increase his purchase amount on the next transaction. The office phones rang but no one seemed to hear it so the calls went unanswered.

After a few minutes, Gwen joined Jay at his desk. Milton and Sharon could not hear her as she sat across from him.

"Okay Jay," Gwen said. "What's the secret?"

"None, just beginner's luck, I guess."

"This is more than beginner's luck sweetie" Gwen whispered. "That only happens once. You've picked two stocks, and they're both winners; you may have the gift as Milton says."

"Milton told you that?"

"Yes he did. You heard him."

"What does that mean?"

"I dunno, I only know about the other gift you have, the good shit."

"Be serious Gwen."

"Never been more. Let's go to lunch today."

"I wanted to study the test today."

"How you doing with the practice exams I gave you?"

"Fine; I passed them both the second time I took them."

"Then take the exam while the stuff is fresh in your mind. It doesn't stay there long."

"I got two more weeks. Milton scheduled me for December 12th."

"Forty –Three- and a quarter" Milton yelled out

"What did you pay?" Gwen asked.

"Thirty-Seven and three quarters"

"That's over a thousand after commission. You selling?"

"Should I?" Jay asked.

"Well, put in a stop loss order to sell at 43; you know what that is, right?" Gwen said.

"Yea I know that. When you want to protect a profit in a stock that may start to fall, you put in a sell order below the current stock price. If the stock trades down to 43, that becomes a trigger then it will automatically sell at the very next price. It could be at 43, it could be higher or less; if it keeps going up, you can raise your stop price."

"What about 43 stop limit?" asked Gwen.

"Again the stop price 43 is the trigger. If it trades at 43, it becomes an order to sell at 43 or higher, but no less."

"So we enter an open order or a day order, and what's the difference?"

"We enter an open order which is GTC; good until it is cancelled. A day order is just that, good only for that day. You testing me?"

"Yes, and you're ready sweetie"

CHAPTER 23

After the market closed for trading and the office quieted down from the excitement caused by the SO story, Jay called Barbara. The stock had closed at 44 ½ and Jay was sitting on a profit of over $1300 less commission. He decided to give Barbara $2000. He had that much in his savings account from his salary and tips working at Shirley's. His brokerage account was now valued at close to $4500. Not bad he thought, for a boy just off the bus.

He met Barbara the following evening for dinner at the chicken and waffle restaurant where they met before. She was radiant. And, it was obvious that she meticulously prepared herself for the date.

While Ida, the same waitress who served them before retreated to the back with their same order of chicken and waffles, Jay explained to Barbara what had happen with the stock.

She listened intently, but he was sure that she didn't understand all that he said. He went on to tell her that Dr. Weinstein was getting rich from the information that he got from his friend Neil Weiss. He told her again that if she felt at all uncomfortable with what he asked of her, she could stop at any time. But, if she was willing to continue getting the information, they both could profit as Dr. Weinstein and his friends did.

He told Barbara to put the $2000 into her checking account. Come to his office in about two weeks and he would open a brokerage account for her and buy the same stocks that Dr. Weinstein buys.

Barbara was sure that she could continue without problems. She was not sure how she should feel about their relationship but she was pleased to get the $2000. The young man had been quite cordial during dinner. In truth, he was so matter-of- fact that she was slightly disappointed that he didn't show more attention to her, the woman.

Barbara ate her dinner quietly and tried not to show her emotions. Jay too didn't have much to say. Ida couldn't talk them into having the peach cobbler like before. So dinner was over. Barbara thought to herself, what's next?

While they were leaving the restaurant, Jay took Barbara's hands and softly squeezed them. As he waited for a taxi to take her home, he said, "You know, I wish I could go with you." Before she realized it, the words were out of her mouth. She said, "Why don't you?" They looked into each other's eyes silently for seconds and more seconds until Jay raised his arm for a taxi to stop. They got in together and headed to Barbara's apartment.

There was no conversation between the two as the taxi traveled across the 138th Street Bridge to the Bronx. Again, Jay took Barbara's hands and held them ever so gently. He could feel the moisture start to form on her silky skin. She looked straight ahead as if in a trance as the taxi bobbed and weaved in the early evening traffic.

Jay thought of the first time with his teacher, Ms. Mack. How he felt so awkward and how she took the lead in their love- making. It happened after three or four innocent visits in which they merely talked, ate ice cream, listen to music and just laughed at some silliness that occurred in school that day.

On that unforgettable day, Ms. Mack was acting rather giddy and playful. Music was always a part of the evening. But on this evening, the music she was playing were all love songs, in particular, an album by the Flamingos, an album that Jay also liked very much. She had also introduced him to songs by Frank Sinatra. Jay grew to really enjoy this time with Carla.

He remembered how she excused herself after some small talk that took place in her kitchen. She reappeared in a black silk nightgown and went to the stereo and moved the needle to a song by the Flamingos called 'Beside You'.

As this ultimate love song began, *'beside you, that's where I want to be forever, I'm like a soul lost in a river searching for a helping hand...* Carla extended her hand and said, "Dance with me."

The high school senior slowly got to his feet not quite sure how to take hold of his dance partner. She took his left hand and placed it around her neck. Then she took his right hand and placed it around her waist. She wrapped her arms around his body, and then snuggled into his hold.

They began to swoon to the music, her head into his chest; his head buried into her sweet smelling hair.

'I love you, I guess my dear, that's why I need you, don't ever leave me bewildered, sad and blue, make all my dreams come through.

They held each other tight; both mesmerized by the lyrics, the music and the feel for each other. They were lost in the moment. Jay, at this stage knew that this must be love. He had no other concerns in the world as he felt this lovely lady in his arms. If Carla said to him right then ' Let's leave Charleston,' he would have said yes with no regards to family, school, or anything else.

The song was ending, their lips met. Jay awkward at first, but Carla maneuvered his mouth and tongue to the right position and the transformation of Jay was beginning the second phase.

The heavy breathing in his chest, the dryness in his throat and the pounding of his heart surprised Jay. He wanted to say something, but no words would come out. He just looked at her.

She then took his hand and led him to her bedroom. She whispered into his ear, "I trust you Jay and I want you. Can this be a secret just between you and me, or will I become the talk of your buddies during gym class? Will your mother run me out of town? Will I get fired?"

Jay replied, "For as long as I live and breathe, no one will hear of this." They kissed and that was the beginning of a young boy making the journey into manhood.

The experience with Ms. Mack gave Jay the knowledge of how to be with a woman like Barbara-or any women; young like him, or older. And so, making love to Barbara for the first time, he was deliberate; he was gentle; he was tender; he was passionate; and he was loving.

Barbara was in a world that she had never been before with men twice the age of Jay. She knew at that moment that Jay was not an ordinary young boy, and she wanted him in her life. They made love for hours and then he left. She lay in her bed spent; in a state of euphoria, and wondering if she was in a dream.

It was after two in the morning when Jay got out of the taxi in front of Sarah's building. Harlem was quiet but still alive. He had as he usually does, replayed the entire evening with Barbara in his mind during the taxi ride. He was tired, sleepy and anxious about the fact that he did not study for the broker exam that night. The exam date was two weeks away.

As Jay reached the second floor, who is there but Maxine. Where the hell is she going this time of night Jay thought; there is no liquor store open. There are bootleggers of half-pint booze in the neighborhood, so that's apparently where Maxine is headed. The bootleggers sell for about three- dollars more than the liquors stores. Good business; especially for people like Maxine.

"Is your aunt home?" Maxine ask Jay. He didn't want to answer.

"I donno"

"She was suppose to give me some money till my check comes in; you got some?"

Without looking at her, Jay handed her the two dollars change he got from the taxi. He realized immediately that Maxine was watching from her front window saw him get out of the taxi.

Then he looked into her face. She looked rather old. The liquor had aged her since the first time he saw her. But then, an amazing idea came into his head and Jay looked at Maxine long and hard. She smiled the look of a woman who senses that she is attractive to a man and the man is interested. In his mind Jay said 'not even if you were the last woman on earth.'

"I'm going to come by and see you one day is that okay?" Jay said to Maxine.

"Sure any time baby, whenever you want to."

She was in a hurry to get to her drink appointment and was down the steps before Jay could reply.

Sarah was in deep sleep when Jay got in the apartment. He showered quickly and went to bed. The new idea with Maxine danced in his head to the fullest detail and he was sure it would work.

CHAPTER 24

The next two weeks were a whirlwind in Jay's life. He passed the broker exam. It was six hours of endurance to flush his brain of all it had absorbed the past eight weeks. He answered 250 multiple choice questions concerning listed stocks, unlisted stocks, municipal and corporate bonds, investment companies (mutual funds), rules governing the security industry, order types, and the New York Stock Exchange floor operations.

There were also questions concerning the National Association of Security Dealers (NASD) and the Security and Exchange Commission (SEC).

The exam is said to rank behind only the CPA, Medical and BAR exams in degree of difficulty. Jay was proud and renewed his respect for Milton and Gwen. He was now one of them.

The stock SO continued to climb and Jay was sitting on a profit of over $2000 on just 200 shares.

Other oil companies stock also moved up in anticipation of other discoveries in the region of Alaska. There was talk of building a pipeline to move the oil to transportation vessels and then to American refineries. This created more opportunities for investors to make money.

Milton and Gwen were waiting for Jay to announce his next pick. Jay was not too happy about that, but Barbara had not called with any news. In the meantime, Jay prospected for himself.

True to her word, Shirley introduced Jay to some of her friends and they opened accounts with him. He also opened an account for the neighborhood's primary numbers banker, Mason.

Jay even tried to convince Sarah to open an account, and she promised to do so after she sends some money home to her parents. She always sent money home.

His mother was next in line and she too agreed to send him $1000 of her savings and his college money. Of course, she warned him that if something bad happens to her money, he could never come back to Charleston.

Jay was feeling pretty good about himself. He had been in New York barely six months and had made a name for himself, albeit just in Harlem, he felt important. He felt, most likely to succeed.

He had other good news also. Merle told him that Mrs. Hall's death had been officially ruled the result of a heart attack and the inquest closed. He was home free. But why shouldn't he be, he reasoned. Over and over again he felt that he did not kill her nor was he responsible for her death. All feelings of guilt were now gone from his fiber.

It was time to go home; to visit Charleston for the coming Christmas holidays. He would get to see his mother and grandmother as well as Harriet, Ruby and all his friends who would be home from college. He knew that they would not be the same but neither would he.

Milton gave Jay the time off that he needed to go home. Jay had no doubt that he would get the two weeks he requested; after all, he was now the star of the office and the object of everyone's admiration. Sharon was now beginning to flirt with Jay more, which did not go unnoticed by Gwen. Jay was cool to Sharon's acts and subtle hints; he did not want to piss Gwen off. That last thing he wanted was some workplace jealously crap. He would get to Sharon in his own time in his own way.

Jay took the train home to Charleston; the East Coast Champion destined for Miami. Jay noticed the passengers were quite different form the ones he rode with on the trip to New York. There were few Negroes and none with brown bags filled of fried chicken. There were more White people leaving the winter of New York for the warmth of Florida.

It was three days before Christmas and everyone it seemed had gifts that they were taking down south. Jay was no exception. He had spent two days shopping. He purchased a ring and cashmere sweater for his mother, a blue wool bathrobe for his grandmother and gold necklaces with hearth shaped pendants for Harriet and Ruby. He made sure the pendants were not the same. He had souvenirs of New York for other friends that may be home also; things such as a bronze colored one-foot likeness of the Empire State building and the Stature of Liberty. Jay also was taking gifts that Sarah had purchased for her family. He had two big suitcases filled with stuff.

Before leaving New York, Jay made sure to call Barbara and wish her a happy holiday. He did not get a gift for her but he planned to get her something when he returned. Maybe he would find something unique in Charleston for her. He also gave Barbara his mother's telephone number in case there was a need to call him. She understood.

Gwen was going home also but just for Christmas; she planned to return on Wednesday the day after Christmas. Jay walked with her to the subway.

"I can't believe you are going to be away for two weeks." She said

"Yes I am, there is so much I have to do."

"Like what?"

"Well, I need the rest of my clothes, I need things for an apartment; you know, stuff. And I've got to spend some time with my grandmother; she's not well."

"Is she the only one you will spend time with?"

"Well, my mom."

"That's not who I mean."

"Who do you mean?"

"The person you said you left behind."

"That person is no longer there Gwen, and I don't know if I will ever see her again."

Of course Gwen was referring to Carla Mack. In the back of his mind, Jay had hoped to see Ms. Mack but several friends told him that she had left Charleston. Not a day went by that he did not think of her.

"And you; are you going to see your preacher?" Jay asked.

"Yea, he'll be there. Probably come to our house for dinner."

There was silence between them as they reached the subway entrance. Gwen said,

"People change Jay. And I know that I have. I don't feel that I'm going home just to see him; in fact I really don't have the same feelings for him that I did. I've moved on. And so have you Mr. Austin, you are not the same person who served me lunch at Shirley's."

"You are so right. I have changed and you can only imagine how. You introduced me to a world that I did not know existed and I love it."

"That world is just going to get better as time goes by Jay, but I guess I wanted to know if you will want me in your world."

He took her hands and squeezed them. "You are in my world silly."

"I'll be totally silly till you get back. Merry Christmas."

"Merry Christmas sweetie."

Jay felt good. He settled into his seat on the East Coast Champion for the long ride home and thought about his past six months in the big apple and what he might do when he returned. The one thing he must assure his mother is that he would be enrolled in college when he returned. Gwen had helped with the registration process, and he brought the college bulletin and the list of courses that he would take to show his mother.

While the plan of college in his life was not the same as it was six months earlier, he would do this just for his mother. He truly felt that his future was secured now that he was a stockbroker with the potential for great income. As least that is what everyone that he came into contact with that knew something about the business told him. Strange, thought Jay. He had never heard of such an occupation until his arrival in New York.

CHAPTER 25

Jay told his mother that he might come home for Christmas, but he did not tell her when he would arrive. He wanted to surprise her. So no one was at the station in North Charleston to meet him. It was nine-thirty p.m. and Jay was surprised at the warm air that greeted him as he got off the train. His immediate thought was this outdoor station was a far cry from Penn Station in New York.

As planned, he took a taxi to his mother's house. She would just be getting in from her beauty salon; dead tired. She was always especially busy around the holidays. Working until this hour would not be unusual this time of the year.

He walked right into the unlocked house; arms full of packages. The taxi driver left the two suitcases on the porch. His mother rushed to greet him. He dropped the packages on the nearest table and hugged her hard and long. He immediately realized how much he missed her as soon as he smelled her perfume.

He also saw how beautiful his mother really is. The thought of Barbara and Ms. Mack, two women he considered very attractive, somehow paled beside the dark, soft beauty of his mother. At the moment, he thought that she deserved much more out of life than she was presently getting. She had made major sacrifices for him and her mother- sort of putting her life on hold for them. She would do so well in New York.

While she still had her relative vitality, health and beauty, she could live with him in New York and open her business there. Shirley, Merle and Sarah would help with customers. There was no man in Charleston suitable for her he felt, but New York might offer more prospects, and she could get married and live a more fulfilling life. Yea; he would like that for her. Yes he would talk to her about this while he was there.

"Why didn't you tell me you were coming tonight? I would have met you at the station."

"Wanted to surprise you."

"How much was that taxi boy?"

"Not much mom."

"My car still works you know; I could've save you that money, I thought I raised you better than that."

"You did. But I also know you would be tired from work and I didn't want you to drive to North Charleston. See; I do know better."

"Let me look at you. You look good baby."

"You look good too mom; how is grandma?"

"She has good days and bad days. Go see her then come back and tell me about yourself."

Jay went to his grandmother's bedroom. She was awake. When Jay entered the room, she sat up in her bed. "I thought I heard my baby out there, come, give me a hug."

Jay was surprised at how frail she looked. It was obvious that she was not well.

He sat on her bed and hugged her tenderly. This lady, who helped raised him and loved him dearly was not long for this world. As he held her, he was suddenly very sad.

"How you doing grandma? You gonna be okay?"

"Why sure sugar, this old lady ain't quite ready yet, I'll be all right soon. Maybe sooner now that you home."

"I'm so glad to see you. I missed you so much. Go back to sleep we'll talk all day tomorrow okay?"

"Yes sweetie, how long you gonna be here?"

"A couple of weeks."

"Oh good."

Jay joined his mother in the kitchen where she was having a cup of tea. "Harriet wants you to call as soon as you get here."

"I'll call her in a minute. What did the doctor say about grandma?"

"He said she has a leaky heart."

"A leaky heart? What is that?"

"I don't know Jay. He gave her some medicine, but I'm not sure it's helping."

Suddenly, Jay got a picture in his mind of his grandmother's heart dripping blood into her body cavity. It just didn't make sense to him.

"The worst part Jay is, I hate leaving her alone all day, you know, I fix food for her before I leave and some times she eats it some times she doesn't. Mrs. Woodson next door looks in on her for me everyday. I'll call her in the morning and tell her you are here okay?"

"You know mom, I've never seen grandma sick; I mean she has always seem well. Not even a headache."

"You're right. My mother is a tough lady, but get use to it sweetie, she is sick this time. When she stays in bed all day and not cook, she is definitely not well."

He placed the gifts under the Christmas tree. His mother had always had one for as long as he could remember. He then retrieved the suitcases from the porch. He called Harriet.

"Jay!" she screamed. "You home? I'll be right there."

"Harriet; it's late."

"I'm on my way."

"She's coming over." Jay told his mother.

"I knew she would."

For the next two hours, Jay, his mother and Harriet sat in the kitchen and talked. Harriet excitedly talked about her short experience at Hampton and how happy she is.

Her mood changed when the conversation turned to the condition of her mother.

In spite of an addiction to alcohol, Harriett's mother, went to work everyday. But that was all she did. While Harriet was distressed over her mother's drinking, she fully supported Harriett's opportunity to attend college and sent money to her every month. For that, Harriet was forgiving of her mother's problem. She prayed for her mother everyday.

Jay's mother told them about all they missed since leaving Charleston. What better place to hear gossip than a beauty salon.

Jay explained, to the fascination of two of the closest women in his life, what Wall Street was all about. He told them what owning stocks meant. He told them that this was how many White people make lots of money. He watched, as they looked wide-eye when he told them about the exam that he had to pass to obtain his broker's license. And there were not many Negroes who hold such a license. And, he is now a professional investment advisor. He went on about his time at Shirley's and the characters he met. Jay also talked passionately about life in Harlem- the great things he has seen in New York and how much he enjoys what he is doing.

Finally, Jay's mother said, "I'm tired. I'm going to bed. I have a long day ahead of me. If you two are hungry, there is plenty of food in the fridge. Good night. Harriet, you staying here tonight?"

"No ma'am, I'm leaving now."

"I'll walk you home." Jay said.

Jay's mother had a car since he was in high school. Surprisingly, he had never learned to drive. His mother was just too nervous to teach him he felt. That he could not drive did not seem to bother Jay. He never had a problem getting around Charleston. JD had a car and he drove the Impalas in and around Charleston their junior and senior years. At this moment, Jay knew that his next trip to Charleston would be in his own car; one that he would buy in New York.

"It's almost one o'clock, stay here Harriet. Jay can sleep on the couch and you in his room." Diane said after a long yawn. Harriet agreed. She offered no resistance.

When Diane left the kitchen, Harriet went over to Jay and sat on his lap. She began, "You have no idea how much I've missed you."

"And I've missed you too Harry. You look just great; more feminine- and you're wearing makeup, you got some guy at Hampton blowing your mind?"

"My mind was blown long before I went to Hampton and you know it; and are you saying I was not feminine before?"

"Of course you were; very much, it's just that maybe, a better word might be, more mature. Yes, that's it you look more mature and still very pretty."

The two close friends- lovers held each other in a long embrace and then they kissed. Jay realized he did indeed miss Harriet.

"Hey" Harriet started. "There are parties all weekend. At the Y, Mark's, the Rouge, you wanna go?"

"Maybe; I do want to see some people, see how they are doing, okay, we'll hang out a little."

"Good. Let's go to my house, my moms asleep."

"It's late Harriet, and I'm tired from that train ride. Stay here like my moms said and we'll go there tomorrow morning."

"Oh all right, but I can't wait to be with you."

"You need something to sleep in?"

"Yea, give me one of your shirts."

CHAPTER 26

It was nearly nine a.m. when the ringing phone woke Jay up from a deep sleep. He paused to adjust his eyes to the surroundings and remembered the look of his mother's living room from the couch. He answered the phone; it was his mother.

"Hi sweetie, you sleep okay?"

"Yes mom, fine"

"Harriet still there?"

"I don't know. Your call woke me up."

"Well look in on mother, there is some food for her in the warmer. What are you doing today?"

"I have no plans, I may see some people later but I'll spend the day with grandma. You want me to do something?"

"No dear, I'll be home by seven, if you want me to bring you something special for dinner, call me."

"I'll fix dinner, mom."

One thing Jay could do, as a young man is cook for himself. His mother and grandmother taught him. He could fry chicken fairly well and of course, cook rice. In fact, Jay had picked up a few ideas from JC the head chief at Shirley's that he was anxious to show off to his two women.

As he was pondering what he might cook, the phone rang again. It was Harriet.

"I thought you were coming to your bedroom last night. I was awake all night."

"You know better than that. What time did you leave?" Jay asked.

"Right after your mother left. I wanted to get home before my mom got up. What you doing today?"

"Nothing much; I've got to take some gifts that Sarah sent to her family over to their house; other than that nothing planned; what you doing?"

"I'm going on King Street; get something for my mom. Want me to stop by?"

"Yea, I'm going to stay with my grandmother today, and fix her something to eat. What time you talking about?"

"In a couple of hours."

"Okay."

Jay knocked on the door to his grandmother's room. He heard a faint reply to come on in.

He entered and looked at her. At this moment, his mind took him to Mrs. Hall bedroom and the last time he saw her alive.

"Hi grandma, how you feeling?"

"Okay darling, it is so good to see you. Grandma miss you so."

"You hungry?"

"I could eat."

"Well I'll fix you something. You want anything special, I learned some good things at my job in New York."

"Diane told me you worked in a restaurant, what you learned?"

"I'm not at the restaurant now, but I'll fix you some grits, bacon and eggs and some biscuits."

"Oh, do show off honey, but I don't want that much."

I'll be right back."

Jay hustled off to the kitchen. There he found the food that his mother had already prepared. He lit the stove to warm the food and heard his grandmother go into the bathroom. She can get up he thought; maybe she is not too bad, at least not bedridden for now.

The food warmed and placed on a bed tray, Jay took it to his grandmother. She was sitting in her rocking chair that for as long as Jay can remember, stood in the corner of her bedroom.

"Here you are grandma."

"Oh sweetie, I could've come in the kitchen, you didn't have to do this."

"No problem, what do you want to drink."

"You know I have to have my coffee."

"Okay, let me set this down, and I'll be right back with that."

Another thing that Jay remembered, as a child, he would see his grandfather and grandmother sitting at the kitchen table every morning sipping coffee and talking –long before anyone else was up.

"You know sweetie, your grandma is not long for this world so I want to tell you that I'm going to leave you a little something. You know that your grandfather worked on the railroad most of his life and he left me his pension. He also left me a life insurance policy. Diane has been putting most of the pension in the bank every month, just keeping some for whatever needs that I might have. I don't rightly know how much is there, but I told Diane to help you go to college with it. Your mother has been just wonderful to me; I couldn't ask for a better daughter. I helped her start her beauty shop and whatever is left will now go to Diane and you."

"Thank you grandma, I know that I love you but you aint going no way right now. You gonna come to New York and see me graduate from college."

Charlotte Austin smiled and said, "I don't know my dear, tomorrow aint promised to you, you know. If the lord willin' I'll see that day, but for now I'm living one day at a time."

Jay knew that his grandmother had some money in the bank but he had no concern about that. That was something that was off limits to children at the time, so he knew not to inquire about it, nor be concerned about it. Now, whatever the amount is, some of it will be his.

Maybe there was enough money to pay his college tuition; maybe he didn't have to go to New York and work like his mother wanted him to. Now, he thought maybe what has transpired the past few months is divine providence. Events befitting someone destined most likely to succeed.

He watched as his grandmother slowly ate the food he brought to her. He was proud of her and his grandfather. He realized how different they were, and how industrious they were, and how fortunate he is because of them. He realized that they sowed the seeds that are now poised to make him most likely to succeed.

His grandfather, John Austin, in spite of the difficulties all men of color in the deep South encountered each and every day, took care of his family. In Kingsville S.C. where he was born, he bought several acres of land and built a fine house for his new bride all by himself. He worked on it every day after work, and all day when he was off from his job on the Seaboard Coastline Railroad. The house had three bedrooms in anticipation of a big family but his wife, Charlotte, had only one child, a daughter that they named Diane.

Jay's grandmother had at one time told him how she almost died giving birth to his mother and that was perhaps the main reason why they were so close. She told him how disappointed she had been because she couldn't give John all the children that he wanted. A mistake by the midwife made Diane the only child that Charlotte would ever give birth to.

When the railroad stopped running through Kingsville, John sold his home there and moved to Charleston to keep his job. He bought the house that Jay and his mother called home.

John Austin was a man with little formal education, but he had a good head on his shoulders, Charlotte would often say whenever she talked about he husband. He knew how to get what he wanted. He started on the railroad as a track maintenance man but soon got a job as a conductor. He worked hard, made a lot of tips, which he saved, and was quite prosperous relative to most Negroes who lived in Charleston. It was he who taught Jay the importance of a polite facade, but not the appearance of an Uncle Tom to get what you want.

In a way, Jay saw some similarity in the lives of Edward Hall and his own grandfather. Both, in their way, were hard workingmen who did not succumb to the obstacles and hindrance that befell Black men in 1930 America. John Austin did not have the education of Mr. Hall, but he had the determination to make it. And both provided for their families even after death. The irony is the fact that he will share in the fruits of labor from both men; one by family and love, the other through cunning and deceit.

Jay's grandmother ate most of the food on her plate and he rushed to remove the tray from her lap.

"That's the most I eat in a while Jay, you brought me a good appetite" she said.

"Good grandma, I'll get those cookies you like while I'm here."

"Oh, I miss my cookies."

"Anything else you want?"

"No dear, I might sit on the porch if it warm up a little later, but for now I think I'll lay back down. Thank you so much for breakfast."

"I didn't cook it grandma, Mom had it done, I just warmed it up, but I'll cook for you later okay?"

Jay went out on the front porch of the house. He wanted to take in the fresh clean air of the Charleston that he knew. He immediately realized how very quiet this town of his birth really is. As he stood on the porch for a few minutes, he saw no cars passing or people walking the streets. The only sounds were the cries of hungry sea gulls heading to the Cooper River a short distance away. He then saw 127th street in his mind and the smell, and the noise and the people. Sarah's words came to mind. "Th're is mo peoples in my block than all a Cha'ston."

He was leaving the porch when he spotted Harriet walking up Pinckney Street. She had a shopping bag and she was coming there. He felt a twinge in his body as he watched how the morning sun hit her light-skinned face; how she moved effortlessly and how she still had that majorette prance in her step. And those legs, he would know them blindfolded. He thought, I will always love Harry.

He left the door open as he quickly went to take a shower. He knew that she would come in the house and wait for him. He peaked into his grandmother's bedroom and saw that she had gone back to sleep. He would take that trip to his bedroom that he failed to take the night before. The memory of the night with Harriet a few months ago danced in his head. But now, he was a new man with new experiences and Harriet, with whom he had his very first sexual exposure, was just the person to show how he had grown. He's a New Yorker now.

CHAPTER 27

After just staring into each other's eyes for a very long time, Jay, with just a towel on his body, Harriet undressing as they touched; the friends, lovers quietly made love. No words were spoken; no lovemaking sounds escaped the bedroom. It was as if the two were aphasic. This was passion at its apex. The passion that the two had built up for the past few months was like an inferno consuming everything in its wake. And when they were finished, the silence remained.

Jay's grandmother was in her bedroom a few feet away, asleep.

Tightly embraced as if they were one, and spent from the high charged exposition of bliss, the two life-long friends in their own minds knew this was a special moment. It was the first time they had been away from each other for more than a week since elementary school. The bond that they had developed over the years was real and they knew without saying, that they will forever be this close. No matter where each would eventually be, their relationship will forever be unbreakable.

They quickly got dressed; remaining quiet and speechless. Harriet was going back to king street to do some more last minute shopping. Jay, he thought to himself, I've got to call Ruby.

The pair stood on the front porch of Jay's house. They kissed and embraced again. Then they made plans for the weekend and for Monday, Christmas day.

Jay called Ruby and listened to her lament about how much she missed him, couldn't wait to see him, how totally bored she was with her senior year, and please, come right away. He promised to see her after dinner that night.

Christmas was always a good time in Charleston. It was never very cold for December.

In the Negro communities, the streets were full of children showing off their new roller skates or new bicycles. There were new cowboy outfits complete with boots, spurs and two cap pistols. There were the new baby dolls, white with blonde hair, and of course the new high-top black tennis shoes that sold for fewer than five dollars at the local Kaybee.

Sarah's family was pleased with the things she sent for them and Jay fully understood what drove Sarah away from them. He gave them one hundred dollars of his own money and said Sarah had sent that also.

Jay saw some of his old friends from school and church. The classmates who came home from college all looked good to him. He was impressed with the change he saw in some people and wondered how he looked to them. He knows he was not the same person who left Charleston months earlier. He also saw the same people who frequented the same street corners of Charleston. Some things and some people will never change he thought.

He did some prospecting at the urging of his mother and to his surprise, got some positive response. He ate dinner at several homes, heard the same stories in the barber shop and after five days back in Charleston after six months away, he was ready to leave.

He had planned to stay two weeks but changed his mind. He spent a great deal of his time with his mother, grandmother, Harriet and stole some time with Ruby. He still could not get Ruby in the situation he desired, but somehow it didn't matter. Charleston would no longer hold an attraction other than his family to him and he would work to change that in time. His mother was not very warm to the idea of moving to New York and living with him but she had not entirely ruled it out.

He would take his very first airplane flight from Charleston to New York's LaGuardia airport, leaving six days after his arrival. Despite the pleas of friends, his mother and Harriet to spend New Year's Eve in

Charleston, he said he had to leave. He was longing for something that Charleston could no longer give him.

Though somewhat nervous, Jay was determined to not show that he was a novice at flying. He dressed in his new Barney's blue suit and looked the part of a businessman on an important trip. In fact, he was the only Negro on the Eastern Airlines flight. He settled into his seat, ever cool and sure of himself. He soon found his cool demeanor changed as the plane thundered down the runway. He felt himself brace against the window attempting to balance the airplane as it banked sharply to the left. He felt silly at his gesture. As the view of Charleston began to fade and the airplane raced to the clouds, Jay looked down on his city in awe. But he knew that the city of his birth Charleston, S.C., is no longer in his blood.

After about fifteen minutes, the pilot announced that he had reached the flight's designated altitude, and they would be landing in New York in about two hours. Jay was amazed at the smoothness of the ride and even more amazed at the attention paid to him by the two White stewardesses. He sat on a row all by himself, and they continually came to him with a big smile while asking him if he needed anything; a pillow, a blanket, a drink. He declined. The attention of White women was definitely not something he had ever experienced in Charleston.

Jay recovered from the rush in his body and began to think of what will happen next in his life. There is the continuing relationship with Barbara and the help he needs from her; the tentative plan he had for the drunk, Maxine; but more importantly, establishing his independence was one of his new agendas. Jay was sure that he and Gwen would grow together in the securities business, but he would have to halt her attempts to control him.

To him, it was not good if people thought that he and Gwen are a couple. To him, it was important if people, women, who will make up the bulk of his business, think that he was available. So, weaning himself off of Gwen without complications was something that would require his talent for getting what he wanted

The taxi ride from the airport in Queens was a new experience for Jay. It seems that everyday there was something new to discover in this great city. The view from The Grand Central Parkway was yet another look at traffic, housing and people of New York. Crossing The

Triborough Bridge that leads from Queens into Manhattan's Harlem and north to the Bronx, made him think of the Cooper River Bridge.

The mammoth Cooper River Bridge connected Charleston to the city of Mt. Pleasant, S.C. The bridge had a span that was one hundred and fifty feet high and was over two miles long with a very narrow single-lane roadway. Jay recalled the many times he crossed that bridge, on the way to Mosquito beach; JD driving, and having white knuckles all the way. The Triborough was more majestic with four lanes of two-way traffic; traffic that reflected the pace of New York.

The taxi driver tossed the twenty-five cent tool into the basket at the end of the Triborough and headed onto the Christmas decorated 125th Street in East Harlem.

Jay saw the stark difference from what he had just seen on the highway in Queens and the streets of Harlem. It was Saturday just before noon and just as he witnessed in Sarah's part of Harlem, it was the same in East Harlem. The trash in the streets was there, the activity, the traffic, noise and people everywhere in spite of the cold weather. The only difference was there were more Porto Ricans in the streets. Jay surmised that it must be the reason why this area was called Spanish Harlem.

After some twenty minutes of the taxi winding through traffic, Jay arrived at Sarah's building on 127th Street. The Saturday morning breakfast, lunch crowd would be at Shirley's he thought. He was afraid to eat on the plane, but now hungry, he decided to change clothes and join them. It would be good to see his new family. He expected to see Maxine coming out of her apartment, suspecting that she saw him get out of the taxi. To his surprise, She was not there. Hearing the music coming from Sye's and smelling the incense indicated that he was home indulging in his favorite pastime. Not now he thought.

CHAPTER 28

Jay hadn't talk to Sarah since he left for Charleston. They spoke briefly when he went to Shirley's for lunch. She was so happy to see him. Every free moment away from her customers, Sarah went to Jay's table to find out if there was any news about her family in Charleston and anything about his trip.

He was deeply asleep, much to her disappointment, when she got home from work that night. Though tempted to wake him in a special way, she fought the urge.

Sarah was dressing for church Sunday morning when she heard Jay in the shower. When she heard him go to his bedroom, she knocked.

"You busy today?"

"No, not really."

"Well dis is New Year's Eve, the las day of the year. Com'n go to church wit me."

"Sure, let me get dressed."

A big smile covered Sarah's face as she retreated to her room to finish dressing.

Yes, Jay had no plans that morning; but that night, New Year's Eve, he was spending with Barbara.

He called her when he returned from lunch on Saturday. It was while eating, that he decided, the person who was most important to his immediate future, is the person who he should be with. Somehow, he felt that way in Charleston and that was the overriding reason why he had to get back to New York.

When Barbara received the call from Jay on Saturday evening, she was washing her hair. She found it hard to believe that he was inviting her out for New Year's Eve celebration. It had been years since she celebrated New Year's Eve in any way other than church service. And she was resigned to do the same as always. Her daughter had her plans that were going to keep her in Westchester where she was in school. Clearly, Barbara was not prepared for this invitation from Jay. When she asked where would they go, he really didn't have a clue. He asked her to think of some place nice, and he would be at her home around nine p.m.

After hanging up, Jay went back out and bought a bottle of champagne. If he thinks of anything else that he should take to her house, it would have to wait until Sunday. He hid the champagne in his room. He planned to put it in the freezer after Sarah goes to work.

On the way to church service, Jay and Sarah huddled against the cold wind that rushed up Lenox Avenue. He began to tell Sarah more about his trip to Charleston. He told of the great time he had and how good it was to see everyone. He mentioned that he asked his mother to join him in New York. Sarah was shocked at this news. She thought that Jay would go back home one day; maybe after he finished college. Then she got nervous; which Jay could sense.

"I said nothing about us Sarah. Remember, I promised you. Besides, we did nothing that I didn't want to do. So, don't feel guilty."

"Ah do feel guilty Jaysun, I'm your god-mother, ah shuld know betta. Ah needs to go to chuch to ask God to forgive me for whut ah done."

"Sarah, please stop that. Just like my mother said, you were the best person for me to be with. She loves you and so do I."

With tears in her eyes, maybe from the cold wind, or from her heart, Sarah stopped and looked at Jay.

"Ah said right off, you is a good person, like yo mamma. And ah loves you. Ah called my folks on Christmas day and they thank me fo the presents an the money. I knows yo done that. Yu give them your own money."

"You're a good person Sarah, and like I said, I love you."

He pulled her close to him feeling her warm wet cheeks against his and the smell of her perfume, he hugged her hard.

"Lets get in church out of this cold. Happy new year."

Barbara was like a schoolgirl getting ready for the senior prom. She changed clothes three times. No place to go came into her mind. She had never been a person who went to the clubs or bars in Harlem. New Year's eve was not a big celebration in her life. There had never been more than a wine toast at home with her daughter after church since her marriage ended. She did go to parties early on into her marriage. But that ended after her husband's infidelity.

Then she got an idea. There was always something she wanted to do, but, didn't or couldn't. She called Jay and asked him to come earlier if he could. She decided that they could go to a show at the Apollo Theater then take the subway to Times Square to watch the ball lowered to bring in the New Year.

Jay agreed and was at her apartment at seven p.m. They had time to have dinner at the chicken and waffles restaurant, see the James Brown show at the Apollo Theater then take the subway downtown to 42nd Street and Times Square

Jay really enjoyed James Brown. The show was spectacular. He and Barbara found themselves screaming and dancing in their seats like all the patrons at the show. The show was over at eleven p.m. and they had ample time to take the twenty-minute subway ride downtown.

The trip, it seems was the same idea that a great deal of people had. The subway was packed with revelers. It was like a party train. Riders were drinking from brown bags that held all kinds of alcoholic spirits. Jay and Barbara standing and holding on to each other were quiet during the ride. They just took in the scene of people having a good time. And for the first time, Barbara had no ill at ease feelings about being with a younger man. She snuggled even closer.

Back at her apartment after witnessing an unforgettable scene at Times Square, Barbara and Jay just sat in the living room sipping the champagne he had brought and talked about their evening. Jay deliberately avoided any conversation about Dr. Weinstein. This was going to be an all pleasure evening.

"You know, I was born in New York and I had never done that." Barbara said.

Done what?"

"Go to times Square On New Year's eve. It took a charming man from the South to make that happen."

"I enjoyed it more than you did." Jay said. "Thank you for a great evening. I had never been is such a big crowd of people having a good time and out in the cold."

"I don't think they were cold. There was a lot of antifreeze in that crowd". They both laughed

Barbara continued, "You noticed I didn't say young man. I don't consider you young Jay, you are surely more mature than most men I've met."

"Does that mean you don't mind being seen with me?"

"Did I act like I minded? You know something else I've wanted to do?"

"What?"

"Watch the fireworks from the East River. Macy's does it every year."

"Well, we'll go next year."

"We will Jay?"

"Yes why not?"

"Jay, where can this go? I mean, we can't dismiss our age differences, I've just met you and you've given me money, you've shown me a great time, I love being around you and I'm afraid to introduce you to my daughter."

"We can go wherever this takes us. We're going to make a lot more money, and we will continue to have good times. I will never embarrass you and I'll meet your daughter when the time is right."

"You sound so positive Jay. But tell me, is this all about making money, is that it?"

"I'm positive about you Barbara, I'm positive about how I feel about you, and I'm positive that we can make this work. I'm also positive that we can make money. But I repeat what I said at first. If you are uncomfortable doing what I asked you to do, don't. It will not change how I feel about you."

Wanting to change the conversation somewhat Barbara asks, "What did you do in Charleston on New Year's eve?"

"Not much." Jay replied. "We went to church, me, my mother and my grandparents. I remember once, my grandfather shot his pistol in the air at twelve o'clock. Then he let me do it. I was about nine or ten. That was exciting. On New Year's day my grandmother would cook collard greens, chitt'lings corn bread and hoppin john for dinner. It was supposed to be for good luck."

"What is hoppin john Jay?"

"It is cow peas and ham hocks cooked with rice. My grandmother made the best."

"Ommm, sounds delicious."

"Tell you what, you doing anything today?"

No. Why?"

"Well, I've watched my grandmother cook it for years, I can come back and cook it for you if I can find some cow peas in New York."

"You would do that Jay?"

"Yes, I would."

"I know where to find cow peas, I can get some in the morning."

Then I'll be back."

"Why do you have to leave?"

"I don't."

"Don't."

Jay thought it ironic, that when he was making love to Harriet just two days earlier, they had to be quiet because of his grandmother. Now in this setting with Barbara, the cries of joy, excitement, desire and passion came rushing from their mouths in a loud and continuous chorus.

Barbara was up early and had gone to the local bodega to buy cow peas. She also bought collard greens and some corn bread mix. Jay teased her about the mix. He told her that his grandmother made it from scratch and he could too if she has some corn meal in the apartment. This mix in a box was not the real thing he told her.

The meal finally got cooked in between passion filled trips to the bedroom, living room and kitchen. There was only energy left to eat.

And eat they did. Jay expertly prepared a meal of hoppin john, collard greens, fried chicken and the Charleston staple, rice with gravy. They were both full of food and full of each other.

As evening drew near, Barbara was looking out on the deserted and cold Bronx streets, she said, "This has been the most wonderful day in my life that I have had in many, many years."

"We shall have many, many more." Jay said.

CHAPTER 29

Jay was back in the office on Tuesday morning. Everyone was surprise to see him because he was not expected back for another week.

Gwen whispered in his ear, "I know, you missed me and couldn't wait to get back. Isn't that right?"

"You are so right my dear. Listen, I got some prospects while I was home, I might open accounts for some people there. How do I do that?"

Gwen said. "Just what Milton did for me. When I opened my parents and some of my relatives in Atlanta, he got me registered in the state of Georgia. He'll get you registered in South Carolina."

"Good."

"Who did you get?" Gwen asked."

"My mom naturally. My pastor wants me to call him and a couple of teachers; my mom does their hair so she told me to come by her shop. I went and met some people. Just like we went to beauty parlors here."

"Good shit Jay. Don't forget to ask for referrals."

Jay knew this but he let Gwen do the talking. With the help of Barbara, he will get the business and the referrals will come.

To his surprise, Jay received a call from Barbara. He was excited at first thinking that maybe Dr. Weinstein was making a transaction with Neil, but, she just wanted to say hello to him. She was still on a cloud from the previous two days with him; she felt compelled to call and hear his voice. He was touched by her gesture; this cements their relationship to his liking.

Jay hadn't talked to his mother since he left Charleston so this he thought would be a good time to call her.

She was disappointed that he left so early, but she understood he had to get back to his new job and prepare for his first semester at CCNY. She reminded Jay that he had to call her customers that he met at her shop. They apparently liked what they heard from him about the stock market and was anxious to do some investing.

At this point there were five prospects including his pastor that he felt he could open accounts for, and they each knew someone who may also have some interest. In his mind Jay imagined a run on the local bank, the Citizen and Southern, on King street. He could see all the Negroes making a total withdrawal from their savings account and sending that money to him. He had gone to that bank many times for his mother to make deposits into her checking account, savings account and of course the Christmas savings account. Maybe his hometown might bear some fruit for him after all.

He asked Diane again to think about his idea to come live in New York. She said she couldn't think about it now and that her main concern was the health of her mother.

Jay spent the next hour calling the Charleston connection and had commitments of $30,000 from six people and referrals for seven more prospects. The office was impressed. Immediately, Milton made arrangements with the home office to rush Jay's registration with the state of South Carolina.

Sharon, who had not said much to Jay since he joined the firm came over to him and said, "Gee Jay, you opened five accounts before lunch, you make this look easy."

"Well, friends and relatives make it a little easy. Jay replied.

Overhearing the conversation, Gwen said, "How many of your new accounts are women?"

"Why?" Jay asked.

"I'm just curious."

"Well, there is my mom, and one of her customers who is single, the others are three joint accounts, husband and wife. Again why."

"Don't make anything out of it Jay. It's just that women, at least Negro women, are more likely to open accounts than Negro men. The idea of investing their money appeal more to them. That's what I've learned and I just wanted to know if you had the same experience. You know how it has been when we went out together; you had more immediate effect with women than men, or did you think it was just your good looks and that smile of yours?"

Jay was annoyed at Gwen's backhanded suggestion, but he would not use this time to show it or comment on it. She was right; he suspected and he knew that most of his clients would be women. And if sex appeal worked for him, then he would use it.

Gwen sensed that maybe she had shown some jealousy, so she decided to change the subject. "You know, we missed Christmas and New Year's, why don't we celebrate your day and go out tonight, or let me fix dinner for you?"

"I'll let you decide what." Jay replied.

Milton told his young staff that normally right after the holidays, there were little opportunities for new business for the obvious reasons. He suggested that instead of prospecting, they should spend the next few days trying to identify people that they might prospect in the coming weeks. He also suggested that they horn their sales techniques.

He suggested that Gwen, Sharon and Jay should role-play with each other and practice the art of getting the order and overcoming objections. It is an art form to successfully get people to first, listen to you, and then get them to trust and believe you, and then write a check for hundreds or perhaps thousands of dollars to purchase something that they could not touch, see, or feel. It was selling the intangible.

One other thing that Milton insisted from his staff is to learn the products offered by his firm. It's important to match product with the objective of the customer. If a customer said that he had a low risk tolerance, low risk mutual funds would be the choice of investment. Everyone else would be introduced to the blue chip stocks of companies that most people were familiar with. So most accounts were opened with the stocks of AT&T, U.S. Steel, General Motors, Ford Motors, Eastman Kodak, Phillip Morris and the like; good dividend-paying American pie companies. The investor was assured that these companies would always be around and always make money and they would make money too.

Milton made sure that his staff also had available the choice of companies that the firm had published the most recent research reports on. Those companies were on a buy recommended list. Jay, of course had his own ideas; the ideas of the winners produced by Dr. Weinstein and his broker Neil.

Jay registered for night school at City College of New York as he promised his mother. The school, in the middle of west Harlem was a group of gothic designed buildings. Jay found the college to be the image of New York, big, bold and grand. He took four subjects and the classes met on Monday, Wednesday and Friday.

For the very first time in his young life, Jay was in a classroom that had White instructors and students. In fact, he was mixed with all kinds of people. He discovered that the White man wasn't just White. He was either Irish, Italian, Jewish or some other derivative. This was fascinating. Most importantly, he learned that they were no smarter than he.

While he attended classes, did the work and excelled in his studies, he felt it all was just a waste of time. He has his career and he was going to be good at it. He was determined however, to make the best of this situation and learn from the experience. Besides, his mother, and his respect for her, remained dominant in his mind.

Gwen was also still attending classes and the two were spending more time together at work and after work at school. They did not have the same classes but the same hours. They traveled together to and after school. They took a bus that stopped just near their office on 125th to CCNY. On the return, they took the bus to 125th street and Lenox. From there, Jay went home and Gwen took the train to the Bronx. On more than one occasion, Jay took the ride to the Bronx also. On more than one occasion, they left for work from the Bronx the following morning together. Jay stopped at Sarah's to change clothes and Gwen went on to work. On the occasional Friday night, Jay got back to Harlem around noon Saturday. The time was not all spent studying.

The end of February was near. New York was in the deep grip of winter. The cold and snow at times had Jay thinking 'what have I done?

When will spring get here?' He was getting a full dosage of life away from the warm South and everything seemed to slow down.

News of this grandmother health was not good. When he talked to his mother, she was not expressing any hopes of her mother recovering from her illness. This made Jay sad but he kept his thoughts of her getting well soon.

Jay continued his efforts to open new accounts and he was developing a pretty good size customer book for a newcomer. His efforts did not go unnoticed by Milton. Milton always took the opportunity to congratulate Jay and even took him to dinner one night when he didn't have school.

Jay expected the dinner conversation to turn to Milton making a pass at him but he was surprised that Milton only talked about their business and encouraged him with new ideas for prospecting clients.

It has been several weeks now and no word came from Barbara about a new stock but that was good. Jay would always call Barbara and managed to see her when time permitted. Getting away from Gwen was becoming more and more difficult. Barbara seemed to understand the demands of his schedule and did not pressure him to make time for her. He liked that about her. She called him with information on a new prospect from what she learned about one of Dr. Weinstein's patients; one that might have some money. She tried to help Jay any way she could.

He continued his practice of putting most of his new clients into mutual funds and blue chips stocks and all was going great. He had learned that you could be successful in this business without inside information. He learned that putting clients into good blue chip stocks was a good thing, and that being an investor in the stock market at this time simply made good sense.

CHAPTER 30

The opportunity for Jay to launch a plan that had played in his head for weeks after the death of Mrs. Hall came unexpectedly one Saturday morning. After coming home from Gwen's apartment where he spent Friday night, Jay was exiting the subway at 125th street. It started to snow the night before, and it was extremely cold. Lenox Avenue was deserted except for one lonely figure trudging through the falling snow.

Jay immediately recognized Maxine walking bent over from the wind and swirling snow. He knew where she would be headed at this time in this weather, the liquor store. He slowed his walk, not wanting to encounter her but let her enter the store and then he would head home. When she entered the store, he hurried his steps to pass by while she was inside. As if she planned it, when he reached the front of the store, she stepped out right in front of him and asked, "Is your aunt home?" Not concerned about showing his total disgust for her, Jay growled, "I don't know if she is home or not why didn't you knock on the door?" He walked around her. He just wanted to get out of the cold and wind. He could hear the crunch of her footsteps in the snow behind him.

"I need a dollar sweetie, just a dollar." Jay continued to walk and didn't respond to her.

"Com'n, gimma a dollar. I pay you back. Soons my check comes."

Jay could hear the desperation and panic in her voice and suddenly felt pity for her but he also felt that now was the moment.

Jay stopped in his tracks, turned around and looked directly at the pathetic figure; the snow was falling into his eyes as he said very deliberately, "I ain't giving you shit no more, but I'll pay you a lot of money if you can do something for me."

"Anything sweetie. I told you before, anything."

Maxine smiled that drunken smile that Jay had seen a few times and in his mind Jay was saying, 'not if you were the last person on earth, bitch.' He heard himself say instead,

"What do you want to drink, I'll get it for you and meet you at your apartment."

"Gin, sweetie Gordon's; ah pint, ah, ah, ah, fifth."

"You go on home. I'll be right there."

"I be wait' in, you coming now?"

Jay did not answer but kept walking ahead.

"The store back this way." Maxine cried out

"I'm not going there, I'm going to 129th."

"This closer."

"Look lady, let me handle this. Now either you go on home, or, forget the whole thing."

"Okay you got it sweetie."

Jay was not about to go back to the liquor store that they had just passed. There must be no connection to him and Maxine. The very few people in the street paid no attention to them. Those few just wanted to get out of the cold like him. Going back to her liquor store would not only give his face away, but would surely connect the gin purchase to him. The store employees surely saw him talking to her. Maxine was well known to the people who worked there, Jay surmised.

He watched as Maxine turned into 127th street and he moved on to 129th. The next thing would be to get into the building and Maxine's apartment without anyone seeing him. Jay walked past Shirley's and saw Sarah putting glasses of water on a table. She did not look up and did not see him. The restaurant was not busy; no surprises on a day like this. Jay's fingers were getting numb from the cold but his plan was developing with each step he took in the snow.

Armed with a pint of Gordon's gin tucked deep into his topcoat pocket Jay made his way to his building. On any given Saturday he would see a number of people on the stoops or in their windows observing the street scene, or kids just playing but not on this day. The snow apparently kept everyone inside. This was perfect.

He quietly moved up the flight of stairs that led to Maxine's 3rd floor apartment just across from Sye. There was no music coming from Sye's apartment that meant he was not home. Sye always did his laundry on Saturday, good weather or not. Sye was a man forced by habit so no amount of snow could change his habit. He would find a Laundromat open somewhere.

Jay quietly knocked on Maxine's door. He felt her eyes fixed on him through the peephole. In fact, he was quite surprised that he had to knock. He thought her door would open as soon as he reached her landing, as it always did, but not today. He had to knock a second time. And then she appeared and her appearance shocked Jay.

She had done something to her hair and put on makeup. This bitch thinks she is going out on a date or something Jay thought. She had tried to quickly clean up the mess that she was. Maxine never had a hygiene problem; while she was truly a drunk and always dressed like a washed up movie queen, you didn't have to hold your nose around her. Jay looked into the face of the Black Loretta Young. That's whom she reminded him of.

"Come in sweetie." Maxine said almost in a whisper. Jay entered without a word. Maxine's eyes were fixed on the bag Jay held.

Her apartment was sparse but not filthy. She didn't have time to do any major cleaning so Jay realized that she was somewhat neat. She led Jay into the living room that was lit by a single bulb in the ceiling. On the walls were album jackets with her picture on them. One such album Jay recognized from one he had seen at Sye's.

There were also pictures of her on the walls posing with some celebrities. Jay recognized Sammy Davis Jr., Duke Ellington, Count Basie and many others that Jay

did not know. Just these few photos confirmed to Jay what Sye told him about Maxine. She was once a star.

She ushered him to a couch while she moved to the kitchen and quickly returned with two glasses.

"You joining me sweetie?"

"No."

"Why not?"

"I don't drink Miss Maxine."

"Good for you sweetie." Her hands were shaking violently as she reached for the bag that held her relief.

She took the bag, removed the pint of gin and with little effort, snapped the cap off and poured a glass more than half full. She took a long drink. Jay saw the relief and calm that took over her body. It looked like someone receiving a dose of a life saving drug. Jay imagined that Harriett's mother must go through the same transformation when she drank.

She poured another glass with hands now steady. "Well sweetie, what can Maxine do for you?"

Jay looked closely at the liquor fortified, smiling reassured person. Beneath the alcoholic worn face was once a beautiful lady. Jay could see that. But now he saw a lady with the right clothes, make up, and coaching could pass for Mrs. Hall; a lady some twenty or more years her senior. Maxine's life style had added those years to her face and body.

"I want you to do a job for me."

"What kind of job?" She replied. The gin had altered her speech.

"I need a actress."

"Oh, I did some parts, I worked on a few movies. I…"

Jay cut her off, "I don't want your resume, I just want you to do what I tell you to do and you can make a lot of money."

Maxine poured another drink; this one smaller as the pint of gin was almost gone. Jay could see the look of concern that appeared in her face.

"I won't do anything weird sweetie, I am a lady." Her speech was fully slurred now.

"I thought you had something else in mind; I thought you wanted to be with Maxine."

"No, you are wrong. And what I discuss with you, you must not discuss with anyone else you understand?"

"Yea, sure sweetie…. You, ah, only got a pint?"

"I'll get you more, but we need to talk now, I need to know if you can really do what I need."

"I can do it sweetie, tell me what it is." Maxine empted the last of the gin into her glass.

"First of all, I want you to pretend that you are my grandmother. I need you to be a woman who is about seventy- years old. Can you do that?"

"Why seventy?"

"Can you do it?"

"I think I can; I mean...I don't think I look seventy."

"Have you seen a mirror lately?"

"You don't have to insult me young man. I ain't seventy but I'm old enough to be your mother."

"Yea, yea. I'm sorry but this is serious."

Jay saw the hurt look in Maxine's face as she held the empty glass in her hands.

"I may be a drunk but I got feelins and like I told you before I ain't no tramp. I'm a lady."

Jay decided to pull back some. Maybe he is being to hard on her he thought. This is not how he gets things done, his way.

"You are right Ms. Maxine; you are a lady. I know you can do this and I'll take care of you. I'll give you some money so you can get another bottle but first, let me tell you what I need you to do."

Maxine managed a smile but clearly she was upset. Not because of the insult but because all the gin was gone. She rarely buys a pint and in her mind she knew she was going to ask for enough money to buy a fifth.

Jay continued. "I want you to go downtown to a bank with me. You will pretend to be my grandmother. Now you don't have to do much talking; I'll do most of that. You will be turning over some papers to me- signing them over to me. I'll pick out some clothes and shoes for you to wear. What size are your shoes?"

"Size six."

"Okay I'll pick some up."

Maxine said, "What kind of papers?"

"I'll tell you about that later. We also got to take a picture of you. Okay?"

"Okay. When we gonna do this?"

"In a couple a weeks. I need you to get yourself in shape first. You need to eat, get your hair done, that kinda stuff, understand?"

"Shit, who you want me to be? I don't even know your name."

"My name is Jay, remember that, I'm your grandson. You were married to a man name Edward. He is now dead. I'm going to be coming here everyday to go over the things you need to know. I'll bring you food. Where is your closet?"

Maxine got up and took Jay to her bedroom and showed him her meager closet.

Jay looked through the clothes but did not see much.

"I can't believe a lady like yourself does not have a mink coat."

"I do."

"Where is it?"

"In the Pawn shop on Lenox Avenue."

"How much is it?"

"I got seventy-five dollars for it. That was about six months ago."

"How do you get it back?"

"I guess you ain't never pawned nothing. I got the ticket somewhere. You pay the seventy plus interest and get it back if he ain't sold it yet."

"Get me the ticket."

Jay was having second thoughts about his plans as he was making them. Can he trust this woman to play the part of Mrs. Hall in order to get control of her small fortune? A drunk?

He thought that maybe he should wait. After all, there was no hurry. There was no need to cash in the AT&T stock and the Treasury bill right away. He could wait for years and perhaps another lady might enter his life that he could use for his plan.

But the need to succeed was too strong so he decided to make this work. He gave Maxine ten dollars and went home to get some sleep.

CHAPTER 31

It was late Saturday evening when Jay woke up. He had gone to sleep with the thought of Maxine deeply imbedded in his mind. He was going to make his plan work. He got up, showered and decided to meet with Barbara. Have a quiet evening with her, or maybe go to a movie.

Barbara's daughter Cheryl was visiting her and had brought a dinner of Chinese food for the two of them. Jay's call came in the middle of their dinner. Cheryl answered the phone, and Barbara decided to talk to Jay on her bedroom phone.

It was not a good time to come over, Barbara told Jay. She suggested that later, after dinner and after Cheryl leaves would be better. Voicing disappointment, Jay agreed. He said he would call later.

Without a sound Barbara returned to her dinner. Cheryl stared at her curiously, but Barbara just quietly ate her plate of Chinese vegetables.

Finally, Cheryl said. "So aren't you going to tell me who that melodious voice belongs to? I don't think I ever heard him before"

"You don't know him."

"So who is he?"

"Somebody you don't know."

"I gathered that mom, so who is he? Is he the flowers at the office?"

"Yes."

"So why didn't you invite him over? I would like to meet him."

"One day you will."

"What's he like mom? I mean, tell me about him; what does he do?"

"He works on Wall Street."

"Mom... not a White man."

"No Cheryl. Do you have to be White to work on Wall Street?"

"Pretty much. I ain't never met a Black man who worked on Wall Street."

"Well, give it time; you're only... how old are you anyway?" As Barbara asked that question, she again realized that Jay and her daughter were about the same age. She knew that one day this was going to be a problem; unless she stopped things now. Yea she thought, when he comes over tonight, I'll tell him we can only be friends.

"I think he is a nice guy Cheryl, but not for me. So I doubt if you will ever meet him."

"Mom, what is it about him that makes him not for you?"

"You wouldn't understand."

"Gee mom you make this sound so mysterious. Just a second ago, you said I will meet him one day. Now you say you doubt if I ever will. We have discussed men in our lives before but this one you..."

"How many men have been in your life Cheryl?"

"Not that many and you know what I mean; we have talked, and you've told me about guys you went out with and I told you about the creeps that I've met. Everything. But you are holding something back on this one. I can see it in your face."

"What it really is, he's teaching me about investments. I opened an account with him to buy some stocks."

"Wow mom, he is a broker? That's great. That's such a great idea. I want to do that too. Can he open an account for me? What are you buying?"

"No individual stocks yet, but something called funds, mutual funds; which is a group of stocks I think."

"Listen to the expert. What else is he teaching you mom?"

"Dr. Weinstein dabbles in this thing everyday. I picked up a few things from him too."

"Well I've got to meet this guy. When can you do that?'

Barbara started to feel uneasy and immediately lost her appetite for any more of the Chinese food. She said, "I'm full. This was great. Your choices of veggies are my favorites."

"My mom the investor. How much did you start with? Do you fully trust him? We gonna be rich. I'm serious mom"

"I trust him." Barbara spoke these words aloud. Silently she said, Lord help me, but I also think I love him.

Jay was hungry but since he couldn't go to Barbara's house immediately, he decided to go to Shirley's for dinner. It was no longer snowing but very cold outside.

He greets Merle, says hellos to the kitchen help, then sat in a booth at Sarah's station. Before Sarah arrives, Shirley comes over and tells Jay she has some more prospects for him to call on. She has kept her word to help him in his business.

Sarah arrives with a big smile and a basket of bread. She knows he had been out all night but she was not going to comment on it. She begins, How you dealing wit this snow Jay; cold nough fo yer?"

"I can't wait till June." Jay says.

"What you wanna to eat?"

"I don't know Sarah. Just bring me something. You decide."

"How bout sum pot roast. It good. I ate sum. JC step on it today."

"Okay that will do. Add some rice, gravy and black eyes."

When Sarah retreated to the kitchen, Jay sees Grace, Mrs. Hall's daughter enter the restaurant. Grace hugs Merle.

Merle was leading Grace to a booth when Grace spots Jay. She tells Merle that she wanted to sit with Jay.

Jay, seeing the two approach, became a little uneasy but still cool.

Grace says, "Mind if I join you?"

"Of course not." Jay responds. He stood up, and said, "Please sit down."

I'll tell Sarah she has someone else." Merle says as she moves away.

"So, How have you been Jay?"

"Just fine Miss Grace and you?"

"Please drop the miss. I've been fine; but tired. I'm working now."

"Oh. What are you doing?"

"Well I lucked out and got a part in this new show on Broadway. It's in the line, but I'm happy."

Jay had no idea what she was talking about. Grace sensed this and began to tell him.

"I'm an actress. That's what I went to school for."

Jay became very interested in the story of Grace's life in show business.

"Really? You know that's what I wanted to do, but my mom would have no part of it."

"So both of your parents were against that."

"Parent. Just my mom. No father."

"Well I'll be the first to tell you to pursue your dreams. But I'll also be the first to tell you to listen to your mother." Grace continued. "I regret the relationship I had with my mother as a result of decisions I made about my career. The only relationship I had with my parents was through my daughter. And, when I tried to make up for that, I was too late."

Sarah came back from the kitchen with a basket of hot corn bread and rolls. She had a glass of water that was about three quarter full. She dropped the bread and water on the table. She did not, as Jay too well knew, place the items on the table. The smile had disappeared from her face; it did the moment Merle told her that Grace would be eating with Jay. Damit; she thought to herself; I can't have him alone at all any more.

She began, "I got bread nough fur two. Whut you wont miss?"

"I'll have whatever he is having." Grace turned to Jay and said, "What did you order?"

"Sarah said the pot roast was good."

"Sounds good to me." Grace said.

"I be rite back." Said Sarah; with her back already turned to the table as she spoke those words.

Jay noticed the change in Sarah's demeanor. He had no control over that. That apartment in Gwen's building may be something to plan for in the near future. But, for now, there is so much to be done.

Grace too noticed the indifference in Sarah. And looked at Jay curiously.

"I understand she is related to you."

"She is my god mother."

"And your mother told her to look after you, right?"

"Yes ma'am she did."

Grace said no more. She knew the attitude of a woman when she was in a jealous funk. She had exhibited the same attitude many times when out with her husband and some floozy paid him too much attention.

"So, you thought about being an actor." Grace asked.

"Yes I did. I had been in a lot of plays in elementary and high school. I loved it."

"Well, you seem to have control of your present career. I mean being and investment advisor, that's what you are right; is an impressive thing. But, you can also seek your dream as you work your career."

"What do you mean?"

"There is a black actors group just forming here. It's called the Negro Ensemble. Why don't you join them There you can interact with others who want the same profession. You learn the craft of acting, as well as other things needed to put on a Broadway stage play. The behind the scene things; and maybe, be part of a production. I just joined and I can introduce you. You interested?"

Jay was genuinely interested and did not try to hide it.

"Yes I am. I mean I'm really interested. When and where should I come? I'm in school three nights but if it's on a night when I don't have school, I can come."

"Okay, I'll let you know when the next meeting is. It may come on a night that I'm working; and I won't be able to go, but I'll tell you who to see and talk to."

Sarah returned with their dinner; two plates steaming with JC's special pot roast. She tried to force a smile for Jay's sake. To hell with this spoil brat lady. She ain't nice like her mother. This thought was on Sarah's mind as she placed the plates with extra portions on the table. The fact is, Grace had not mistreated Sarah, ever. The few times Sarah had served Grace, she received a good tip. And Grace had been quite cordial to her. Sarah always had a problem with attractive women; and to her, Grace was pretty, well off and not a nice person. To think that her Jay was even remotely familiar with this lady was just unnerving to Sarah. She ignored the fact that Grace was older than Jay's mother, her friend.

Their plates were nearly empty when Jay said, "Your daughter interested in the stage too?" He wanted it to appear that he did not recall the name of Grace's daughter.

"Joyce? No she has not shown any interest yet and I hope she will not. I don't think she has given much thought into what she plans to do or maybe she just hasn't shared that with me yet. By the way, she talked about you quite a bit. Joyce don't talk about men very much; I kind of think she likes you. She'll be home soon on spring break. I'm sure she is going to come by here." Jay tried to suppress the smile he had on his face.

Sarah returned again to remove the plates and looking just at Jay says, "Peach cobbler?"

"Yes, we both will."

"Nooo not me." says Grace. "I can't; besides I have to go"

While never looking at Grace, Sarah heads back to the kitchen.

Jay says, "Are you staying at your mother's house?"

"You mean my daughter's house. No I can't stay there yet. It's just too big for me to stay there by myself. I'm living with two girl friends on Amsterdam Avenue. One is in the same production with me. I'm going to the house just to pick up a fur coat that belonged to my mother. I can use it in this cold weather."

"Would you like me to walk you there?"

"You are always the gentleman everyone has says you are. No thanks Jay. Enjoy your cobbler. I don't want your caretaker to get a bigger attitude with me."

Grace took twenty-five dollars from her purse and put it on the table. "Dinner is on me."

"No miss Grace, I'll take care of it."

"Please let me." With that, Grace left the table. She hugged Merle again and was out the door.

Jay lost his appetite for the cobbler just as Sarah returned with it topped with vanilla ice cream.

"She left you a good tip Sarah."

"Oh, that nice."

"She is a nice person Sarah. She asked me if you were feeling okay."

"Why she ask you dat?"

"I don't know. Maybe she thought so."

"I don't know why she think I ain't feeling good. Whut you tell hur?"

"I told her she might be right because you are always good with your customers and you always talk to them and give them good service."

"I give you good service."

"Yes, you gave *me* good service; you didn't look her way."

Sarah was shocked at the thought of Jay scolding her. She wondered if her jealousy was that obvious. She stood at the table unable to say anything when Shirley save her further embarrassment by coming over with the list of names she promised to Jay.

After thanking Shirley, Jay was out the door and into a taxi to the Bronx. It will be good to be with Barbara. As the taxi crossed the 149th street bridge the thought of the peach cobbler and the vanilla ice cream brought back memories of Carla.

CHAPTER 32

Barbara was startled when the bell on her apartment door rang. At the same time, her heartbeat began to accelerate. It had to be Jay. Again she was surprised by her feelings and the arousal that took over her body. She stood at the door, took two deep breaths to calm herself, and then opened the door.

Jay entered, shoulders hunched from the cold. He put a hand gently on her cheek. She recoiled from the cold touch but felt warmth enter her heart.

"Your hands are cold. Come on in and warm up." She said.

"I got warm as soon as I got in the building downstairs."

"You did?"

"Yea. The thought of you made me warm."

"Is that right? Your hands don't feel like it. You want something to eat? I got some Chinese food left."

"No, I'm not hungry I ate at Shirley's."

After Cheryl left, Barbara had quickly showered and changed into a black lace nightgown. Jay had told her that black was his favorite color. She felt his eyes burning into her flesh as he removed his topcoat.

"You look dreamy; In fact, you look good enough to eat"

"I thought you said you weren't hungry."

"You mentioned Chinese food. That I don't want."

"Then what can I offer you my good man?" Barbara was feeling devilish and she enjoyed this exchange.

"What's on the menu?" Jay asks.

"I'm sure we can satisfy whatever taste a gentleman like yourself desires." Barbara was so immediately overwhelmed that the notion of telling Jay that they could only be friends was the farthest thing from her mind. She knew this when she put on the black nightgown.

In a flash, Jay was fingering the small buttons on the gown and gently pushing her towards the bedroom. By the time they had moved the short distance from the living room to the door of the bedroom, the gown had fallen on the floor and Barbara was in her naked beauty. They started to work on Jay's clothing. Frantic, as if in desperate need, the two clutched and pulled at the shirt and underwear that stood between the wanton bodies.

At last Jay was free of the encumbrance, and he kissed her long and hard. They fell on the bed. Jay began to kiss her body all over. He made his way to her thighs slowly and softly. She started to moan from the pleasure. That soon gave way to sheiks of ecstasy as the kisses reached her special place. The kisses were planted with deliberate care and a gentleness that a woman appreciates. The gentleness continued even after he was inside her. Carla had taught him well.

After they both reached heights that only people who genuinely care for each other can, they lay silent and tightly embraced. Each had their thoughts. Barbara's thought was, what am I going to do. I don't want to let him go. Jay's was don't hurt this lady whatever happens, don't hurt her.

They spent the down time caressing each other's body. Finally Barbara said, "You know, Neil Weiss called Dr. Weinstein last Thursday."

This News excited Jay, but he did not want to show it in his response, so he nonchalantly said,

"Oh, and did he hit on you as he always does?"

Barbara sat up and with a big bright smile said, "How do you know he hits on me?"

"I know he does. What man wouldn't?"

"I don't pay him any attention. He always says he is coming to Harlem to take me out."

"You tell that White man to keep his mind off you."

"Oh. My sweetie sounds jealous." Barbara turned to her lover still lying down and kissed him softly on his forehead.

Still tempering his anxiousness, Jay says, "So what are the boys doing now?"

Barbara said, "Well I didn't call you because this was different. You know, he went to his book as he always does, but he didn't write down how much he was buying, and I was listening this time. I heard him say something like 'You say we sell short?' Barbara continued, "He wrote in his book, SS 1000 Phillips Pharmaceutical. Do you know what that means?"

"Yea I think so, but I don't know a lot about it. I have to check with Gwen and Milton."

"Forget Gwen, go to Milton." Barbara said

"Now who sounds jealous?"

"Yes I am." Barbara said. "And I don't mind saying so. She is a cute young girl."

"That she might be, but you are a beautiful woman." Jay kissed her on the cheek.

"You didn't say young."

"I don't want young."

The lovemaking began again. But now Jay's mind was somewhere else. He did not entirely neglect Barbara. She just did not have all of him; like before.

Sell short; that was a strategy that Jay remembered from the broker's exam. It is a way to profit when a stock declines in price. Jay recalled vividly Milton telling him that buying stocks was the simplest of strategies. That anyone can profit from a rising market; a bull market it is called. The real smart person Milton said, is one who knows how to profit in a bear or declining market.

To sell short means that you don't own the stock. Your firm borrows the stock for your account to sell in the belief that you can buy it back at a lower price than you sold it. Simply stated, sell high, buy low. The reason for a short sale is that the company may be subject to some bad news; news that may affect their earnings. If earnings are affected negatively, the stock price will move downward as holders will lose confidence and sell their shares.

The risk in a sell short strategy is that the stock price increases. If the stock price should increase substantially or even slightly higher than your sale price and you must buy the stock back, you will incur a loss.

Milton emphasized that no customers in his office would qualify for such a strategy. Maybe in the future, after some experience would he allow a short sale. He also told his young staff that there were other ways beside the short sale to participate in a declining price; something called put options.

Jay knew that thus far, the good doctor and his friends did not have any risk. They brought stocks on information that indicated a price increase was imminent. The latest information simply meant that they now knew of a stock that was going to decrease in price. He couldn't wait to get to the office on Monday. First order of business was read up on Phillips Pharmaceutical.

After the second round of pure sex and joy was over, Jay asked Barbara rather casually, "Did Dr. Weinstein have a price in the book?"

"No, just what I told you SS 1000 Phillips Pharmaceutical. No price."

"Okay."

The dilemma in Jay's mind is, should he exhibit his new found knowledge of a short sale with Neil and Weinstein's pick or should he just let this one go but watch the stock.

The decision came on Monday morning. Gwen had an attitude because she had not heard from Jay all weekend. The two had spent Friday night together after school but had no contact since then. She telephoned him several times Saturday and Sunday but there was no answer. She wondered where could he have been. While this question was on her mind, she knew better than to ask him right out. She decided to wait for the appropriate moment.

Jay went to Milton's office and asked him to request a research opinion on Phillips Pharmaceutical from the home office. He had checked the price as soon as he got into the office and noticed that the last sale on Friday was forty-eight and three-eighths.

Naturally, Milton asked why. Jay replied that he was just curious. Milton wanted to know if this stock might be another selection that Jay felt was a buy. And if that was the case, Milton had some clients sitting on cash and he was going to make a purchase of that stock for them. He was very surprised when Jay said that he has been doing some reading at the library on Saturday and felt that the stock might be over-price.

"How did you come to that conclusion Jay?" Milton asked.

"I'm not definite." Jay replied. "I just think that the whole drug industry is selling above earnings."

Milton heard these words and could only think to himself that this kid is special. He should not have the experience or knowledge to think like that after only four months in the business. He is talking like an experience analyst. This kid had two winners in his four months so you must at least listen. Milton concluded.

Jay continued. "Actually, it was an article from the Journal that was written five years ago. I like to read old stories. It's like studying history to me. And what better way to learn than to read history."

"And what did this history tell you?" Milton asked.

"Well there have been no new breakthrough drugs in the treatment of some of the major diseases affecting Americans, namely heart disease and cancer. Further more, there is nothing new in the way of research and development in the pipeline." Even Jay was surprised at his bullshit response. Mr. Most Likely to succeed was using his gift to gab.

By Now Gwen's, curiosity was uncontrollable. She too went to Milton's office.

"What's up?" she asked.

Milton replied, "Jay here thinks PPH is a short."

"A short, you mean like a short sale?" Gwen asked. "I thought we couldn't do that?"

"I don't allow it for customers, but a broker can do whatever for their own account."

"Is that how you would play it, a short sale?" Jay asks; not wanting to show too much confidence.

"Well, that is one way." Said Milton. "But, your risk is unlimited. You can determine your risk in a transaction like this through options. Buy a put option."

Both Jay and Gwen were lost at this point. They had read about options; put options and call options but that's all. They heard Milton briefly mention the product one day but had very little knowledge about how options worked.

"Where did this come from Jay?" Gwen asked.

"What do you mean where did it come from?"

"I mean where did you get the idea?"

"Reading."

"Is that what you did this weekend." Gwen thought this may be the opportunity; even in the company of Milton. There was no need to hide from Milton her feelings for Jay.

"Yea, I went to the library to do some home work. I read some old Journals and came upon this idea.

"Tell you what." Milton said. "I'll order some research. If it is bearish, we can buy some puts. No customers, just us okay?"

"What are we talking about, how much?" Jay asks.

"I'll get put options prices too. Something for ninety days.

Jay and Gwen leave Milton's office and she says to Jay as he sits at his desk.

"So you spent the entire weekend reading?"

"I didn't say the entire weekend but I did spend some time doing homework and reading at the library. It was too cold to do anything else. I also watch the football game with Sye on Sunday. Anything else you wanna know?"

Gwen felt the irritation in his voice.

"I didn't mean anything sweetie, It's just that I was calling you. I hadn't talked to you since you left Friday."

"I wanna be good at what we do Gwen. You got me into this business and I love it. It also means that, if I'm going to be good at it, I've got to work at it everyday; not just in the office but everywhere."

"You are already good at it Jay. In fact you are good at everything you touch, and that includes me. I'm sorry. I didn't mean to sound... I was just worried and..."

Jay put his forefinger to his lips in the sign to be quiet or speak softly. He then put the same finger on Gwen's forehead to let her know that it was okay. That everything was okay. She smiled and felt that way.

It was two days later when a courier arrived at the office with the research report that Milton ordered. There was a great deal of anticipation surrounding this report, so Gwen, Sheryl and Jay rushed to Milton's office to see what it said.

The four pages report said the usual things about PPH; all extremely positive. To their extreme disappointment, there was nothing, not even a hint of a reason to believe that this stock was headed for a downturn. The report, written three months, earlier when the stock was selling at forty-two, concluded with a strong buy recommendation. In fact, the stock's price had increased over twelve percent since the report was written.

Jay was unmoved by this development. He knew that Dr. Weinstein was profitable on every transaction he saw in his notebook; profitable because of the inside information. He was sure that public information on PPH would be forthcoming, and it would not be positive.

"I don't know Jay." Milton said. "There is nothing here to indicate overprice. The financials are good, management good, labor good, product good, sales great and distribution good."

"Tell me about puts Milton." Jay said.

"You still wanna play it?"

"Yea I think so."

"Well here it is. For cash, or the premium, you can lock in a sell price, or the strike price, on PPH within a specified period of time. When you buy a put option, you have the guaranteed right to sell one hundred shares of that stock at the strike price no matter what the current price is. It is a contract. That contract expires on a predetermined date.

Milton continued. "For a period of ninety-five days and at the current price, forty-eight and change, you can buy a put option for three hundred dollars plus commission. The worst that can happen is if you are wrong, and the price of PPH does not fall below your strike price within the next ninety-five days, you will lose your three hundred. But if you are right, and the stock falls more than your three hundred dollars or at a price of forty-five or less, you will profit. It must happen within your time frame. You can buy a put for a longer period of time; say six months or even a year. Of course you will pay more premium for more time."

"Where would you buy a put or a call for that matter?" Gwen asked. Jay thought she would always know what questions to ask.

"Our option department downtown would call the put and call dealers. They would find a seller."

"Jay asked, "Why would anyone sell a put?"

"The seller is an investor just like us. He is betting that you are wrong and PPH is not going to fall. So for your premium of three hundred dollars, he guarantees by contract, that he will buy PPH from you at the strike price at any time before the expiration date. If you are wrong, he has your money.

Gwen had a puzzled look on her face that Milton noticed so he continued. "Now you're wondering how do you sell the stock if you don't own it. Sounds like a short sale doesn't it?"

"Yea that's what I'm thinking." Gwen said.

"The deal is, if the stock is lower, you simply buy the shares in the open market. Then exercise your put option and sell it at the strike price guaranteed by the terms of your contract. Sounds complicated but it is very simple."

"Well I wanna buy puts; each one is for one hundred shares?" Jay asked

"Yes." Milton answered.

"I wanna buy six."

"As I stated Jay, if the price of PPH does not decline within your time frame, then your puts will expire worthless and you will lose your entire; six you said? At three hundred each, that will be eighteen hundred dollars plus commission."

"Don't do it Jay." Gwen said. "Did you hear what Milton said? You can lose all your money."

"Put the order in." Jay said with the utmost confidence.

"Jay, are you crazy?" Gwen screamed.

"I'll call it in. Tell you what Jay; I see a conviction in you with this. I'll buy two with you. I'm willing to gamble six hundred." Milton said.

"I don't think you will be sorry." Jay said. Sounding cocky now.

"You're both crazy. I can't throw away my little bit of money." Gwen said.

Jay responded, "Gwen, you shouldn't do this if you feel that way, but I would like to try it, and I'm going to. Call it in Milton."

Milton called the downtown office and asked for the option department. He proceeded to place the order. "Buy eight puts for ninety-five days on PPH at forty —eight and one half strike price for three hundred dollars; two accounts."

Milton was waiting for a confirmation of the order from the option clerk when Sharon entered Milton's office. "Jay, you have a phone call, It's your mother."

Jay knew this call was not good news. A chill came over his body the moment Sharon said its your mother. He hurried to his desk.

There was no need to delay the news. "Jay, sweetheart, mom is in a very bad way. She has been asking for you."

"I'll be on the next plane."

"Let me know when, I'll pick you up."

"No, stay with grandma, I'll take a taxi."

Milton and Gwen sensed what the call was about. Milton said, "Take all the time you need. I'll get you a ride to the airport when you're ready to go."

Gwen said, "Anything you need me to do?"

Jay did not answer. He knew he would be going home to bury his dear grandmother.

CHAPTER 33

The Green Chapel Baptist church was full for the funeral of Charlotte Austin. The only family of Charlotte, her daughter Diane and grandson Jay sat alone on the front pew. Everyone else was a friend of the family or a member of the church. Jay's grandparents had been active and very respected members of Green Chapel for many, many years.

Jay recalled the funeral of his grandfather John Austin ten years earlier and all the people present. He recalled the pastor saying, their presence spoke of the man and how much he was loved and respected. As Jay looked around the full church, he knew the same would be said of his grandmother. She was loved and respected.

Harriet insisted on coming home from Hampton, so she was there with her mother. Ruby came with her mother. Jay also saw a few of his friends from high school who were at this point, still living in Charleston. Most of Diane's customers from the beauty shop were also there.

Jay's mind wandered back to another loved and respected lady that he looked down on in her coffin a very short time ago. The words his grandfather spoke to him shortly before he died came to him. The words were, 'you are going to die one day; we all will. What's important is, what will people think of you as they look upon you in your coffin. What will they say?' What will they be thinking about you?'

Jay thought he would have some time to write the script for what will be said about him.

Mother and son sat holding hands; dignified in their grief. The pastor delivered a moving and very eloquent eulogy. Jay was cool as always, even in this moment. But when a soloist from the church choir sang in a voice capable for the opera, the song, *Swing low Sweet chariot, coming for to take me home*, Jay lost it. He had heard the song before at the funeral for Linda Hall. Jay lost it.

With tears flowing like a stream, Jay started to shake uncontrollably. Diane put her arm around his shoulder and held him close. She had not seen her baby cry since he was a baby. She too lost it and screamed out like a lost child, motheeerrr.

Charlotte was buried next to her husband in a small somewhat unkempt graveyard in North Charleston. The families of loved ones buried there took it upon themselves to cut the grass and clean debris left by beer drinking youngsters and the unemployed men who spent the time sitting under the nearby trees. The White people's graveyard, just a short distance away, had full time caretakers.

At the conclusion of the graveside service, Jay's mother said to him that she must now find time to come back and clean the area that held her parents. Jay just looked at her. He would not be in Charleston so he simply told her that he would arrange for someone to do the upkeep, and he would pay for it.

A number of people came to the Austin home after the burial. And as is the custom, they brought food that they had prepared for the occasion. Harriet and her mother donned aprons and just took charge of the kitchen. They fixed plates of fried chicken, macaroni and cheese, collard greens, dressing, black-eyed peas and other southern goodies for anyone wanting to eat.

Jay and his mother went to visitors and thanked them for coming. When Jay made his way over to Ruby, he hugged her close. She whispered in his ears, "Your grandmother looked so peaceful and beautiful. I started to cry when you cried."

"Thank you sweetheart. It's so good to see you; even like this. How are you doing in school? Have you decided on college yet? I saw your mother, where is she now? Are your parents doing okay? I'm sorry, I've asked you ten questions and haven't given you time to answer."

Ruby just looked at Jay and smiled the smile that attracted him to her and said, "School is okay. You know I've missed you. I think State is going to be the one, but I haven't quite made up my mind yet."

Not knowing what to say. Jay responded. "You'll love State, it's a good school."

"How long will you be in town Jay?"

"A few more days; spend some time with my mom. She told me she fixes your hair now."

"It was one way I could get some news about you." Ruby said. "You stopped writing me Jay, so it was good to hear your mother talk about you. She is so proud of you."

Still not quit knowing what to say to Ruby, Jay says, "I would like to see you before I leave. Will you have time?"

She looked at him strangely. "Of course Jay. I was hoping you would find some time for me."

"Then I'll call you in a day or so."

Jay went out to the front porch to sit and be by himself for a while. Mr. Earl, his boss from the Francis Marion Hotel and other men who knew his grandparents were out there also.

Diane had told Mr. Earl what her son now did in New York, the job on Wall Street. Mr. Earl was very interested and tried to get Jay to talk about it. Jay knew he had to be polite so, he tried to explain what the stock market was all about. He just wasn't very enthused at this time and so he labored through the conversation.

At last, Harriet came on the porch and said, "There you are. I've been looking for you. I fixed a plate for you. Come on eat something."

Although not hungry, Jay moved toward the house. He said to the men on the porch. Y'all come on eat something with me."

Harriet said, "Yea, y'all come on. There is plenty."

As Jay moved through the house he called home for all his short life; he suddenly realized it would now be without two of the three people who lived for him, loved and molded him. This development was all the more reason why Charleston is no longer a place he wanted to be. First thing in the morning he decided, he will ask his mother again to move to New York with him. There really is no reason to stay there now.

He also came to a realization that the game he played with Ruby and to some degree Harriet, was no longer fun. In a few short months, his life had changed so much that it also changed some of his personality. Yea, he would see Ruby, but it will never be like it was in high school. As for Harriet however, there will always be a place for her. He saw a mature person who would come to the aid of friends when they were in need. He and Harriet were friends before they were lovers. That friendship will endure forever he felt.

It was late in the evening when the last of the visitors had left; only Harriet remained. Her mother had left earlier after cleaning up the kitchen and only at Harriet's insistence because she had to go to work the next morning. Harriet felt that her mother was surely tired from the day's activities.

Jay, Diane and Harriet sat in the living room opening the many cards of condolences that were received. Some held small amounts of cash. Then they moved to the cards that came with the many flower arrangements that were left at the gravesite. One such flower card that pleased Jay to see was signed, 'from your friends at Shirley's.' Another came from Milton, Gwen and Sharon. These two cards made him feel good. People, that only recently came into his life wanted to acknowledge his loss. The sympathy cards and flowers cards were arranged in a neat stack. Diane said she would respond to all of them in the coming days.

Then Diane got up, reached out to Harriet to stand up. She embraced the young girl and told her thanks for being there for her and Jay today. She told her she loved her like a daughter and that she expected her to always come to her home whenever she is home from Hampton.

Jay observed this scene and thought that what his mother did and said was typical of her. She did not let a good deed go unmentioned. That's where he got his personality traits. So, he too got up and gave Harriet a hug. His a bit more sensuous. Harriet and Diane noticed.

"You both have always been there for me." Harriet said. "Besides my mom, you are the only family I know." Then the three hugged each other and the tears flowed from all eyes.

Harriet was going back to Hampton the next day. To her disappointment, she did not have any personal or private time with Jay.

Jay sensed that Harriet wanted to be with him and he wanted to be with her. He just didn't make it happen. That also told him something about the change in him. Maybe it just wasn't the right time or maybe deep down, he just didn't want to. He promised Harriet that he would visit her at Hampton one weekend soon and he meant it. For now, at the Greyhound bus station, it was just a goodbye peck on the cheek for his dear friend.

It was Thursday, and Jay decided that he would stay through the weekend and return to New York on Monday. Diane promised him that she would consider New York in the near future; in fact, would visit in the summer. She also took this time to tell Jay that Mr. Leyland; his English teacher was one of the first people to call after her mother died to express his sympathy. She told Jay that Mr. Leyland was extremely disappointed that he did not attend Talladega College and that he wanted Jay to call him if he had an opportunity.

Jay decided to call Ruby. He made plans to visit her Friday night. He then decided to walk to King Street. At the corner of King and Calhoun Streets is a drug store that sold out of town newspapers. There he could buy the Wall Street Journal. The clerk looked at him curiously, obviously wondering, what is he doing with this paper, it must be for his boss.

Jay slowly walked out of the drug store reading the Journal. He wanted to be seen. He wanted someone to ask him about Wall Street. Someone White.

There were no startling or unusual headlines in the paper and nothing about PPH, at least on the front page. The news Jay was expecting would easily be front page.

He decided to return home the long way, that is, walk down King Street. Jay passed a men-clothing store that was one of his favorites when he was in high school. He had been in there only once and that was to pick up a suit for a hotel guest.

Today, he was drawn to its window. It was time to increase his wardrobe. He went into Jack Krawcheck. This was a store that always attracted his attention whenever he passed by. Now is a good time. Of course, the salesmen ignored him so he was left alone to wander.

He looked at suits, shirts and ties. He had enough cash on him to buy three shirts and two ties. He also saw a couple of suits that he liked but would need to come back before he leaves for New York. After his purchase, Jay headed to Market Street and then through the market place.

This place always fascinated him. He enjoyed watching the many old Negro women weaving straw baskets. The baskets were made into all shapes and sizes- all with intricate designs. Besides baskets, there were place mates, coasters, flowerpots and other things that can be made from the straw that grew in the South Carolina countryside. They were artists at work.

He watched the White tourist offering ridiculously low payment for the works of art, only to be rebuffed by an old woman, dressed in Aunt Jamima clothing, telling them in her best Gullah, "No dawlin, dis ma price. You ang go fin nun betta. You loks roun, Ah ant gwning no ways. Ah be rite char."

Word is, this group of Negro women, artist, entrepreneurs, were the first to devise price fixing. They decided among themselves what each item they made was worth and agreed not to sell for any price less. This kept them equal competitively, and profitable collectively.

At the rear of the market is the area where local Negro farmers from the surrounding islands sold their vegetables. Jay and his grandmother visited there often to buy fresh butter beans, peas, tomatoes, and corn. The market ended at East Bay Street and a short distance away is the Cooper River.

Suddenly, the smell of fresh seafood filled Jay's nostrils. This was one of the areas where fishing boats returned with their fill of great seafood, which Charleston was famous for.

That was one thing he missed about Charleston. He grew up loving seafood; his favorite being shrimp, oysters, blue crabs and when he worked at Henry's restaurant, their   famous she-crab soup.

As Jay turned off East Bay onto Pinckney Street, he saw a familiar figure emerge from a taxi in front of his house. There was no mistake as she walked up the steps that led to the porch. It was Sarah. She had come from New York.

He hurried his walk now and reached the porch as Diane was opening the door to let Sarah in. Jay called out her name. "Miss Sarah, I didn't expect to see you here, what a surprise. At that same moment, Diane was out the door and hugging Sarah. Saying, "Oh Sarah, I'm so glad to see you. Now I can tell you in person thanks for what you have done for my Jay."

Sarah wrestled with the idea of coming to the funeral. She was not sure she would be able to mask the feelings she developed for Jay.

Finally, the feelings and love she had for Diane were strong enough to overcome her great fear. She felt that Jay would honor his word to keep their secret. She was in a way relieved, when he called her Miss Sarah. It told Diane that Jay still had respect for her.

"I didn't come for thanks, I come for you. I figga when everybody gone, you here by yuself. So I stay wit you fo a while. I needs a vacation anyway. Sorry I couldn't make the funeral. How you doing?"

"I'm doing okay Sarah. Doing okay. This is so sweet of you. Come on in."

Sarah turned to Jay and asks, "And how you? You okay? Ah couldn't tak no plane had to ketch the train. Everybody at the restaurant send dey love. Diane, everybody just loves this man. He jest bout take over Shirley's. Everybody sorry he gone."

Jay just smiled; then he too gave Sarah a hug being mindful that it can't be like the hugs that started in New York. He asked Sarah, "You took some time off?"

"Yes, I had no problem. I told Shirley I had to be with yo mamma a while. She say okay."

"How long are you gonna be here?" Jay asked.

"Jest as long as Diane needs me. When you going back."

"Monday."

'Well amma stay here if it okay. Diane, my mamma house full."

"Of course." Said Diane. "I *want* you to stay here."

"When did you get here?" Jay asks.

"Last night. I went to my mamma. I left my stuff dar, can you take me dar to pick it up?"

"Whenever you are ready to go; mom will let me drive you. Right mom?"

"Okay Jay. Boy I don't know why you didn't get your license."

"I'm gonna do that soon as I get back to New York."

Jay turned to Sarah "I ask mom to come live with me Miss Sarah."

"Oh dat be great Diane. Com'on, I takes care of you. The three of us do good in New York. You go do it?"

"I'm thinking about it Sarah, I just might, just might."

Jay enjoyed the company of the two most important women in his life. Sarah's presence had changed the atmosphere somewhat. She brought a lot of laughter and that was good.

Diane drove them to Mount Pleasant, across the Cooper River and bought live crabs and fresh shrimp for a seafood dinner. Over dinner of boiled crabs, fried shrimp, with baked potatoes and corn on the cob, Diane and Sarah talked about their high school days together and the boys in their lives. Then Sarah told Jay how all the boys at Avery High School loved his mother. Little did Diane know that her dear friend was now in love with her son, and had been intimate with him almost from the time he arrived in New York.

Jay met Ruby Friday evening; practically after she got home from school. He thought he would make it a short evening by taking her to a movie on King Street, then take her home and be back with Sarah and his mother by seven. He really didn't want the date but he had made a commitment.

This sweet high school girl whom he had strong feelings for just a few months ago, just did not excite him now. But Ruby made plans of her own. When Jay got to her house and suggested that they go to a movie, she said she didn't want to go out. She went on to say that her parents weren't home and wouldn't be back until very late. And that her younger sister, who was a sophomore at Burke, was going to a dance at the YMCA. They would be alone.

Jay was surprised by this development and the take-charge attitude of Ruby. He liked that. They had both been disappointed at the only time they had been alone, and their one opportunity for lovemaking was interrupted by her period. She wanted to end her virginity and it had to be with Jay. She saw his being in town, even for the reason that he was, as a sign that must not be ignored. Furthermore, her parent's plans and sister's plans fortified the sign that this was going to be her time. Her time to become a woman with the man she loved.

Ruby ushered Jay to her bedroom. She was taking deep breaths, nervous but in control. She closed and locked the door, pulled Jay close to her and kissed him like she never had before. She whispered, "I want to give myself to you; all of me."

"Are you sure you want to do this?" Jay whispered.

"Yes."

"Are you sure about your family?"

"Yes Jay, no one will be here until later."

With that response, Jay took charge. He knew that this must be a moment to remember for Ruby, the virgin. At his young age, he had been made well aware of the importance of the very first time for a woman. His experiences with Carla, Sarah, Barbara, Harriet, and to some extent Gwen, taught him that gentleness, patience, passion, and preparedness is required on his part, if this is to be a pleasantly memorable experience for Ruby.

So He started very slowly. He moved her to the small twin bed. He kissed her gently all over her face. He had always enjoyed kissing Ruby and so this gave him pleasure too. She immediately started to breathe heavily.

He pulled the baby blue sweater she wore up over her head and off with extreme care. He then patted her hair back in place, took her sweet face into both his hands and kissed her hard and long, but passionately. He stood her up, moved his hands over her breast, then down to her waist around to her back, and then up to the hook on her bra. He unhooked the bra and let it fall to the floor at their feet.

The one button that held her skirt was loosened in a flash. While kissing her, the zipper was down and the skirt also fell at their feet. Jay felt a sense of exhilaration from the softness of Ruby's skin. He wondered if his hands, through free of callous or rough skin, felt to Ruby as her skin felt to him.

He stopped the enduring message only to quickly remove his own clothing. While doing so, he took a full look at the body that fascinated him for over two years. Her skin was perfect over every inch. Not a pimple, blemish, or any other imperfection was visible.

The two stood naked and continued the kissing. He lifted her off her feet and gently laid her on the bed. She was light as a feather; he felt her submission as if she was to be sacrificed to some deity. Patience Jay, he heard his mind say.

His caresses now moved to her legs, first one and then the other. Ever so slowly down to her ankles and slowly up to her thighs but avoiding the pleasure palace. He made small circles with his finger all over her stomach and breast. He took the nipple of her breast and teased it with his tongue. First one and then the other. Ruby began to emit pleasure groans. He then repeated the small circles with his tongue and brushed the hairs of her pleasure palace but careful not to enter yet. He stopped to look at her face to see if it had a look of approval.

Her eyes were shut tight and a grimace of concern covered her face. Jay knew he was on the right track. Now the pleasure palace that had never been opened, was moist from wanton desire. The pleasure juice had risen to the surface for the first time ready to assist the entrance of the deity. Patience.

Jay then took her young supple breast into his mouth; felt them getting firm. First, a light bite on the nipple followed by a soothing bath by his tongue. First one and then the other. The tongue bath moved from nipples to full breast to stomach and to the outer rim of the pleasure palace. But not to touch yet.

Jay remembered Harriet telling him, when neither of them knew what they were doing, how much pain she had that night after the trip from Columbia. Hell, he had pain too he told her. He was determined to minimize the pain that he and Ruby was about to encounter with as much foreplay pleasure for as long as he could.

Ruby was ready. In fact she had been ready for a long time. She had been discussing with some of her girl friends, what to expect from that first sexual encounter. She believed that she was the only virgin among her friends. She was on her bed waiting for the moment that Jay, whom she adored, to remove the blossoms that the rite of passage says, you are a woman. She was waiting and waiting. She wanted to scream out, now Jay, now.

Jay had been taught by Carla to locate and find the diamond that guarded the pleasure palace. She explained that the diamond is a woman's sensual center and much care should be taken with this spot. She demonstrated how and what he should do to take her to the heights of sexual bliss.

Sarah, with her many years alone and choosing to bring on her own ecstasy, also coached Jay with the details of effective diamond mining.

So, that was the next step. With extreme tenderness, Jay placed a finger into the pleasure palace and quickly found the diamond. With that single finger, he slowly made small circles around the diamond. Then, he made slow up and down strokes then a combination of both. Make your finger a feather Carla had said to him.

After a few minutes, Ruby's low murmurs turned to shrieks of rapture. The room was spinning around, she had difficulty breathing, her forehead and body was wet with perspiration, she wanted to talk but couldn't. Finally, she took a deep breath and screamed out his is name. "Jaaaaaayyyyyy."

Now was the time. Her legs involuntary opened up to allow the deity to enter at will. Then he was inside her and she screamed out his name over, and over and over again. Soon. He reached the same place that Ruby had visited, nirvana- and he screamed out her name.

"Jay, I love you, I love you, I love you." Ruby repeated those words over and over. Jay said, "We should get up and get dressed." She heard him, but could not move. He helped her up but she felt dizzy and sat back down on the bed.

"Are you okay?" he whispered.

"Yes, I think so."

"How do you feel?"

"I feel wonderful." She began to wipe tears from her eye.

Jay kissed the tears. "Are you sure?"

"Oh yes Jay, yes.

She got to her feet, threw her arms around his neck and just held him tight. "Are you pleased Jay, did I make you happy?" she said softly.

"I have always been happy with you Ruby, but today was about making you happy."

"Well you did. But I'm also sad because you will be leaving again."

"Yes I will, but like I've said before, I will never forget you.

CHAPTER 34

Diane gave Jay two thousand dollars in cash. It was from the bank account that she held jointly with her mother. Jay protested, but she assured him that it was for him. He didn't need the money but he couldn't say that. Jay went back to Jack Krawcheck and bought two suits. He had more attention than he wanted this time after all the salesmen witnessed him paying over one hundred and fifty dollars for three shirts and two ties the day before.

The suits purchase created quit a stir in the store; especially with the Wall Street Journal under his arm. A deliberate act. This act could not go unnoticed by the salesman who served Jay and asked him about it. Just what Jay wanted. He expounded for a few minutes about New York City and the stock exchange. Of course the salesman asked him which stocks did he like. His reply was, "Everything, the market is the best place for your money to grow."

The suits were a perfect fit. Only the trousers needed a cuff, which the store did for him while he waited. Good service for a good customer.

Jay was dressed in one of the new suits, shirt and tie for the flight back to New York on Monday morning. He settled onto his seat, buckled up and prepared himself for a nice smooth flight on the Eastern Airline whisper jet. He enjoyed flying, and the train will only be a distant memory now.

After reaching cruising altitude, the stewardess came through the cabin with newspapers and magazines for the passengers. Jay naturally asked for the Journal. The stewardess, with a surprised look on her faced replied that there were only two copies on board and they were both being read by passengers who were sitting in first class. She told him that she would bring a copy to him as soon as one was available. She offered him the New York Times. He accepted. At least, he felt, the Times had a financial section that he could peruse.

The bold headline of a story on the front page caught his eye; '*Morning sickness drug causes birth defects.*' Jay decided to read further. The story disclosed that European health officials discovered that a drug called thalidomide that was prescribed as a sedative and for nausea has caused birth defects. The drug thought to be extremely safe, was given to women who were in the early stages of pregnancy. The manufacturer of the drug Phillips Pharmaceutical called the discovery a tragedy.

Jay could read no more; he dropped the paper and said to himself, 'that's it, that's the story. The stock is going to take a beating today.'

He wondered immediately what was happening in the office. What was Milton and Gwen thinking; he could only imagine but he was sure the mood would be one of exhilaration.

He knew there would be shouts of joy coming from Dr. Weinstein's office. Now having the knowledge of what goes on when news like this surfaces on Wall Street, he imagined stockbrokers phones ringing off the hook and customers saying 'Sell my PPH. All of it.'

Jay called the office from the first phone booth he could find at LaGuardia airport. Sharon answered.

"Jay where are you?"

"La Guardia airport."

"We called your house in Charleston, there was no answer."

He heard Gwen in the background say, "Is that Jay?" She picked up.

"Jay, You did it again."

He was cool "Did what?"

"The stock... Phillips is in a free fall. It's down eight so far."

"Really?" he said.

Milton picked up. He joined Sharon and Gwen on the line. "Jay how did things go. How are you?" At least, Jay felt, Milton was concerned enough to ask about the reason he was where he was."

"I'm fine Milton, everything went very well. Thank you very much for the flowers. My mother and I really appreciated that."

"It was from all of us."

"Gwen said something about Phillips?"

Gwen said. "Didn't you hear me, the stock is in the tank."

"What's the news?" asked Jay.

"They distributed a drug in Europe that is causing birth defects. They didn't manufacture it but they sold it. They have some liability." Milton said.

"Wow." Said Jay.

"You coming in today?" Gwen asked.

"Well I just got off the plane. I didn't plan to; should I Milton?"

"No. Call me when you get home in case we need to do something today. As long as the stock is falling we are okay."

Jay then called Barbara. It was important that he let her know that she made money also. But he also had another idea. It would be interesting; he thought if Barbara could get off for lunch and meet him at Sarah's apartment for a sort of a mid- day quickie. He could get a taxi and be home in half an hour. It was just 11:15. He quickly dismissed this idea. Just call her and let her know that you are back he decided. You can see her later that night.

Barbara was indeed happy to hear from Jay. She lamented that she felt helpless the past few days because she was unable to comfort him. Jay assured her that his thoughts of her were comforting enough. He expressed to her that he would share some good news with her later that evening.

Before hanging up Jay inquired about the mood of Dr. Weinstein. She told him that he had been singing like a bird all morning. Jay knew exactly why.

As soon as he unlocked the door to Sarah's apartment the phone rings. It is Gwen. "You had lunch yet?" she asks.

"No I just got in why?"

"I wanted to take you."

"You can tomorrow." Jay wondered why was Gwen talking so softly. Then he realized that she didn't want anyone in the office to know that she was talking to him.

"What's wrong with today?" she continued.

"Nothing I just wanted to unwind, get some rest, I didn't get much in Charleston, you know, just, get ready for work tomorrow."

"Your god mother at work?"

"No she's in Charleston. She came down to be with my mother."

"She's not there? I'm coming over."

"I don't know if that's a good idea Gwen."

"Let me come Jay. I missed you. I need to talk to you."

"You know where I live?"

"I have the address you know. You're my customer. Remember?"

"Okay. I'll be looking for you."

What the hell, Jay figured. He might as well have that quickie after all. He waited a few minutes to allow Gwen time to get out of the office. It was not unusual to leave the office. In fact, Milton encouraged that. Sometimes you have to go get the business, and that meant calling on prospects face to face.

Then, Jay called Milton. When Sharon answered, he could hear the admiration for him in her voice. He asked for Milton.

"Jay my man. I don't know how you do it. It's like I said, you have the gift."

"What's the next step?" Jay asks.

"Well the stock has settled down now. It's at thirty-nine and seven-eights. Some orders to buy the stock obviously came in. But our puts guarantees us the sale of the stock at forty-eight and one-half. So, the next step is buying the stock in the open market. Right now, we can but the stock at forty. That's the offering price. Do you want to buy the stock today or see if it's going any lower?"

"I don't know Milton. What do you think?"

"The stock could go lower. We don't know if all the news is out. But, as I said, there is some buy orders coming in. It traded as low as thirty-nine and one-half. But it's trading up now." Milton replied.

"Maybe we should get out then and take our profit." Jay said.

"That's what I wanted you to say. No need to get greedy. And even though we still have lots of time left on the puts, we are looking at a profit of five hundred per put. That's three thousand for you Jay. Not bad. A profit is a profit."

"Okay, let's do it." Said Jay.

"Okay, I will be putting in an order to buy six hundred PPH in your account at forty. At the same time, I will exercise the puts to sell the six hundred at forty-eight and one-half. You won't have to put any money up to buy the stock. It's called a same day substitution."

"That's pretty good huh?"

"Pretty good? Jay, that's the easiest thousand I've ever made. I only wished I had bought more than two."

"Next time Milton. Let me speak to Gwen please." Jay ever cunning, tries to cover all bases.

"She just went out on a call. I'll tell her to call you when she gets back. I'll see you tomorrow?"

"Yes, I'm going to take a nap. See you tomorrow."

Seconds later, Gwen rings the bell to Sarah's apartment. Jay lets her in and she hugs him and buries her head into his chest. This felt good to Jay; and he found himself closing his eyes and enjoying the feeling.

She found his lips and kissed him ever so affectionately. Finally, she releases him, steps back and say, "I knew there was something special about you the first time I saw you at Shirley's."

"Gwen, I'm not so special."

"Yes you are my sweet and I love you."

"Because I picked a couple of stocks that made some money?"

"No, because you are you. I missed you so much while you were gone. Did you think of me at all?"

"Of course I did. I bet the flowers were your idea."

"Well we all wanted to do something; like send you a telegram to let you know that we were thinking about you, so Sharon called the restaurant, spoke to your god mother and got the details. We decided to send flowers."

"Thanks very much. That made a great deal to me and my mother."

"Were you close to your grandmother?"

"Yes, very."

Jay took Gwen to his room and put on some music.

"There is no food here. You hungry?"

"Only for one thing."

"And what might that be?"

"You."

Again they embraced and they both knew what would be next. Jay whispered, "What will you tell Milton about your appointment?" Jay asked.

"I'll tell Milton that I made mad, passionate love to him."

"Hmmmmm."

With the music of John Coltrane playing on the stereo, the two were out of their clothes and into the bed.

Milton called the option desk at the Wall Street office and instructed the clerk to exercise the eight put options.

The clerk said," looks like you guys hit a good one."

"Yes just luck."

The clerk followed the instructions then called the operations manager, Leo Romanelli.

"Guess what?"

"What is it?" Romanelli responded.

"The Harlem office had puts on PPH."

"No shit. They did, how many?"

"Eight."

"Who the fuck do they know. When did they buy em?"

"Early last week. I bought em from Shearson. We gonna exercise all eight now."

"I'll be dam. Okay thanks." Romanelli said.

Romanelli called the regional manager, Robert Clayton. He is the person responsible for the creation of the Harlem office. Clayton saw a day when Negroes would, like a great deal of Americans, invest in corporate America through the means of stock ownership. So he urged the executive committee to open an office staffed by Negroes in Harlem.

A native New Yorker, Clayton was proud of his forward thinking and liberal background.

Clayton met Milton when they were both students at the New York University School of business administration. They became close friends and after graduation, they joined the same firm Hamill, Rhodes and Peck. Clayton, with his contacts and influential family, was on a fast track at the firm and soon became a vice president.

Milton, relative to the White brokers in the firm, was an above average producer. He had well-to-do Negro and White clients, thanks to his father's contacts. He would not be considered as an officer at the firm because of the quiet whispers about his life style, but he had good management skills. There was no one besides Milton considered for the manager of the Harlem office and there was no opposition to his appointment.

The opening of the Harlem office did not go unnoticed by other Wall Street firms. They were monitoring the situation to see if such a move was one that they too should make. The Harlem office was one of nine Hamill branch offices located in the Northeast that reported directly to Clayton.

Clayton was in his office on the fifty-six floor of Two Broadway in the financial district of lower Manhattan. The view from his window included Battery Park, the Hudson River, the stature of Liberty and Staten Island. The ports of New Jersey could also be seen in the distance. He told his secretary to get Milton on the phone.

"Milt, I've heard some good news, congratulations. Was it you?"

"No, Bob, one of my new brokers."

"Really. Who is this hot shot?"

"A kid literally, Bob, never seen anything like it."

"What's his name?"

"Jayson, with a Y Austin."

"How old is he?"

"Turns twenty on his next birthday. This is his third pick"

"We're hiring teenagers now Milt; does he know someone?"

"He's just off the boat Bob. He knows no one. He's good *and* he opens accounts."

"I've seen the branch numbers, I just assumed that it was you. Didn't look at individuals. I would love to meet him; Are you free for lunch tomorrow?"

"Yea, I think we can make that"

"Good. I'll see you then. My office at noon."

"Okay Bob."

Yes, Clayton was happy with the state of the Harlem office. The numbers indicated that they would start to show a profit in the very near future. Milton's production was important as it stood. The expectations were, that Milton would improve his numbers, and hire up to five more brokers who had the ability to be outstanding. The plan was to attract one or two Negro brokers from another brokerage firm who had a good client base, and try to get them to transfer to Milton's office. The plan hasn't worked yet because no such brokers were in New York at the time, but there was indeed good reason to be optimistic.

Milton wanted to call Jay right away but he thought, maybe he is taking a nap as he stated. He also knew that Gwen might be on her way to see him and may already be with him. It could wait until tomorrow he decided.

The next morning, Milton told Jay about the invitation to lunch with the regional vice –president. The reaction by Jay was surprising to Milton. Jay was not as pleased as Milton thought he would be. In fact, Jay displayed some reluctance to wanting such an honor. Milton thought that perhaps Jay, at his young age, was just simply nervous about meeting a higher up in the firm.

Jay was indeed nervous, but cool. He just wished he had more warning about this meeting. He was not concerned about what this VP might ask him; he would just look at the results and assume, beginners luck and leave it at that. What could he know?

Gwen was ecstatic and happy for Jay. If there was any resentment or jealousy on her part, it was not visible. She had her time with Jay last night; the entire night. She had only left at six that morning to go home and change clothes for work. She would have a good day regardless.

The office went about its normal routine of trying to open new accounts to increase their assets under management. That's the key to being successful. Get cash under your control each day and get more the next day.

Milton planned that he and Jay would take the subway at eleven o'clock and that would give them more than adequate time to get to Wall Street. At ten thirty, Jay went to Milton's office and said Gwen should go too. This gesture surprised and pleased Milton. This showed a sense of team play as well as loyalty. To Jay, it was an opportunity to score more points with Gwen. He felt he scored enough the previous night to last for a while, but Gwen is responsible for him being where he is at the firm and she should share in this small gesture of recognition. At least that's what Milton called the meeting with Clayton

He scored more than planned with Gwen, to the expense of Barbara. He didn't see nor talked to her at all. He planned to go by Barbara's office after lunch, and then go to her house after school that night. It is Barbara who needs the attention.

Before the three left the office, Jay went over to Sharon who he felt was being left out. She could go to lunch with them and just forward calls to the downtown office as is done when they all went out at the same time, but Milton wanted her to stay this day because he was expecting some important calls.

Jay said to Sharon, "I'm sorry you're not going. Would you like me to bring you some lunch back?" She smiled the big smile she always have for Jay and replied, "That's sweet of you Jay, you don't have to, but thanks. I'll go when you all get back."

"What would you like?" Jay asks.

"Oh anything, surprise me."

As the southbound number two subway roared past the fiftieth Street station, Jay and Gwen exchanged glances; each remembering the night at dinner and the night at her apartment after dinner.

Jay had not been below Fourteenth Street since the ride with Sye to Barney's to get his suite. The conductor announced 'Wall Street'. This was the last stop in the borough of Manhattan. The next stop would be in Brooklyn, another place he had not been.

The three made their way down the narrow sidewalks of Wall Street. The lunchtime crowd made the streets even narrower. Milton pointed out sites to Jay such as, the New York Stock Exchange, the Federal Reserve Bank building, the JP Morgan building and the mammoth Chase Manhattan Bank building. Most impressive to Jay were all the high-rise office buildings.

Jay did not see Negroes on the streets like he saw in Harlem. In fact most of the people he saw were White men and women, all nicely dressed.

They reached number two Broadway. This was another high-rise building with a huge lobby. They took the elevator to the fifty-six floor. Hamill Rhodes and Peck had operations on three floors in the building. On the fifty–fifth floor was housed the order room.

This operation is the heart of the firm. From the many branch offices of Hamill located   around the country, orders to buy and sell the various investment instruments were teletyped or telephoned in to be executed and processed.

Gwen suggested that they stop there for a minute to show that room to Jay. Having the time, Milton agreed and thought it was good idea.

The order room, a little over half the size of a football field, took up most of the entire floor. In the middle of the room was a large high-speed conveyer belt that was slotted and color-coded. At the center of the conveyer belt was a bank of teletype machines that were buzzing with incoming data. Several workers were tearing off the sheets of data and placing them into slots on the conveyer belt to be transported to various locations. These locations were the order desks for the various investments products. Other workers removed the data from the belt and proceeded to call in the orders to the trading floors of the various stock exchanges. The workers placed the order in a file then waited for the execution report.

The floor below was the boardroom where the brokers worked. This is where Gwen first worked for the firm. She was hired to be an administrative assistant to three brokers. Her job consisted of answering the phones, taking messages, and doing whatever the brokers needed to make their job more productive. She was good at it. Milton, the only Negro broker in the boardroom, noticed her and her abilities, asked her to work with him in the Harlem office.

Gwen was flattered by the offer and did not hesitate. She had seen him in the office and thought he was very handsome. He was merely cordial to her but was always business- like. He never hit on her like the White brokers did. She knew that he was much older, but she was still attractive to him. To her surprise and disappointment, she understood why when Milton's friend, lover, came by the Harlem office soon after it opened for business.

Jay was again amazed by the activity happening all around him. He noticed the turning heads of the White and the few Negro employees observing them as they moved through the order room. Milton stopped to chat with the order room manager for few minutes then they were on their way to Clayton's office.

Clayton's secretary escorted them into his office. Clayton immediately was on his feet and greeted Milton with a handshake and hug. Milton quickly introduced Gwen then Jay.

Entering Clayton's office, Jay immediately realized what wealth and power meant on Wall Street. The splendor of just this regional manager's office was a display of success and power. Jay could only imagine what the chief executive's office must be like.

Milton said, "I asked Gwen to join us, you hadn't met her; she started in the boardroom. She is doing good things for us and I feel she has a bright future."

"I'll tell you one thing Milt, we are getting old. They both look so young. I'm very pleased to meet both of you. Let's get some lunch."

After a short walk, they arrive at the New York Stock exchange for lunch at the Exchange Luncheon club. This is a member only dining room located several floors above the main trading floor.

The luncheon club is the bastion of well to do White men; where they exude wealth, eat extremely well, dress well and discuss big business. Jay had seen this type of White men at the many banquets he worked while employed at the Francis Marion hotel in Charleston. He served them just a few months ago. Now he would be sitting and eating among them. He was living up to his destination. Most Likely to Succeed.

Jay observed the headwaiter greeting Clayton by his name, then ushered them to a round table in the middle of the dining room. Jay also observed the many diners who waived to Clayton as they walked to their table.

"The steaks here are excellent, in particular the New York strip." Clayton said.

"That's me; medium." Milton said.

"Me too; well." Said Jay.

The waiter arrived shortly and he too greeted Clayton by this name. "New York strips for the men, and I'm not sure the lady has decided yet."

All eyes turned to Gwen who was engrossed in the menu. She looked up. "Oh I'm sorry. I just couldn't decide, but I think I'll have the Caesar salad. You could see the look of awe on Gwen's face. She was one of only a few women in the dining room.

She was worried about her dress that day after being told she would be having lunch on Wall Street. So worried, she wanted to go home and change, but Milton and Jay assured her that she was fine.

"So." Clayton began, "I've head good things about you young man, your third? Do you use a crystal ball?" They all laughed.

"No sir, I don't have a crystal ball, I've had what you might call beginner's luck." Said Jay.

"Well I've been in the business, what, Milt, now twelve years, and I'm still waiting for my beginner's luck." Laughter again.

"What about college?"

"They're both just out of high school but enrolled at CCNY at night." Said Milton.

"That's good. Milt will tell you, I've made your branch office my passion. I've felt all alone that the Negro people did not participate in stock ownership because of exposure. So the mission of your office is to create that exposure. And, from your beginning, I'm pleased to see that Milt is on the right track. High school! We spend a great deal of money recruiting from the finest colleges in the country and none of our expensive recruits has the start you have. How is the staffing going, Milt?"

"I've got a couple more candidates that I'm looking at. Maybe fill three desks soon.

"That's great. You know you can run an ad in the papers; The Times, Journal or any other paper. It's up to you."

"Okay." said Milton. He wondered to himself, if that also meant the local Harlem newspaper, The Amsterdam News. He will find out.

Turning to Jay and Gwen, Clayton says "We also pay a great deal of money to analysts. Their job it is find and identify investment opportunities for our clients. Most have not picked one real winner and you have three, with practically no experience. Maybe we need to put our resources somewhere else huh Milt?"

"Yea, Rice high school is right down the street." Said Milton. Clayton had to stifle his laugh.

The steaks and salad arrive and everyone enjoyed the meal. Jay savored every bite of the steak. He declared this would be his dish of choice in the future.

Half way through the meal, Clayton asks, "So how did you come up with Phillips?"

Jay looked at Milton who nodded his approval. "I read a lot, and what I saw was a bearish trend in the entire pharmaceutical industry. I thought Phillips was the most over priced. I had no idea about this drug and the birth defects problem." Jay responded.

"So you brought puts?"

"Well yes, I wanted to short the stock at first but Milton thought the least amount of risk would be to buy puts."

Milton said. "We don't allow short sales or options for our clients yet. But, I allowed it for Jay and of course, Gwen if she wanted to. They understand the risk. As you know, if the strategy was wrong, the loss is limited to the cost of the puts. On the other hand, if we shorted the stock, we would have unlimited upside risk."

"That's good thinking Milt; a good sound approach. So other situations that you might identify, that looks purely bullish, you will open to clients?"

"Of course. The firm's recommendations are a straight buy of what ever it is. It is clients transactions that will drive our revenues." Milton said.

"That's right. And happy clients lead to more clients. Looks like you will keep your clients happy without downtown's input." Said Clayton.

"Well, we still look at everything, not just some high flyer."

"I like what I hear and anything I can do to help you, just name it." Clayton, looking directly at Jay said "And, I want to hear about number four, okay Jay?"

After the meal, and as they were waiting for the elevator to take them back to the ground floor and the entrance to the trading floor, Clayton said, "I have a treat for our young prodigies Milt, how would you like to go on the trading floor?"

Both stunned; neither Gwen nor Jay said a word. They just looked at Clayton. Finally, Gwen realizing the magnitude of this gesture screamed out "Yes, Yes."

Clayton went to the trading floor entrance, wrote something on a piece of paper that he handed to a clerk. Jay and Gwen could see some of what was going on from their vantage in the lobby, but they were not prepared for the experience they were about to have.

A middle age White man soon came to the lobby. He extended a hand to Clayton. "Hi Bob, Hello Milt; what's going on?"

"I have some guest with me from our uptown office. I wanted them to see how the floor works if you're not too busy."

"Sure, we're covered." The man replied.

Clayton said, "This is one of our floor brokers Frank Weston. He will be your tour guide."

"Pleased to meet you. Come inside with me. You'll need ID badges. You coming too Milt?"

Milton had this tour years ago so he declined. He told them he would see them back at the office. Gwen had seen the trading floor from the visitors' gallery. Now, she and Jay were about to walk the trading floor that had over three thousand men and watch them in a chaotic but organized fashion, buy and sell the shares of American corporations.

Weston led the pair through the maze of all male bodies; some standing still, some moving, some waiving pieces of paper in the air, some shouting and some just plain having fun. And they were all wearing a tie.

The New York Stock exchange is an auction market. Shares of all the listed companies are traded in an open out cry. The steady din was punctuated by loud cries of '*buy* and *take em*, or *sold.*'

With so many men in the mission of making money, and with time and timing being a huge factor on the trading floor, invariably they bumped into each other in movement. Jay and Gwen were jostled a few times before they reached what is called the booth.

This is an area with banks of telephones, most ringing, and clerks taking orders or giving reports of a transaction. A Hamill employee manned one of the position phones. Other positions represented other brokerage firms

Jay and Gwen drew the stares of many, for it was perceived that the pair must be important. There were only a very few Negroes employed on the floor and to see two being showed around was just extremely unusual.

Jay was simply lost for words but cool as always. Weston was particularly cordial and answered patiently every question Gwen and Jay asked him. He took the time to explain as simply as he could, how this market place, called the nation's heartbeat, could effect a change in ownership of millions of dollars of securities each and every day in a matter of minutes, with relatively minimal errors. He told them that you couldn't buy a house for far less value in less than thirty days. And the process would involve a host of people led by lawyers, at least two real estate brokers and a mortgage banker. The paper work alone would be volumes. Stocks are trades each and every day with just the words of two people.

The entire process of an order execution from the time it is received at the booth and subsequently reported to the office from where it originated was demonstrated to Gwen and Jay. Then, they saw that execution print on the ticker tape and viewed around the nation. It was indeed fascination. Weston pointed out the responsibilities of some of the men. Men like him called floor brokers, and the specialist, various clerks, reporters and squad boys.

After about thirty minutes, the tour ended and Jay and Gwen were back on the train to Harlem. They were silent until Gwen said "Not one woman, not one."

CHAPTER 35

It was nearly three p.m. when Jay and Gwen got back to 125th Street. Jay told Gwen he would see her at school later, but he was not going back to the office. He decided that the person most directly responsible for the day he so much enjoyed deserved his attention. He went to doctor Weinstein's office to see Barbara.

Like weeks earlier, he stopped at the florist first and brought a dozen red roses. Barbara was in the office alone. Doctor Weinstein had gone home early because there were no appointments. Barbara was merely doing some unimportant paper work to keep her busy until she leaves for the day. She became annoyed when she heard the outer door to the office open and thought who the hell could this be at this time. Her eyes widen the moment Jay walked into the office, roses in hand.

"Jay, I didn't expect to see you; what are you doing here?"

"I came to see you." Seeing no one in the reception area, Jay walked behind Barbara's desk, pulled her to her feet with his free hand and hugged her tight. She felt so good in his arm.

"Jay, what is it, are these for me?"

He didn't say a word. He savored the feel and aroma of her for a few moments.

Finally he said "They're for Dr. Weinstein."

"No they are not; they're for me, let me see them."

He put the flowers on her desk then hugged her with both arms wrapped around her.

"Jay."

"Yes"

"Let me see the flowers."

He did not let her go. "Is the good doctor here?"

"No, he left about an hour ago."

"Anybody else here."

"No. Jay, let me see the flowers"

He was still hugging her. He then kissed her lightly on her cheeks, then her ears, then her neck.

"Jay, somebody is going to walk in here and…"

"Let em, I missed you."

"I've missed you too."

Then, their lips met in a long hard and sensuous kiss. He felt her swoon in his arms. "You can see these flowers all night and tomorrow. Right now, I feel like taking you in the back and ravishing you."

"Jay stop."

Jay repeated the gentle kisses all over her face, her neck and ears. He could see her light complexion start to turn the color of the roses and he could see and feel her breathing increase. He started backing her towards the treatment rooms in the back remembering a leather couch he saw in Dr. Weinstein's office. She resisted slightly.

"Jay, we can't do that here." Barbara whispered

"And why not?"

"Somebody might come in."

Jay released her. He went to the door and turned the bolt on the lock that would lock anyone out. He was back to her and again pushed her to the back; all the time kissing her.

He pushed her into Weinstein's office. The lights were off but not dark. Jay quickly glanced at the desk that held the secrets to his success thus far on Wall Street. His attention then turned to the couch. He removed the few magazines and newspapers that littered the couch then pushed Barbara towards it.

"Jay, not here, I…."

He found her lips and cut off her talking in mid sentence. He unbuttoned the top of her uniform and exposed the full round breast that were now heaving. Reaching behind her, he quickly released her bra and kissed her breast. He was frantic from anticipation so he was not as gentle as usual.

In one continuous motion, Jay reached down and pulled up the skirt of her starch white uniform and pulled down her white panties. Barbara no longer offered her token resistance. His gentleness returned just to stroke the hair of her vagina to feel the moisture. Again in one continuous motion, he loosened the belt to his trousers and let it fall to his knees. He pushed her onto the couch and was immediately into her.

Jay wondered as they made passionate love, had Dr. Weinstein ever did what he and Barbara were doing in his office.

Barbara cried out in ecstasy and joy. "What are you doing to me?"

When they were finished, the lovers were rearranging their dress and Jay said. "I wanted you so bad I couldn't help myself after I saw you. I'm sorry for acting like an animal. I've been thinking about you since I left."

"I've been thinking about you too. Don't apologize to me. I didn't let you do any thing that I didn't want. I have never done that before."

"Done what?" Jay teased.

"You know."

"Well, I'm gonna come here everyday after from now on after the good doctor goes home."

"No you 're not. Barbara laughed.

They were both dressed and went back to the reception area. Barbara went to the flowers.

"These are beautiful Jay "

"I have something else for you also."

"You do, what is it?"

"Money. I don't have it with me now but we made some money on Dr. Weinstein's last entry."

"You mean that stock called Phillips; you know I saw something in the paper about that, something about birth defects; we made money on that?" Barbara asked.

"Yes and so did the doctor. He made a lot of money."

"I don't understand how, but I told my daughter about you and she wants to open an account too."

"You told her about me?"

"Yes Jay; I hope you don't mind. You don't have to do it right away. Besides, she might forget about it."

"No I don't mind. I am surprised you mentioned me. What did you tell her?"

"Well I didn't tell her everything, but she is not stupid."

"She is your daughter. I know she is not stupid but how do we handle this?"

"I don't know Jay. Let's see if she mentions it again."

"Okay sweetie. I've got to go to school. I'll call you later."

Jay was feeling great about this escapade with Barbara. It took their relationship to a new level in his mind. He was sure Barbara felt the same way. He didn't care if her daughter knew about them. In fact, he thought, it might be about time he met her. A mother and daughter tryst sounds intriguing to him. No, his mind said. Don't mess up this thing with Barbara. Besides, he did like her very much.

He hurried the short walk to Sarah's apartment. He planned to call his mother before he goes to school. When he reached the landing to the apartment, as usual, he heard music coming from Sye's apartment. He recognized the sounds of the saxophone genius Charlie Parker. Sye had played one of his albums for him recently. He loved it. Jay played the sax for years from grade school through high school and never realized the instrument could sound the way Charlie Parker made it sound

He raised his hand to knock on Sye's door then changed his mind. No time today. Turning to Sarah's door, he heard the door unlock at Maxine's apartment. He waited for her to come into the hall.

"Hello Jay, I haven't seen you for a few days" She said.

Jay was surprised she remembered his name. She didn't look as ragged as she usually does. In fact she looked sober.

"I've been out of town. How you doing?"

"I'm okay; I been wondering when we gonna do that thing you wanted me to do. I thought you were coming to see me bout that."

"I am. You ready? You look good."

Maxine smiled and ran her hand over her hair. It was definitely a long time since anyone gave her a compliment. She was still drinking but not as much, and it showed in her face. Jay saw the tremble in her hands and he heard the nervousness in her voice. He recognized the unmistakable traits of an alcoholic from the times he had been around Harriett's mother.

"We'll be doing that thing soon. You keep taking care of yourself." He then reached into his pocket and gave her ten dollars.

"Thanks Jay, I'll be looking for you."

Jay did not know what to make of Maxine in this half sober state, but it was good for his plan. He may execute it sooner than he planned.

Jay called his mother. She assured him that she was adjusting to the death of her mother and that Sarah had been such a good friend. Sarah was staying one more week and then would be back in New York. Once again, Diane promised Jay that she would think seriously about relocating to New York.

Several weeks went by and a hint of spring was in the air in New York. The daily temperature was starting to average out to the low fifties. Jay had gotten through his first winter in New York and none too soon. He recalled that during Charleston winters, he never wore more than a jacket. Since living in New York, he had added several sweaters and two topcoats to his wardrobe.

Jay spent his time, as well he should, prospecting for new clients. From that effort, his list of clients was growing and his personal production was growing. His commission checks showed that. Though modest by the standards of a seasoned White stockbroker, Jay was doing well. His commission income was much more than the draw that Milton started him with so the draw was discontinued. His income was just his commission from purchase and sale transactions.

Jay went to school every night, studied hard and was excelling in his classes. He saw Gwen everyday at work and school, but the romance time was on his own terms- only when he wanted to. Barbara never demanded his time so he saw her only when he wanted to. He was never a person to waste time or efforts.

Jay and Gwen were quite successful harvesting accounts from the small business owners in and around Harlem. Their success with this effort encouraged them to prospect in other areas where there were small business owners like The Bronx, Brooklyn and Queens.

One day, as it often happened, several ministers were having lunch at Shirley's. One of them, pastor of a prominent congregation of middle income Negroes in Brooklyn, was discussing with his fellow pastors a situation that involved securities. He told them that his church, once an all White congregation, now about ninety-nine percent Negro, had this investment portfolio that was handed down to them. The former White members of the church managed the account. Those members now deceased or had moved away were no longer in touch with the brokerage firm where the account was domiciled.

The dilemma, the pastor said is the fact that the church's current treasurer, although very capable of the day-to-day financial operations of the church, had no knowledge of stocks or bonds. The treasurer could not talk the language nor understand whatever suggestions the broker who handled the account would make whenever he called the church. And no other member of the church had even a little stocks investment knowledge. The broker grew increasingly frustrated and impatient with the church. He could not do any business with them. The results of this is, the account has been inactive and laid dominant for a number of years but the pastor was sure the account's value was substantial.

The pastor further explained that the broker was reluctant to come to the church and discuss the portfolio with the trustees since it would have to be late in the evening.

He had no desire to be in New York, much less Brooklyn, after five o'clock was the conclusion of the pastor and his financial board. The board felt that a visit to the brokerage firm was somewhat intimidating and inconvenient. It is the church's funds they reasoned so the broker should come to them. They refused the broker's invitation. Meanwhile, there was this account of securities that belonged to the church but not under church management or scrutiny.

One of the ministers in the group said it was his understanding that Shirley, owner of the restaurant where they were at the moment enjoying lunch, was familiar with such matters. He suggested that the pastor of the Brooklyn church talk to Shirley after lunch.

Shirley, proud to talk of her limited experience, assured the pastor that she indeed knew just the person he should be talking too. And she, of course had Jay in mind.

Jay took Gwen to Brooklyn with him for the first meeting with the church financial committee. He only told her that he had a lead that he wanted to pursue. It was nearly eight o'clock when all five members arrived for the seven o'clock meeting.

By design, Gwen took the lead in the opening discussion. She explained their background, their expertise, the commitment of Hamill to the Negro community, and the many reasons why this church should consider in its overall financial plans, the value of stocks investments. She explained the sound strategy of owning pieces of corporate America and the financial security it provides.

When the treasurer showed Jay and Gwen the most recent account statement, they barely held their excitement. What was revealed is an account valued at over three hundred thousand dollars. The account was made up of the most successful and well known American corporations. The number of shares held varied from one hundred to one thousand. There were also a number of corporate bonds in amounts of five to twenty.

Jay, taking note of the age of the pastor and the committee members was sure that his and Gwen's age would be an issue. He told them that he and Gwen were not qualified at this time to take over the management of an account this size and importance. He told them that he was sure that the members of the church charged this committee to make sound decisions. He also told them that he and Gwen lacked the experience necessary to properly manage their account but their manager, who was one of the first Negroes to work on Wall Street and had far more years experience, including managing accounts like theirs, would be more qualified. Finally, Jay told them that Milton would be happy to meet with them.

It was after nine-thirty when Jay and Gwen got on the subway for the ride back to Manhattan. The A train was not crowded so the two sat close together and were letting out shrieks of joy for their apparent good fortune. The committee agreed to meet with Milton one week from that day at the church.

"That was very smart of you Jay to talk of our age; what made you think of that?" Gwen said.

"Two teenagers? Would you turn over that kind of money to two teenagers? I don't think it mattered what kind of experience we had.

A group like that looks for experience that you get from maturity. We should call Milton tonight. When you get home, call him; this kind of news should not wait." Jay said very excitedly.

"Okay I'll call him. Like I said Jay Austin, you are so smart. By the way, I am no longer a teenager."

"I don't think you ever were. You have been all woman to me. The older woman." They both laughed.

Gwen took Jay's hand, squeezed it, then kissed him on the cheek. She said, "Why don't we call Milton together and tell him the good news."

"We? Does that mean I'm going to your house?"

"Yes you are my sweet."

CHAPTER 36

One week later, Milton met with the Emanuel Baptist Church finance committee. Milton was dazzling. He was just himself. He was careful not to try and impress the members with his knowledge of the securities industry. Instead, he approached the group as if he was a teacher- a teacher of American economic history.

He took with him a chart that displayed the growth of the market since its earliest days. He explained that world wars, the great depression of the thirties, Pearl Harbor and other conflicts, domestic and international had not stopped the growth of stock ownership and the increasing value of those holdings. Milton told how American corporations used the market as a means to raise capital to expand their business thereby increasing jobs and growing the economy.

Finally, Milton told them that his mission as a broker was to help his clients reach their investment goals through careful planning; and that the strategies he employs will incur minimal risk.

The finance committee asked what should they do to transfer management of the account to Hamill.

This was a major accomplishment for the Harlem office. When Bob Clayton, the regional manager learned of it, he called Milton to congratulate him. Milton told him that his two young brokers were totally responsible for bringing the account to Hamill. Jay sent two dozen roses to Shirley.

This development disclosed another source of prospects and more fertile ground for Jay and Gwen to explore. With all the churches in Harlem from 110th Street to 155th Street and from the Hudson to the Harlem Rivers, the weekly collections was perhaps in the hundreds of thousands; maybe much more. Where were the churches putting that money? The office was going to find out.

The plan of prospecting Harlem churches disclosed that the lack of knowledge of the stock market in the Black community was far deeper than anyone imagined. Milton, Gwen and Jay discovered that it was difficult or near impossible to approach the decision makers about the merits of investing when they had no idea what they were talking about.

Since there was little or no study of the stock market done in schools, the only contact for Black folks of this subject was on a television newscast when the Dow Jones industrial average was mentioned. In Harlem, the business pages and stock tables in the local newspapers were bypassed for the most part.

Gwen came up with the idea of bringing the subject to the people through a series of seminars. The staff of the Harlem office developed an elementary guide to the stock market that they could present in a classroom setting. They presented the seminars at churches on Saturday mornings. They entitled the seminars 'Own a piece of America, you helped build it.'

Introducing the fundamentals of investing to Black people in this setting was very well received in the churches. The pastors were pleased because the staff had the foresight to tell the audience to make tithing a part of their overall financial strategy.

Hamill supported the effort by providing all the marketing materials Milton and his staff would need. The Harlem office was staging a seminar practically every Saturday at a different church and at times a repeat presentation at certain churches. They decided to do two a day with Jay and Gwen at one and Milton and Sharon at another. This went on for several weeks.

Spring was finally full blown and the staff's Saturday mornings were not so bad. The hard work was paying off. Everyone's commission checks were good from the business coming in but the staff had little time for themselves. Milton said this was the sacrifice needed to build and grow your client base. The month of March was going to be the last of the seminars. They decided to just seek referrals from the current client base for the time being.

Jay had little time for Barbara or anyone else. He managed to talk to her now and then or stop by her office just to say hello on his way home. She did not complain. She understood what he was doing. He found himself tired from the schedule of work, school at night and the seminars on Saturday. While he saw Gwen everyday, they had little time for extracurricular activities. Occasionally, they would spend time after school together or after one of the seminars. But for the most part they only went to go to Gwen's apartment to rest and sleep.

No one in the office expected Jay to come up with another success stock because he, like everybody in the office, had been extremely busy planning and conducting the seminars, then following up on the prospects that were generated. With the time required for his studies in school, there was no time that he could say he spent looking for the next one.

When he least expected it, Jay got a call from Barbara. Dr. Weinstein got the call to buy the shares of Financial Trust Company of New York. FTN. At first, Jay wasn't sure how to handle this. Should he quietly buy the stock for his clients, or should he tell the office that he was playing another hunch.

Jay knew in his heart that he could not play the stock by himself. He had to let Gwen and Milton in on it. In fact, that was a part of his make up. He had to let people know or at least think that he was special, that he had abilities beyond others, that he was smart. The one way they would think the way he wanted them to, would be, to share his find.

Jay also knew he had a few days at least to buy the stock FTN. So, he casually mentioned to Milton that one of the seminar attendees told him that she worked for FTN and that they were always very busy. She was undecided, however, about whether she should buy the company stock after it was offered to the employees at a discount.

Jay said he told the young lady that he would look into the company's performance and get back to her. He said his study suggested that she should buy FTN, but he would feel better if Milton ordered a research report from the main office. Milton agreed and ordered the report. The report arrived a day later, but it had a neutral recommendation. In other words, it said neither buy nor sell at this time. The report also said that the banking industry was primed for major growth and some major New York banks would lead the way.

Jay told Milton and Gwen that he wanted to put some of his clients into this situation and would it be okay. Milton was not about to disagree. After all, FTN was a solid company that paid a dividend uninterrupted for many years. The stock could be an income generator even if there was no immediate prospect for price appreciation. More importantly, Milton said from his track record, Jay deserved the benefit of any doubts. That was just what Jay wanted to hear.

The three of them went to work. At the current price of thirty-two, they convinced their clients who had the available cash to buy the stock. The others who had purchased other shares were strongly advised to sell them and buy FTN. This created two commissions.

New accounts were opened with the purchase of FTN for whatever monies they had available. Even if they had only enough for five or ten shares, Jay reasoned that if a person's first experience was successful, he would always be a client and bring others to him. He wanted everyone to make money.

Jay opened Mason for one hundred shares, even convinced him to get a bank checking account. He also opened Sarah, JC and Sye. He bought FTN for his mother and all of his Charleston clients. He included Barbara and all the accounts generated at the seminars. Lastly, Jay reminded Milton to call Grace and Joyce. They bought two hundred shares each.

The Harlem branch was responsible for buying thirty thousand shares of FTN. Their activity caused the stock to move up one –half point. All that was left is to wait for the news that Jay knew would be coming soon.

It was three weeks later when the Journal broke the news of a mega bank merger. Hudson bank was buying out FTN at forty dollars a share. It would be the biggest merger in US banking history.

CHAPTER 37

The activity of the Harlem branch did not go unnoticed by the regional manager, Bob Clayton. He was impressed with the number of new accounts opened and the stock purchase activity but he did not call the office. He didn't call, even after Milton left a message for him informing him of the FTN play by the Harlem branch. But now, Clayton was on the phone with Milton as soon as he read the story in the papers. This story said something else. It said this office had uncanny timing and insight or someone was plugged in.

Milton told Clayton that it was his young gun again. And that he just did old fashion reading and research. Clayton said have Jay in his office for a lunch meeting the next day.

Milton saw that Jay had developed a quiet swagger in the office, but he was not prepared for the response from Jay to Clayton's invitation.

"Tell Mr. Clayton to come up here for lunch. We can go to Shirley's to eat and talk if he wants to."

"Yea" said Gwen."

"You know, you're right." Chimed in Milton.

Clayton had no trouble getting a taxi from Wall Street to Harlem; although the driver looked at him a little curiously. He had not been at the office since the grand opening two years ago.

Milton asked his friend to come to the office and answer the phone and take messages. Sharon, who is taking the brokers test in two weeks, deserved to be at this meeting also.

Clayton was going to see just what Jay wanted him to see. Jay remembered how Clayton was revered and recognized by all at the Exchange Luncheon Club. Now, he will observe how Jay will be received in his world at Shirley's.

With no prior notice or any type of advance warning, Jay and his party of Milton, Clayton, Gwen and Sharon walked into Shirley's. As if on cue, Merle immediately greeted Jay. She then hugged him, fawned over him and treated him as a special customer. Milton smiled inside. Gwen felt proud and Sharon just looked starry eyed.

After Merle sat the party at the best table, Shirley herself came out to greet them. Jay introduced her to Clayton. Then JC, the chief, came out to say hello to the young blood. Then Sarah came to wait on them. The other servers came by to say hello. Mason said hello; Sye waved to him; and most of the customers that knew Jay from his days at the restaurant felt compelled to acknowledge him this day.

Of course everyone greeted the young blood from the south. He had just made money for them. Jay was saying to himself, check this out Clayton. The reception Jay received was not all the result of the FTN stock success, or the fact that several people in Shirley's restaurant will profit from Jay's inside information. It was a genuine affection everyone had for Mr. Most likely to Succeed.

"Everything on the menu is good at Shirley's but let me suggest, the baked chicken with stuffing, black eye peas, macaroni and cheese, and butter beans." Jay said.

Clayton just looked at him and replied rather meekly. "Okay, I'll take it."

Everyone agreed.

Jay added, "Sarah, bring plenty of hot corn bread and ice tea. Oh, and please, a little rice and gravy on the side for me."

Shirley knew this must be an important White man. She and Merle were both in the kitchen to oversee the preparation of their order. It wasn't necessary. JC and the kitchen staff knew exactly what to do. And that was just doing the usual. The food will take care of everything. And take care it did. Clayton totally enjoyed his meal. He repeatedly lamented how good it was. Over the peach cobbler, he told Milton, the coming regional meeting, attended by all the northeast branch managers will be at the Harlem office and lunch will be at Shirley's. She was delighted when Milton relayed this to her as the party was leaving.

Back at the office, Clayton and Milton cloistered in the small conference room engaged   in deep discussion. After about twenty minutes, Milton called Jay in.

Milton began. "Jay, you are wanted at the big house."

"What do you mean Milton?"

Clayton replied, "A man of your talent should work at the main office. I would like for you to work downtown."

"What would I do?" Jay asked

"I would like you in the sales office.

"Why? I like it here."

"We'll increase your payout to forty percent."

"I don't know Mr. Clayton. I mean Gwen is my partner. I like working with Milton. There is so much more we need to do."

"Listen Jay, I appreciate your loyalty to Milton. I really do. Milton told me that he has two people he is going to hire. I understand that Sharon will be into sales soon. So, it's not like your leaving will hurt the branch. I'm not saying they will replace you. I think you have a special talent that can't be replaced but I'm thinking of the firm as a whole."

Milton said, "Jay, this could be good for you. Think about it. I'm sure if you find that the move is not good for you and the firm, Bob will let you come back here. Am I right Bob?"

"Of course. But I can assure you we will do everything to make you happy."

"I'll think about it, and let you know tomorrow." Jay said.

Gwen was very upset at this news. The joy of the FTN transactions was no longer on her mind; losing Jay was. While Jay told her that he would still be in touch everyday and see her in school at night, the only change would be where he worked. Their relationship he promised, will not change.

Jay had other ideas about the move. It was obvious to him that Clayton just wanted him in the downtown office just to take advantage of his apparent talent for picking winning stocks. Jay knows his talent, which is Barbara will not last forever. Barbara will still help him in the time being. But what will happen if she decides not to; that she is no longer able to. Dr. Weinstein has talked about retirement she once mentioned.

So, Jay told Clayton that he will accept the move but not in the sales department. He had become fascinated with the options product. He wants to work in that department; learn all there is to learn about put and call options. Then he could pick another department if he so chooses. More importantly, he will work for a salary only and not have to open accounts. He told Clayton, he will continue his research, and any ideas will be brought to him directly.

Clayton could not resist Jay's plan and agreed. He was also impressed with Jay's thinking. Here he felt was a young man who had just profited eight points on thirty thousand shares of stock. Just think what he could do when he really learns the business. He said the firm will pay Jay a salary of twenty-five thousand, and he would also get a Christmas bonus.

This was more than Jay expected, and he was very pleased. He called his mother, then Barbara. Then he told Sarah.

There was so much Jay had to do. He told Clayton he would start downtown in one week. First he transferred his clients. He decided he would continue to manage the Charleston clients. He let Gwen pick which clients she wanted then he gave the rest to Sharon. He expected to collect from this gesture at a later date. The next step was to resurrect Linda Hall. He went to see Maxine.

Maxine had not fallen any deeper into the gin bottle but she was still a drunk. The difference between Maxine and Harriett's mother is Harriett's mother would drink until she was drunk. Maxine would drink until all the liquor was gone. Jay found her at one of those moments.

When Jay knocked on her apartment, it was like she was expecting him.

"Hi Jay, you come to see me?"

"Yes Miss Maxine we gonna do our plan now. You ready?"

"Yea I ready."

"Did you tell anyone about what we talked about?"

"No, I don't talk to nobody. I stays by myself."

Jay knew this was probably true. Maxine had worn out her welcome with most people in the neighborhood. Fact is, most people avoided her.

Then he laid out his plan. He told her to meet him at the subway station on the downtown side. He purchased tokens for the trip to Forty-Second Street to get a passport photo of her made.

Before returning, they stopped at a thrift store on Broadway where he bought her a dress, a handbag, a hat and gloves. The items were fitting for a well- to- do but elderly woman.

Maxine was being very cooperative. She listened to Jay as he told her how to walk, how to look distinguished, and how to look like a loving grandmother. He cautioned her again and again that he would do all the talking. She was prepared for her acting role. The production was planned for the next morning at ten o'clock. Jay saw that she was starting to tremble a little so he rewarded her with just enough cash for a pint of gin. He couldn't have her smashed in the morning.

Letting Maxine get inside their building first, Jay walked slowly so he could look into Shirley's window to see if Sarah was working. After he saw Sarah, Jay hurried home.

Working meticulously, he removed the picture of Mrs. Hall from the passport and replaced it with the picture just taken of Maxine. Satisfied that it will pass inspection, Jay put the passport back in the Miles Davis album jacket where he had it stored for months.

He then left the apartment for an evening with Barbara.

Jay took two dozen roses and two thousand dollars in cash. He was going to tell Barbara about his move downtown. While Jay always enjoyed being around Barbara and the lovemaking was always especially good, tonight he was merely going through the motions.

Barbara, on the other hand, was glad to see him since there had been little time between them for weeks. The flowers and the money was a special treat but neither was necessary in her mind. The touch, the tenderness, the presence of Jay was all she wanted, but She could never say that.

Jay was not all there. He had his mind on tomorrow. After what he felt was his obligation to pay homage to Barbara, he was ready to leave. Tomorrow was a big day.

Maxine met Jay at the subway station exactly on time. She had prepared herself just as he told her to. Jay was sure no one on the block recognized this old woman in the hat and gloves, especially the nosy Mrs. Knowles. She knows every person, place, and thing on 127th Street. From her window seat, she watched everyone who walked this block day and night. Even she, Jay felt would not think that this is Maxine. She was ready for her performance.

Jay was dressed in the stylish gray suit he purchased in Charleston. The white shirt and blue silk tie gave him the look of an Ivy League student. They sat together on the train and looked the role of grandson and grandmother.

Maxine asked, "Do I look okay?"

"Yes you do. You've been taking care of yourself the past few weeks."

"Yea, I'm just tired of the life I been living Jay, I'm gonna change. I wanna go home after this if you can help me."

"Where is home and how can I help you?" Jay asked.

"I'm from St Louis. Got a niece there. She says I could stay wit her if I wants to. She got a big house and can get me in a program, help me stop drinking."

The pity that Jay felt for Maxine the first time he met her returned. Finally, she realizes the self-destructive life and path she was following can be changed before it's too late.

"Of course I'll help you. If you mean money, I will give you enough to take care of yourself for quite a while. Okay?"

"That be good Jay. My niece got three kids; a girl and two boys. The girl, she wants to sing. I'm gonna teach her all I know. Maybe that something I can do before I die. I wasted bout twenty years of my life and now maybe I can salvage some of what I lost."

"What happened to you Maxine? Sye played some of your music for me. I really thought it was great."

"Unfortunately, we don't control our music son. My manager, the studios, made the money and controls the money. When I complained, they blackball me. You know what that means?"

"I think so."

"They used me. They used my talent, they used my body. And when they felt I was used up, they kicked me out. That's what happened. I tried to forget everything by drinking. But I don't forget."

Jay thought to himself, now I'm using you.

It didn't take long for the ride to Fifty-Seventh Street where the Eastern Bank and Trust Co. was located. Jay had found out that this bank was one where he could negotiate the Treasury bill and stock certificates with little scrutiny.

Sure enough, a young trust officer, eager to get this business was more than happy to handle the transfer of the AT&T stock to the name of Jayson Austin. The treasurery bond, being a bearer bond, which means whoever has possession owns it was no problem at all.

The young banker didn't even ask for identification of Linda Hall. He took Jay's word that his grandmother who worked at AT&T for thirty years had accumulated this stock and was now giving it to her grandson. When Jay told him that he wanted to open a new account in his name, liquidate the stock and bond then leave the cash proceeds in the account at the bank, may have been the reason the officer was so accommodating.

It was all much easier than Jay imagined. Maxine was quiet and a loving grandmother. She merely nodded her approval of the plan as laid out by Jay. In less than one half hour, the transaction was done. In less than a week, the sale of one thousand shares of stock and one Treasury bond will be converted into more than one hundred and fifty thousand dollars in cash in an account for Jay.

The opening of such an account, even though most unusual, blinded the banker. These two people aroused no suspicions in him. Gushing from his good fortune from walk-ins, he thanked Jay profusely and then said, "And thank you very much Mrs. Hall; you must love your grandson very much."

Maxine did not miss a beat. "I do love him very much."

Jay took her arm and ushered her out of the bank.

They were quiet all the way back to the subway. Once inside the station, Maxine, voice trembling said, "Who is Mrs. Hall?"

Jay ignored her. Instead he simply replied, "You were absolutely great Maxine. I'm proud of you. When do you want to leave for St. Louis?"

"I'll leave soons I get the money; how much you gonna give me?"

"Well you heard him say it will take a week to get the cash, but I had ten thousand in mind. Is that okay?"

"Oh that be great. Boy do I need a drink now."

"I'll take care of that when we get back. We'll ride in different cars going back. When you get to 125th Street, you go on home. I'll be there with some; what kind of gin?"

"Gordon's." Maxine said.

Maxine, feeling good about herself, continued her obedience to her new young benefactor. She sat alone on the noisy, dirty train and was thinking; I'll be out of this dam city in about a week. She also thought, where did I hear that name before?

Jay saw Maxine ahead of him as he emerged from the subway. He had to make three stops before he goes to her apartment. He walked back to 124th Street to the liquor store and bought a fifth of Maxine's favorite gin. Then to 126th Street and bought another fifth. His last stop would be at 128th Street where he purchased a third bottle of gin. He wanted to make sure she enjoyed herself tonight. Permanently.

Jay briefly entertained the idea of giving Maxine some money; ten thousand and let her go to St. Louis and live out her life. That thought changed the moment she asked who is Mrs. Hall? He couldn't afford to have her pursue the answer, even if she moved to St. Louis.

What did the neighborhood say about Maxine? One day she is going to drink herself to death. It was four days later when she was found dead in her apartment.

CHAPTER 38

After a week off, Jay reported to the downtown office of Hamill. Clayton arranged for him to work at the options desk as an order clerk. Hamill had a total of twenty-eight branch offices. All Jay had to do was enter orders that came in from those branches to buy or sell put and call options with an outside dealer. He was being trained by a man in his mid thirties name John Riccardi. Jay found him to be a fairly nice person who willingly told Jay what he needed to know about the product. Clayton had instructed the order room personnel that this young man Jay Austin, was to be treated with respect and everyone was acting accordingly.

Jay did not act like he was anyone special and the order room staff grew to like him and made him just one of the boys.

Jay was adjusting to his new life. He was adjusting to the subway ride downtown to Wall Street and the ungodly crowd of people at seven-thirty in the morning. Then there was the ride uptown at five-thirty in the early evening. After first walking to work at Shirley's and then the Harlem office, Jay was not quite prepared for rush hour in New York. This scene was unbelievable. The first week, he witnessed several fights between riders who didn't like being pushed, shoved or just touched in an inappropriate way. For the most part, he found the subway scene amusing. To him, they were just New Yorkers with attitudes.

Jay had no further thoughts of Maxine. It was Sye who aroused suspicion about her whereabouts when he heard no sounds coming from her apartment for four days. He always heard her coming and going out. He contacted the building superintendent who finally went into Maxine's apartment and discovered her body. The police, seeing the empty liquor bottles, and her lifestyle being common knowledge among the neighborhood, quickly ruled the cause of death as from acute alcoholic consumption.

No one had seen Jay with Maxine and no one saw him enter her apartment with the three fifths of liquor. He went to Maxine's after first knocking on Sye's door and not getting an answer. He was home free again.

Jay poured himself into his new duties. He made it a point to turn himself into a sponge and absorb all that John could teach him about options. The one thing that he learned is, this department was not very busy. While all other departments were busy all day, the options order desk had only a few orders during the day to work on. There was only one conclusion to draw from this and that was, the customers and brokers of Hamill just did not know this product and management did not place much emphasis on it.

Jay celebrated his twentieth birthday by inviting Gwen, Sharon and Milton to join him for dinner at the Hawaii kai, the restaurant that Gwen introduced him to.

While Jay often saw Gwen at night school, he hadn't seen Milton or Sharon since he left them. Sharon was now a broker herself and she looked great. Jay thought he would soon invite her out.

The dinner conversation was all about the business. Milton had finally added two more brokers, one a young college grad who had attended one of the investment seminars and the other, also a college grad who responded to a New York Times ad. Milton also had a new administrative assistant who replaced Sharon. So, the Harlem office was growing as planned. Life was going on without Jay. This pleased him, because he was going on without them. There still was the feel of love for each other that Jay felt will always exist. He continued the celebration later that night with Barbara.

Jay discovered just how little importance the options department had on Wall Street when news came from Dallas, Texas that the president of the United States, John F. Kennedy had been shot and killed.

The noise in the order room became a loud continuous roar. The teletype machines started spitting out an ocean of papers. The papers were all orders to sell stocks. Every phone in the office was ringing and the staff, some with tears in their eyes were trying to keep up with the demands of their jobs. The scene was totally chaotic. The market was like a runaway train in a downward fall. No one thought about a break for lunch during this time. Jay and John were asked to help out in other areas because they were not busy at all.

After three days of this hectic scene, the market settled down and America paused to bury a beloved president.

Jay was perplexed by the lack of business at the options desk. The product was more and more fascinating to him every day. But the rest of the world at Hamill did not think that way.

He wanted to learn more so he arranged to have lunch with several put and call dealers. These experts of the product told him more than John could teach him. He learned how Hamill's competitors handled options and why they had more business. Jay learned a great deal from these lunch dates but he had to wait for the right moment to approach Clayton with the latest plan his mind was hatching. He had learned so much that after a few months, John, his teacher was asking him questions.

The moment Jay was waiting for came with a call from Barbara. Dr. Weinstein had gotten another call. Weinstein was told to buy Mesa petroleum. This was a small oil company in Texas. That didn't matter to Jay. He didn't care who the company was or what they did. The fact that it was going to go up soon was all he needed.

Jay went to Clayton and told him that the client base of Hamill were not taking advantage of stock options and that he had a plan to stimulate interest thereby increasing business and increasing revenues.

Clayton was somewhat reluctant but he could not ignore Jay's recent track record. He allowed Jay to solicit quotes to buy call options on Mesa Petroleum. He then allowed the recommendation of this purchase to a select group of clients and also approved the purchase of calls in the firm's own trading account.

Three weeks later with the positive news that came about Mesa, Jay was a made man.

From this point, Jay became the options department. With the help of his dealer friends, Jay wrote a weekly newsletter in which he explained the many uses of options. He wrote how options could be used to control the risk associated with stock ownership. He explained how to protect a profit or use options as an insurance policy on owned stocks.

He explained the leverage factor that options allowed the holder, and how to increase the yield on owned stocks. Jay also taught the firm's brokers how to use options to acquire stocks at a lower cost.

Jay no longer worked on the options desk. He had his own office near Clayton. He traveled to the branches to explain the product in person to the brokers and in some instances their clients. Soon, the order room had to put more people on the options trading desk to handle the business created by Jay. Clayton was no fool. He knew that Jay had become a valuable commodity; a commodity that Hamill's competitors could lure away with a much higher salary that he was currently getting. So, Clayton went to the executive committee and asked that Jay's salary be increased to forty thousand annually.

It was time to leave Harlem. It was time to move into the big apple, Manhattan.

With the help of Clayton, Jay found an apartment on Manhattan's upper west side on Columbus Avenue. This building still represented what Harlem was before its transformation into a Negro ghetto.

The apartment was on the sixteenth floor. It had two bedrooms, a large living room with white walls and parquet floors. The living room, overlooking Columbus Avenue, had two large windows and a fourteen-foot ceiling with decorative moldings.

This was a niece clean neighborhood. Jay observed several different ethnic groups of people living in his building.

When Jay rode the elevator, he got curious stares from his neighbors, double looks from the White women especially when they saw him dressed in his Wall Street uniform, as he was everyday.

Jay invited Barbara to the apartment to solicit her ideas on decorating it. He also asked her to go shopping with him for furniture. With his account at the Eastern bank and his salary, he was able to fully furnish the apartment with all that he needed. So he bought furniture for both bedrooms, the living room and kitchen.

Barbara was impressed. He thought about asking Gwen for her help, but he felt that Gwen would become attach to him all over again. The move to the downtown office had helped the weaning. He only saw her at night school, and then the conversation was short. When he felt alone, he could always go to her apartment if he didn't go to Barbara's. He was in control.

The next step was to get a drivers license. A car is in the very near future. Jay had his mind on a small sports car. A red Sunbeam convertible had caught his eye once so that was going to be his next purchase.

Jay was the talk the Hamill main office. The White girls in the office were now noticing him. If he didn't go to lunch with Clayton, he often ate lunch by himself in the cafeteria. There was always some White girl dropping hints to him that he ignored. He may be out of the south, but there were some things that was never going to leave him and one was, don't mess with White women. There were a few that drew his attention but he reserved his attention to all the Black women that he came in contact with on Wall Street.

The option business continued to grow and Jay grew with it. He found out that if you could produce money for the White man, it didn't matter what color you were. On Wall Street, the only color that mattered was green.

The option product was his baby and his entrée into the inter-workings of the Street. His position afforded him the opportunity to attend Broadway shows, sporting events and dinner at the finest restaurants in New York, all gratis.

Jay invited Sye to join him at a Knicks basketball game where he had courtside seats.

After the game, they went to dinner at a restaurant that featured live topless dancers. Sye really enjoyed that.

He took Barbara to a Broadway show on one occasion and Gwen on another. He went by himself to see the show that Grace, Mrs. Hall's daughter was in. He took her to dinner after the show but fought the urge to press further.

Grace talked about her daughter Joyce and urged Jay to call her at college. Jay promised to do that.

There really wasn't much time for Jay to spend with women. His schedule didn't permit that. He was traveling to the Hamill branches on days that he didn't go to night school and studying and preparing his options strategy newsletter other days.

The job also permitted Jay to see other cities like Boston, Philadelphia, Washington, D.C. and Princeton, N. J. The boy most likely, had succeeded.

Jay found time to fly to Virginia on one occasion to spend the weekend with Harriet. That was great fun for both of them. He also paid for her to come to New York to spend the weekend with him. He found that being with Harriet was still enjoyable. He introduced her to New York and suggested that she move there after she graduates.

Harriet, now a senior at Hampton was excited by the idea. While she had met and become involved with a fellow student at Hampton, she still loved and adored Jay. She promised Jay that she would think about it.

CHAPTER 39

Three years passed by. Jay was still doing exceptionally well. He had received news of the death of two of his classmates from Burke High School who had been killed in the war with Viet Nam. This news saddened Jay, and he thought how fortunate he was to have been his mother's only son. Otherwise, he would have been in that war also.

He witnessed on many occasions, students, religious leaders, some politicians and others marching down Broadway, right in front of his building to protest the war. He was sympathetic but fought the urge to join in.

Hamill as a firm was growing. The company had recently taken over another firm name F. A. Kidder. They had fifteen offices located in several southeast cities including Charleston. This was extremely exciting to Jay. There was going to be an opportunity for him to go home one day and teach the good old boys about options. He was sure he would see some gentlemen that he waited on at Henry's restaurant back in Charleston.

The other feeling of excitement that engulfed Jay was he was about to graduate from CCNY. Going to night school year-round had paid off. He was preparing for his mother to come to his graduation in the spring 1966.

Jay became close friends with several young Black men who also worked on Wall Street. These relationships gave him male buddies to hang out with and also talk the street   language. It was if his high school club, the Impalas had been reborn. Of course women were always the subject of conversations.

Diane Austin too was doing very well. Her business in Charleston had expanded. She opened a second location in North Charleston to serve the wives of navel and air force personnel stationed in the area. And, she met a man. For the first time in many years Diane trusted her heart to a man again. He was the principal at an elementary school in North Charleston. She had been seeing him for over a year now and she felt that he was going to propose marriage to her one day soon. She planned to discuss this development with Jay when she arrives in New York for his graduation.

Bob Clayton was growing alone with Hamill. He was now on the executive committee and destined to become president and chief executive officer in the near future.

Jay left an invitation to his graduation for Clayton with his secretary so he was not surprised when he received a call from Clayton to come to his office. He was sure it would be to discuss his graduation. Jay didn't expect him to come but he invited him.

He developed a good relationship with Clayton but aside from the many times he dinned with him to discuss business or traveled with him to a branch office, the relationship in Jay's mind was employee and employer. He was not prepared for the reason he was invited to his office.

Clayton was busy on the phone when Jay arrived. He motioned to Jay to sit down while he continued his conversation. This act reminded Jay of the time a few years earlier when another White man did the same thing. That White man was Dr. Weinstein and overhearing that conversation was the beginning of his Wall Street career.

As Jay sat there looking at the great view of the lower Hudson River and hearing Clayton discuss the affairs of a branch office on the phone, Shirley's restaurant came to his mind. Then Barbara, Mrs. Hall and Sarah and his arrival in Harlem engulfed his thoughts.

Shirley was enjoying added success with her restaurant business. From that, and her investments with Jay, Shirley purchased the building next door and added a room for private parties. Jay was going to have his graduation party in this new room.

Deep into the thoughts of the past few years, Jay did not hear Clayton speak to him until he said hello the second time.

"Jay, you okay?"

"Yes, I'm fine, I was just thinking." Jay responded.

"Thinking about what?"

"Oh nothing in particular, just when I first came here."

"Well, you've done well for yourself Jay, and quite frankly, well for me."

"I have?"

"Of course. Some of the success I've attained can be attributed to you. So I want to repay you somewhat."

Jay thought to himself, wow, a raise. That's great.

Clayton continued. "By the way, I got your invitation and I'll be there. I'm also bringing my wife; she has heard me talk about the food at Shirley's so she will be with me."

"That's great." Jay said.

"What are your plans after graduation?" Clayton asked.

"Oh, I'm just going to relax. It has not been easy the past few years but I promised my mother that I would get my degree, and now I'll have it and she'll be happy."

"That's one of the things I wanted to talk you about." Clayton said.

"Oh."

"Yea Jay. You know I'm in line for CEO. One of the things I intend to do is recommend, no not recommend, I intend to make you an officer of the firm; Vice President."

"Really?"

"Yes, really."

"That's just great. I mean that's wonderful." Jay said; his voice full of glee.

While Jay was overjoyed to hear this, he also heard something else in Clayton's voice.

"I don't anticipate any problems, but I've always tried to be one step ahead in my dealings with the powers to be." Clayton said.

Here it is Jay said in his mind.

"So what is that step?" Jay asked.

"Well your performance has been exemplary, your production unparallel, your abilities unquestioned and, everyone loves you."

"Thanks Mr. Clayton. It means a lot to me to hear you say that."

"I believe I told you the first time I met you to call me Bob."

"That you did."

Clayton glanced at the scenic view from his office window at a passing cruise ship then he continued.

"What I would like to see, so that there is no question of the appointment, is you getting a MBA. Most of our officers have or are working on their MBA. What do you think?"

More schooling was the last thing on Jay's mind. He didn't see why having a master's degree meant any more in light of his accomplishments. He will not learn any more about options in school. He knew enough about all the other products the firm offered. He was delighted about the prospect of being an officer, but he was not warm to the idea of more college; he had to be delicate in this response.

"To tell you the absolute truth Bob, I didn't think about a masters. I want to spend more time getting the options product out there. There is talk of an options exchange for standardized options. I've got to be on top of that and I've got to get out to the new branches and bring them up to speed, and I just don't see the time for school right now."

Clayton replied, "I understand that. Tell you what I think. You can't do all these things by yourself. Get an assistant. Make him you. You can go to school two nights a week and on Saturday mornings. I've heard that options exchange talk, but that's some time away. We are going to beef up our investment banking and I want you there. Your talent in the front of people will add to your success. I really think this is important Jay. I'm also talking about you making history. You can become the first Black officer in a Wall Street firm. Think what that will mean."

Jay let the words spoken by Clayton sink in. The first Black officer. He is Mr. most likely to succeed, how could he not do what Clayton is asking.

"Okay Bob. I'll get on it right away."

"Good. I have some contacts at NYU. There is a good chance that you will take most classes at the downtown center next to the Amex. You can walk there after work."

"What about Columbia." Jay asked.

"Columbia is fine. We can do that too. You investigate and make the choice. We'll reimburse the tuition."

Clayton walked Jay to the door and one of the lawyers of the firm was waiting to see him next. Clayton introduced Jay to Morris Levy. Levy, it seems, did all of the personal work for the officers of the firm such as preparing wills, trust funds and other legal matters for a fee smaller than they would pay otherwise.

Clayton told Jay that Levy could handle any matters for him if he had such a need and it would not be disclosed to anyone in the firm. Jay and Levy promised to have lunch one day soon.

Jay retreated to his office to contemplate this new phase in his life. He has been looking forward to some time for his personal life and school was not to be a part of it. As he sat at his desk, he thought this might be a natural order; a master's degree. Wouldn't that be impressive. His mother would surely be very pleased. While he had done very well thus far and had completed college only to please his mother, now he had to continue to please his boss. A couple more years won't be so bad, he thought.

He picked up the phone to call his mother. He was going to see her in a few days but this news could not wait. Then he called Barbara.

Jay had invited Barbara to his graduation party, but she is hesitant about coming. He assured her that it was important to him that she is there. Their relationship has been ongoing for over four years now and she still did not want nor asked more of him.

Jay's mother asked him if she was going to meet his girlfriend at the party. He told her that she would meet several of his girlfriends at the party but there was no one particular girl in his life; he didn't have time for a personal or serious relationship he explained to her. Diane also told Jay during one of their recent conversation that she wanted to be a grandmother and that she was looking forward to him getting married.

She also told him that Harriet, now a Hampton graduate was home and teaching in North Charleston. And that she looked so pretty. For the first time, Diane was hinting to her son that Harriet would make him a good wife.

Diane also asked him about Ruby. He thought about the times he had spent with Ruby when he flew down to Orangeburg, SC. to visit her at State College. The pretty young high school virgin now in her last year of college still excited him.

Jay only smiled inside. He knew more about Harriet than his mother did. He found his mother's wish for grandchildren curious. That made him think. Why is it that with all his affairs with women, counting Harriet, Gwen, Sarah, Barbara, Ruby, the quickie with Sharon, and a few others, that no one turned up pregnant. He had never used a prophylactic; didn't even know how to put one on. This made him think was it luck or was he sterile?

Marriage was the last thing on Jay's mind. What he would like to do is introduce Barbara to his mother as his girlfriend. He felt closer to Barbara than anybody else, but he knew he could not do that. His mother would think that he had lost his mind. Diane and Barbara were nearly the same age.

Jay never forgets that it was Barbara who made his big splash on Wall Street possible. He continued to give her gifts whenever he saw something that he felt she would like. He took her out to dinner or Broadway shows often.

Once, when he was in Boston to conduct an options seminar, he stayed the weekend and had Barbara fly there to stay with him. They had a grand time sightseeing and feasting on the seafood of New England. And of course, the lovemaking.

At this point in the relationship, Barbara did not care what people thought about she and Jay. She even gave Jay a key to her apartment to use whenever he chooses. She no longer cared what her daughter Cheryl would think. She was in hopelessly in love and she was quite sure that Jay loved her too.

Jay never used the key. He would always call before going to see her. He preferred that Barbara come to his apartment. He was more relaxed there. She likewise would never come to his apartment without calling first. This affair had been more than Barbara hoped it would be. Jay treated her extremely well and she had more than twenty thousand dollars in a savings account.

She never told him about the abortion she had several months ago. All she told Jay is that she had a female problem and was under doctor treatment. He did not know that she aborted his son.

CHAPTER 40

Shirley and Merle wanted Jay's party to be the best affair that the new party room would stage. They planned a buffet of the favorite foods from the everyday menu. The invited guest would be dining on fried chicken, roasted chicken, pot roast, fried smothered pork chops, baked meat loaf, rice with gravy and all her sumptuous vegetables. There will also be peach cobbler, apple pie and strawberry short cake for desert.

Making the food self-serving allowed the restaurant employees such as Sarah, JC and Merle to enjoy the party and not be concerned with service. Merle also arranged to have music for dancing.

On the day before the graduation, Jay met his mother at LaGuardia Airport. She was still uneasy from her first flight. He had seen her often enough; never missing the holiday seasons. And once, he flew home on her birthday to surprise her. Yet he thought, he had never seen her looking so stunning.

"Well hello Ms. Diane Austin. You look great." Jay said to his smiling mother.

"I don't feel great. I'm so happy to be on the ground. Boy, why did you want me to fly by myself? You know how nervous I am."

Jay laughed. "I knew you would be all right. You didn't like it?"

"I was okay until we hit some, some air pockets they said. Then I got scared."

"Oh that happens all the time. That's nothing." Jay said.

"Listen to the expert. You fly all the time now. You're used to it. But I nearly lost the food we ate."

Jay laughed again. "Well let me get you home, I guess you're not hungry."

"No. I don't want anything now. But I'll be fine soon. Let me look at you, my college graduate. If only mother was here to see you now."

"Yea I wish that too."

Jay helped his mother into his sunbeam for the drive to Manhattan. She had never ridden in a car so small and that was her first comment.

"So, this is the sports car you told me about."

"Yea. You like it? Wanna drive it?"

"Jay, as wrecked as I am from that flight, I'll wreck this car. Besides, I can't drive a standard"

"It's automatic mom."

"Well, I still don't want to drive.

"It's a convertible mom and it has a hard top that I leave in the basement of my building. Want me to let this top down?"

"No Jay, my hair will be all over the place and I'll look like a witch tomorrow."

"You'll be beautiful mom, just like you were at my high school graduation."

Jay pulled the sunbeam into the early evening traffic of the Grand Central Parkway heading to Manhattan.

"I'm going to take you all over New York; show you this city and then down to Wall Street where I work. You'll ride the subway; see a show at the Apollo, the Empire State building, there is so much. I'm so happy you're here. My graduation party is tomorrow night at Shirley's. You'll see Sarah and you'll meet the people I worked with when I first came here. I still want you to move here. I think you will like my apartment; maybe we can buy a house. You can sell your house. How about that?"

Diane sensed the excitement in her son and could only smile, as he talked non-stop.

Jay thought to himself, I must sound like Sarah. I'm running off at the mouth. It was hard not to be excited with all that was happening in his life. He wanted his mother to see and feel his enthusiasm.

Diane was looking for a moment to mention that she recently got engaged and will get married soon. There was no way she would move to New York now. She felt that Jay appears to have his life in order. The dreams she had of his success are very visible. And now his job is going to pay the tuition for him getting a master degree. All the years she devoted to him and the care of her mother were now behind her. Now she was going to put her life in order. She was tired of the loneliness. She decided to wait and tell him after his celebration.

"So, what's happening in Charleston? How are things at your new shop?" Jay asked.

"Not much honey, the shops are going okay. The work is hard and long but I'm making a decent living."

"That's' good mom, but I still say you could do so much better here."

As Diane watched the skyline of New York appear as they cross the Triborough Bridge, in her mind, the life that she had always longed for was in back in Charleston.

The weather was perfect for the graduation ceremony. Jay was expecting everyone from the Harlem office to come. He knew Gwen would be there. So would Milton and maybe Sharon if she has gotten over the many times he had broken dates with her. Barbara promised that she would be there, and his mother would arrive with Sarah and Shirley. His Wall Street buddies would be at the party later.

After the ceremony, Jay met all his people to pose for picture taking. Another gesture provided by Shirley. She hired a photographer for the occasion. Shirley told Diane that she was very proud of Jay and that she loved him like a son.

Jay reveled in the moment and posed with everyone. Gwen quietly insisted on a picture of just she and Jay. He obliged her. He looked around for Barbara but she was nowhere in sight. She quickly left after the ceremony was over. He wondered if he would see her later. For a moment, Jay's mind returned to his high school graduation when he looked for his teacher Ms. Mack. That was the last time he saw her.

A tap on his shoulder interrupted his thoughts. He turned and got a passionate hug from Sharon.

He whispered, "I'm glad you came."

"Are you really?" she asked.

"Yes I am. Are you coming to the party?"

"I'm not sure. I don't want to piss Gwen off. I do have a gift for you but you have to come and get it. I didn't bring it with me."

"Please come, I want you there."

"May be I'll come for a little while." She replied

Sharon had surprised Jay. He learned that she was not the shy quiet person he met in the Harlem office. In fact, it was in the Harlem office late one night that he received that revelation.

They planned to meet and discuss the accounts that he had turned over to her management. No one else was there and as soon as he walked in, she threw her arms around him and proceeded to kiss him all over his face. Each time he tried to talk, her lips found his. He decided to just be cool and let her take charge. When her tongue and hands began to make him breathe the way she was breathing, they made a mad rush to pleasure; right on the floor of the office. It was a quickie that he would never forget. He promised her that the next time it would be different. He just never found the time.

Shirley was anxious to get to the party back at the restaurant. She announced that one last picture would be taken, and then everyone should be on his or her way to the restaurant. Only one person could ride with Jay and Gwen made sure it was she. Diane, Sarah, Shirley and JC rode together in Shirley's car.

Jay and Gwen arrived just as Clayton and his wife were getting out of their chauffeured limo.

Gwen wanted to ride with Jay for two reasons; one, to send a signal to all at the ceremony that she and Jay were close, and to voice her jealously over Sharon. She asked him had he slept with Sharon and how well did he know Barbara. The ride to the party was not pleasant and Jay began to act indifferent to her.

He scolded her. Then told her that she had no right to ask him such questions. He made it clear that whatever happened between them when they worked together was nothing more than two people enjoying moments of lust. He had moved on with his life and told her to do the same thing. Then he toned it down and told her that he will always cherish their friendship, but do not expect more from him.

Seeing Clayton and his wife caused the conversation to change. Clayton greeted them and introduced his wife Joan.

Joan, tall and blond came from a wealthy family in Virginia. She is a graduate of an all women college in the northeast. This was her very first trip to Harlem and she was taking in the street scene. The few minutes they spent chatting on Lenox avenue and 127th Street, Joan saw perhaps more Black people that she had seen her entire life on this Saturday afternoon.

"I'm sorry we didn't make the ceremony, but I was not going to miss your party." Clayton said. "And, as I told you, I wanted Joan to taste Shirley's food."

"That's the most important reason to be here, not me but the food." Jay said.

"I understand you worked here before you joined the firm?" Joan asked Jay.

"Yes." Jay replied. "Until Gwen talked me into the business. In fact, she, more than anyone else is responsible for my being on Wall Street. She was my first trainer and I'll always be grateful to her.

Jay saw this as a way to soothe Gwen's feelings that he had just stepped on in the car. He took Gwen's hand and looked into her eyes as he replied to Joan. He could see the hurt somewhat ease.

"Well I'm starving. Let's get inside and eat." Clayton said.

The private dining room could be entered from the front door of the building next door or through the main dinning room. Merle supervised the construction and decoration so the room reflected her good taste. The lighting was subdued. The walls were painted a light peach and the wood grain floor stained and highly polished. There were five rows of ten seat round tables. The tables here were arranged to be more intimate.

"It is a party room." Merle's replied when someone asked her why the tables were so close together. Merle reasoned that it should not be like the dining room where there was more space between dinners. The room had space for more, but Jay's party was planned for only forty people. The rear area of the floor was covered with linoleum tile for dancing.

The buffet table, more than forty feet long, greeted the guest with the captivating aroma of Shirley's menu. The music of Ray Charles was blearing from the sound system but no one was eating or dancing yet. The thirty or so guests were waiting for the arrival of the graduate.

As Jay entered the room, he immediately saw Merle, his mother, Shirley, and Sarah sitting at a table. Then he saw Sye and several of Shirley's employees who he worked with. There was Milton, Sharon, and Reverend and Mrs. Michaels, pastor of the Brooklyn church that led to the idea and entrée to the church investment seminar program.

He saw his Wall Street friends, Joe, Richard, Bernard, Donald Washington, Don Tyler, Bill, and Ralph. Some were alone, and some brought their girl of the day. Now the party would start, and the buffet table would be attacked.

While the music of Motown artists were playing, Jay's friends ate, danced, and drank to the success of one destined most likely to succeed.

The Hamill employees sat together, but Clayton and Joan did not see the arrows that Gwen and Sharon were slinging at each other. Joan made several trips to the buffet and her only conversation seems to be just the non-words, uhmm, uhmm, uhmm.

In between plates, Milton and Clayton talked business. Milton, as usual was impeccably dressed. He was dressed in a simple but expensive blue blazer, white shirt with button down collar, no tie, gray slacks and oxblood penny loafers. All of Milton's dressed shirts are custom made with no pocket and his initials monogrammed on the right front breast area. Jay, always an admirer of the way Milton dressed, asked Milton who made his shirts. Now all of his are custom made; including his initials JAA monogrammed in the same area.

Jay moved to sit at the table with his mother, Sarah and Shirley. There were a few people dancing now including Sye and Merle.

Shirley said, "Jay you and your mother could pass for sister and brother."

"Why what a nice compliment Shirley. You are so nice just as Jay said you are. Thank you so much." Diane said.

"Everyone has been very nice to me mom. Sarah, Merle, everybody. I can't thank you enough for this party Mrs. Shirley. You know I love you."

"Don't mention it Jay. You deserve it with all that you have done for me. Your mother says you are gonna get a master?"

"Yes ma'am. I'm waiting to hear from Columbia."

"That's just great Jay. What do you plan to do after that?

Just then, JC came to the table with a plate of peach cobbler in hand.

"Well I want JC's job. I wanna cook the way he cooked today." Jay replied.

JC had a confused look on his face. "What?" He said.

While laughing, Shirley said, "Jay wants your job."

"Sure young blood; you come on back to my kitchen. I teach you everything."

JC turned to Diane and said, "I liked this boy the first day I meet him."

Jay turned to Shirley and said, "I honestly don't plan to do any more than I'm doing right now. I love what I do but my boss said I should I get a master, so I will."

"Well, he must have a reason for suggesting that so you do what he says." Shirley replied.

Sarah was very quiet at the table. Her mind was on the first year that Jay lived with her. She looked at Jay and thought to herself, how handsome he looked. She wanted to scream out, I know him better than anybody here. ' He wus my lover. Ah still loves him.'

Jay saw the look on her face and said, "Come on Sarah, dance with me."

"No." Sarah protested. "I don't dance. Yur momma wus a good dancer in school; dance wit hur."

"All right. C'mon mom. Show me the stuff y'all did in the forties."

Diane said, "I can do what they do in the sixties too c'mon."

Mother and son joined others on the dance floor and all eyes were on them. Diane indeed, was a good dancer. Jay was too cool to be good. But he was adequate. He wished he could dance like Donald Washington or Joe, but he didn't work at it.

Diane said to Jay as they danced to Smokey Robinson and the Miracles singing 'Tears of a clown, "When am I going to dance at your wedding Jay?"

"I don't know mom. No time soon. I can tell you that."

"Would you come home and dance at mine?"

"What do you mean?"

"I'm engaged sweetie. I'm gonna get married."

"You are? Why didn't you tell me?"

"I wanted to wait until after today."

The news stunned Jay momentarily. They continued to dance. Then he stopped, hugged her, and said, "That's great mom. I'm really happy for you. Who is he? Is he nice? Will I like him?"

Diane smiled. She looked into her son's eyes and said, "He is very nice Jay, and you will like him. I'll tell you all about it when we get home tonight. Okay?"

Back at the table, Jay said to Shirley, "I want you, and you too mom to meet my boss and his wife. She just loves the food."

"Well, we'll fix her a big doggie bag."

Jay proceeded to introduce his mother first to Clayton and Joan. When he started to introduce Shirley, Clayton, said, "I met you a couple years ago when we had our regional meeting here. My people still talk about it."

"Oh yes I remember. Thank you sir. I appreciate that. Y'all must come back. We have this big room for you now."

"I promise you we will." Clayton said."

Joan said, "If you are coming here. I'm coming too. Just for lunch. Mrs. Shirley, I've never had such good fried chicken. And the dressing, the collard greens, and, the corn, the peach cobbler. My oh my; I just stuffed my self."

"Why thank you Mrs. Clayton. We'll fix you something to take with you."

The party guests were all stuffed and feeling good. The feel good that makes you sleepy after a terrific meal. It was near eight o'clock and Harlem was just waking up for its nightlife. Clayton's chauffeur was outside waiting for him, and Jay's Wall Street buddies were planning the rest of their evening. Jay suggested that they would *really* have a great time if they all went to Sye's apartment afterward. Sye, Jay said would be a great host. His buddies understood what he meant.

Sye was very gracious and extended the invitation. Jay, naturally, could not join them.

The main restaurant was starting to get busy with the dinner crowd and Merle and JC had to go to work. Jay and Diane were going to

Sarah's apartment and just visit with her for a little while. Then Mother and son would spend the rest of her stay in New York together just the two of them.

First Gwen then Sharon hugged and said goodbye to Jay. He whispered something to each.

Just before leaving, Merle said to Jay, Remember Mrs. Hall's granddaughter Joyce?"

"Yes I do. How is she?"

"She's fine. She graduated last year. She is a social worker in the Bronx and hates it."

Jay did not hear any news about Grace nor Joyce. Since he had turned over management of their investment account to Gwen, he had not been in touch with them. He was sure the account was doing well because the market was doing very well.

"Is she living in her grandmother's house?" Jay asked.

"Yes she is." Merle replied. "I see her all the time. I told her that when I saw you, I would talk to you about a job. She wants to get away from what she is doing."

"Oh sure; here give her my card and tell her to call me."

CHAPTER 41

Diane decided to return to Charleston on Thursday rather than Sunday as originally planned. She was really enjoying New York and all it's glitter and grandeur. Jay had taken her everywhere just as he promised. Diane saw a Broadway production for the first time. She went to the top of the Empire State Building, visited the stature of liberty, went shopping on Fifth Avenue and had lunch at a chic restaurant in Central Park. As much as she enjoyed being with Jay and as much as she appreciated his attention, she missed her lover back in Charleston. She wanted to go home.

Jay did all he could think of to make his mother feel good. He didn't go to work the week that she was in New York because he didn't want to leave her alone. Now that she was gone, he will do what's been on his mind since the graduation party. That was to see and spend time with Barbara.

He decided to do something different. Thursday evening after seeing Diane off, he went to the local delicatessen in his neighborhood and ordered several sandwiches and other snacks to go. He packed a small bag, drove to Barbara's apartment and told her to pack a bag. He was taking her upstate New York and spend the weekend in any small town to their liking. As always, Barbara was overwhelmed by Jay kindness and thoughtfulness. She had been very lonely the past week but as was her nature, she would not call Jay to complain. This weekend with Jay would take the gloom away and bring back the radiance in her life.

On Monday morning, Jay was happy to be back to work. The time with his mother and weekend with Barbara was gratifying but he missed the Street.

Jay did not have nor wanted a personal secretary. All telephone calls for him when he is away, went to the options department where Karen, a young White girl who handled all clerical duties, took the messages. She gave him a stack of pink note sheets. This says he got a lot of calls while he was out. He flipped through them and the only one that caught his eye was a call from Joyce Freeman. This was Mrs. Hall's granddaughter. She had called on Monday morning a week earlier.

The message slip had two numbers. Jay called the first one and it was her work number at the South Bronx social services office where she worked. The impatient female who answered the call only took the time to say that Miss Freeman was not there. She did not offer to take a message. The second number Jay assumed to be her home number. He decided he would call that number before he leaves his office that evening.

In the meantime, there was much to be done. He had more calls to make but first, he took a quick trip to Clayton's office. He wanted to thank him for coming to the party and to inquire about Joan and her impression of Harlem.

For the next hour, Jay made calls to Shirley and Merle; also Gwen, Milton, Sharon, and his buddies Don Tyler and Joe. All commented on the party and the great time they had.

Joe especially complemented Sye. Sye had been quite a host to them in his special way; which included his music and the contents of the cigar box.

Gwen asked him to call her at home that night. She said she had a client on the phone, but it was important that she speak to him.

Merle asked had he heard from Joyce. Jay told her that he received a message that Joyce left for him and he expects to talk to her soon. Merle also said, "I saw Barbara at the graduation, why didn't she come to the party?"

Cool in his reply, Jay said, "I don't know. She left before I had a chance to talk to her."

Finally, Jay called Sarah. She was not at the restaurant when he called there. He just wanted to assure her that their secret is still a secret and that she will always have a place in his heart. She melted right there on the phone.

Personal stuff over, it was time to get to work. Jay had to prepare his weekly options newsletter and his suggested call and put play for the week. He went to the order room to see what was going on.

The options department now had three traders and two clerical people who were responsible for processing the transactions. Looking over the busy options staff that is all White, and over the huge order room, Jay saw only three Black faces.

The options staff reported to the order room supervisor but in fact, the options department is Jay's department. He felt that now it might be the time for him to see if he had any influence. The options product is going to grow in importance he realizes, the staff will need to be increased. At least two more traders will be needed; one of them he wants to be a Black man.

Still on a high from his conversation with Clayton about his future, the party and the weekend with Barbara, Jay was feeling extremely good and with that feeling, came a sense of power. He planned to test it.

It was nearly seven o'clock when Jay left his office for home. He had completed his newsletter and left it for Karen to type and disseminate throughout the firm in the morning. He stopped at the deli on Columbus Avenue to get another sandwich like the one he had with Barbara last weekend. This was going to be his dinner.

After his quick meal, Jay called Gwen. They exchanged cordial greetings but Jay detected a melancholic mood in her voice.

And then she began. "Jay, I'm sorry for what I said to you last week. I was wrong and I just wanted to apologize to you."

"Not necessary." Jay said.

"No Jay. You win sweetheart. I must tell you; I was really feeling jealous about you graduating and you started school after me and...."

"Well, I went year round Gwen. That was hard. You'll finish next semester right?"

"It's more than that Jay. I thought about how successful you are now and you are gonna get your MBA and well...I don't know. I just felt left behind. I mean, you started the job after me, you started school after me and now you're so far ahead of me."

"Is that what's bothering you Gwen?"

"I know that I've done well as a woman. As a Black woman, I've done extremely well. My production has been great, and it's gonna get better. But I'm not happy."

"Gwen, what is happiness? You are all of twenty-six. Can you define happiness? You have entered a world that we both know is reserved for White men. And you decided that you could survive in it. Even your family doubted that you could. Doesn't succeeding bring some measure of happiness?"

"But you were there with me everyday Jay, and when you left to go downtown, I lost some of my desire. I didn't see you in school anymore, and I only saw you briefly other wise." I've tried to get you out of my mind; you know, see other men. And when I tell them what I do, they get stupid. My preacher friend in Atlanta asked me to marry him and move back to Atlanta. I turned him down flat." After a few moments of silence, Jay replied, "I don't know what to say Gwen."

"You asked me what is happiness? My happiness would be if I had you in my life Jay. "But now I realize that won't happen."

"Remember the first time we were together? And you asked me what will happen next? I said we didn't know the answer to that but we should let things take it's own course. Well, I think it has Gwen. When I said to Clayton's wife that I owe my career to you, I meant that sincerely. So you will always be in my life you will always be a part of my life."

"Thanks for saying that Jay. Milton said you had the gift; if only he knew. Bye sweetheart."

Jay hung up and said to himself, 'What was that all about?' After a few minutes to reflect on Gwen's conversation, he called Joyce.

The noted change in this female from the previous was startling. She was in a good mood and her voice reflected it.

"I was beginning to think that I wasn't going to hear from you." Joyce said.

"I'm sorry, I was out of the office all last week. I just got your message today. I tried to call you at your job this morning."

"You did? I didn't get the message. But that's how things are there. I was probably out in the field." How have you been?"

"Just fine Joyce and you?"

"Oh, not bad, but I've been better."

"And your mother?"

"She is doing great. She is on the road with the Hello Dolly show. I think she's in Chicago the rest to this week."

"Merle said you're living in your grandmother's house."

"Yes, me and my mom now live here."

Jay wanted to ask her if she was there by herself now but stopped short of asking her.

"Merle told me you were having your graduation party in the restaurant."

"Yes, why didn't you come?"

"She told me too but I didn't want to come uninvited by the host."

"Joyce, I won't hold it against you, but that reason is very disappointing to me. I'm sure you know, that Merle knows, that I would have loved to had have you there."

Jay immediately knew that what he just said was confusing to her and that was because he was feeling a little nervous. He imagined the brown eye beauty with a curious look on her face.

"Merle also told me that you graduated last year?" Jay said.

"Yes. Thank God. I thought I was going to change the world but the world is changing me. I understand you are Mr. Wall Street now."

Jay laughed. "Well I wouldn't say that. But I do like what I do."

"I wish I could say that. In fact I'm very unhappy. That's why Merle suggested that I talk to you."

"Well what can I do for you?"

"I would like to know about your business, I want to explore what you do to see if I can do something meaningful. You help people, right?"

"Yes I do. I'm still a registered broker but I don't actively sell. My job now is to promote this one particular product that potentially help people realize their financial goals. Do you think something like that would interest you?"

"That's what I wanted to find out. I know that our account with your firm has done very well. Mom has said over and over again that what you did has been very impressive."

"Thank you. Tell you what. Are you busy tomorrow? Can you get away for lunch?"

"What time?"

"Whenever you can. You can also make it after work if you want to."

Jay wondered for a moment if he sounded too anxious. He remembered how very pretty Joyce is and the sudden urge he got the first time he saw her at Linda's wake.

"I Think dinner is better. Do you like Cuban food?" Joyce asked.

"Well I don't think I've ever had any, but I do love rice and beans."

"Then you'll love this place. Its called Victors. It's right on the coroner of Broadway and   Seventy –Second. How about seven tomorrow?"

"Great I'll see you then."

After watching the Knicks on television, Jay went to bed where he replayed the entire conversation with Gwen and Joyce. He still did not know what to make of Gwen's rambling, but Joyce's was intriguing.

At work the next day, Jay kept watching the set of clocks in the order room with his eye keenly on the one that showed Eastern Time. This was silly, he thought after doing it several times. Surely the time on that clock was not going to move faster than the time on his expensive wristwatch. Finally, he left work at five- o'clock so he would have time to shower and change. He was going to wear the new blue blazer he purchased when he and his mother went shopping at Bloomingdale's. He was going to have the elegant casual look that Milton had at his party.

Parking would be a problem Jay thought so he decided to take a taxi. The restaurant was only a few blocks from his apartment building and he could have walked. But if he did, he would have arrived sweated, and he didn't want that. A family curse his mother once told him. The Austins sweat quite easily. It was warm out and he could have done without the jacket, but that would not give him the look he wanted. He must look relaxed and casual but professional.

He heard the roar of a subway train arriving in the station below. It stopped, and then started up again leaving the 72nd street station. In the middle of the exiting horde, he saw Joyce walking up the stairs like a queen going to her coronation.

Jay felt perspiration rise on his forehead. He reached into his back pocket to retrieve his ever-present handkerchief to dab the beads away. His immediate thought was she is more gorgeous than he remembered. She had darkened her naturally curly hair and let it grow out so it reached her shoulders. She wore a simple black skirt, knee length and a light gray blouse.

She smiled as she saw him from the short distance and a poem Jay once read in high school came to his mind. *She walks in beauty.*

Her smile grew wider as she got closer; then she extended her hand. Jay took her hand. He suddenly realized that his palm was wet from perspiration and he could not shake with the firm, vigorous grip as he always does. He was embarrassed to shake with his limp wet rag of a hand. You are losing it he thought.

"You're right on time I see." Joyce said.

"I was not going to keep you waiting. Besides, I live near here."

"You do? Where?"

"Over on Columbus." Jay felt dryness in his mouth. This doesn't happen to him but he can't help it.

"Well that's a coincidence. I didn't know that."

Jay wondered if that was indeed true. Merle could have told her where he lived.

Then she said, "You look very nice, I love that jacket; very Wall Street."

"You look very nice also." Jay replied as he brushed his moist hand against his blazer.

"If you have another restaurant in this area that you like, we can go there instead."

"Oh no. I've been looking forward to something different. This'll be fine. Let's go in."

They were ushered to a booth and Jay found his handkerchief again for another dab at his forehead.

He asks, "You've been here before?"

"Yes. Many times. I come with my mom. She and her actor friends hang out here. And the food is good. You like sangria"

"Yea, I like it." Jay had no idea what that was.

"Okay we'll get a pitcher. And of course, rice and beans."

"Okay that's fine with me."

Jay ordered chicken and Joyce ordered beef with the plan to share each other's dish. When the waiter brought the pitcher of red wine with ice and orange slices, Jay was surprised but he did not show it. This must be the sangria he assumed. Not being much of a drinker, this was going to be a test for him.

The waiter poured two large glasses and Joyce said, "Here's to perhaps a new beginning for me." She took a small sip then another. Jay followed. The smooth grape flavored wine tasted good to him and right away, he liked it.

Before their food arrived, they had both drank a full glass of the wine and was on the second. Joyce was relaxed and telling Jay about her job and how much she disliked it.

Jay was wondering why his tongue was feeling thick and loose. And the more he drank the iced wine, the more he sweated. But he didn't care. He stared into the eyes of this lovely person across the table from him listening to her talk and he was totally captivated.

The meal came and after sharing each other's plates, they ate and Joyce asked Jay if he was pleased. Assuring her that he was indeed pleased, Jay indicted that his plate was empty and so was his wine glass.

By now, Jay was feeling quite good. The wine had given him courage and he no longer visibly perspired, but there was still some anxiety in his mannerism.

Joyce finally asked Jay to tell her about his work. The wine induced intrepidity and having complete confidence in his knowledge of options, Jay talked endlessly about what he does on Wall Street. The words flowed on an on. Mr. Most Likely to Succeed, after all, does have the gift to gab.

He could see that she was impressed because she looked directly at him engrossed in his every word. Then she said, "Wow, you really love what you do and it sounds so fascinating."

"It is fascinating and as I said before, I do enjoy what I do."

"Well I've made up my mind. Can you help me?"

"Are you asking for a job?"

"Yes I am."

With a triumphant look on his face, Jay asked, "When do you want to start?"

"You can really hire me?"

"When do you want to start?"

"Well, I must give notice at the agency but I guess...in two weeks?"

"Come down to my office as soon as you can and fill out some paper work."

"Okay. I'll come down on Thursday." Joyce replied.

Jay had no concerns about making this commitment to Joyce. He was sure that Clayton or anyone else at Hamill would not object to him bringing someone into his department. In fact, he thought, tomorrow morning he will talk to Clayton about moving the option department out of the order room and into a separate room totally under his control.

The waiter brought the check and Joyce took it right away. She was not going to let him pay for dinner. Jay insisted but Joyce persisted and prevailed.

It was somewhat cooler outside and Broadway had the usual busy New Yorkers doing their thing. Jay hailed a taxi for Joyce and told her that he would be expecting her in two days.

He decided to walk home and let the cool air clear his head. The wine and Joyce had filled him with exuberance.

CHAPTER 42

Edward Hall Jr. returned to his cell at the Peekskill, N.Y. prison after his second parole hearing. He didn't have a good feeling about his chances for an early release, but that's always the way it is. The parole board members never give any indication which way they might vote.

After Ed was denied the first time, he was in a state of depression that lasted for over six months. This time he was not going to live on hope only to be turned down, so he conditioned his mind for whatever happens.

The one thing that had made the last six years somewhat bearable was the little money Grace his sister had put into his bank at the prison commissary. With money, he was able to sustain some friendship and power behind bars. He could buy cigarettes and other goods to use as barter for what others could provide for him. The few times Grace and his niece Joyce came to see him encouraged him to work hard on his release. So the for the last few years, he has been a model prisoner. He attended drug counseling. He completed his college degree through a correspondence program. He took part in a program to inform young men about life behind bars. It was designed to scare at risk teenagers into a life style away from crime. Ed taught fellow inmates how to read and write. He also acted as a mediator and settled disputes between the different ethnic groups behind the walls. All the inmates trusted him.

Ed's actions did not go unnoticed by the prison officials. So, even the warden was pulling for Ed to get the early release. Yes, in his mind, Ed paid his debt to society. There was no way he would ever come back to a place like Peekskill.

He also has some money waiting for him when he is released. Some time ago, Grace told him about the life insurance proceeds from the death of their mother Linda Hall. Grace invested Ed's portion for him. The thirty-one thousand dollars that was his share is now worth close to forty-five thousand.

Unlike most ex-convicts, Ed won't come out of prison with problems like no job and no money. These are the conditions that often times led them right back.

There was one thing that bothered Ed but he never mentioned it to Grace. In all her visits and letters, she has never mentioned the Treasury bond that their father told him about. That was another hundred thousand. Maybe, he thought, she is saving that as a surprise for him when he comes home. Ed decided that he would not make it an issue now. He has nothing but time on his hands. The most important thing now is to first get out, and that could be just months away.

It was just after 11p.m. when Grace got to her Chicago hotel room after that day's performance. She knew that it would be midnight in New York but she wanted to call Joyce. She was happy to be with the traveling production but didn't like that she would be away from home for three months. She and Joyce were having a great mother daughter relationship, and this was very important to her at this stage of her life.

It was Joyce who convinced her to take the part and Grace was finding the experience both rewarding and enjoyable. Even thought late, Grace wanted to call just to say hello.

Joyce was not asleep when the phone rang. In fact, she was hoping her mother would call so she could tell her about her new job with Jay Austin.

On the first ring, Joyce answered, "Hi mom."

"How did you know it was me?"

"No one else calls me. Especially at this hour." Joyce replied.

"How you doing sweetheart?"

"Just fine. How is Chicago?"

"Good. All shows are sold out, great audiences. But you know how hotel beds are, so I'm not sleeping that well yet. We're in Detroit next week then I'll be home for a couple days before Boston."

"I've got good news mom." Joyce said.

"What is it?"

"I've got a new job."

"You do, where?"

"On Wall Street"

"Wall Street, that's great. Doing what?"

"I'm gonna work with that guy Jay, remember him?"

"I sure do. He is very cute and you like him. How did you manage that?"

"I met him yesterday. We had dinner at Victor's and he offered me the job."

"Well how about that. That *is* good news. Anything else going on between you two?"

"No mom. He is all business."

"Hmm, that's for now. I got a feeling he likes you too."

"I don't know mom. He probably has a lot of women."

"But none as good looking as you. How much will you be making if you don't mind my asking."

"You know, we didn't even discuss that. That really just didn't matter. I'm sure it will be decent."

"Yes, you *are* a college graduate." Grace said.

"Oh mom. I just wanted to get away from what I was doing. That job was killing me."

"Well, I'm happy for you sweetie. Tell me all about it when I get home. I'm going to bed now I'm tired. Bye."

"Okay. Oh, by the way. Uncle Ed wrote. He had a parole hearing. No word yet though."

"I sure hope this one goes good for him."

"Yea, we'll see. Bye mom."

Grace got ready for bed. She was glad she called Joyce and was happy for her. Jay would be good for her she thought. Joyce is a good person and she deserves a good man. A grand marriage for Joyce danced in her head as she drifted off to sleep.

Jay went to see Clayton as soon as he got to work the next day. As he assumed, Clayton told him to hire whom ever he wanted. As for the separate room for the options department, Clayton told him it made sense, and he would make the arrangements.

Knowing that Joyce had no knowledge of the securities business, Jay arranged that she would first work in the listed stocks operations. She would learn how customer transactions to buy and sell stocks are executed then processed. After three weeks there, she worked in the mutual funds department, and then two weeks at bonds trading. Then Jay moved her into the options department. There she would stay. Joyce's first duties were to help the traders. She obtained quotes, which is the best possible price that Hamill customers might pay for orders to buy, or the best amount that they might receive to sell options. The quotes came from the options dealers. Jay reasoned that this would help her get familiar with the product and the dealers. His plan was to make Joyce a trader.

Joyce loved the job. She got along with everyone in the department and her personality made it easy for the traders to teach her. She didn't interact with Jay very much at work and she sensed that he wanted it that way. When she did see him in the order room, he would be without his jacket, very impressive, very much in control and very respected. She became even more attracted to him. After several weeks, Joyce's knowledge of the option department was evident and the traders now entrusted her with actual orders to execute. Jay was aware of this because John Riccardi was giving him daily updates on Joyce's progress. He invited her to have dinner with him at Victors after work that night.

Jay made it a point to keep the relationship with Joyce all business but he couldn't keep his mind off her. She totally unnerved him like no woman had in his young life. As hard as he tried to treat her like Gwen, it was useless. She was on his mind constantly.

At dinner, he was as fidgety as he was the first time he met her there. He let her order for the both of them while he was wolfing down the sangria. Joyce noticed his uneasiness and asked him if he was okay.

"I'm fine" he replied. "Just have a lot of things on my mind."

"Like what?" she asked. "You're not going to fire me are you?" she laughed.

"Fire you, I'm told that you are doing great. I knew you would."

"Well I'm glad to hear that. I love the job Jay. It really is fascinating just like you said."

"We'll be moving to our own room soon, and I'm going to be on the road a little; and then, I start grad school. I'm just thinking about all that."

The wine was starting to mellow Jay out a bit so he started to talk more.

"Bob, Mr. Clayton, thinks I should have an assistant and I have to find someone for that too. So I have a full plate for now."

Joyce was listening very attentively. Just then their order arrived.

"Well, you can start to empty the plate in front of you, it looks great." Joyce said.

"That is does." Jay replied after a long sigh.

They ate in silence for a few minutes then Jay said, "You know, when Merle told me you wanted a job, I immediately felt that... that you could work with me. Like, I mean, I knew you could do the job, but I didn't think.... that, ...that I would fall in love with you."

Jay did not plan to say that. It just came out and now he started to sweat all over again.

He took a sip of the wine.

Joyce stopped eating and with a look of disbelief on her face said, "What did you say?"

"I think you heard me Joyce."

"Jay, I didn't think that you even knew I existed. You never talk to me about anything other than options and, and you are always all business and now you say this to me."

"I didn't want to make a fool out of my self. And I just knew that you had somebody and..."

"Jay, sweetheart, sweetheart, didn't you know how I felt about you? Didn't you feel anything the past few weeks? Are you telling me that you didn't see the look on my face every time I was around you? And not just now, but also the very first time I saw you? Are you really saying that you couldn't tell?"

Jay too stopped eating. He looked at Joyce, sighed deeply, and then said, "Joyce, I couldn't see anything but your beautiful face, I saw it constantly. I saw it when I tried to sleep, I saw you when you were nowhere around me. And when you were around me, like at work, I was a wreck. I may have looked in control but I wasn't. I also thought that someone like you wouldn't have anything to do with me."

"I can't believe you Jay. I can't believe you said that. What do you mean someone like me? Did I come off to you as some kind of bourgeois Black girl? That I wasn't appreciative of what you've done for me? And, and that you took me from a situation that was making me depresses? I know I didn't. I'm hurt and surprise that you would say that."

"Please don't be hurt Joyce. See what you do to me. What I mean is someone like you …. don't happen to me."

Neither had an appetite for the chicken, with red beans and rice that sat before them getting cold. Joyce said, "Jay, it was I who fell for you, long ago. Whenever I saw you at work, I had to control myself. And when I would hear the ladies talk about you at work I tried hard not to show my jealousy."

He reached across the table and took Joyce's hand. He put her hand on his face and closed his eyes. Finally Jay said, "let's get out of here."

Joyce stood up almost immediately ready to go. The waiter came to the table with a concerned look on his face. "Is everything okay? You don't eat nothing." He said.

"Everything is fine Manuel. I think you can bring the check and maybe make this take out for us. Okay Jay?" Joyce said.

Jay seemed in a fog. He just stared at Joyce who stood over him with a big smile on her face. She was waiting for him to say something, or just get up to leave like he suggested.

Jay emptied the last of the sangria, and then stood up. He took money out of his pocket to pay the check then Joyce took his hand and nestled up against him. Jay didn't know if the wine suddenly drugged him or the touch of Joyce but his head was swinging.

Jay and Joyce stood on the sidewalk of Broadway and 72nd Street and watched the New York crowd pass them by. The noise of the city was loud as usual. Joyce asked him again if he was all right. Jay replied that he was but clearly he wasn't. She then asked where should they go. He replied, to his apartment.

She took his hand and said, "Let's walk. Looks like you need to clear your head."

His speech slurred, Jay said, "My head is very clear. I'll get a taxi."

"No, let's walk sweetie you don't live far right?"

"Five blocks, Seventy-Seven Street." Jay said.

"Then we can walk. Com'n, It is so nice out. Are you sure you're okay?"

"We're not married yet and already you're telling me what to do."

"I'm not... what did you say?"

Again words came out of Jay's mouth that he didn't plan to say. Joyce stopped walking and turned to him and said, "Jay you are acting kind of strange but it's very intriguing to me. Are you trying to tell me something?"

"I think I've already said it."

The two just stared into each other's eyes. Jay held the bag with the unfinished dinners. With his free hand, he pulled Joyce closed to him and said "Joyce you are truly adorable. you have taken my heart and I'm... I'm in love with you."

"Oh Jay, you can't imagined how I've wanted to be in your arms; to just be held by you. I have prayed that you would want me too."

At that moment, they saw no one else on the streets of New York. It was just the two of them alone and in love. So they kissed long and hard.

They walked faster now to get to Jay's apartment. There was a sense of urgency to consummate this new romance. As Jay closed and locked the door, Joyce was into his arms and they just held each other in a frantic grip. They released and began clutching at their clothes while moving to the bedroom.

This first time in bed together for Jay and Joyce was for the purpose of immediate release of repressed emotions. And to extinguish the rage that burned in the both of them. They both knew that the love making of exploration, passion, and patience would come in the future. But for this moment, they both just wanted the joy of being with and into each other.

CHAPTER 43

How to handle their relationship at work was the immediate concern of Jay and Joyce. It would not be a good idea if Clayton and all the options staff thought of them as lovers. Every move that Jay might consider to benefit Joyce would be suspect, and neither wanted that.

As they lay in bed tightly embraced and spent from the sex, Jay shared with Joyce his idea of her being his assistant. It was going to be awkward at best just working in the same department but being lover and assistant, would bring unwanted scrutiny.

So, they decided to show no evidence of their relationship at this time. In fact, Joyce dismissed Jay's idea of being his assistant. After careful thought, they both decided that it would be best if Joyce just learn all that she can from Jay and others in the department.

After some time, she should then move on to another firm. She would be a unique person in the world of stock options and her knowledge would position her for a supervisory job whenever the exchange for listed options opened for business.

Jay felt that Joyce is the woman of his dreams. While he had very strong feelings for Barbara and totally enjoyed being with her, it was not love. It was more loyalty for the Wall Street career she made possible for him to enjoy. The age difference would always be an issue for them Jay thought.

At that moment, while still in bed embraced with Joyce, the thought of Barbara entered Jay's mind vividly. What should he do? Should he tell her about Joyce? Should he continue their relationship? The answers to his questions would come later. For now, the passionate love making and the joy of just holding Joyce consumed his mind and body.

It was near midnight when Joyce stirred from the blissful moments she shared and dreamed about since the time she first met Jay. He was asleep and she gently kissed him on his forehead. Jay too came alive and returned her kiss.

"I've got to go." Joyce whispered.

"Why?" Jay asks.

"You know why my sweet."

"Stay with me. You can go to work from here."

"If you have clothes in your closet that I can wear to work tomorrow, I won't be back ever again." They both laughed.

"Besides, my mom will be wondering where I am and she will be worried."

"Did you call her?"

"I did. I told her we were going out to dinner."

"So, will she spank you for coming home late?"

"No, I'll tell her you've already spanked me." Again they laughed. This was another thing Jay loved about Joyce. He liked her wit. She made him laugh.

"Okay my sweet, I'll drive you."

"No Jay. Don't get up. I'll take a taxi."

"No you won't. I'm getting up so I'll take you. I'm hungry, so I'll get up and drive you. Get something while I'm out."

"You have all that food from Victor's. Why don't you just eat that?" Joyce said.

"That's right. I forgot about that. You want some?"

"No Jay. You eat my sweet. I'm full of you."

They both got out of the bed and pressed their naked bodies together. They held each other tight in silence. For that moment, Jay had the feeling he experienced only one other time in his life. He closed his eyes and tried to block out that moment when he felt he was truly in love.

Reluctantly, Jay released Joyce. She then moved like a feather blowing in the wind to the bathroom. Jay put on his night robe and turned on the oven to heat the food that they brought home from Victor's.

After a few minutes, Joyce reappeared with that radiant look that Jay saw earlier in the evening. Her smile was brighter and bigger now. Again she nestled into his arms.

"Did you say you were going home?" Jay said.

"Yes honey."

"If you don't let me go, you won't be leaving here."

"I'm not holding you Jay. You've got me locked in your arms" She kissed his cheek.

"And your heart." She kissed the other cheek "And your body" she kissed his lips

"And…"

"Joyce, you are gonna make me rip your clothes off again."

"If you promise that you will always love me and *make* love to me like tonight, you will never ever have to rip my clothes off." There was that quick wit of Joyce that captured him.

Jay stared into her eyes and said, "I'll get a taxi for you. Let me put some clothes on."

In the elevator, Joyce again found her way into Jay's arms. She said, "You know what I want to do sweetie?"

"No what?"

"I wanna go dancing this Saturday at the Palladium. Celia Cruz and Joe Cuba are in a concert there. You know how to dance Latin?" Joyce asked.

"No but I love the music."

"Then I'll teach you. Imagine me teaching you something Mr. Austin."

"I'm sure you can teach me quite a few things. In fact I learned something tonight."

"And just what did you learn?"

"I learned that loving someone, is more exciting than *making* love to someone. I felt wonderful just being around you Joyce and I've felt that way I suppose, since that first time I saw you. You know, one of the things your grandmother said to me was that I should meet you and that I would like you."

The elevator opened on the ground floor of Jay's building and the lovers held hands and moved into the ever-bustling New York scene. Even at this late night, the city, as usual was alive and busy.

282

Joyce said, "So in a way, my grandmother arranged for us to meet?"

"Well I wouldn't say that; given how we met. If she were still alive, I think she would have arranged for us to meet." Suddenly, Jay felt a little uncomfortable talking about Linda Hall. A taxi appeared just in time and he practically got in front of it to make sure the driver stopped.

"Call me when you get home." Jay said.

Joyce gave him a peck on his cheek and was in the taxi.

"See you tomorrow." She said.

Jay watched the taxi disappear in the traffic then he hurried back to his apartment to eat the food he left warming in his oven.

After wolfing down the warmed chicken with red beans and rice, Jay was not sure if the euphoria he felt was from the food or his evening with Joyce. What a silly thought he said to himself. He turned on the TV to watch nothing in particular and wait for Joyce to call him.

Joyce arrived home in twenty-five minutes after a taxi ride in which the driver was surely practicing for a career in the racing circuit. She said to herself, I've just made love to the man I'm going to marry and this taxi driver is trying to kill me. To show her disgust, she only tipped him a dollar. That'll give him a message she thought.

As Joyce suspected, her mother was awake and waiting for her. Joyce and Grace had made some changes in the house that Linda Hall left her granddaughter. Grace lived on the top floor that had a full apartment with kitchen, bath and dining room. Joyce slept on the third floor in the front master bedroom and had her own bathroom. The second floor parlor that was Linda's bedroom after climbing the steps became difficult is a parlor again.

Grace greeted Joyce on the parlor floor where she had fallen asleep on the couch.

"Hi mom, you still up?"

"Yea. I just woke up when I heard your key."

"Well I'm getting to bed right away. Everything okay?" Joyce asked her mother.

"Yes. How was dinner?" Grace asked.

"Just wonderful mom. I…ah, ah think I really like him."

"That's no news to me sweetie. I've seen that look in your eyes. Just go slow. It must be a little bit touchy since he is also your boss."

"Not at all mom; we kinda got that worked out too."

"Okay honey but still go slow."

"By the way," Grace continued, "Your uncle Ed called. Great news, he made parole."

"He did?"

"Yep. He will be out soon. He needs a place to stay before he is released so he asked me if he could stay here. I told him this is your house now and he must ask you."

"Of course he can stay here. This is his home too."

"He'll also need a job. I told him I would make some calls." Grace said

"Good. I'll call some of my social- service friends. They can help too. Oh, that's just great. I'm so happy for him." Joyce said.

"Well I'm going up. We can talk about it tomorrow. Good night honey."

"Good night mom."

The next day at work, the lovers were no different outwardly but each stole glances at the other and smiled an inner smile. This is going to work Jay thought.

Jay was going to be out of the office for the next three days. The much-anticipated trip to the new branch office in Charleston was on the agenda. While he was looking forward to seeing his mother and meet her husband to be, he didn't want to leave Joyce so soon.

He planned to spend two working days in the branch then the evenings and weekend with his mother and his prospective step-father.

Suddenly he got the idea that Joyce could fly down Friday evening and join him there. But, is time spent like that too soon? He wanted her with him, but he was not sure of what to do. Then he thought he should not interfere with his mother's plans for the weekend. So he quickly dismissed the idea.

The Hamill branch office was located on Broad Street near the Battery. When he drove the rented car to the office, he passed the spot where he and Carla were parked in her car on East Bay Street eating ice cream six years ago. In those years, Jay often thought about his teacher and the precious moments of his senior year in high school. Now his thoughts are of Joyce and the precious moments now and joy of the future with her.

Jay did not stay at a hotel on this trip as he did on most of his travels. Where to stay was not a problem in northern cities. He could stay wherever he wanted to.

But in southern cities like Charleston, he was not welcomed to the better hotels downtown or near the branch office he was visiting. Often times, it was some small out of the way Black owned motel. But in Charleston, he stayed at the house he grew up in.

He did not expect any trouble in Charleston. After all, he is a native. Clayton also made sure that Jay was never disrespected wherever he went representing the firm. On one trip, he overheard some brokers refer to him as a 'colored big shot from New York.'

It really didn't bother him. In his mind, what he heard them say was simply the truth.

Jay used his ability to control an audience by using techniques he learned in speech and marketing classes at CCNY. He would began by saying, 'I'm going to give you a colorful presentation of the word of options. In fact, I can't help being colorful. I was born that way.'

That always got a laugh from the all White audience and then he had them in his hands.

After two days of introducing the brokers to the options products and other company business, he was ready for the weekend with his mother. But he longed for Joyce. He called her from Charleston as often as possible; two and three times a night. They talked late into the night about the office and their love for each other.

Jay liked his mother's fiancé right away. Richard Glover appeared to be about the same age as Diane. Jay saw him as a good man, who has a good education, a good job, worked hard, is respected in the community, involved in his church but had never been married. He might want a child Jay thought. It was very possible. Diane was only forty-four.

Imagine, having a sibling twenty-five years younger. That would be quite the conversation in Charleston. Imagine further, if Joyce and Diane were to give birth at the some time.

His mind was running away like the train he heard in the distance in the quietness of the Charleston night.

He was happy that his dear mother finally met a nice man and he hoped the marriage would bring joy into her life. Diane prepared a great dinner of fried shrimp, roast chicken, rice, fried corn, string beans, macaroni and corn bread.

CHAPTER 44

Arriving back in New York on Sunday evening, the first thing Jay did was call Joyce and asked her to meet him at Victor's for dinner. She agreed. Over their meal of braise beef with rice and beans and the usual sangria, she filled him in on things that happened in the office the past three days. Jay never expected anything out of the ordinary, but it was good now to have eyes and ears that he could trust.

After the meal, they spent the rest of the evening in bed at Jay's apartment. Their lovemaking now developed into the deep passion that got in the way of that very first time.

With their bodies at rest, Joyce told Jay about her uncle Ed and that he would be coming home after a stint in prison.

She told Jay the story of her uncle's involvement with drugs, the subsequent murder conviction and that he is finally being paroled. Jay listened intently and was fascinated with the story. He did not mention that Mrs. Hall expressed her disappointment in her son Ed Jr. to him or that she ever mentioned him at all. Jay also said he would inquire of any employment opportunities for Ed in his growing network of friends and contacts.

Later that day, Jay called Barbara. He hadn't talk to her for several days and felt that he should at least say hello to her. There was nothing else that he really wanted to say. He felt a need to tell her that he found someone else, Joyce; but the words did come out. He promised to see her soon; when office business allowed him too. As always, Barbara was understanding and made no demands on Jay.

After work, Jay went to Columbia University to register for the graduate program. This is   the first step to his master degree. The Ivy League school located in the Morningside Heights area of New York was yet another gem of the city that Jay was seeing for the first time.

The campus features a collection of buildings each displaying some of the greatest example of classical architecture in the world. Jay walked through Low Plaza, which has been described as an urban beach and observed students studying, socializing, or just hanging out enjoying the sun. He was going to love it here was his first impression.

He found his way to the school of business. A graduate school advisor helped him choose the courses that would garner the MBA degree in two and one-half years. He would attend classes on two nights and half day Saturdays. Jay realized that the schedule was grueling and it will take a great deal of his free time. But the reward will be an opportunity of a lifetime. He can become an officer in a major Wall Street firm.

His travel to the firm's branch offices extolling the value of options will continue but not as often. He decided that his trips would be limited to just Thursdays and he will return on Friday for his Saturday classes. He will also suggest to Clayton that it may be more beneficial if some of the managers and other branch personnel visit New York to hear his seminar that address options as a valuable investment tool.

After finishing the registration process, Jay decided that he would take a taxi to Shirley's for dinner. The restaurant was a short distance from Columbia and of course, Joyce lived just around the corner from there.

As usual, the staff at Shirley's was glad to see Jay. Merle, Sarah and Shirley sat in a booth with Jay and listened to details about his work, his plans for grad school. Sarah wanted to know about Diane's wedding plans. She said she was going to the wedding.

After dinner, Jay's initial thought was to go to Joyce's house, but then he got the idea to take a taxi to Barbara's apartment in the Bronx; surprise her and have some passionate moments. The visit was not disappointing. Barbara was esthetic as she always is to see Jay and there was not much conversation, but plenty of sex. Jay again did not mention Joyce. He decided to just play this out. To what end, he did not know.

CHAPTER 45

For the first time in nearly twelve years, Edward Hall Jr. was a free man again. He first took a bus from the upstate New York prison and was now on a train that would take him to New York City. His only luggage was a small bag that carried three books, his diploma from the correspondence college, some letters and a few pictures.

Grace sent him a ticket for the train and she planned to meet him at the 125th Street station in East Harlem. On the train, Ed said to himself, he would never go to a place like Peekskill ever again. He resolved to make the most of his life now; the life his parents envisioned for him. He is fortunate that he will have some help with his readjustment to society and some money to ease the transition. He is excited and at the same time concerned about his future. He will have a place to stay and a job that Grace arranged with a Broadway production company. The job will not pay a lot of money, but being employed was one of the requirements of his parole.

Ed knew that he would have at least thirty thousand dollars from his mother's life insurance policy. Grace invested that money for him, but he was not going to make a big deal out of whatever the sum is that she will turn over to him. If it has grown or not, he will show nothing but appreciation for her efforts on his behalf. Right now his sister and niece are his only allies and he will do nothing to lose their help and support. He will ask Grace about the Treasury bond that his father told him about but he will not inquire immediately. He will wait until he feels the time is right.

After a three-hour ride, the train is finally approaching Westchester, just North of the Bronx. None of the sights are familiar to Ed and that is what twelve years away will cause. When the train arrived in the Bronx, Jay knew that he was minutes away from his second chance in life.

Grace was there waiting at the station and Ed ran to her and embraced her. He could not stop the tears that flowed from his eyes. He did not cry once during his incarceration. That would have sent the wrong message to the other inmates. But now he cried for the minutes, hours, days, months and years he was away. Grace too, cried for her brother.

Grace was not a great cook so naturally she had Shirley prepare some of the restaurant's specialties for a dinner at home. She reasoned correctly that Ed would rather stay at home his first night and have dinner with just her and Joyce. There would be a great deal of things for the three to talk about.

Ed savored every morsel of food that he put into his mouth. Being able to eat without hundreds of men around you and noise, fights, misery and fear for your life on the menu, was just pure joy. Ed did not talk very much at the dinner table, but Grace and Joyce did. They knew he would have more to say when he is ready.

So mother and daughter told about their lives the past few years. Grace told of her failed marriage, failed career, regrets about the relationships with her parents, then revived career and happiness to be in the place she is now.

Joyce talked about Jay. She talked about this mature men who in such a short time has meant so much to her. He brought her true happiness, a job that she loves, and then she told Ed, "You know uncle Ed, grandma loved him too. In fact, he was the last person to see grandma alive. He brought her last meal from Shirley's when he worked there."

Ed listened attentively to everything his sister and niece were saying to him, but this last statement was of particular interest to him, but he showed no reaction to it. He realized that his niece is in love this guy she was talking about.

Grace also listened to her daughter talk about Jay. She realized at that moment that Joyce sound and act as she did when she was that age. This is how she sounded when she first fell in love and didn't listen to her parents. And how vulnerable she became to disappointments. Grace said to herself that she has got to talk to her only child whom she loves so very much; and try to be the parent her mother tried to be to her. While Jay had not shown any signs of a dog, he is still a man and only time will tell his pedigree.

Grace then said to Ed, "Jay is quite a young man. In fact, he is the person I invested your insurance money with."

"He is a stock broker?" Ed asks.

"No. Well, yes he is but he doesn't handle individual accounts now. He runs the department I'm in." Joyce replied

"He sounds like a big shot. He's your boss and boyfriend?" Ed asks.

Joyce just blushed. Before she could answer, Grace said, "Yea she likes him and he is also very smart Ed. He made some money for me, Joyce and a lot of other people we know. Your account is over Forty thousand. This girl on 125th Street handles it now."

"Wow, That's great sis. I didn't expect that." Ed looked at Joyce and said "Well what should I do with it now; you're the Wall Street person?"

"I have some ideas to make it grow. We'll teach you about options." Joyce said.

Dinner apparently finished, Grace gets up from the table and walks behind Ed and rubs his shoulders with genuine affection for her brother. She says to him, "You'll have the basement apartment Ed. You remember; it has its own entrance. You can start work Monday. It's just moving props around on stage. Doesn't pay much but it's a start till you find something better."

"Me and Jay are also looking for something better." Joyce said.

"That's fine. Thanks you two. Thanks for being there for me. You don't know how much I appreciate what you have done for me. I know I screwed up my life. Mom and dad really tried to be good parents to me. And what happened was none of their fault. It was all me. What I regret most is, neither lived to see me make something good out of my life. I plan to make sure you two see some worth in me."

"I know you will." Grace said. "Look, why don't I take you to 125th Street tomorrow. You can take some money out of your account, or all of it. Whatever you wanna do. You'll need to buy some clothes and other things that you may want for downstairs. Okay?"

"That's fine sis. We'll do that. I'm sleepy now. Not use to a meal like what we had. So if you don't mind, I'm going down to sleep. This is the first time in a long time when I can turn off the lights myself or leave em on if I want to. Good night. See you in the morning." Ed hugged and kisses them the both

Ed retreated to his new home in the basement. Remembering his youth for a moment as he looked around the apartment, he saw images of his father and mother in this home that they were so proud of. He brought shame to this house and that he will not be able to change. What is in his power to change is the perception people will have of him. Once again, he vowed that he would work on that.

As sleep seeped into his body, he thought of the t-bond again. He decided to ask Grace about it on the way back from 125th Street in the morning.

CHAPTER 46

Jay was adjusting to his new schedule and courses at Columbia. After six weeks, all was going great. He found no interference with work or his time with Joyce. There had been some days when Joyce brought a change of clothes to work and stayed over night at Jay's apartment. She would have dinner ready for him when he came home from school.

They both knew what would be next for them, but it was not spoken. For now, the important thing was getting Jay through grad school. Then look for his appointment as an officer in the firm. The devotion and commitment to each other in private was evident. Their love for each other grew stronger day by day. Their secret remained just that at work.

One Saturday after his eight-thirty class ended, Jay had some time before his eleven-thirty class on finance and economics. He decided to visit one of the many campus coffee shops just to sit and read a little before that class. He walked past some lecture halls in session and looked into one such lecture hall and could not believe his eyes. There was no mistake in who he saw. She stood radiant as ever, beautiful as ever and more elegant than the last time he saw her at his high school graduation. Carla Mack was conducting a class at Columbia University.

Again, Jay looked into the small window in the door to make sure. Then his knees started to shake. She is absolutely gorgeous. She has changed her hair. No longer is there the bang and comb back look that gave her the look of a student. Her hair is shorter now and styled to enhance her soft features and hazel eyes.

Suddenly, Jay felt silly peering into the window. He moved away then wondered what should he do. He can't just stand there and he can't leave. His class starts in fifteen minutes, and he didn't know when her class would end. He quickly decided that at best, he will be late for his class but he had to talk to her. He glanced at his watch, and then just paced the hall. Then he saw a place where he could sit, and wait and watch the door to her room.

Fifteen minutes later, students started to exit the room. He waited a few seconds then entered. She had her back to the door and was arranging some papers that she was preparing to put away. She did not see him standing there.

Feeling a presence, Carla turned and looked at Jay. Her face slowly evolved into a magnificent smile that made Jay's knees shake again.

"Is it really you?" Carla said

"I can't believe it's you." Jay replied.

Carla rushed to him, extended an awkward hand then pulled him close into a tight embrace. Jay dropped his briefcase then wrapped his arms around her.

Suddenly, there was silence in the outer world around them. Jay pulled her closer and closer. It was as if he was not going to lose her again and holding her now would make sure of that. The sweet aroma of her perfume as he remembered, brought on the intoxication that he always fell into whenever he was around her. There were no words spoken.

Finally, they released after remembering where they were. They stepped back from each other.

"What are you doing here?" Carla asked.

"I'm on my way to a class that I'm late for."

"You're enrolled here?"

"Yes I am."

"What... I mean, how long have you...where?"

"School of business. I'm working on my MBA. Just started. I see you're a professor."

"Not yet. Working on that."

"Carla, I've got to go to this lecture. Can we meet and talk later? I'm done by one."

"Well I guess so. This was my only class today. I could come back, I guess. Where should I meet you?"

"Why not right here?"

"Okay, I'll see you at one."

They embraced again and Jay was off to his class.

Jay took his seat in the finance and economics class, but he really wasn't there. While the professor was talking about the fundamentals of corporate finance, Jay was thinking back to a time in the recent past when he was hopelessly in love with his math teacher. Instead of learning how American corporations raised working capital through the issuance of securities, Jay was thinking about the woman who made him a man.

He took brief notes. After all, this subject was not entirely new to him. He kept glancing at his watch, and thought about leaving the lecture early. But why, he reasoned, she said she would be back at one. So Jay resigned to the time he would have to wait to see the object of his boyhood desire again.

Carla took a taxi to her apartment on Broadway and Ninety-Eight Street. All she could think of at the moment, was what should she wear to the meeting with Jay. Nothing in her closet came to mind during the taxi ride. When the weather is nice like it is today, Carla would walk the fifteen blocks to her apartment. But today, she needed time to get home, shower, change clothes and get back to the campus.

Why is he coming back into my life at this time is the question that consumed her mind. It's been over seven years since Carla has seen Jay and she thought about him everyday for those seven years. Even the affair with her advanced mathematics instructor at Cornell, where she earned her master, did not erase memories of Jay Austin.

Realizing her life's dream to be a secondary school educator, led to the position at Columbia. And Carla has been very happy with that. Even living in New York has been good for her. Previous attempts at love and happiness however, have been disastrous for Carla. She has vowed to not rush things with any man that might enter her life now. She found that some Black men for the most part were intimidated by her education and looks. Those men felt a need to establish their manhood by being abusive, and being less then gentle. She wondered, as she entered her apartment what will Jay be like, now that he is a grown man.

She changed clothes three times before deciding on simple gray pants and a burgundy colored blouse. She would be Saturday casual.

Finally, the professor said he was finished for the day. Jay ran to the men's room to freshen up. Always impeccably dressed, it was not his attire that concerned him. It was Saturday and he had not shaved. He needed a haircut, which he planned to do later that day and he just didn't feel confident in his look. Too bad. She'll see me again when I'm at my best, he reasoned.

He went to the lecture hall where he saw her but it was now empty. He glanced at his watch, looked up and down the hallway, then waited. It was just ten minutes to one o'clock. The thought occurred to him that maybe Carla was married and has children. It has been a few years. If not married, maybe involved with someone. She was just too attractive to be alone.

Jay's thoughts ended when he saw her walking toward him. She had changed clothes so that meant that she lived nearby. Maybe in that high-rise apartment building on 110th Street that housed some of the faculty, Jay thought. That's interesting if true. At any rate, she lives not too far from me was his last thought before she greeted him with that smile again.

"Hi again Jay. While I was gone, I was wondering where did you go for undergrad?"

"Here at CCNY."

"You've been in New York since you graduated?"

"Yes I have. And You?" Jay asked.

"Well I was fortunate to get a grant to Cornell where I finally got my MBA."

"How long have you been here at Columbia?"

"This is my second year. I've got some more work before I'm a full professor."

"That's great. Well look, how about some lunch, you hungry?"

"I could eat something. Where would you like to go?"

"What would you like?" Jay asked.

"Anything. Why don't you pick."

"Well, when I came here after Burke, I worked at the best soul food restaurant in New York. I've always wanted to go to the second best so I've got a place for us."

"Okay." Carla replied.

"I've got my car so let's go."

Jay drove his Mercedes Benz to school as he sometimes did. He drove to a restaurant called Wilson's on Amsterdam Avenue and 157th Street. He had heard about this place since arriving in New York but never ate there before. He was glad he had his new car so right away Carla would be impressed.

Wilson's lived up to all that he heard. They had a bakery on the premise so they sold fresh baked cakes, pies, cookies, and pastries. The food was excellent. It was just as good as Shirley's Jay thought as he ate fried chicken with bake macaroni, collard greens, and of course rice with gravy. Carla ordered the same plate.

They did not talk much during dinner. It was as if they both were shy and meeting each other for the first time.

After desert of peach cobbler, Carla said, "You know what I do, you haven't told me what you do Jay."

"I work on Wall Street. I'm a broker and a department head."

"Really? So that's why business school?"

"Yes."

"I don't know anything about the stock market."

"Well I can teach you."

"So now you wanna be *my* teacher." Carla said. They both laughed.

"It looks like you are very successful at what you do. I love your car."

"I'm been lucky."

"Is that what you call it."

"Well yes. I happen to be in the right place at the right time."

"I recall Jay, you were voted most likely to succeed in your class. Looks like that came true. There aren't many Black men doing what you do."

"No, but like I said, I was lucky. Ready to go?"

"Yea. The food was great. I don't think I will eat any more today."

The two were back in Jay's car driving through West Harlem. Again there was no conversation. Finally Carla said, "I've been dyeing to ask you if you are married?'

"No, not yet."

"Not yet? Does that mean not now but soon?"

"No it doesn't mean that and it doesn't mean I'm engaged either."

"You mean Harriet hasn't snagged you yet?"

Jay laughed."No. She hasn't."

"Where is Harriett? Are you in touch with her?"

"We stay in touch; she is working at a bank in Charlotte. She graduated from Hampton."

"That's great. When have you been to Charleston?"

"Recently, I was there working."

"Working, doing what?"

"At one of our branch offices; teaching the brokers there about stock options."

"So you *are* a teacher. Stock options, what's that?"

"It's a long story. And what about you?" Jay asked.

"What about me?"

"Are you married?"

"No."

Jay said nothing more. They were now on Broadway near Columbia and Jay asked, "Where should I take you?"

"I'm on Ninety- Eighth and Broadway."

"You're not far from where I live."

"You live in Manhattan?"

"Yes, Columbus."

Carla directed Jay to her building and he pulled into a parking space out front.

They just looked at each other for a few moments and Jay said, "There is so much I want to talk to you about; I've thought about you so very much the past few years. I always wondered if I would ever see you again."

Carla said nothing but instead looked straight ahead at nothing in particular. She turned to Jay and said. "I've thought about you too, I have to admit. I've thought about that time in Charleston and not without some guilt and some pain. I don't regret what happened between us, but I was in pain because it was hard to forget you. I look at you now and I'm so very proud of you. I don't know how to describe the other feelings I have right now."

"Carla, we can't bring back that time. We're not the same people. I know I have changed and I'm sure you have too. But one thing has not changed for me, and that is how I feel about you and I cherish that secret."

"Jay, are you telling me that you never told anyone about us, not *one* of your friends?"

"Not one. Never wanted too."

"And what about the lady in your life now. There must be one."

"There is, and I like her I admit but it's nothing serious."

"When are your other classes?" Carla asked.

"I'm there Tuesday and Thursday nights."

Carla sat in silence for a moment, sighed deeply, then reach into her handbag and got a pen and a piece of paper. She wrote her phone number on it then handed it to Jay.

"Call me if you like. I'm home every evening." Carla said.

"I will." Jay leaned across and kissed her on the cheek.

He opened the door on the driver's side to get out to open her door. She told him not to.

Jay watched as she entered her building, then drove off.

Joyce has probably called and was wondering where he is. They planned to go to a movie that night.

CHAPTER 47

Ed decided to stop at Shirley's for dinner one night. Grace and Joyce were not going to be home and with the exception of his job at the theater, he had not been going anywhere very much. Being a stagehand at the theater was not much work, and the pay is modest but the job serves its purpose for now. So instead of being home alone on a night that he is off, Ed thought he would have dinner out. He also thought it was about time he thanked Shirley for her kindness to his mother. Grace told him how Shirley and Merle had been so helpful and how she took care of his mother when she was alive.

After Ed finished his dinner, he went to Merle to pay for his meal. Merle knew him but respected his privacy and made no attempt to converse with him. Ed asked Merle if Shirley was there and would she call her for him. Merle obliged and told him to wait.

Shirley came and greeted Ed with the warm personality she has for all her customers.

She told Ed how happy she was to see him then invited him to her office to talk. They talked for nearly an hour. As he was leaving, Ed promised to come by more often. He went home thinking about all that Shirley told him. The thing that stuck in his mind most was the story of her former waiter, Jay. He was the last person that saw his mother alive.

When Ed finally asked, Grace assured him that she knew nothing about a t-bond or any other securities that their parents had. But at the same time, he was convinced that his father would not have told him that if it were not true. He continued to make no big deal   about the situation with Grace. He trusted her but it never left his mind. This Jay character somehow plays in his head. The big shot Wall Street guy. He is so successful now. He made a lot of money for people according to Shirley.

Ed had the urge to talk to Jay but did not know how or when that might happen. And if his thoughts about Jay took on a new meaning, he would have to take a different tact. His mother liked and trusted the guy. His sister likes him. His niece loves this guy and wants to marry him and he is also her boss.

Ed went home and called some old friends from the big house in upstate New York. They all lived in and around New York City. Terms of his probation prohibited his association with former criminals but a call to them would not be detected. He might have a job for them one day soon. He had the money to pay and he was sure that they had a need. He just wanted to establish their availability if he might want their services one day. For now, a visit with Jay was off limit. He was his niece's lover and he did not want to hurt her in any way.

Jay wasted little time in calling Carla. He couldn't believe the encounter earlier that day and that she was really back into his life. After he and Joyce went to the movies on Broadway, he took her home early. In fact, he couldn't tell you the name of the movie or what it was about. All he could think of was Carla. He told Joyce that he was not feeling well, and that he had a lot of things to do for school and the job and he was going home to rest. Joyce did not object. She knew his schedule. In fact, she knew that he didn't get home from his Saturday classes until rather late because he had to go to the library. So she urged him to go on home and that she will go home and call him later.

Joyce was surprised to get a busy signal when she called Jay. His phone was busy for more than forty-five minutes. She wondered whom could he be talking too for so long when he had so much to do. She became really annoyed after more than an hour passed and assumed that he obviously took the phone off the hook so he would not be disturbed.

Deciding to just go to bed, Joyce said to herself, Jay must have known that I would call him.

Jay indeed talked to Carla a very long time. Carla was more relaxed now than she was at dinner so she was more talkative. They took the time to fill in the gaps of the past seven years. They reminisced about that special trip to the battery, Burke High school, classmates, teachers and the city of Charleston.

She told of her failed relationships, her disappointments with men and the pursuit of her personal education goals.

Jay told of his entry into the world of Wall Street but omitted certain details. Details that he will never share with her or anyone else. He also omitted details of the women he has encountered. Then they talked of the secret past that they shared.

Jay asked Carla if she recalled the last conversation they had the night of his graduation. She responded, "Yes I do remember. You were celebrating with Harriett and others at Mark's house, I think. You wanted to come over to my house. I said no."

"I was crushed." Jay said.

Laughing, Carla said," No you weren't."

"Yes I was."

"You can still be dramatic I see." Carla said.

"I was crushed and even more so when you said we will never see each other again."

"Yes I did say that."

"And I said you are wrong, I will see you again."

"So I guess you were right." Carla said.

There was silence. Jay was tempted to ask, 'Can I come over now?' but he hesitated. He must go slow and careful now. He could feel the sensation in his body that he always felt whenever he was around her. The feeling that he got in her classroom and in her bedroom.

The next day at the office, Joyce noticed that Jay seemed somewhat detached. His mind appeared to be preoccupied. He did not even come to the trading desk as usual to see how business was going. She just assumed it was the rigors of school and the job.

They went to lunch as they sometimes did at a restaurant not frequented by their fellow employees. The secret of their romance was still intact. Joyce again noticed the same mood in Jay. Finally, she asked him if he was still feeling poorly. He replied that he was well, just tired.

Then she mentioned that she tried calling him the night before but his phone was busy. He replied that he had called his mother and probably fell asleep and didn't hang the phone up. This sounded believable to her.

Whenever Jay wanted her to come to his apartment, he would give her his key. He told her more than once that he would give her one but he hadn't done so yet. Nothing thrilled Joyce more than to be at the apartment when Jay came home. She was not a great cook but was learning certain things; all to please the man she so loved. It was such a pleasure for Joyce to see the look on his face when she presented Jay with a late night meal followed by a trip to the bedroom. To Joyce, this was the preview of their marriage.

While Joyce had been tempted to just get a duplicated key made when he gave it to her again, she did not. She was going to wait until he actually gave one to her. Jay did not give her a key on this day so Joyce thought nothing of it. It means, she assumed that either he will be getting home from school late, or he will be busy.

They returned to the office. Jay's mood was still the same. At the close of the market, Jay came to the trading desk and whispered to Joyce, "I don't have school tonight, you wanna do something? Have dinner maybe?"

Joyce was thrilled and said, "You sure, you're not tired?"

"No. Come on over. On second thought, maybe you should go home first and get a change of clothes."

This brought a smile to Joyce's face and she blushed all over. She looked around to see if anyone saw her response then whispered, "I'll be there boss."

"Instead of that, I'll pick you up. There is a restaurant in Harlem that I want to go to."

"Not Shirley's? Joyce asked.

"No I want to go to a place called Wilson's."

"Shirley will stop speaking to you."

"You gonna tell her?"

"I'll be ready when you get there boss."

Jay knew his mood had been funky. But he also knew that he loved this woman and Carla coming back into his life just had him disjointed.

Tonight he will cement his love for Joyce and rid his mind of Carla and Barbara. The older women will be gone forever.

Jay was surprised that he wanted to go to Wilson's. He was just there a few days ago for lunch with Carla. After dinner, they returned to this apartment and did indeed cement their love for each other. The next day at work, Jay had lunch with Morris levy, Hamill's general counsel. Jay had some legal papers prepared and took advantage of the discount fee Levy charged for his services. Jay felt it was time to get serious with his personal life. A will was a part of serious thinking. Joyce is the person with whom he wants to spend the rest of his life with. And Carla and Barbara and all the other women in his life will be just a distant memory now.

That thought came and went the next time Jay saw Carla at Columbia. In fact, Carla made sure that he would see her. She knew his schedule and waited until his class ended. She just casually walked toward the lecture hall that he would be exiting.

When their eyes met, their body language said this was no accident. With few words spoken, they were in a taxi to Carla's apartment.

Jay had played this scene over and over in his head since graduation when he dreamed of seeing Carla again. But his deepest dreams, his strongest imagination, his most ardent vision, paled to the reality of this encounter. He was a young boy again. His teacher was again in charge. He was hopelessly lost.

CHAPTER 48

Jay faced another dilemma in his young life. His professional life was on the fast track. He had money. His future looked very bright but he was not happy. This was not suppose to happen to one deemed most likely to succeed. Why must he now choose which woman he should share his future with? This was never in the equation before. It seemed unfair to him. Carla and Joyce brought him great joy but it was getting more and more difficult to play the role of lover to both. The lies to each were increasing, the deception problematic and his work started to suffer a little. Since he began distributing the weekly newsletter on suggested options strategies, he missed issuing one. While no one complained about it, the options staff noticed. They assumed that his new schedule in school made it difficult, and he has just forgotten about it.

He had no one to talk to about his situation. There were times he would call his mother, or Harriett and even Gwen. He did not discuss his situation or how he was struggling with his life. He was hoping that during the conversation, he might get a hint of how he should proceed. That was a futile idea. No ideas were forth coming. They had their own situations to talk about and Jay would just listen to them for a while, say goodbye and slip back into his despondent state.

In spite of the constant regard for discretion that Jay faced with Carla and Joyce, there was no denying the joyous time he had with each. There was so much bliss, that he was now accepting the challenge of being with two women without a single thought of guilt. He was enjoying it. In fact, at times he was reminded of his time in high school. None of his women ever caught him in a lie; or so he thought.

Grace was given two tickets to a Broadway show and she invited Joyce to go with her. Joyce agreed and went with her mother. After the show ended around nine-thirty, they boarded the subway for the ride back uptown. At the 77th Street stop, Joyce told her mother that she was going to stop by Jay's apartment and would be home later. Grace said okay.

Grace again saw in her daughter the young woman she was when she was at the same age and in love. Realizing that Joyce was full grown, successful and sensible, she accepted the fact that she could make her own decisions. But as a mother, she still worried about her.

Joyce, full of exuberance, walked hastily to Jay's apartment on Columbus Avenue. She knew that if Jay wasn't home from school yet, he soon would be. She couldn't wait to see him. She was going to ask him for a key tonight.

At the entrance to Jay's building, she pushed the intercom button to his apartment several times but received no answer. Somewhat disappointed but undeterred, she waited at the outside entrance. Just then, a male tenant was leaving the building. The tenant, assumed that this attractive young lady was not a person who may cause harm to anyone, allowed her to enter into the lobby.

Her first thought was to take the elevator and wait outside his apartment. Instead, she went down the stairs behind the door in the rear of the lobby that leads to the tenant's parking garage. The door had a small window with a view of the lobby. She could find out if Jay's car was in its parking space, or did he drive it to school. His car was there.

Joyce returned to the ground floor and heard someone opening the lobby door. That may be Jay she thought. Before opening the garage door, she looked through the small window. She saw a woman enter the lobby followed by Jay. Her heart started to pound. She immediately stepped away from the window in the door to the parking deck so she could not be seen. She heard them talking as they waited for the elevator. Her heart began to beat faster, and she could hardly catch her breath.

That can't be Jay. She thought to herself. Yet there was no mistaking his voice. It was he and he was with another woman. They continued to talk as she heard the elevator door open. Her immediate thought was to enter the lobby and ask him who is this lady, but her legs would not move. She felt as if she suddenly became paralyzed. Before she knew it, tears were falling from her eyes in big drops.

When the elevator left the lobby, Joyce ran to the exit and into the New York City street sounds and people on Columbus Avenue. She could hardly see because of the tears falling from her eyes. She walked into several people who tried to avoid her because they were not sure what kind of state she was in. Unable to walk on steady feet, she stopped at a streetlight pole to gather herself. She found a napkin in her purse to wipe her eyes, and then she saw people staring at her.

There must be a reason for this. Joyce's mind raced with calming thoughts. This is *not* what it seems. I know Jay loves me like I love him and I'm going to ring his apartment again and he'll let me in and introduce me to this woman. He'll tell her how much he loves me and… Oh this is so silly. It may even be his mother; I've never met her.

Joyce made her way back to the entrance. With a nervous finger, she managed to find then push the right button after several tries. One long ring. Seconds go by. She expected to hear Jay's voice come through the intercom almost immediately. He should know it's me. He would say 'Come on up babe' and release the locked lobby door from his apartment. Another ring . No acknowledgement. She wanted to push the button again but her finger would not let her. Finally, she left the building and searched for a taxi. She was shaking uncontrollably and barely managed to give the driver her destination.

On the ride to Harlem, she lost all remaining control of her emotions. She did not care what the driver thought. She was in pain. She did not hear him ask if she was okay.

After arriving home she took cash out of her purse but not sure how much. She just handed it to the driver. He did not complained so it must have been enough. She fumbled with the key to the gate then ran to her room in the elegant house that once belonged to her grandmother. She threw herself across her bed and cried like a baby.

CHAPTER 49

The next day, Joyce was inexplicably absent from work. No one heard from her and Jay felt very uneasy. Jay thought it might have been Joyce who rang the lobby buzzer to his apartment last night. Now he was thinking that it was very likely her. What he was not sure of is, did she see him with Carla. The ring came very shortly after he opened the door to his apartment so it was very possible that it was she. He didn't give Carla time to question who that might be ringing his apartment. He was all over her as soon as he heard the ringing. At the second ring, Jay was kissing her, caressing her, and at the same time, removing her clothing.

He was hesitant about bringing Carla there but being confident of his control of the situation, he was sure that he would get away with it. Carla had no scheduled classes the next day and it was her idea to spend the night with him until he left for work. He agreed reluctantly.

The sex was overwhelming as usual but Jay was not relaxed as usual. He kept Joyce on his mind. In his mind, he pictured Joyce ringing the buzzer in the foyer with a concerned look on her face. He was surprised that she did not call his phone but was also relieved that she didn't.

Having no idea what he was going to say to her, Jay called Joyce's home number but no one answered. He knew that her mother is normally home and thought that she may have her own phone number. After obtaining it, he called and Grace answered.

"Ms. Freeman, this is Jay. I'm calling for Joyce, is she all right?"

"Is she all right? Isn't she at work?"

"No ma'am that's why I'm calling."

"Hold on, let me see."

Grace raced down stairs and knocked on the door to Joyce's bedroom. There was no answer. She knocked again then called out her name.

With a voice barely above a whisper that indicated she was not well, she answered "Yes"

"Are you okay honey, Jay's on the phone; he said you didn't call into work are you sick?"

"No."

"Can I come in?"

"Not now mom. I'm okay."

"What should I tell Jay?"

"Nothing."

"Nothing, what do you mean nothing?"

"Tell him whatever you want to."

"What's wrong sweetie, you wanna talk about it?"

"No."

Grace went back to the phone and told Jay that Joyce was not feeling well and would not be coming in to work. Jay thanked Grace, and then asked her to tell Joyce that he would call her later.

Grace felt that something was wrong. She felt that way after she heard Joyce come home shortly behind her. When Joyce told her that she was going to Jay's apartment, Grace did not expect her home that night or to come home as early as she did.

She wanted to go back to Joyce's bedroom but decided to wait until Joyce wanted to talk. It was near noon, and Joyce had not surfaced. Grace could not wait any longer. When she knocked on Joyce's door, there was no response. After a second knock, she heard Joyce slowly moving towards the door.

Finally, the door opened and Joyce stood in the doorway looking down at nothing in particular but avoiding her mother's gaze. She was wearing the same clothes she wore to the theater but now they showed wrinkles and tearstains. Her hair and make up was a mess.

Grace could see the puffiness in her daughter's eyes and it was obvious that she had been crying for some time, maybe all night.

Grace took her into her arms to comfort her.

"What's the matter sweetheart?" Grace asked

Joyce started to sob again. She tried to say something to her mother but was only able to   choke out some non-word sounds. Grace knew in her heart, that Jay was the reason for her daughter's discontent. She didn't know what he did but he was the reason.

She just held Joyce in her arms stroking her matted hair, trying to sooth the emotional pain that she was going through.

Finally Joyce blurted out, "He was with another woman. I saw him with her."

So that was it, Grace said to herself. She had no words of comfort for Joyce immediately she just continued to hold her.

She looked Joyce in the eyes; she tried to maintain a soothing, comforting voice. She asked, "Are you sure sweetheart, are you sure there is something going on between them?"

"Yes. I'm sure."

"Seeing people together doesn't mean that..."

"I know what I saw mom; you weren't there. I saw him with my own eyes."

Grace could see that Joyce's sorrow was now turning to anger. This is normal. She knows from her own experience. First the shock, followed by pain then anger. She was not going to do or say anything to defend Jay. In fact she emphasized with Grace and was starting to feel anger build up within her. In her mind Grace said, how dare he hurt my daughter. I know she loves him. How could her hurt her like this? Bastard.

"What are you going to do Joyce? He said he is going to call you later."

"I don't want to talk to him if he calls, and I'm not going back to work there."

Grace offered no indifference or agreement to Joyce's comments. She realized that first reactions are just that, a first reaction. It is born of rage, fury, disappointment and irritation. First reactions are often modified by time and rationale. And it appears that only time will take care of this situation.

Grace asked, "What do you mean you're not going back there?"

"Just what I said. I can't work there and look at him everyday after what he did to me. I can find another job. I'm not going to work with him again. If he calls, you tell him that. Tell him I quit and don't call here any more."

With that outburst, the tears started again and Joyce ran into her bathroom; closed and locked the door. Grace knew it would be useless at this point to try to talk to her any longer. She decided to give her more time to get the hurt out. She went to prepare a light lunch for Joyce. She will need that later.

Joyce found herself getting physically sick besides the emotional pain she was feeling. She just made it to her bathroom and threw up all the contents of her stomach. This brought more anguish to her. That she is actually sick over Jay.

Grace went to the downstairs kitchen where she sometimes drank coffee with Ed. They used this time to bring each other up to date with events in their lives. Ed in particular used the time with Grace to fill in the gaps of the past twelve years of his life. He found out about family and friends from as much as Grace knew about them.

Ed was sitting at the kitchen table when Grace came in. She had a worried look on her face and went right to the refrigerator without so much as a good morning to Ed.

Ed knew something was not right as he sat sipping coffee. He thought he heard Joyce on the floor above sounding somewhat distressed. At least he was sure that Joyce did not go to work that morning and that was news. Joyce loved her job and this guy that goes with the job.

After a few minutes, Graced acknowledge Ed's presence. He sensed her preoccupation with cooking something and thought he should just get out of her way. He was about to leave the kitchen but stopped to ask Grace, "How is Joyce. She didn't go to work today?"

Without looking away from the can of soup she was opening, Grace said,

"She says she ain't going back."

"She's not going back to her job?" Ed asked.

"That's what she says. He hurt her bad."

Ed's interest suddenly peaked "What do you mean hurt her; did he put his hands on her?"

"No nothing like that, but he might as well. She saw him with somebody, another woman; and that hurt her. She loves that boy. I could tell. I kept telling her to go slow."

"She'll get over it." Ed said.

"Maybe. But if she says she is not going back to work with him, I believe her."

"Aw, Joyce will be all right. She is too smart and too pretty to be that caught up on any body like that."

"I agree Ed but you should see her this morning; she's a mess.

Ed left the kitchen and went to his bedroom. There he placed a telephone call to his friend. When his friend answered, Ed simply said, "What we talked about is on. I'll meet you after work tonight."

Jay was having a terrible day at work to say the least. His heart hadn't stop pounding since he spoke to Joyce's mother early that day. He found that he was not able to concentrate on anything he tried to do that day. He wanted to talk to Joyce and planned to call as soon as the market closed. He's got to make this situation right was the thought that dominated his mind. He didn't have a clue as to what he should do but he had to do something, and right away. Joyce means too much to him and he can't afford to lose her.

When he left for work that morning and left Carla in his bed, he knew it would be the last time with her. He still loves the woman and perhaps always will. She was his first but Joyce will be his last. He was suffering big pangs of guilt that made this a day full of torment. Jay had never experienced this feeling even after all the things he had done in his life. His feelings told him that it is Joyce that he will surrender his heart to and he will tell Carla that the very next time he speaks to her.

As the bell was ringing to end the trading day at the New York Stock Exchange, Jay was ringing the phone of the woman he truly loved. It rang and rang and rang. Joyce did not answer. On the third day after she still refused to take his calls, Jay knew he was indeed in trouble.

CHAPTER 50

It was time, Ed determined, that he have that conversation with Jay. He had a few things that he wanted to talk to him about. One was, did his mother Linda Hall, discuss a treasury bond with him.

Now that Jay has fallen out of favor with his niece and sister, he is fair game to Ed and his plan. Ed has paid out five thousand dollars to implement this plan. Ed will not be present when his friends question Jay. In fact, during the planning meeting that Ed arranged, he stressed that Jay must never know that he is involved.

Ed hired Jackson, a fairly intelligent ex-con, to seek answers to the questions that plagued him. Including, what happened to the t-bond and the stock certificates. This smart guy stockbroker is one person who would have the knowledge to negotiate these things.

Ed learned about Sarah, Jay's god mother from Shirley. The plan Ed devised is that   Jackson, and three other men that he hired, will lure Jay into 127th Street under the guise of an urgent telephone call from Sarah. When he arrives, he will be subdued, blindfolded and taken to another location where he will be questioned. Ed will be at this location but Jay will not see his face or the face of anyone else. Sarah had to be involved because it was easier to abduct Jay from the streets of Harlem than his own neighborhood on Columbus Avenue. And Sarah could get him there.

The most unpleasant thing that must be done is to convince Sarah to call Jay. Jackson has a special talent for causing people pain. That is one of the reasons why Ed recruited him. Persuading Sarah could be unpleasant to most men, but not Jackson.

Using one of his other talents, Jackson and his accomplice got into Sarah's apartment unnoticed and just waited for her to get home from work. He had no problem hurting Sarah until she did as she was told. Sarah protested at first and refused to call Jay. But she soon changed that tact when Jackson threatened to cut up her face and leave her scared for life. Jackson assured her that no harm would come to Jay but she would suffer great harm if she did not get him to come to her apartment right away.

Sarah could not cry out for help, for Sye or Mason would surely come to her rescue. But Jackson made sure she was gagged and bound. The heavy tape was removed from her mouth after she agreed to do what the two men wanted. They held a knife to her throat as she spoke to Jay.

After the call was made to Jay, Jackson and his helper left Sarah battered bruised and tied up in her bedroom closet. The men joined two others who were waiting in a car on Lenox Avenue. Jackson called Ed and informed him where they were with the plan. As soon as Jay arrives on 127th Street, part two of the plan would be put into effect. Jackson asked Ed what should they do if for some reason, they run into a problem. Ed replied, "I want some answers from him, but if we get him and he is unable to talk I won't be disappointed."

Jay hung up the phone after Sarah's call and proceeded to get dressed for the trip to Harlem. She sounded weird on the phone but her company, he felt, was just what he needed. He had been feeling miserable since Joyce refused to speak to him. It's been over one week and while he is confident that if given the opportunity to talk to Joyce face to face, he could convince her that it was all a mistake. Once he explains to her that the lady she saw him with was his high school teacher, she would know that there was no affair. He planned to tell her a line his mother once told him ' believer none of what of you hear, and only half of what you see.' Yea that'll work he felt.

Grace told Jay during his latest telephone call that Joyce would not be back to work at Hamill. He dismissed such talk and told Grace that he has informed the company that Joyce is sick and will be back to work soon. Grace said suit yourself.

Breaking up with Carla was not easy but he had to. Jay told Carla that he was in love with Joyce and that he is going to ask her to marry him. So to get over his misery, a night with Sarah could be a pleasant distraction.

CHAPTER 51

The news reached Charleston the next day after it happened. On the bottom right side on the first page of the Morning News and Courier was the headline:

LOCAL MAN MURDERED
ON THE STREETS OF NEW YORK.

Jayson Austin, a 1961 graduate of Burke high school was shot dead in an apparent robbery attempt on Lenox Avenue in Harlem. Police reported that Mr. Austin had escaped his assailants and was trying to get away in a taxi. He was fatality shot in the back as he opened the taxi door. There have been no arrest or reported suspects in the shooting.

Mr. Austin was a department head at Hamill, Rhodes and Peck, A major Wall Street investment firm. He is the son of prominent Charleston businesswoman, Diane Austin Glover. She could not be reached for comment.

Robert Clayton, CEO of Hamill, says "Mr. Austin had a very promising career and was destined to be the first Negro officer of a Wall Street firm. I, along with my wife, and everyone at the firm were very fond of Jay and will miss him very, very much".

After graduating from Burke High school, Mr. Austin went to New York and enrolled in the City College of New York night school while working as a stockbroker during the day.

At the time of his death, Mr. Austin was enrolled at Columbia University graduate school of business. He specialized in an investment product called puts and calls. He was highly respected by his peers.

Harriett White, a classmate of Mr. Austin said, "Jay was usually affable and we all loved him. He was voted most likely to succeed in the senior class. To learn of his success in New York was no surprise to anyone who knew him. His death will affect me for the rest of my life."

Friends of the family say Mrs. Austin-Glover will have her son's body returned to Charleston for burial.

EPILOGUE

Shirley arranged a memorial service for Jay in Harlem. This allowed her employees and the many people he touched in New York to pay their last respects. Among attendees were Mason, Sye, Sharon and some of Jay's Wall Street co-workers and high school friends.

Jay's body was placed in the same chapel where Linda Hall was reposed several years earlier.

Barbara came and sat alone in the rear of the funeral home. She wept silently during the entire tribute to Jay.

Diane had her son's body brought home to Charleston for a funeral at the Green Chapel Baptist Church. The small church was overflowing with grief stricken friends of the popular Jay Austin. The New York contingent that made the trip to Charleston, included Shirley, Merle, Gwen, Milton, Carla Mack, Joyce and her mother Grace.

Sarah also made the trip after receiving medical treatment. After leaving the hospital, Sarah told the police of her ordeal with the men in her apartment. The police surmised that she was used to lure Jay to her apartment in an apparent robbery attempt but it did not go as planed. She could not identify the men who beat her and held her captive.

Joyce recognized the woman she saw get on the elevator with Jay. She sat alone during the solemn service. After the service, the woman approached Joyce and whispered in her ear, "I was one of his teachers in high school. He told me how much he loved you."

This brought a broad smile to Joyce's face and all she simply said was "Thank you." They embraced.

Joyce had news for Diane Austin Glover that she was waiting to tell her at the right moment. It came after the burial and during the gathering at Diane's new home in North Charleston. She whispered to Diane "I'm carrying Jay's baby. You've lost a son but you will have a grandson soon"

Several weeks later, Morris Levy rang the bell at Joyce's home in Harlem. He informed her that Jay had a will. And that he left a Treasury bond and cash for her. Ed and Grace were stunned by this but just looked at each other and never said a word. Joyce said that Jay must have known that she was pregnant and this was his way of taking care of the child she was going to deliver in six months.

Levy also paid a visit to Barbara with a sizable check.

ARNOLD POWELL was born in Charleston, S.C. After attending Talladega College in Alabama, he moved to New York and began a career on Wall Street that lasted over 30 years. His writings then consisted of industry news letters, informational memorandum and investment compliance literature. This is his first novel and he is currently working on his second. Now retired, he lives with his family in Georgia.

LaVergne, TN USA
11 December 2009
166763LV00002B/7/P